Knights Club

THE BANDS OF BRAVERY

Club

SHUKY · WALTCH · NOVY

QUIRK BOOKS

PHILADELPHIA

Originally published in France as Chevaliers: Journal d'un héros
in 2012 by Makaka editions.
Copyright © 2012 MAKAKA. All rights reserved.

First published in the United States in 2018
by Quirk Productions, Inc.
Translation copyright © 2018 by Quirk Productions, Inc.

Library of Congress Cataloging in Publication Number:
2018933926

ISBN: 978-1-68369-055-9
Printed in China
Translated by Mélanie Strang-Hardy
Cover design by Andie Reid
Typeset in Sketchnote
Production management by John J. McGurk

Quirk Books
215 Church Street
Philadelphia, PA 19106
quirkbooks.com

10 9 8 7 6 5 4 3 2 1

Halt!

THIS ISN'T A REGULAR COMIC BOOK!

In this comic book, you don't read straight through from first page to last. Instead, you'll begin at the beginning, and soon be off on a quest where you choose which panel to read next. On your adventure, you will answer riddles, solve puzzles, face mighty foes, and collect bracelets of bravery—because YOU are the main character!

It's easy to get the hang of it once you see it in action. Turn the page for an example of how it works!

HOW TO PLAY COMIC QUESTS

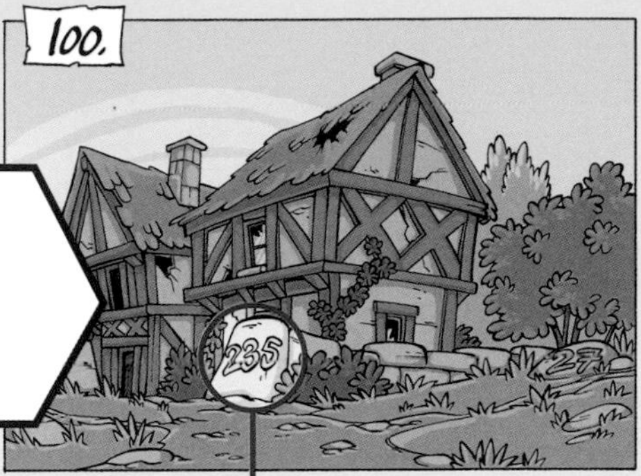
100.
235

1 First, pick where you want to go in the panel—doors, paths, signs, and objects can all have numbers.

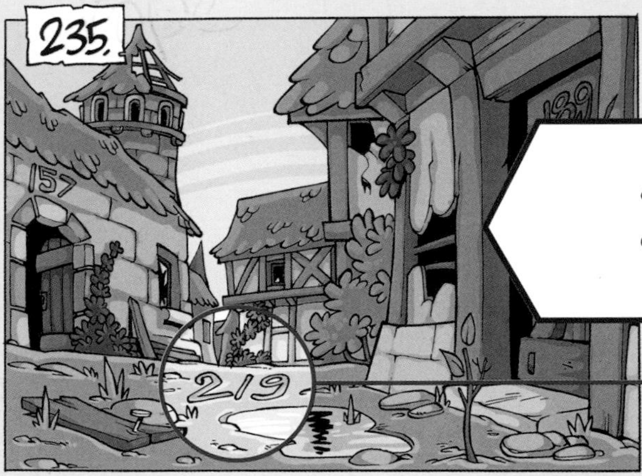
235.
157
189
219

2 Flip to the panel with the matching number.

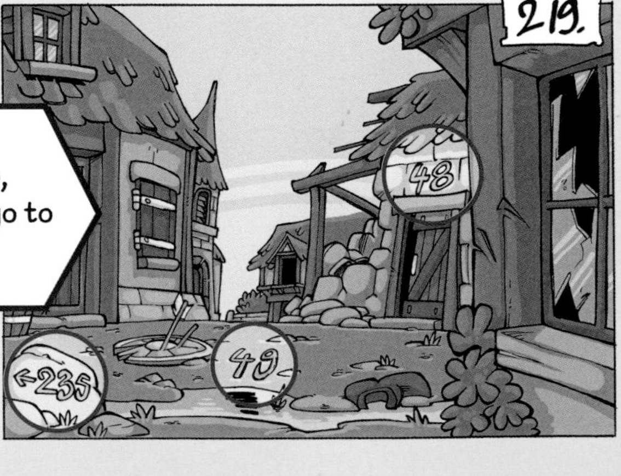
219.
48
←235
49

3 Continue reading from there, making more choices as you go to complete the quest!

HOW TO PLAY COMIC QUESTS

As you go, use the handy Quest Tracker sheets on the next few pages to log your progress. Use a pencil so you can erase.

(You can also use a notebook and pencil, or download extra sheets at comicquests.com).

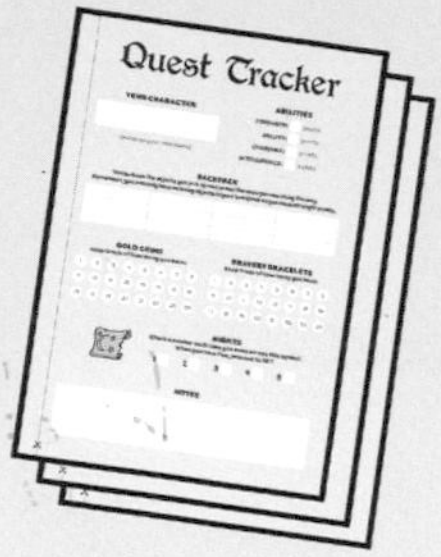
Quest Tracker

THE RULES OF KNIGHTHOOD

While playing the game, be sure to follow the rules to preserve your honor as a knight.

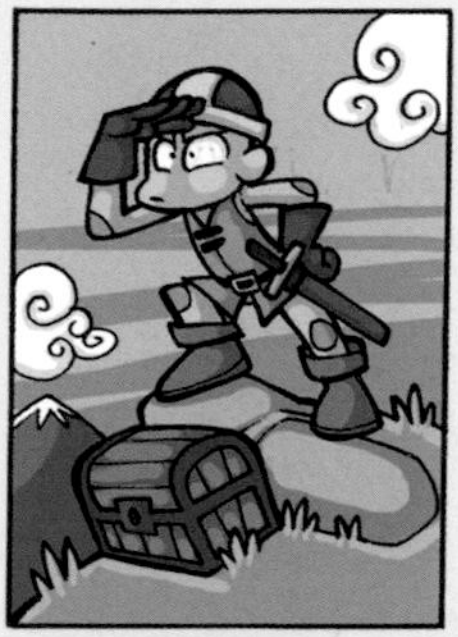

BE WISE IN BATTLE: You can only attack a foe if you have a weapon in your possession (because to do otherwise would be foolish!)

REMAIN VIGILANT: Always examine your surroundings for hidden passages, objects, and bracelets of bravery—they may be hard to spot.

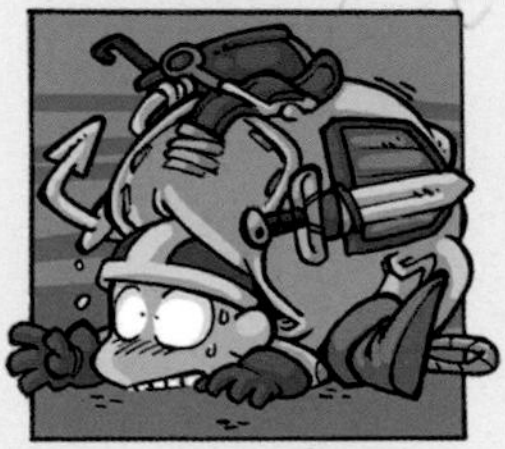

STAY TRUE TO YOUR STRENGTHS: You may only carry as many objects as you have strength points. However, you can unload an object whenever you need to make room for a new one. Bracelets of bravery and gold coins weigh nothing, so they won't count against your strength points.

REST WELL: Each time you encounter this symbol, make note of it on your adventure tracker—another night's rest has passed. After five nights, you'll need to return to the castle to show your cache of bracelets of bravery.

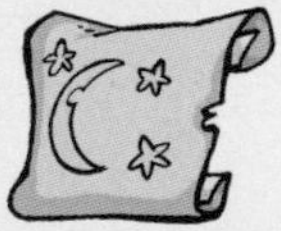

BE HONEST: An aspiring knight does not steal. Only take the objects you are offered or that no one else owns! If you pass through the same place twice or more, you should mark the nights on your adventure tracker, but not take the same object twice or collect double bonus points.

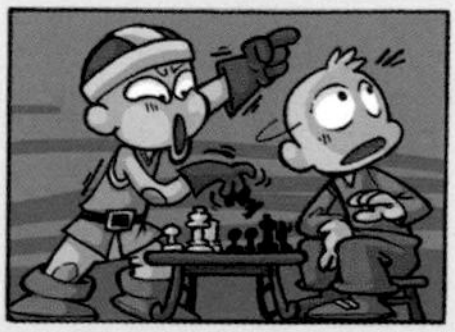

GOOD LUCK! LET THE ADVENTURE BEGIN...

Quest Tracker

YOUR CHARACTER

fane

(make up your own name)

ABILITIES

STRENGTH:	4	points
AGILITY:	10	points
CHARISMA:	[illegible]	points
INTELLIGENCE:	13	points

BACKPACK

Write down the objects you pick up and erase the ones you use along the way.
Remember, you can only have as many objects in your backpack as you have strength points.

rope	rope	rinig	sapd

GOLD COINS

Keep track of how many you have:

1	2	3	4	5	6	7	8
9	10	11	12	13	14	15	16
17	18	19	20	21	22	23	24

BRAVERY BRACELETS

Keep track of how many you have:

1	2	3	4	5	6	7	8
9	10	11	12	13	14	15	16
17	18	19	20	21	22	23	24

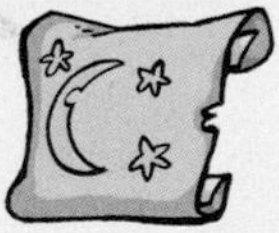

NIGHTS

Check a number each time you come across this symbol.
When you have five, proceed to 387.

1 ✓ 2 ✓ 3 ✓ 4 ✓ 5 ✓

NOTES

Quest Tracker

YOUR CHARACTER

(make up your own name)

ABILITIES

STRENGTH: 4 points

AGILITY: 10 points

CHARISMA: 3 points

INTELLIGENCE: 13 points

BACKPACK

Write down the objects you pick up and erase the ones you use along the way.
Remember, you can only have as many objects in your backpack as you have strength points.

GOLD COINS

Keep track of how many you have:

1	2	3	4	5	6	7	8
9	10	11	12	13	14	15	16
17	18	19	20	21	22	23	24

BRAVERY BRACELETS

Keep track of how many you have:

✓	2	3	4	5	6	7	8
9	10	11	12	13	14	15	16
17	18	19	20	21	22	23	24

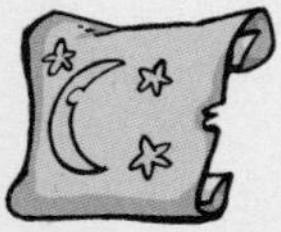

NIGHTS

Check a number each time you come across this symbol.
When you have five, proceed to 387.

1 2 3 4 5

NOTES

Quest Tracker

YOUR CHARACTER

(make up your own name)

ABILITIES

STRENGTH: points

AGILITY: points

CHARISMA: points

INTELLIGENCE: points

BACKPACK

Write down the objects you pick up and erase the ones you use along the way.
Remember, you can only have as many objects in your backpack as you have strength points.

GOLD COINS

Keep track of how many you have:

1 2 3 4 5 6 7 8
9 10 11 12 13 14 15 16
17 18 19 20 21 22 23 24

BRAVERY BRACELETS

Keep track of how many you have:

1 2 3 4 5 6 7 8
9 10 11 12 13 14 15 16
17 18 19 20 21 22 23 24

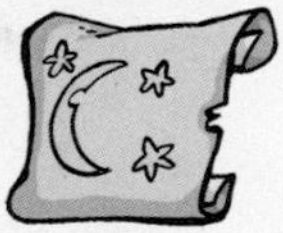

NIGHTS

Check a number each time you come across this symbol.
When you have five, proceed to 387.

1 2 3 4 5

NOTES

Quest Tracker

YOUR CHARACTER

Hether

(make up your own name)

ABILITIES

STRENGTH: 10 points

AGILITY: 30 points

CHARISMA: 29 points

INTELLIGENCE: 100 points

BACKPACK

Write down the objects you pick up and erase the ones you use along the way.
Remember, you can only have as many objects in your backpack as you have strength points.

rope	ring		

GOLD COINS

Keep track of how many you have:

1 ✓	2	3	4	5	6	7	8
9	10	11	12	13	14	15	16
17	18	19	20	21	22	23	24

BRAVERY BRACELETS

Keep track of how many you have:

1 ✓	2 ✓	3 ✓	4 ✓	5	6	7	8
9	10	11	12	13	14	15	16
17	18	19	20	21	22	23	24

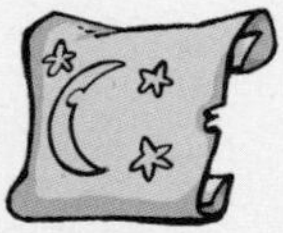

NIGHTS

Check a number each time you come across this symbol.
When you have five, proceed to 387.

1 ✓ 2 ☐ 3 ☐ 4 ☐ 5 ☐

NOTES

Quest Tracker

YOUR CHARACTER

(make up your own name)

ABILITIES

STRENGTH: points

AGILITY: points

CHARISMA: points

INTELLIGENCE: points

BACKPACK

Write down the objects you pick up and erase the ones you use along the way.
Remember, you can only have as many objects in your backpack as you have strength points.

GOLD COINS

Keep track of how many you have:

1 2 3 4 5 6 7 8
9 10 11 12 13 14 15 16
17 18 19 20 21 22 23 24

BRAVERY BRACELETS

Keep track of how many you have:

1 2 3 4 5 6 7 8
9 10 11 12 13 14 15 16
17 18 19 20 21 22 23 24

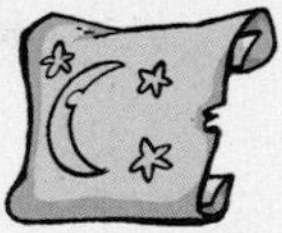

NIGHTS

Check a number each time you come across this symbol.
When you have five, proceed to 387.

1 2 3 4 5

NOTES

Quest Tracker

YOUR CHARACTER

(make up your own name)

ABILITIES

STRENGTH: points

AGILITY: points

CHARISMA: points

INTELLIGENCE: points

BACKPACK

Write down the objects you pick up and erase the ones you use along the way.
Remember, you can only have as many objects in your backpack as you have strength points.

GOLD COINS

Keep track of how many you have:

1	2	3	4	5	6	7	8
9	10	11	12	13	14	15	16
17	18	19	20	21	22	23	24

BRAVERY BRACELETS

Keep track of how many you have:

1	2	3	4	5	6	7	8
9	10	11	12	13	14	15	16
17	18	19	20	21	22	23	24

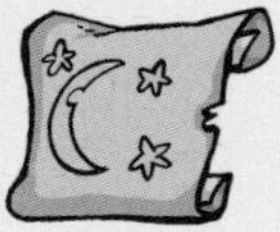

NIGHTS

Check a number each time you come across this symbol.
When you have five, proceed to 387.

1 2 3 4 5

NOTES

Quest Tracker

YOUR CHARACTER

(make up your own name)

ABILITIES

STRENGTH: ___ points

AGILITY: ___ points

CHARISMA: ___ points

INTELLIGENCE: ___ points

BACKPACK

Write down the objects you pick up and erase the ones you use along the way.
Remember, you can only have as many objects in your backpack as you have strength points.

GOLD COINS

Keep track of how many you have:

1	2	3	4	5	6	7	8
9	10	11	12	13	14	15	16
17	18	19	20	21	22	23	24

BRAVERY BRACELETS

Keep track of how many you have:

1	2	3	4	5	6	7	8
9	10	11	12	13	14	15	16
17	18	19	20	21	22	23	24

NIGHTS

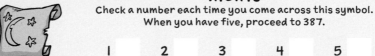

Check a number each time you come across this symbol.
When you have five, proceed to 387.

1 ___ 2 ___ 3 ___ 4 ___ 5 ___

NOTES

Begin Your Quest!

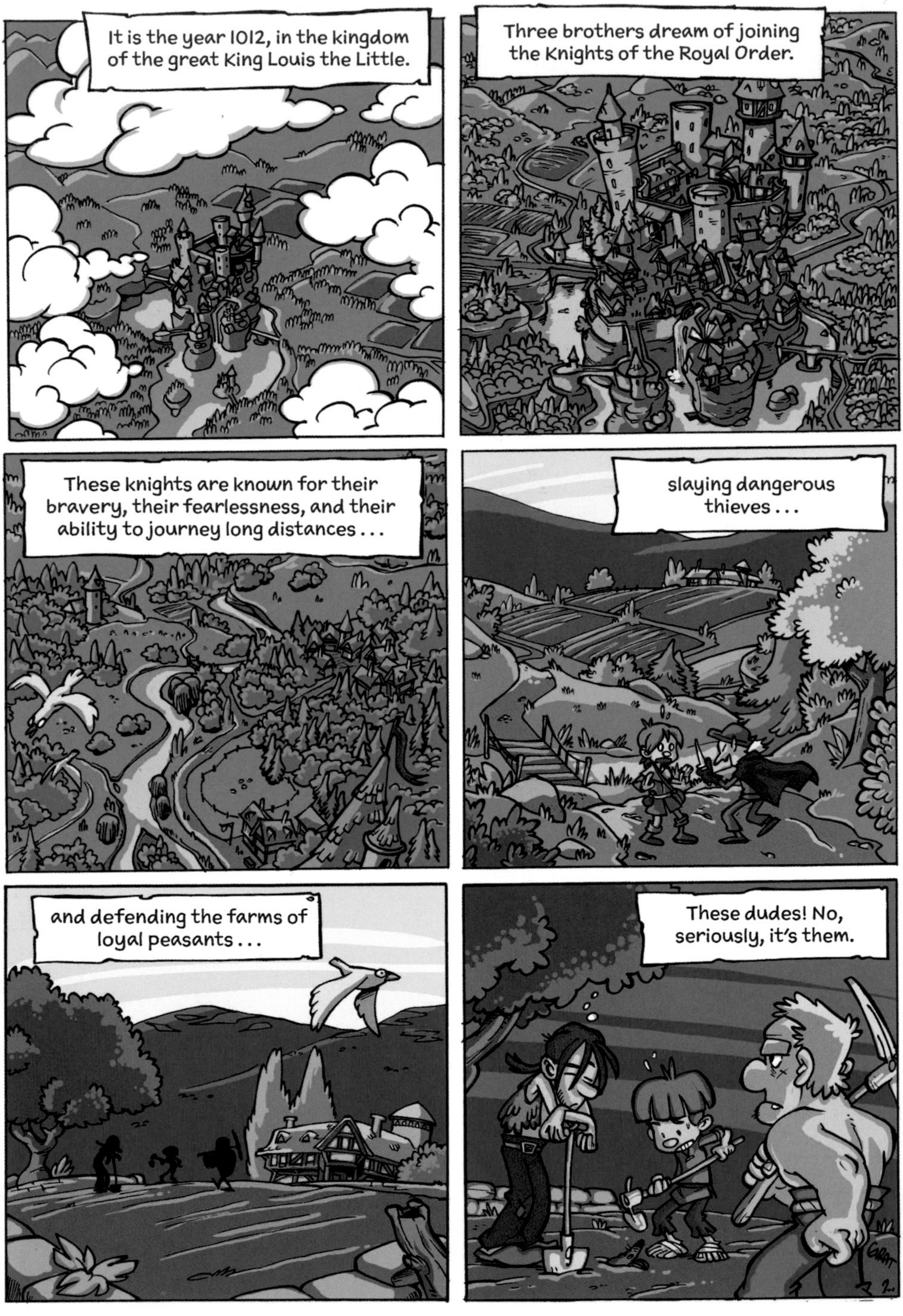
It is the year 1012, in the kingdom of the great King Louis the Little.
Three brothers dream of joining the Knights of the Royal Order.
These knights are known for their bravery, their fearlessness, and their ability to journey long distances . . .
slaying dangerous thieves . . .
and defending the farms of loyal peasants . . .
These dudes! No, seriously, it's them.

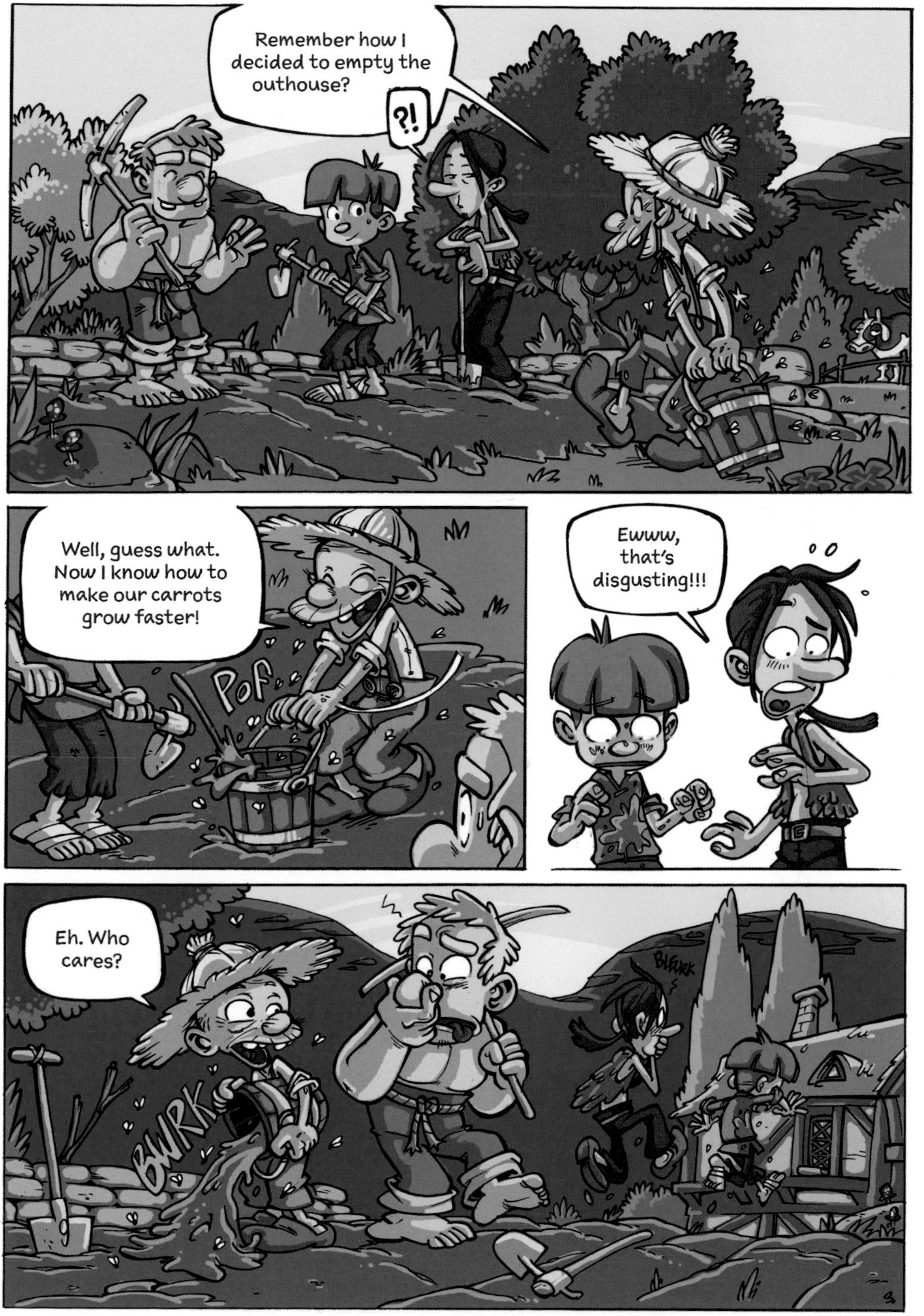
Remember how I decided to empty the outhouse?
?!
Well, guess what. Now I know how to make our carrots grow faster!
POF
Ewww, that's disgusting!!!
Eh. Who cares?
BWRK
BLEURK

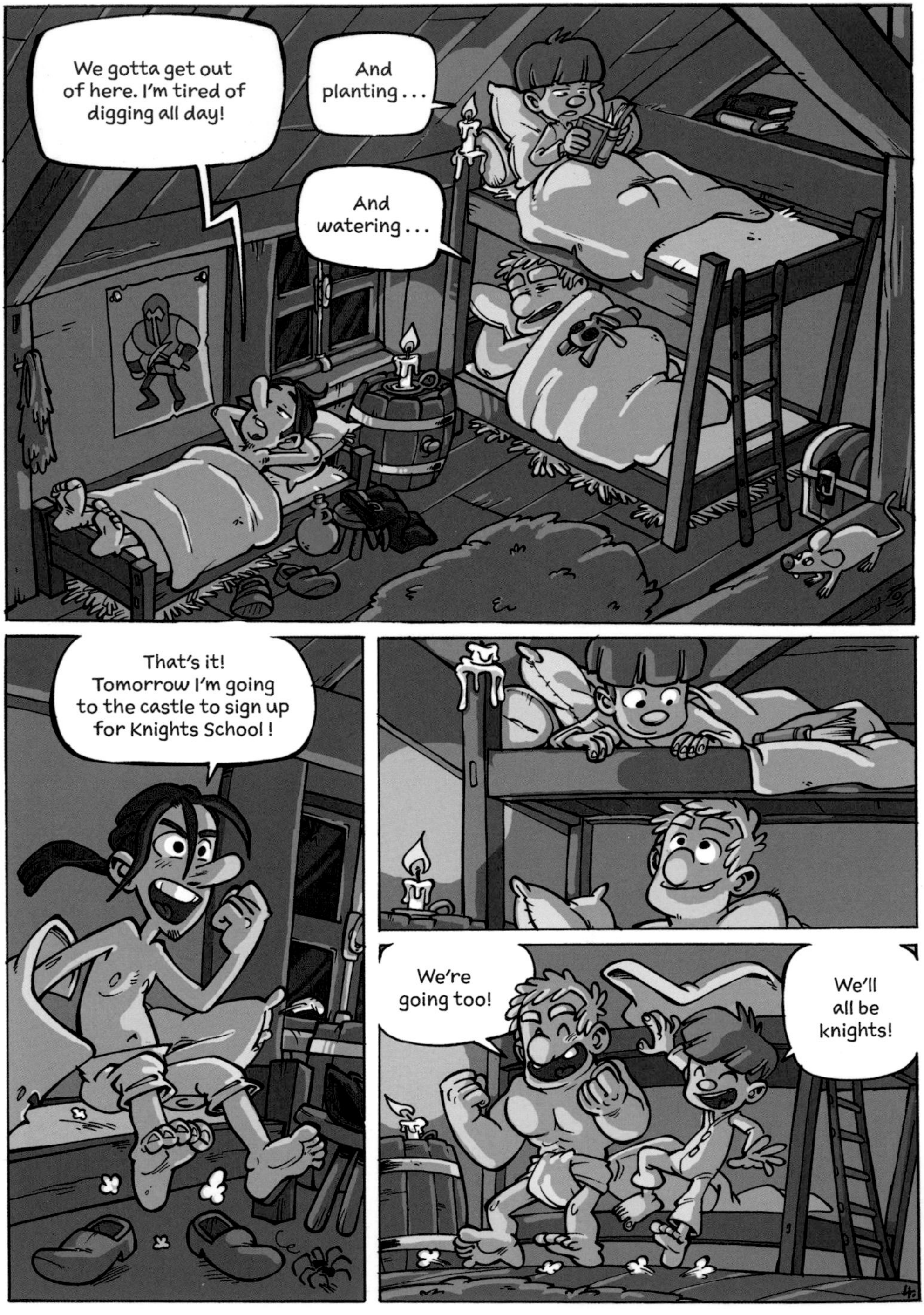
We gotta get out of here. I'm tired of digging all day!
And planting . . .
And watering . . .
That's it! Tomorrow I'm going to the castle to sign up for Knights School !
We're going too!
We'll all be knights!

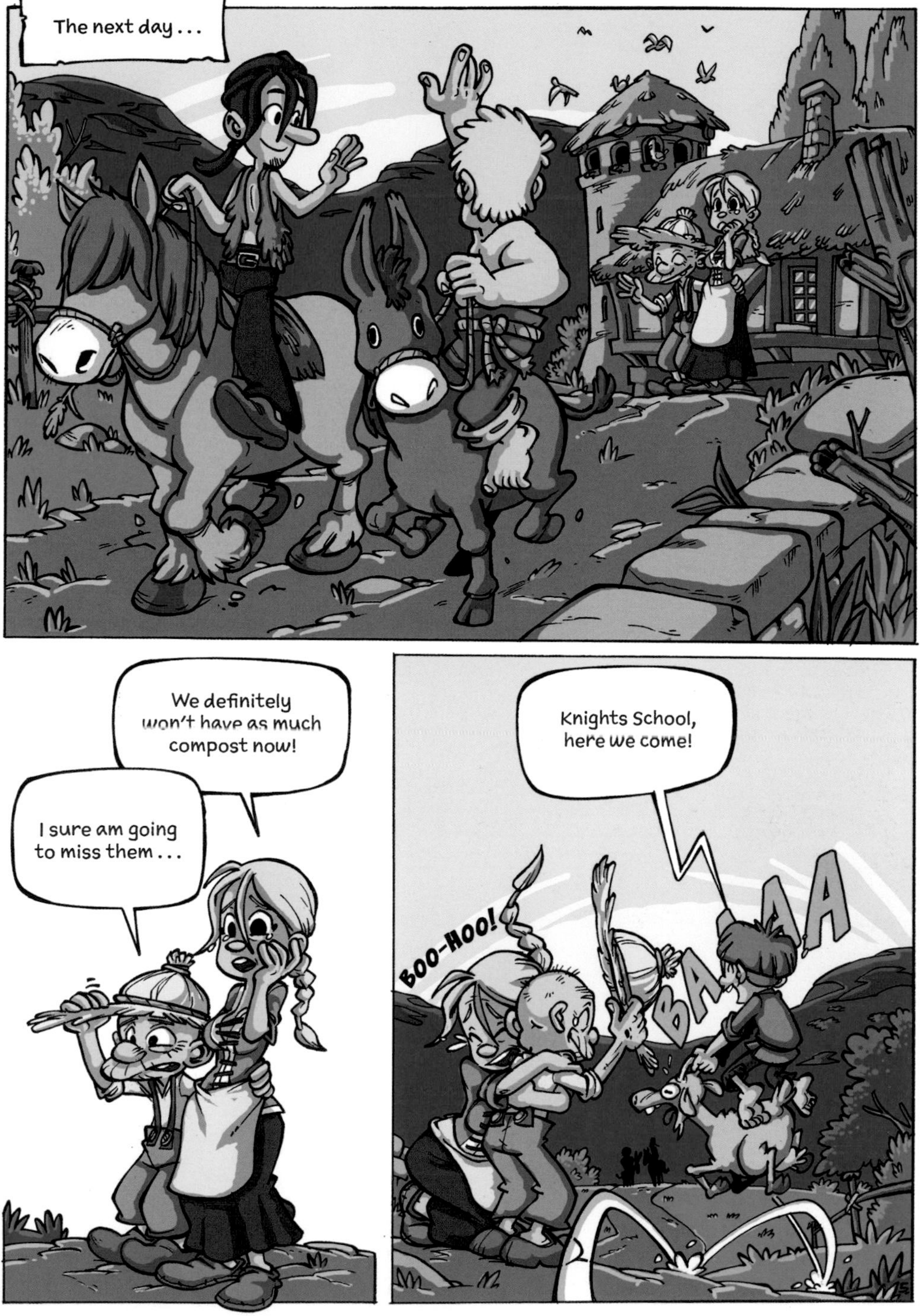
The next day . . .
We definitely won't have as much compost now!
I sure am going to miss them . . .
Knights School, here we come!
BOO-HOO!
BAAA

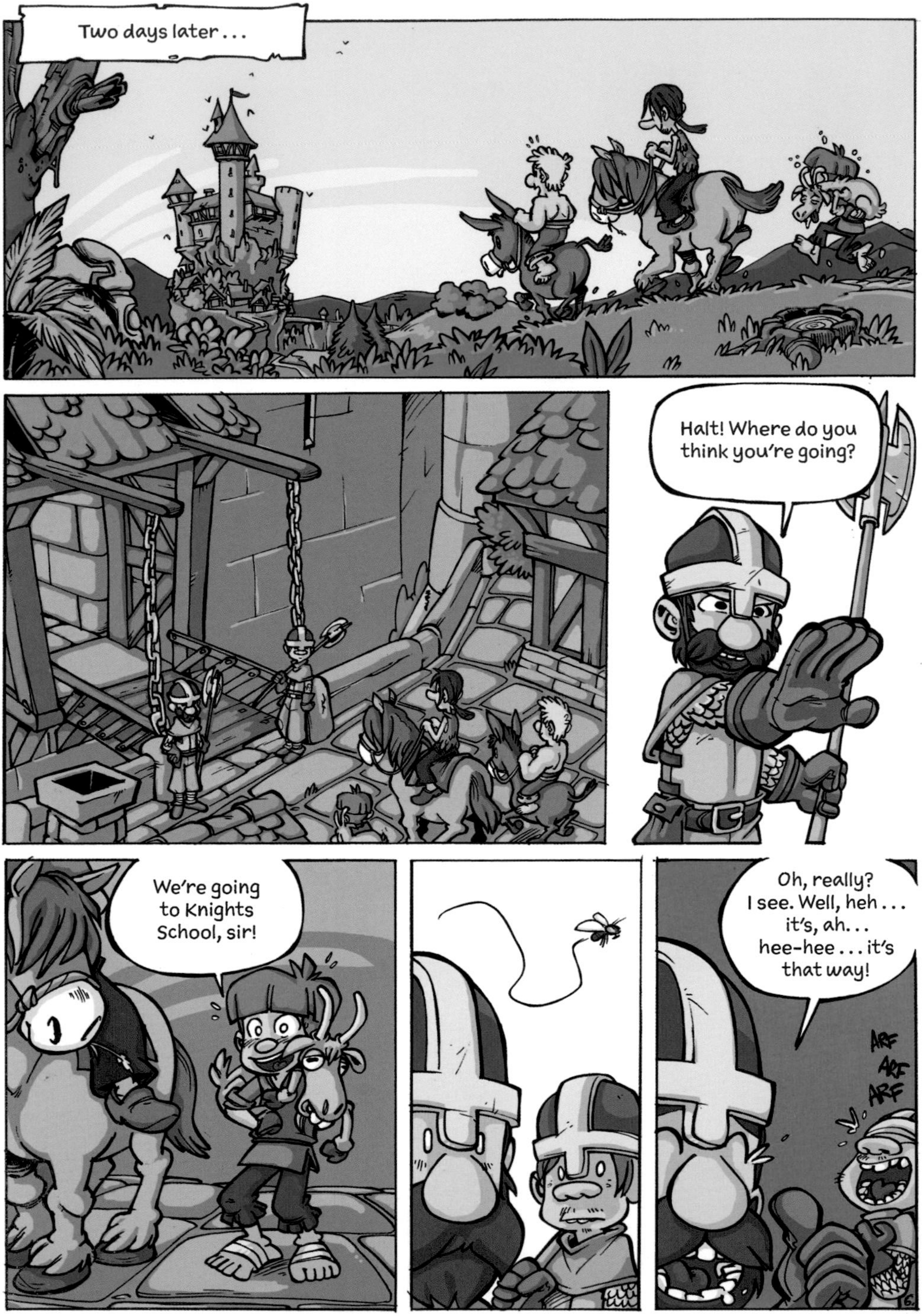
Two days later . . .
Halt! Where do you think you're going?
We're going to Knights School, sir!
Oh, really? I see. Well, heh . . . it's, ah. . . hee-hee . . . it's that way!
ARF ARF ARF

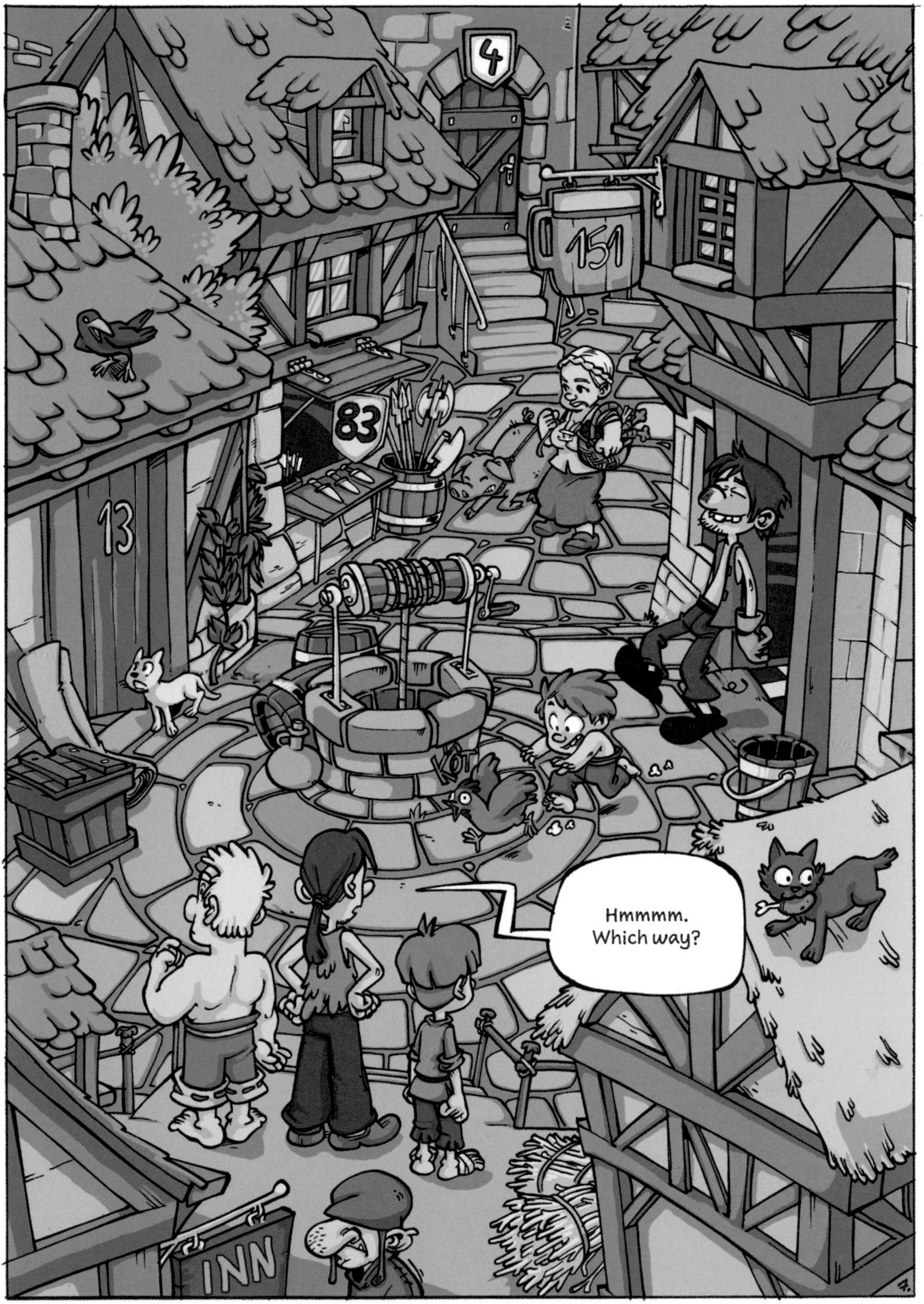
4
151
83
13
KOT
Hmmmm. Which way?
INN

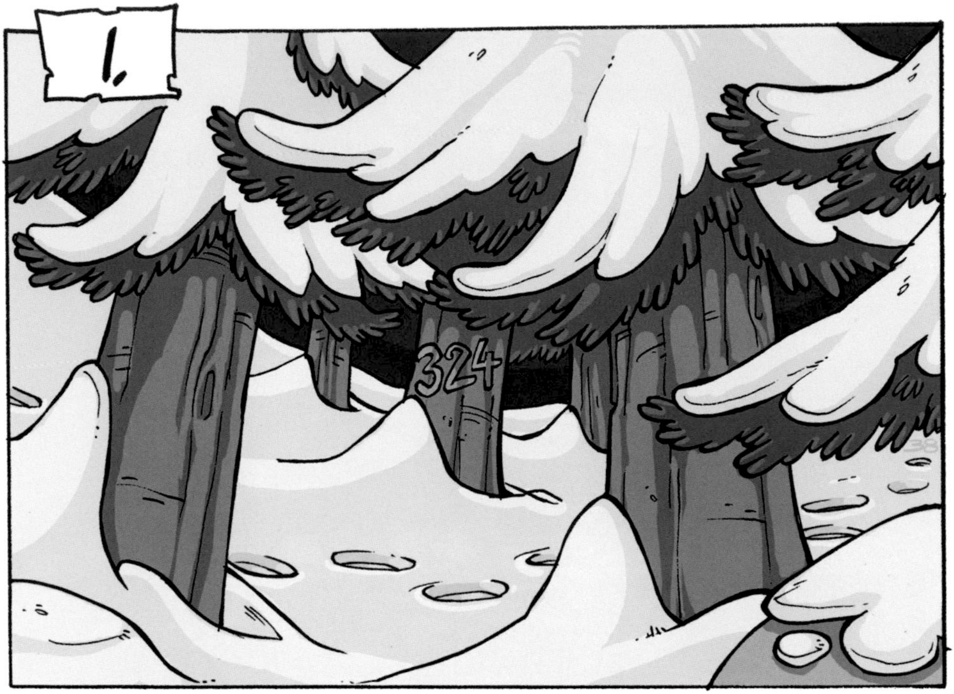
1.
324

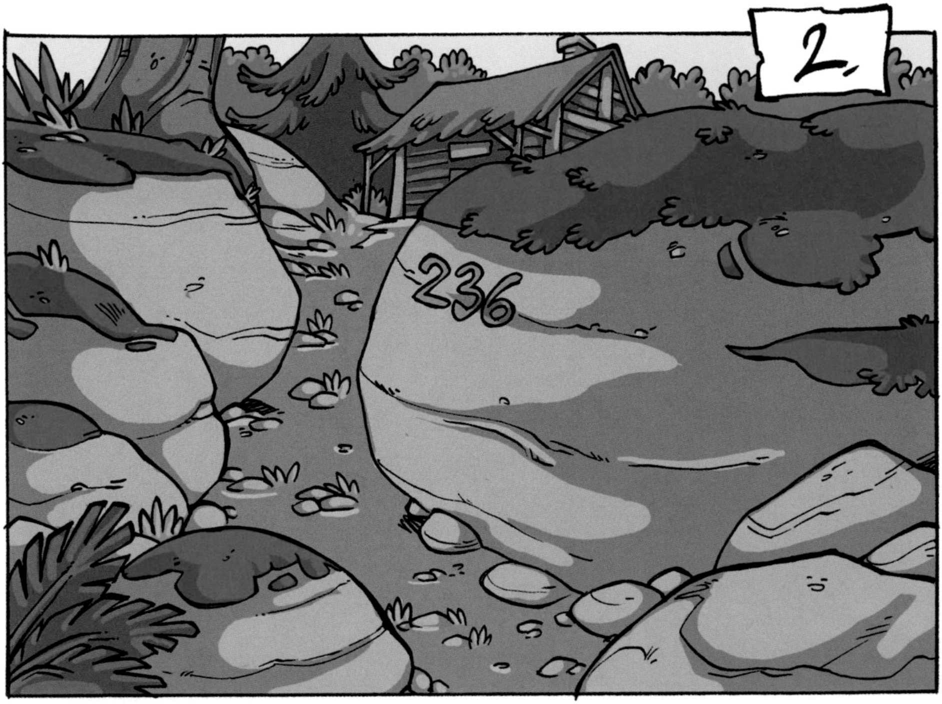
2.
236

3.

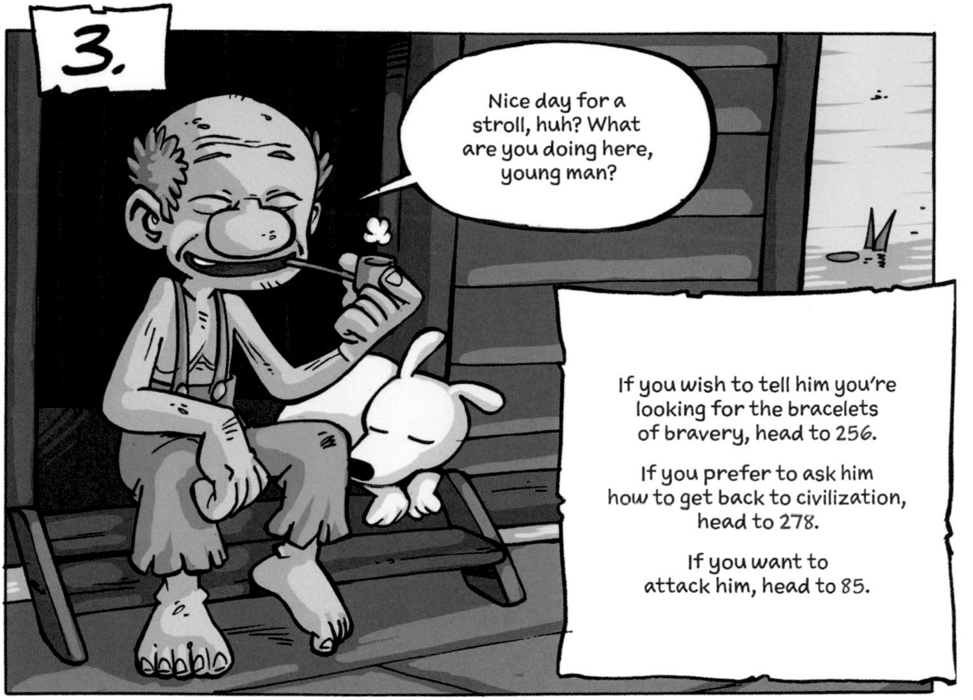
Nice day for a stroll, huh? What are you doing here, young man?
If you wish to tell him you're looking for the bracelets of bravery, head to 256.
If you prefer to ask him how to get back to civilization, head to 278.
If you want to attack him, head to 85.

4.

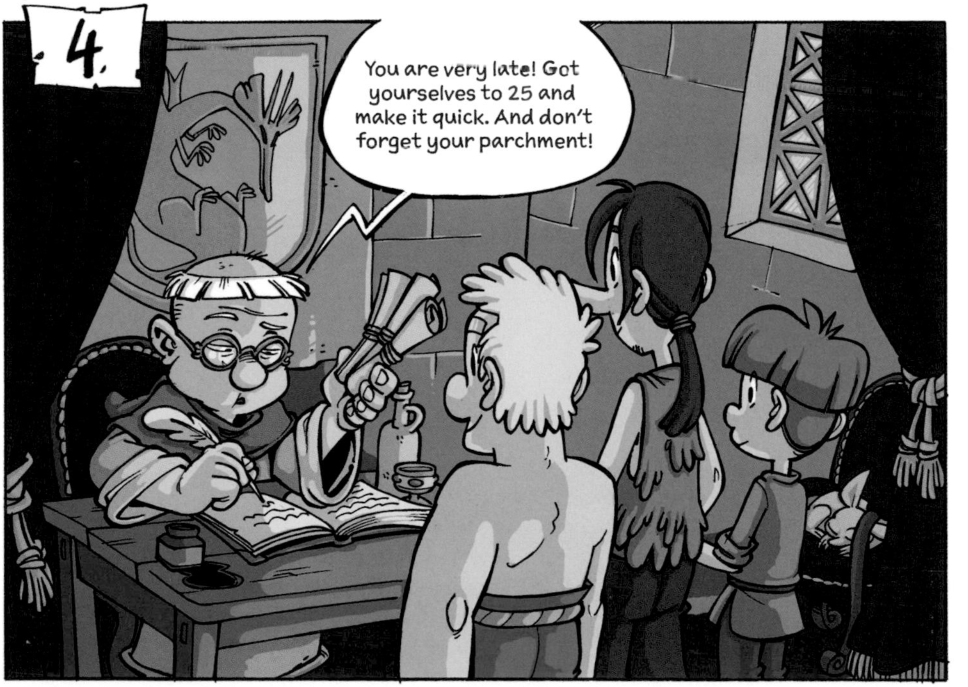
You are very late! Got yourselves to 25 and make it quick. And don't forget your parchment!

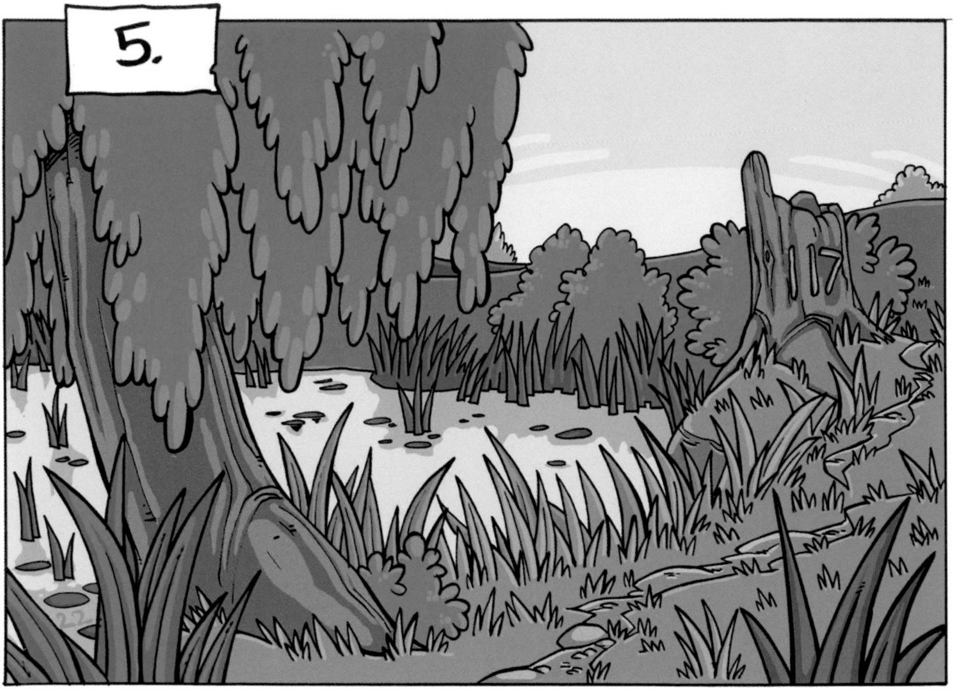
5.
17
22

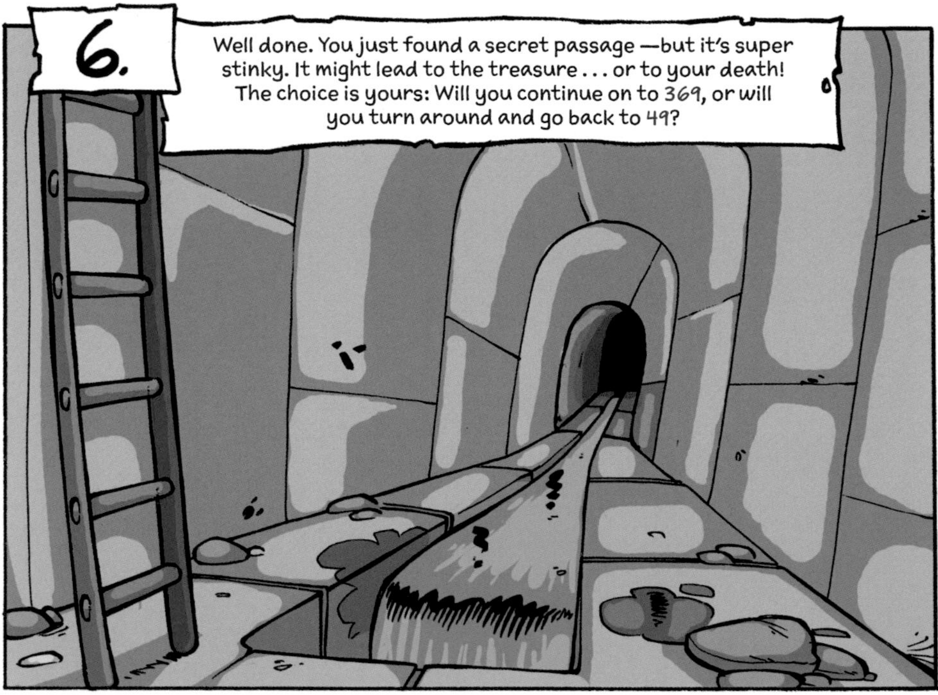
6.
Well done. You just found a secret passage —but it's super stinky. It might lead to the treasure . . . or to your death! The choice is yours: Will you continue on to 369, or will you turn around and go back to 49?

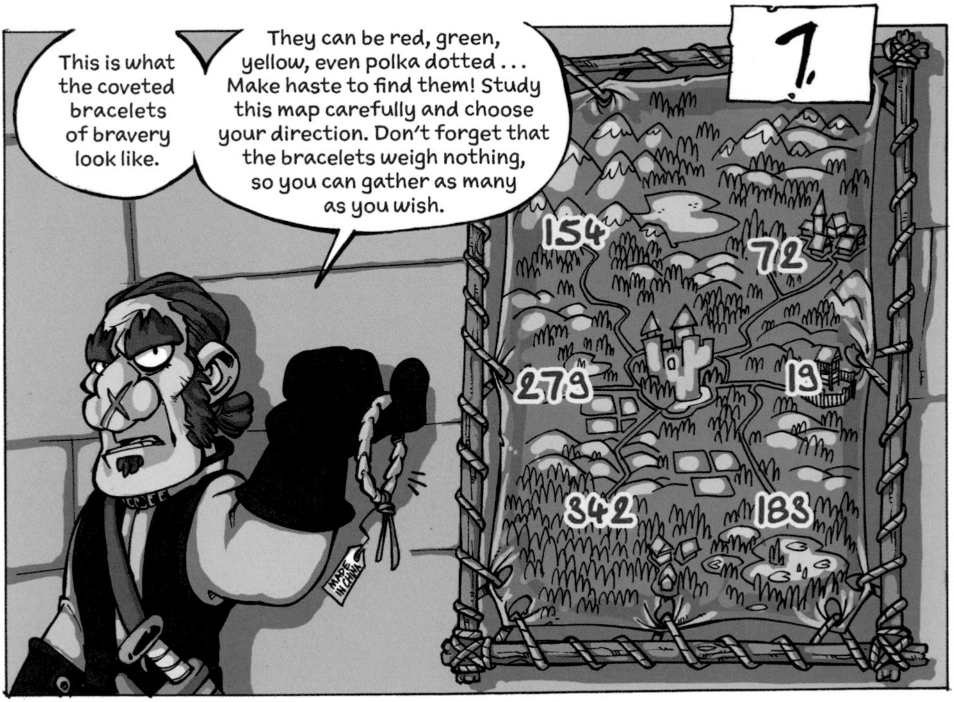
7.
This is what the coveted bracelets of bravery look like.
They can be red, green, yellow, even polka dotted . . . Make haste to find them! Study this map carefully and choose your direction. Don't forget that the bracelets weigh nothing, so you can gather as many as you wish.
MADE IN CHINA
154
72
279
19
342
183

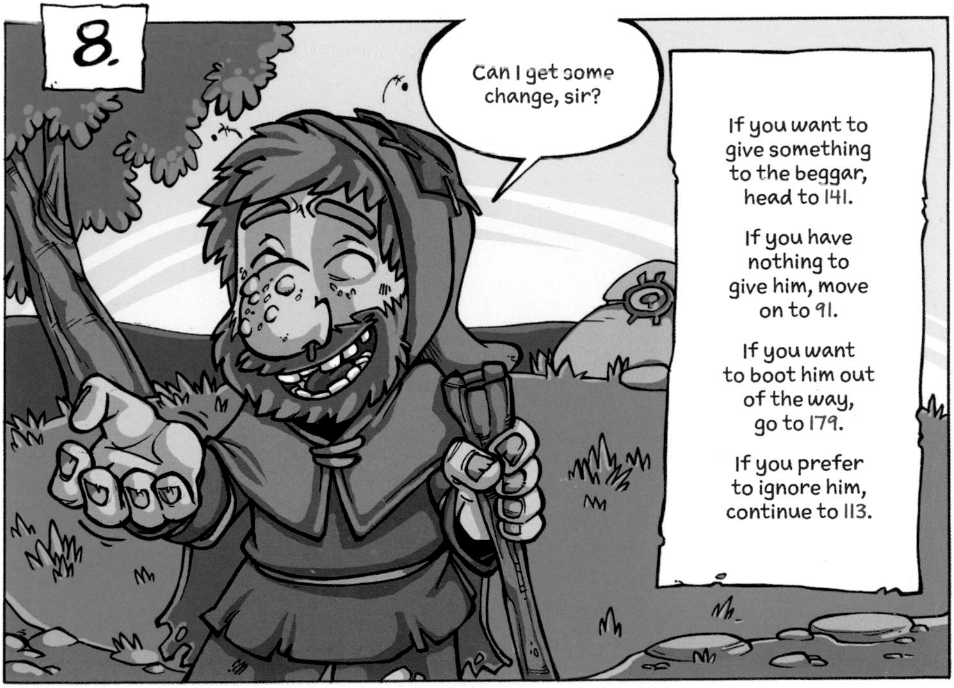
8.
Can I get some change, sir?
If you want to give something to the beggar, head to 141.
If you have nothing to give him, move on to 91.
If you want to boot him out of the way, go to 179.
If you prefer to ignore him, continue to 113.

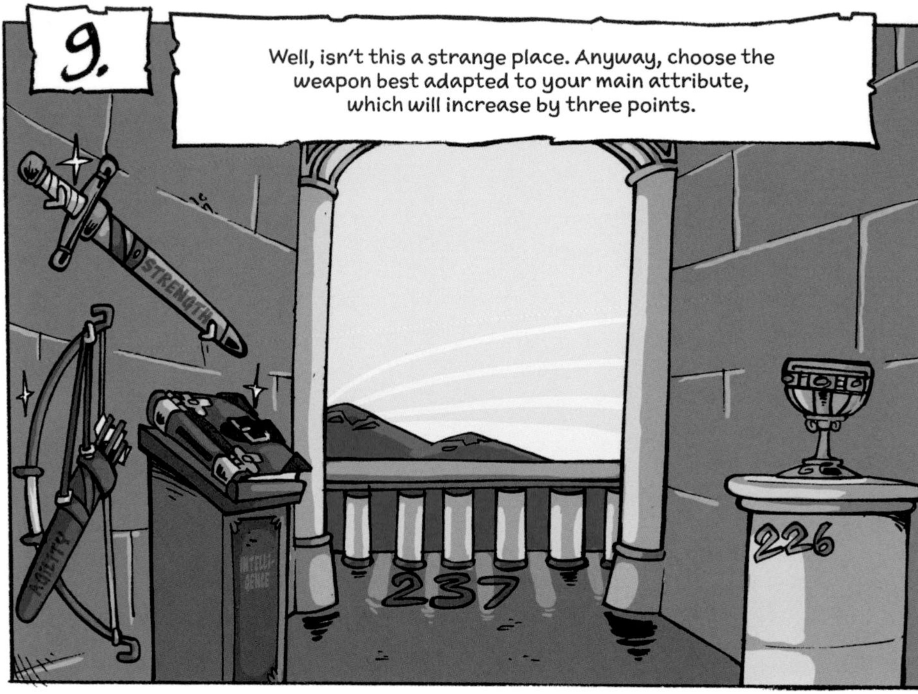
9.
Well, isn't this a strange place. Anyway, choose the weapon best adapted to your main attribute, which will increase by three points.
STRENGTH
AGILITY
INTELLI-GENCE
237
226

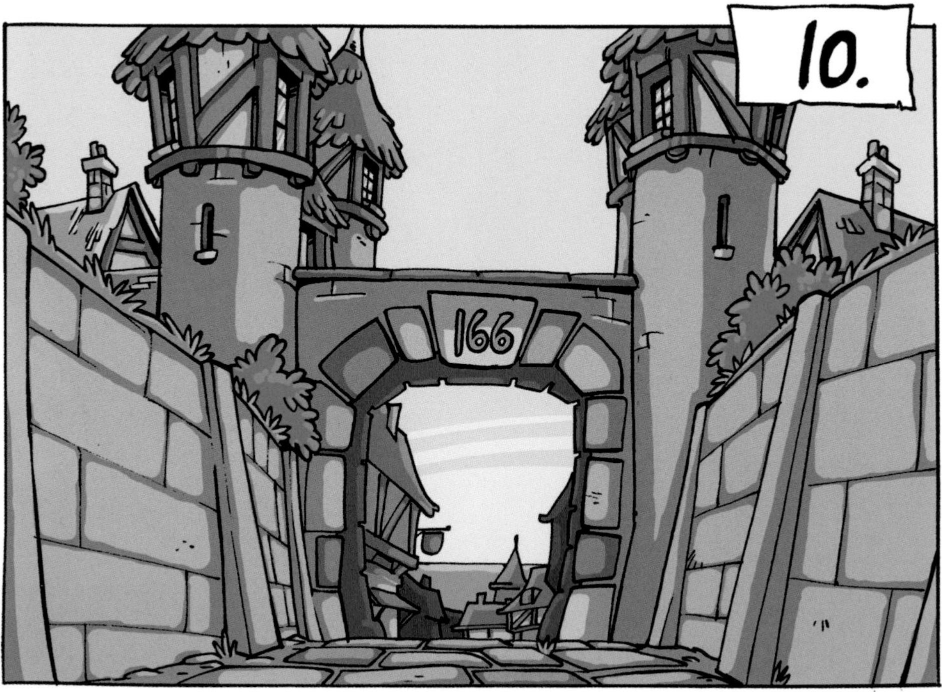
10.
166

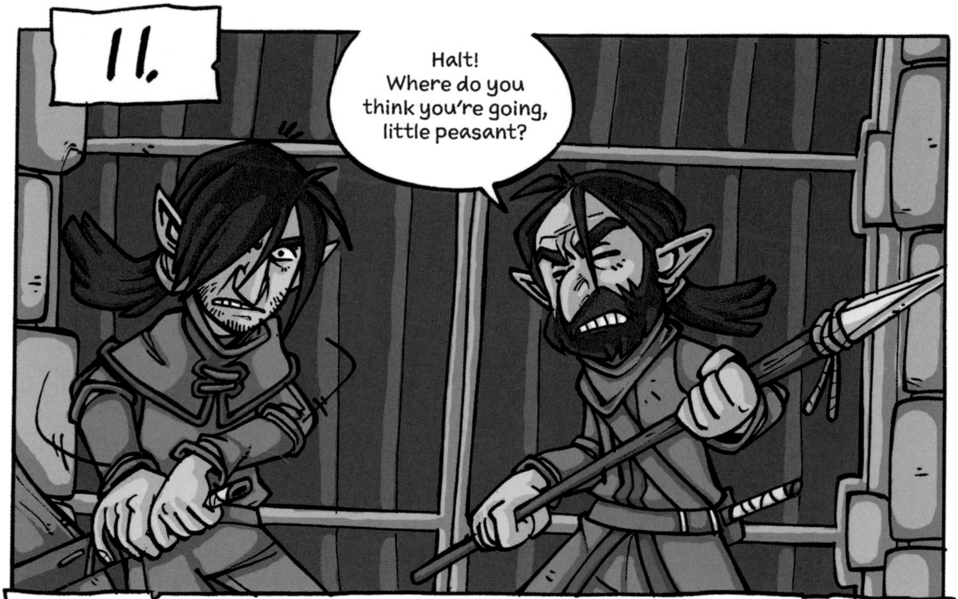
11.
Halt! Where do you think you're going, little peasant?

If "I'm going in your . . ." is your first reaction, then 252 is perfect for you! If you'd rather not engage in bathroom humor, but just want to ask for directions to Land of the Nod, then head to 43. If you hope to find out more about the woods, whose entrance is guarded so fiercely, then go to 84.

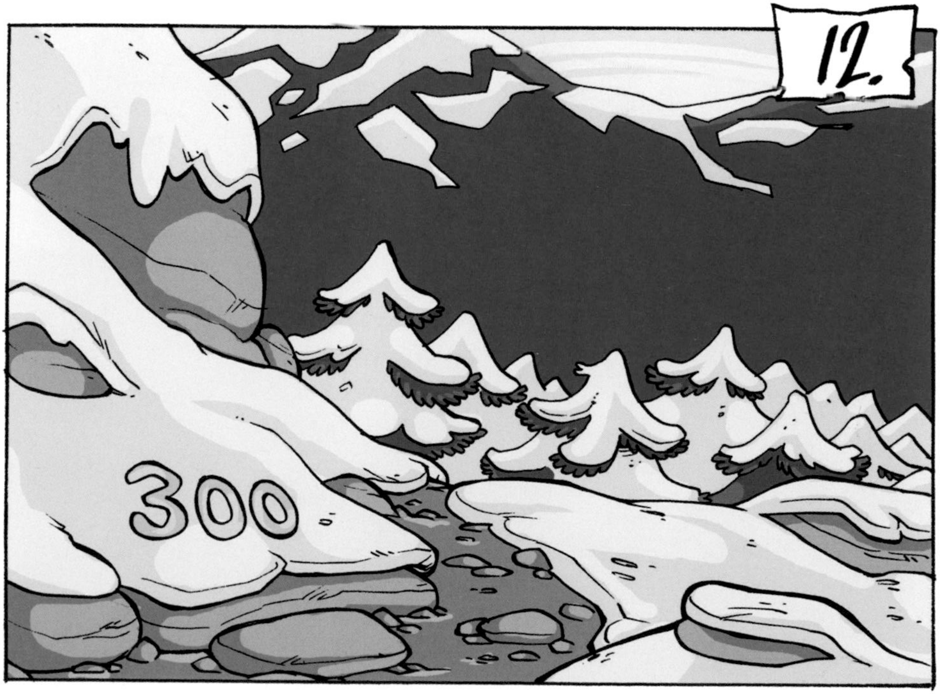
12.
300

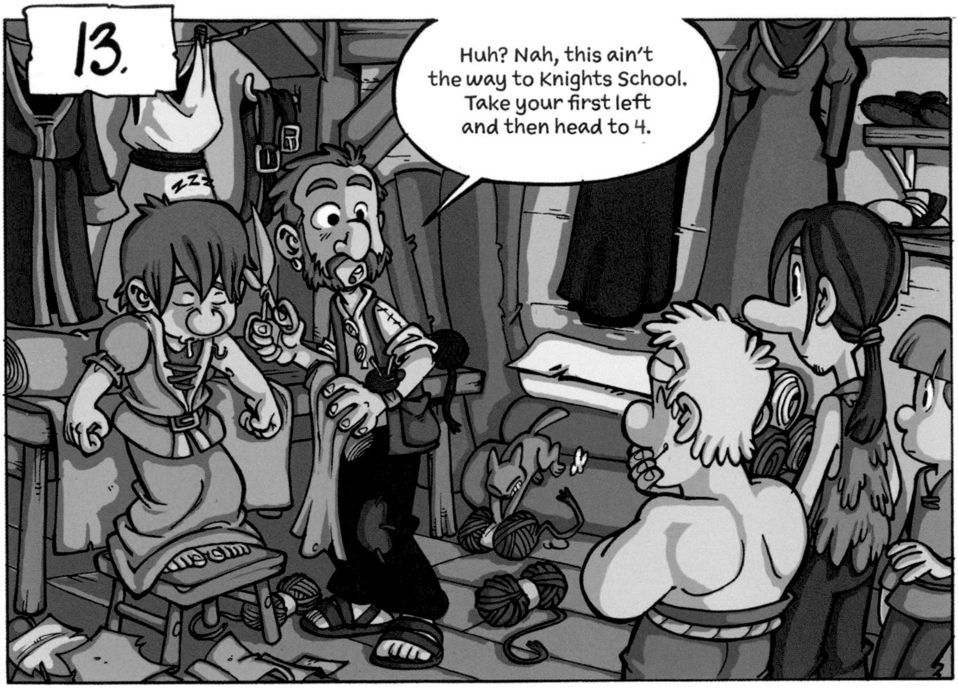
13.
Huh? Nah, this ain't the way to Knights School. Take your first left and then head to 4.

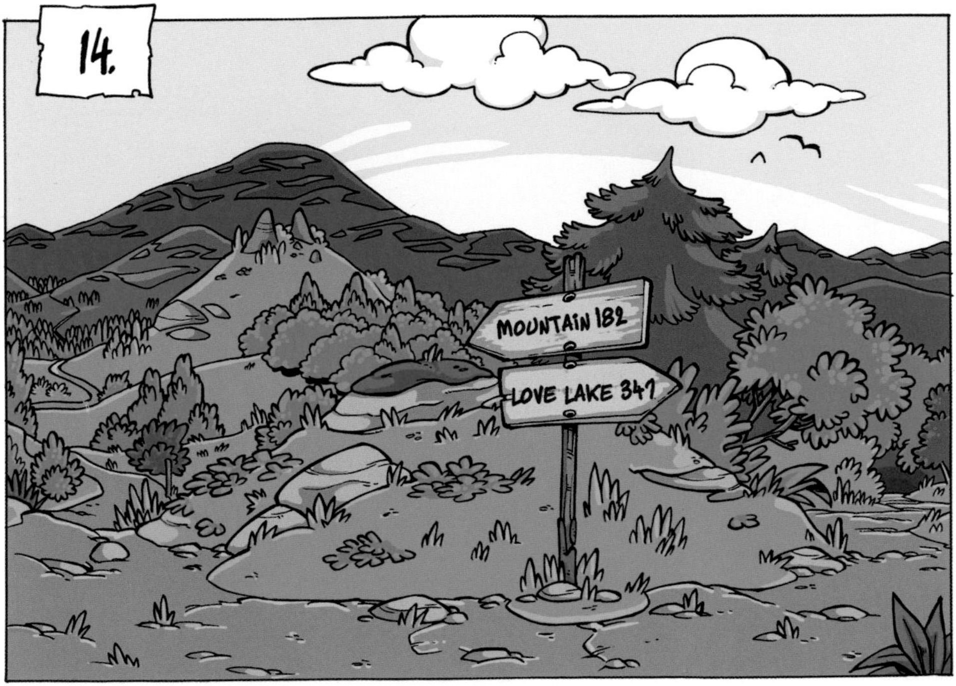
14.
MOUNTAIN 182
LOVE LAKE 347

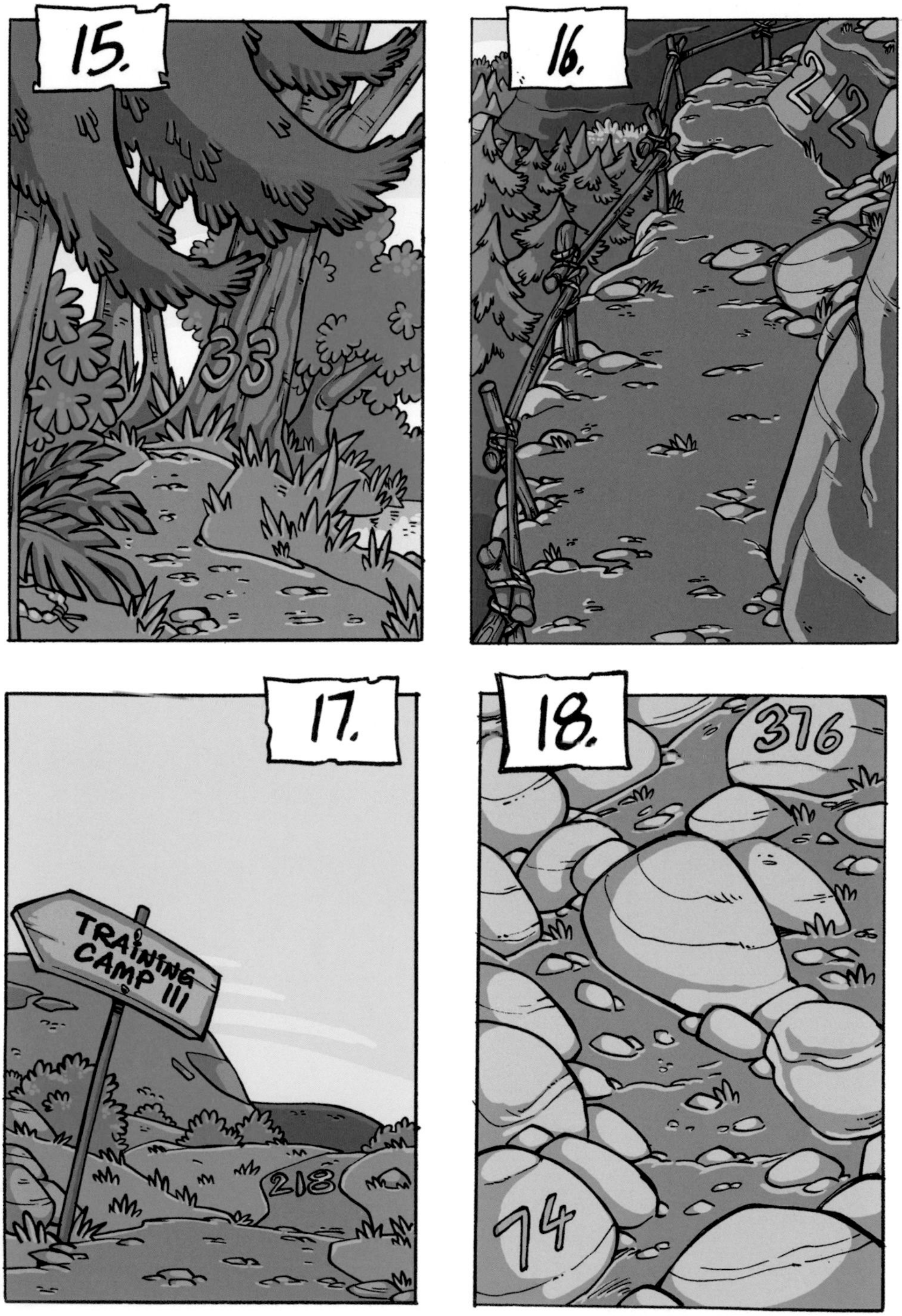
15.
33
16.
212
17.
TRAINING CAMP III
218
18.
376
74

15-16-17-18

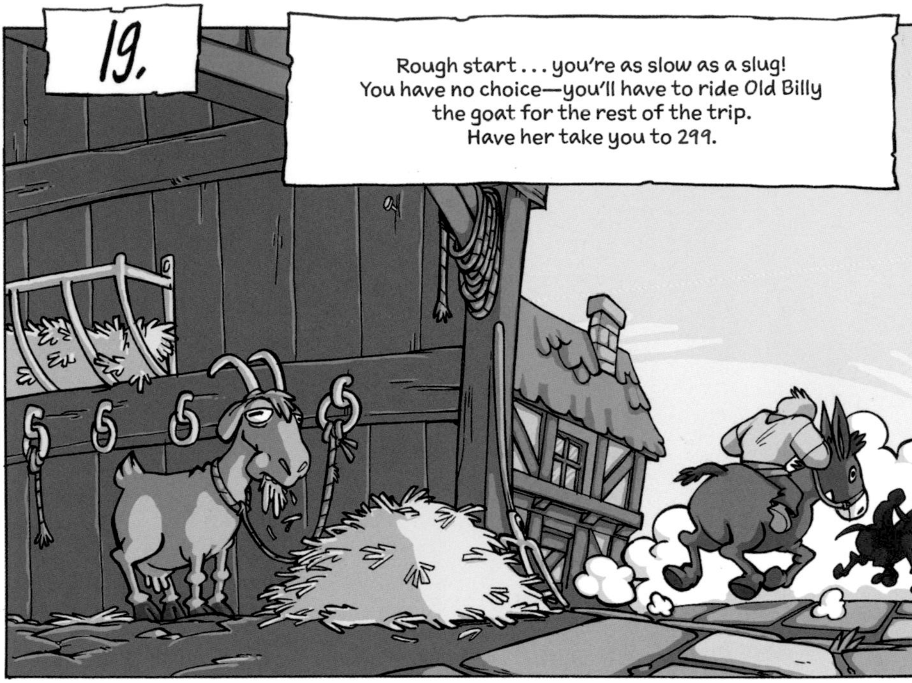
19.
Rough start . . . you're as slow as a slug! You have no choice—you'll have to ride Old Billy the goat for the rest of the trip. Have her take you to 299.

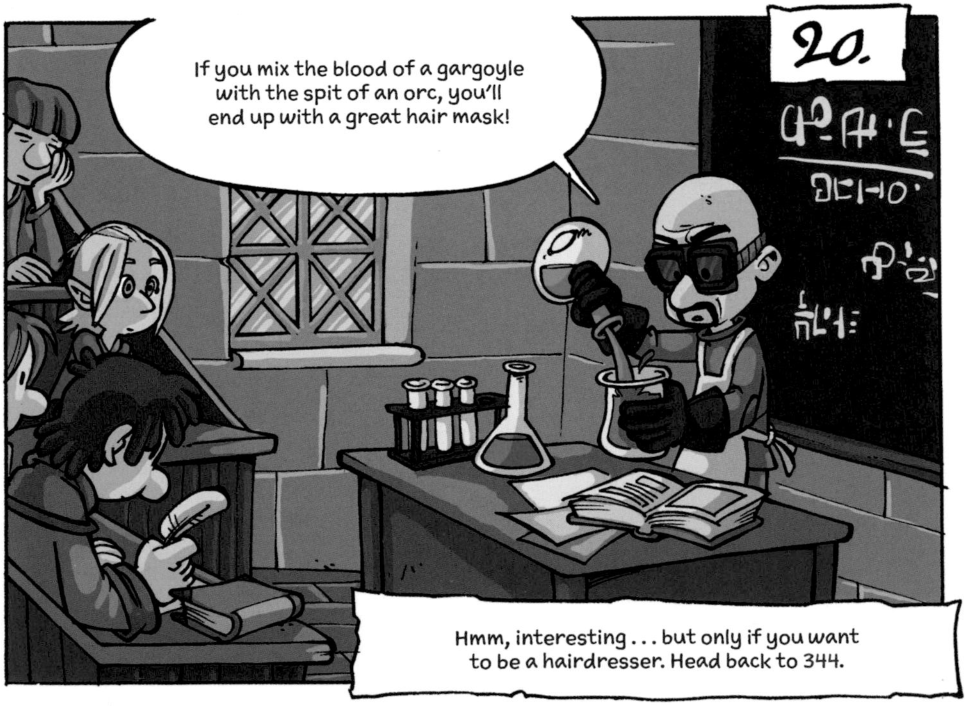
20.
If you mix the blood of a gargoyle with the spit of an orc, you'll end up with a great hair mask!
Hmm, interesting . . . but only if you want to be a hairdresser. Head back to 344.

21.

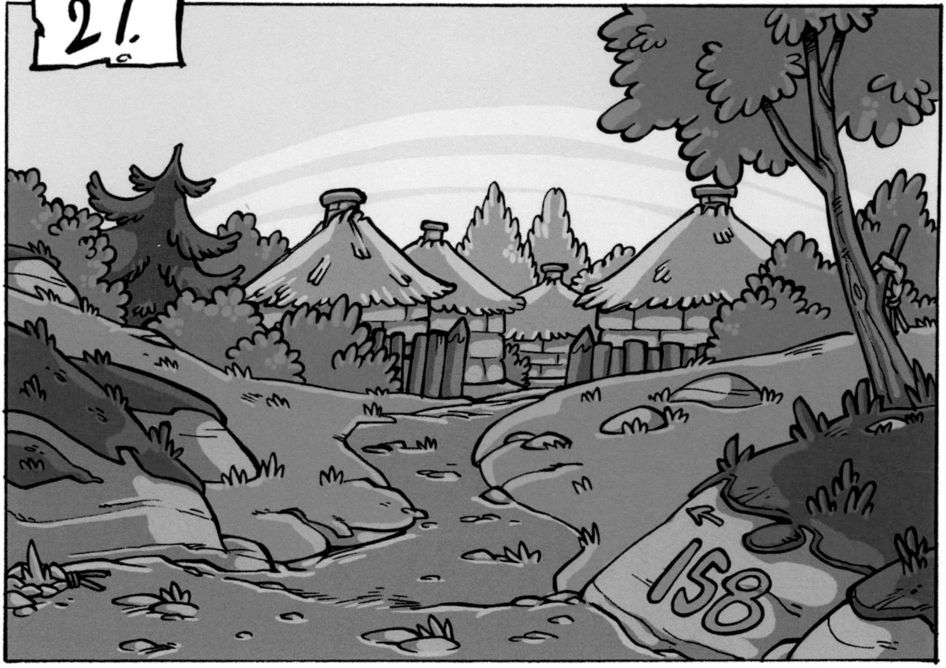
158

22.

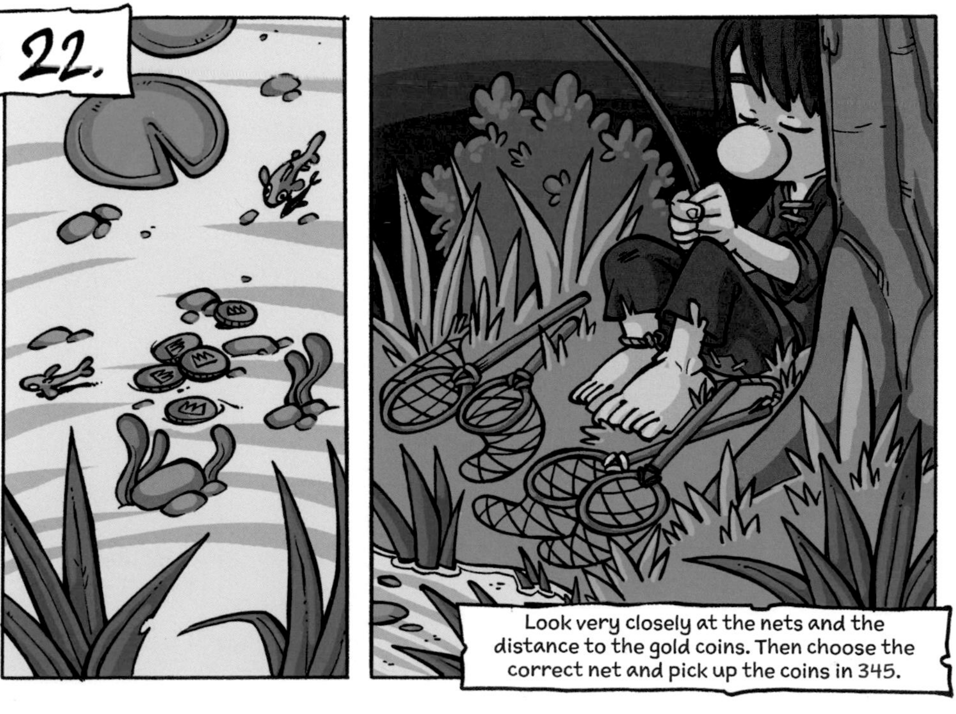
Look very closely at the nets and the distance to the gold coins. Then choose the correct net and pick up the coins in 345.

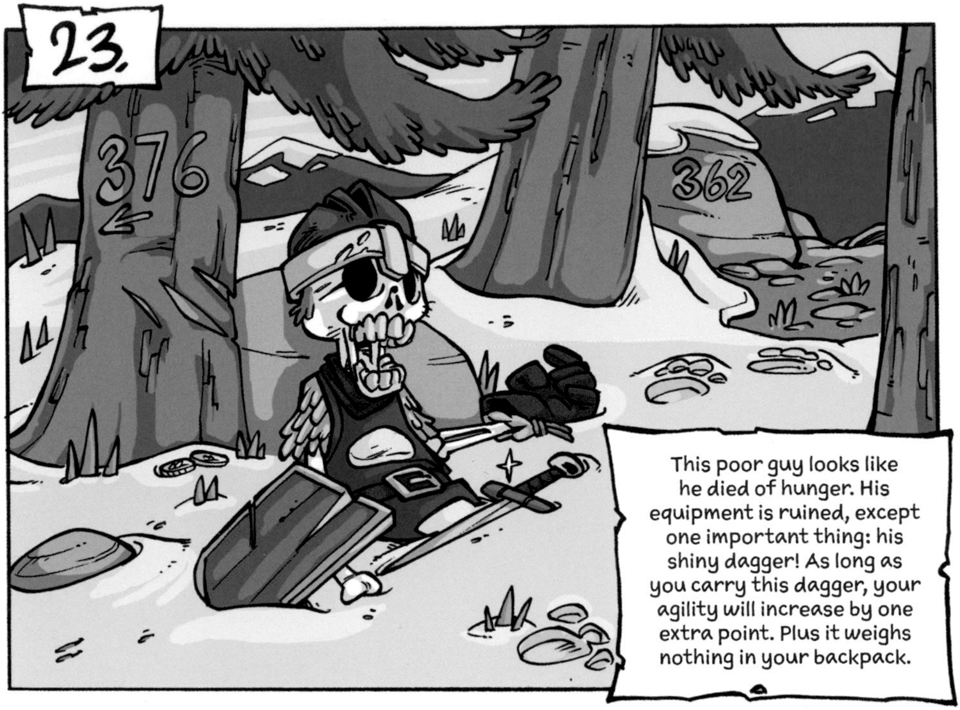
23.
376
362
This poor guy looks like he died of hunger. His equipment is ruined, except one important thing: his shiny dagger! As long as you carry this dagger, your agility will increase by one extra point. Plus it weighs nothing in your backpack.

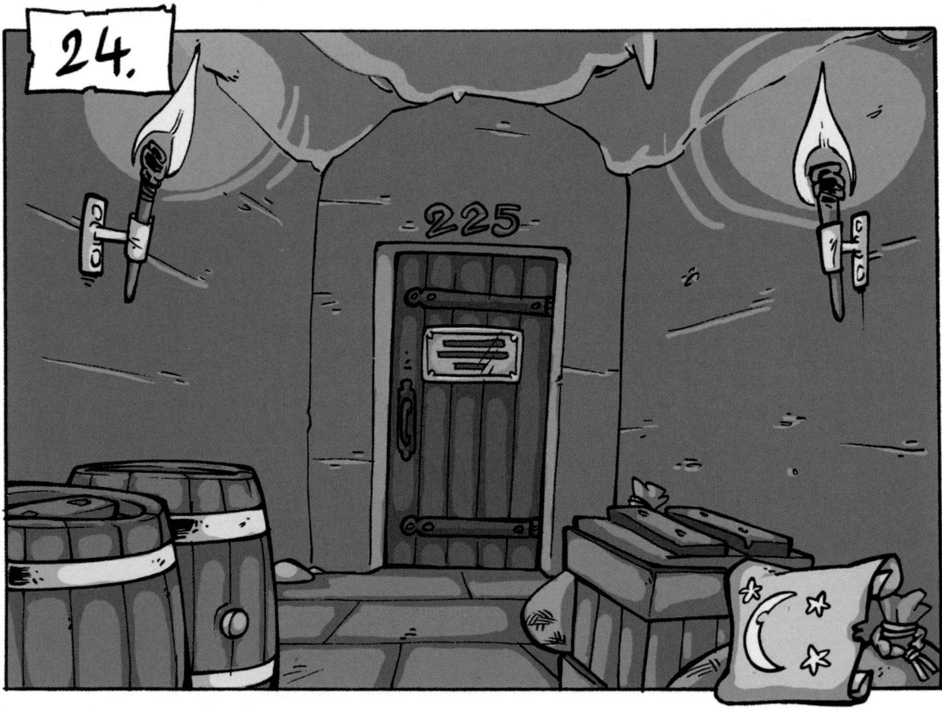
24.
225

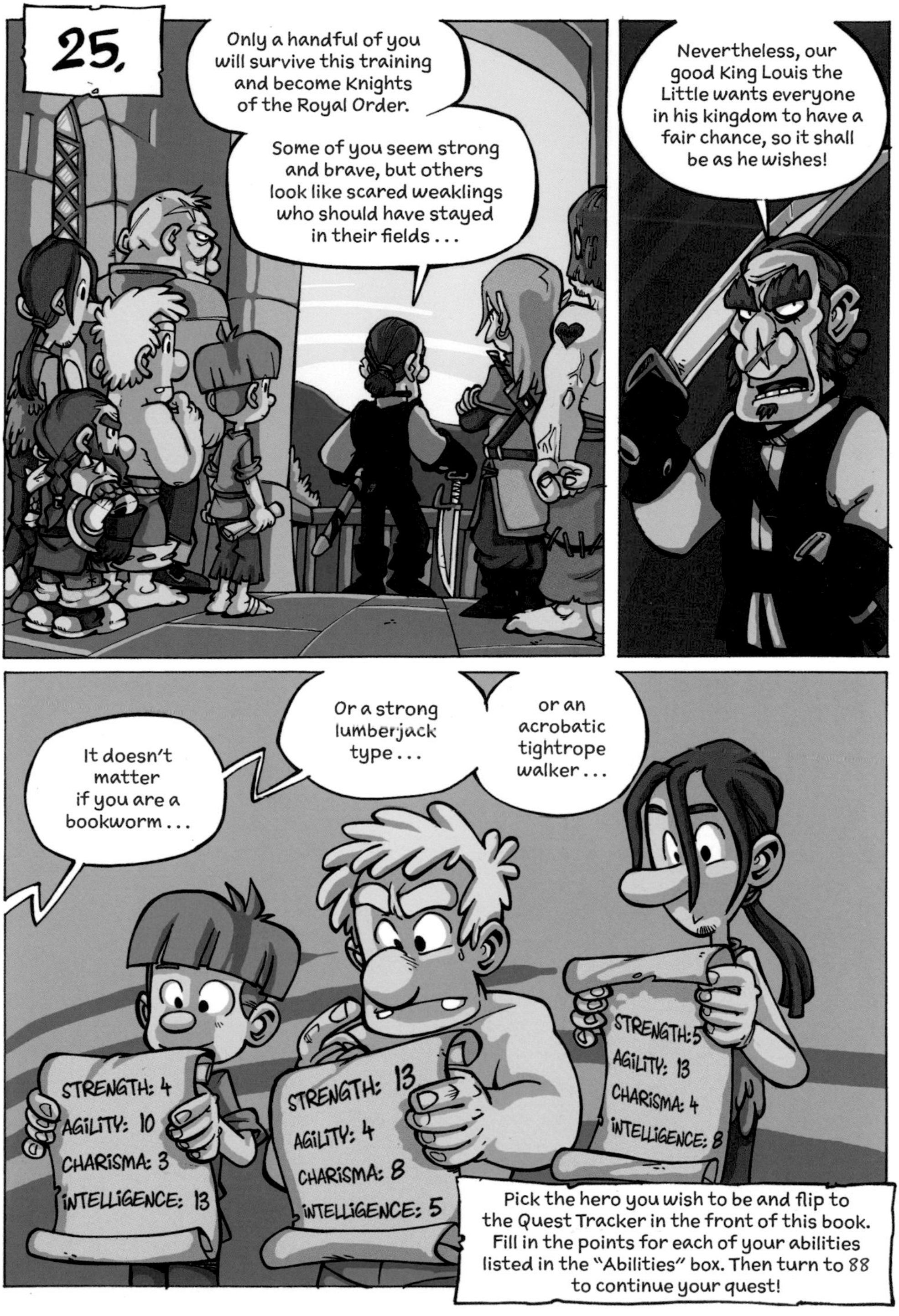
25.
Only a handful of you will survive this training and become Knights of the Royal Order.
Some of you seem strong and brave, but others look like scared weaklings who should have stayed in their fields . . .
Nevertheless, our good King Louis the Little wants everyone in his kingdom to have a fair chance, so it shall be as he wishes!
It doesn't matter if you are a bookworm . . .
Or a strong lumberjack type . . .
or an acrobatic tightrope walker . . .
STRENGTH: 4
AGILITY: 10
CHARISMA: 3
INTELLIGENCE: 13
STRENGTH: 13
AGILITY: 4
CHARISMA: 8
INTELLIGENCE: 5
STRENGTH: 5
AGILITY: 13
CHARISMA: 4
INTELLIGENCE: 8
Pick the hero you wish to be and flip to the Quest Tracker in the front of this book. Fill in the points for each of your abilities listed in the "Abilities" box. Then turn to 88 to continue your quest!

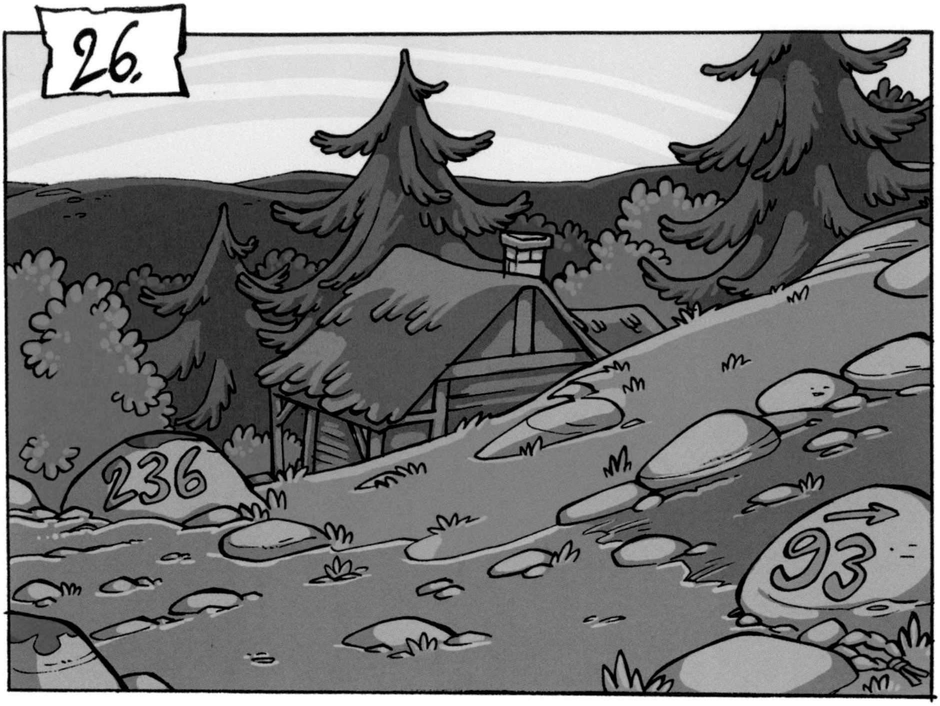
26.
236
93

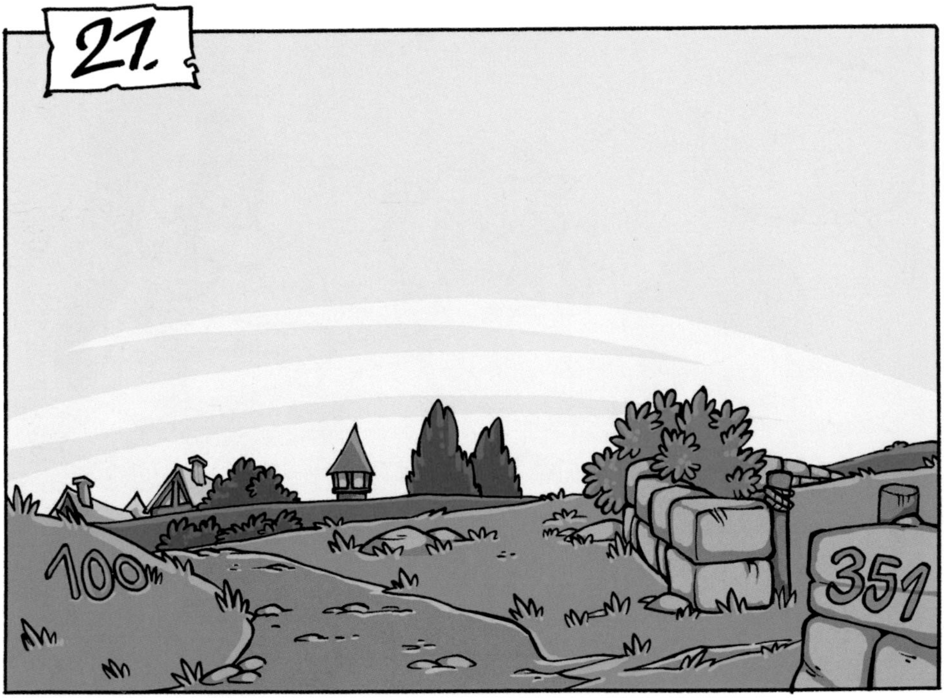
27.
100
351

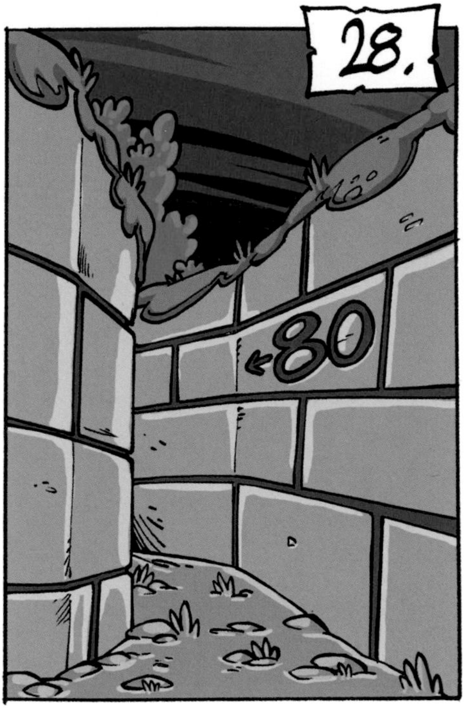
28.
80

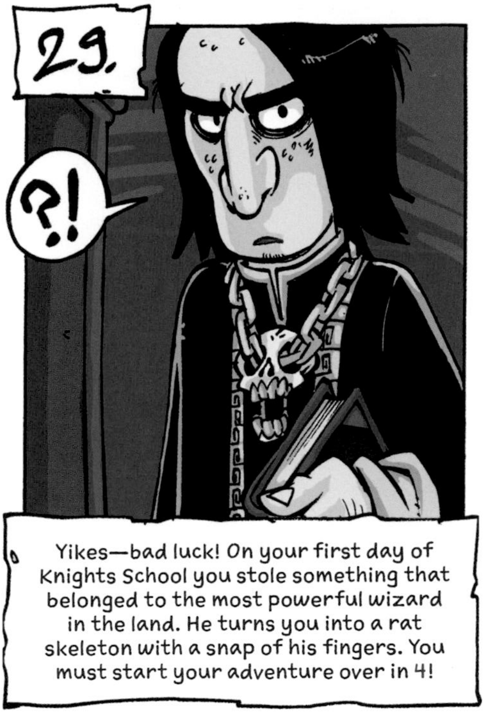
29.
?!
Yikes—bad luck! On your first day of Knights School you stole something that belonged to the most powerful wizard in the land. He turns you into a rat skeleton with a snap of his fingers. You must start your adventure over in 4!

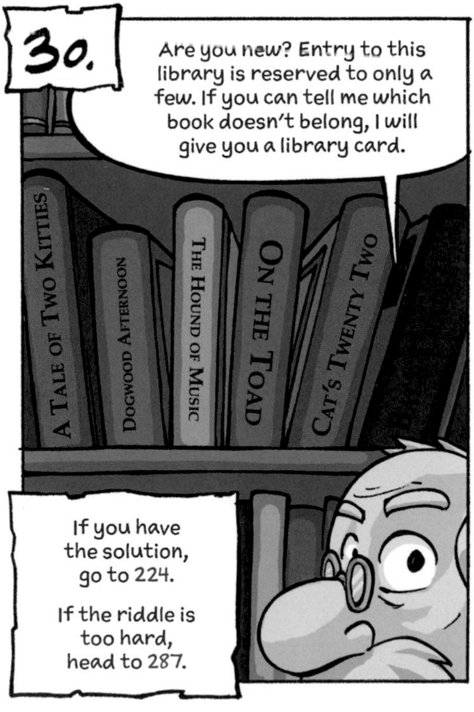
30.
Are you new? Entry to this library is reserved to only a few. If you can tell me which book doesn't belong, I will give you a library card.
A Tale of Two Kitties
Dogwood Afternoon
The Hound of Music
On the Toad
Cat's Twenty Two
If you have the solution, go to 224.
If the riddle is too hard, head to 287.

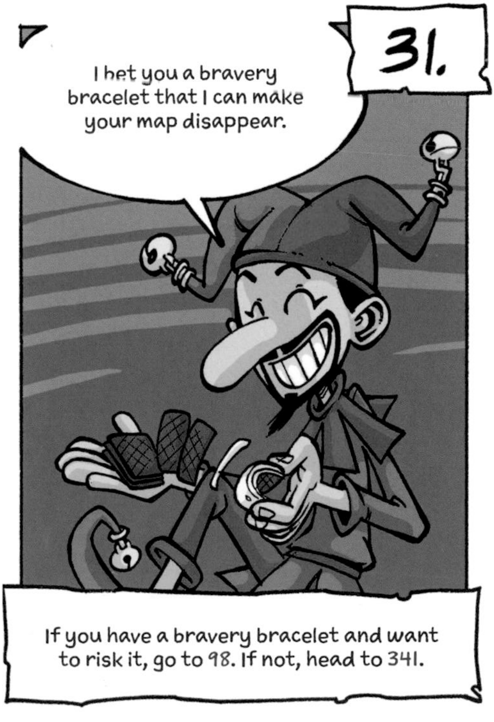
31.
I bet you a bravery bracelet that I can make your map disappear.
If you have a bravery bracelet and want to risk it, go to 98. If not, head to 341.

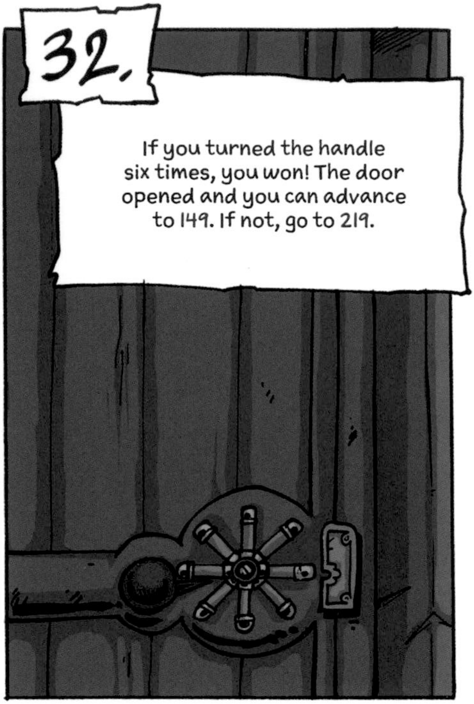
32.
If you turned the handle six times, you won! The door opened and you can advance to 149. If not, go to 219.

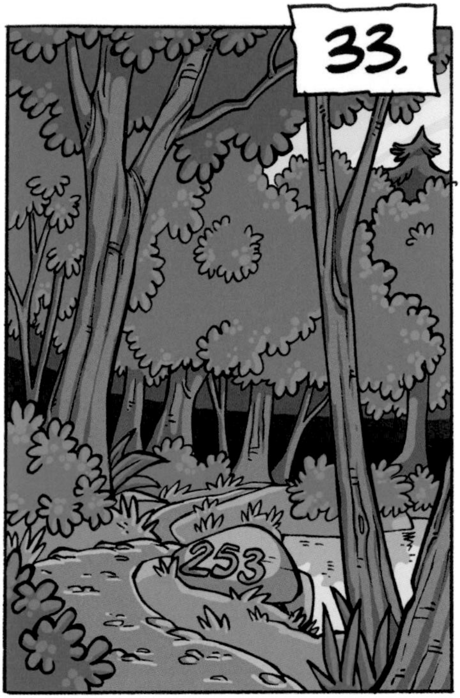
33.
253

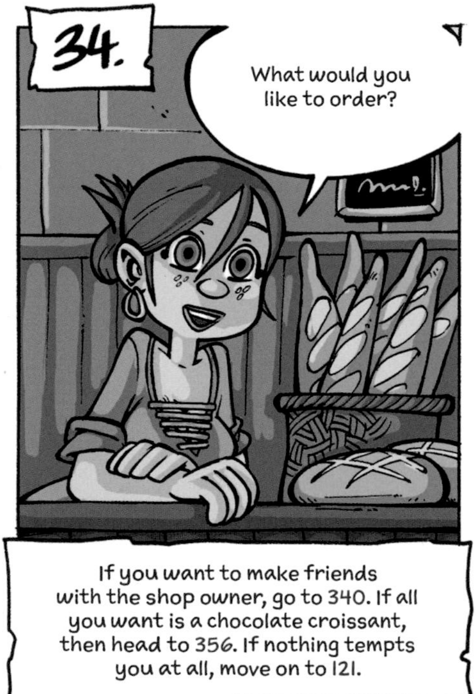
34.
What would you like to order?
If you want to make friends with the shop owner, go to 340. If all you want is a chocolate croissant, then head to 356. If nothing tempts you at all, move on to 121.

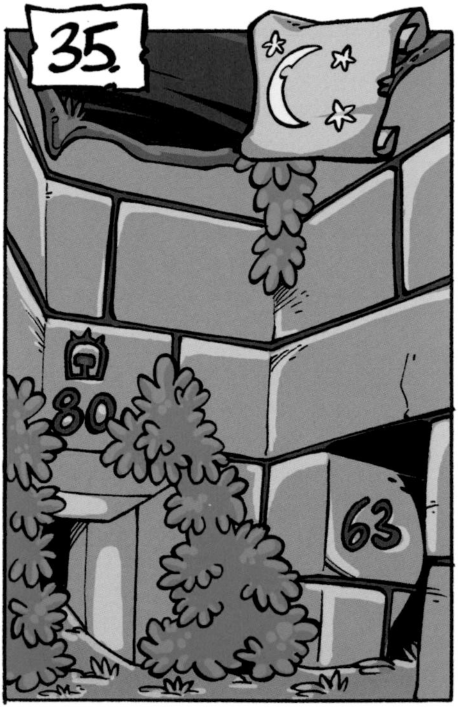
35.
80
63

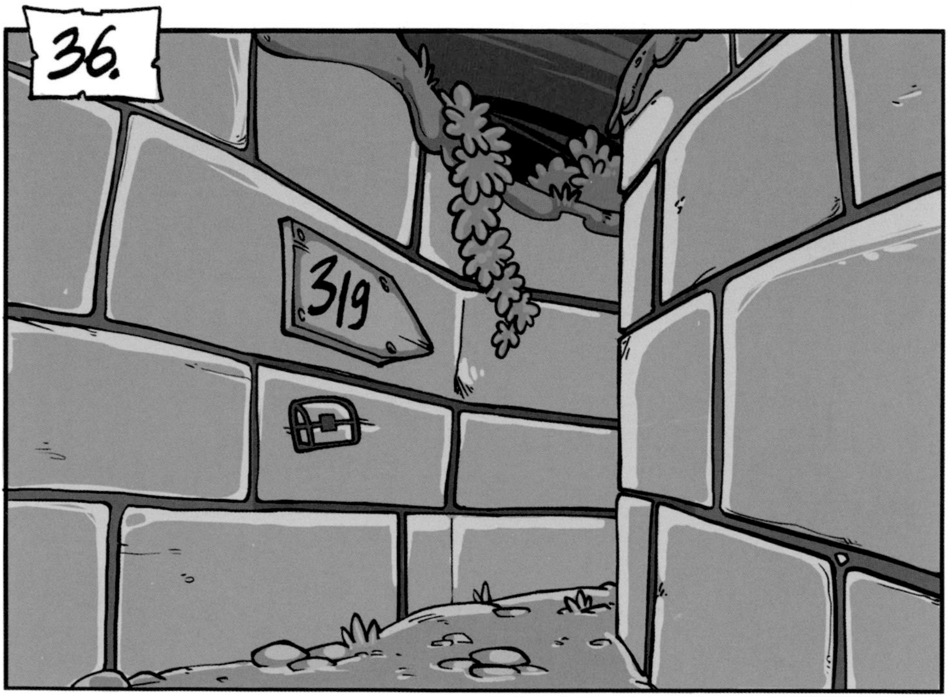
36.
319

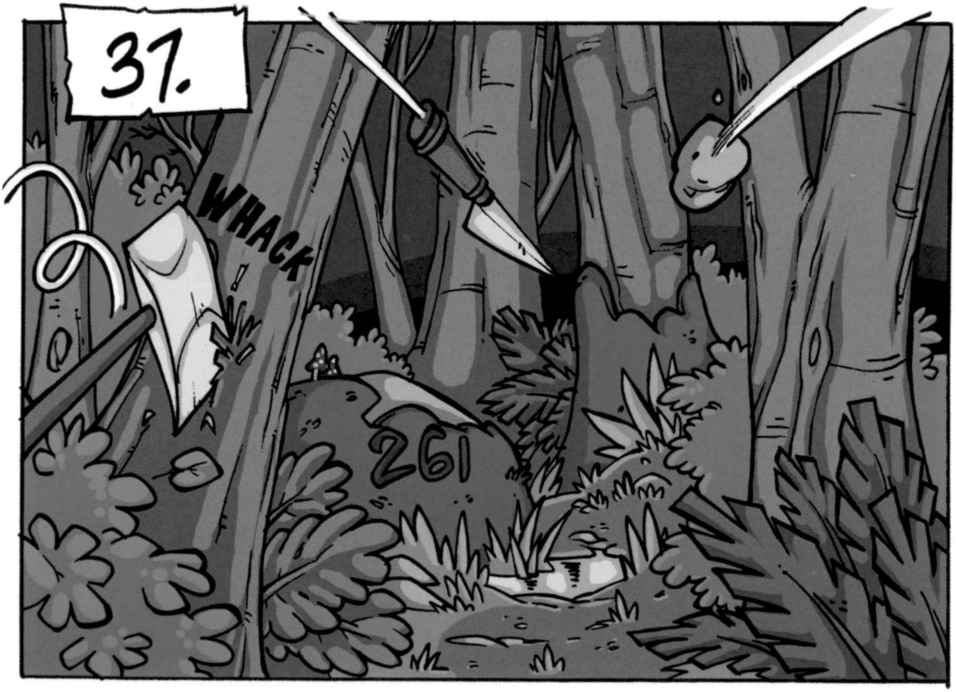
37.
WHACK
!
261

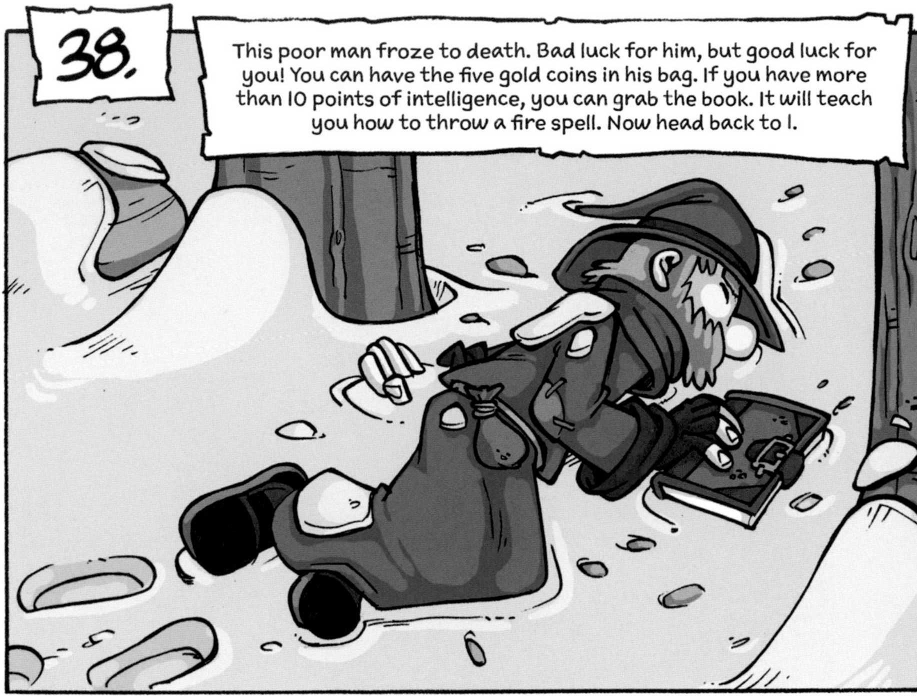
38.
This poor man froze to death. Bad luck for him, but good luck for you! You can have the five gold coins in his bag. If you have more than 10 points of intelligence, you can grab the book. It will teach you how to throw a fire spell. Now head back to 1.

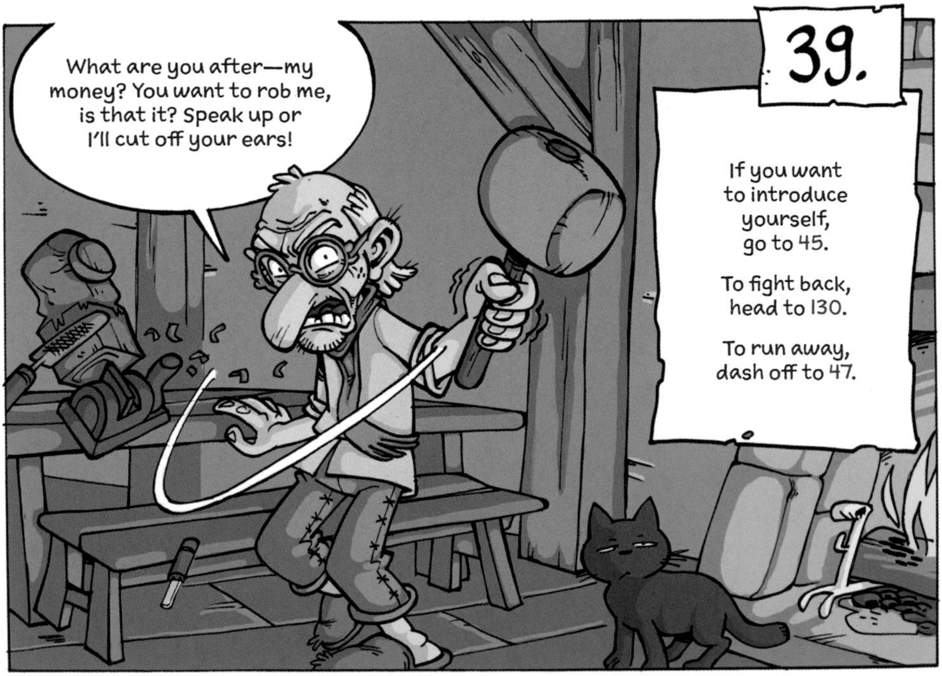
39.
What are you after—my money? You want to rob me, is that it? Speak up or I'll cut off your ears!
If you want to introduce yourself, go to 45.
To fight back, head to 130.
To run away, dash off to 47.

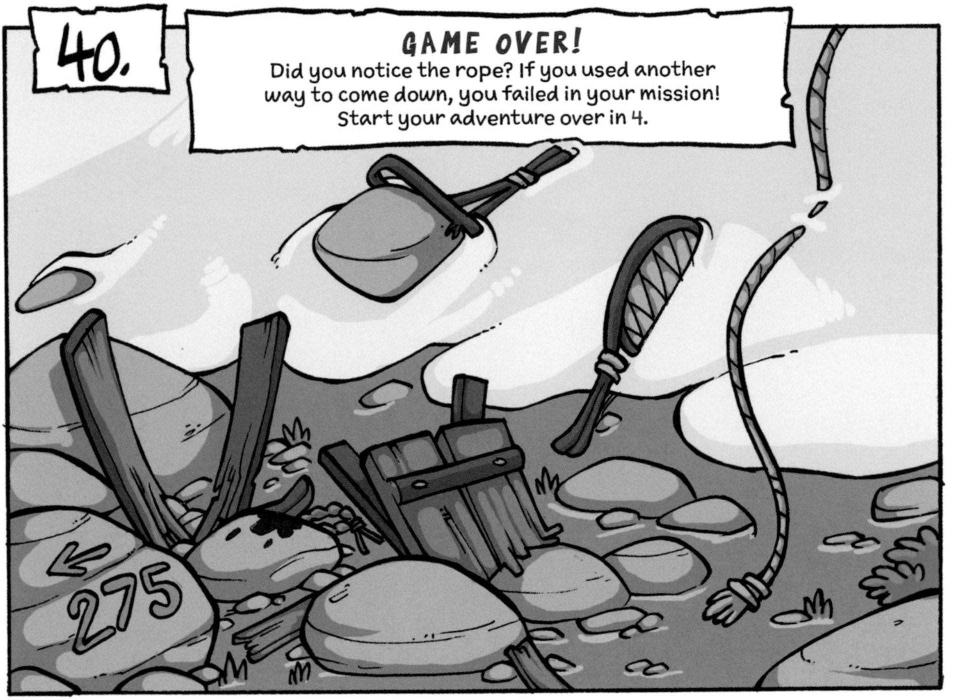
40.
GAME OVER!
Did you notice the rope? If you used another way to come down, you failed in your mission! Start your adventure over in 4.
275

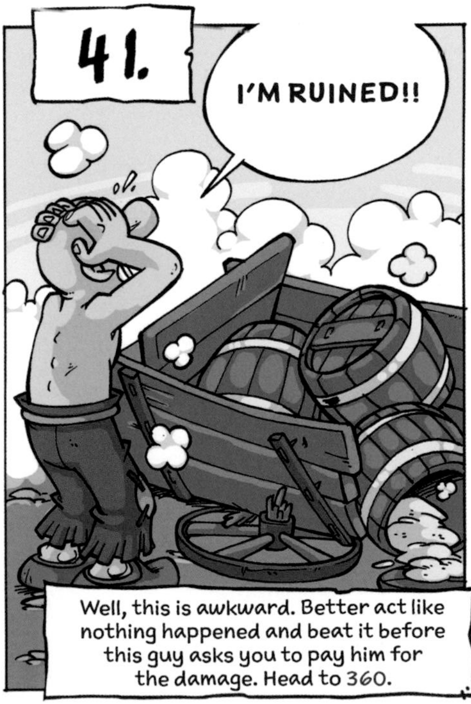
41.
I'M RUINED!!
Well, this is awkward. Better act like nothing happened and beat it before this guy asks you to pay him for the damage. Head to 360.

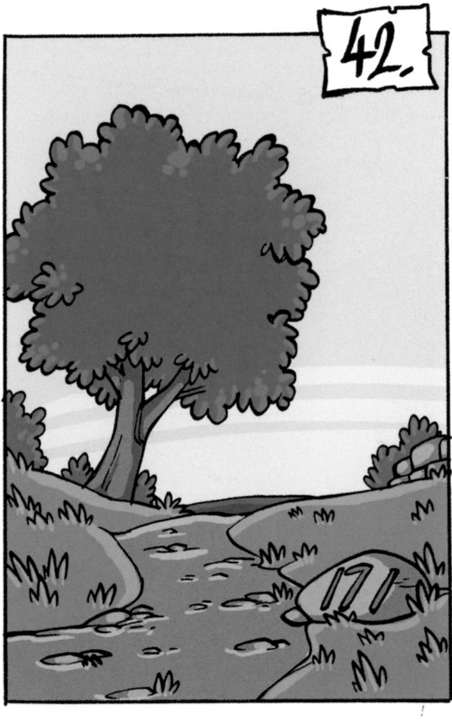
42.
171

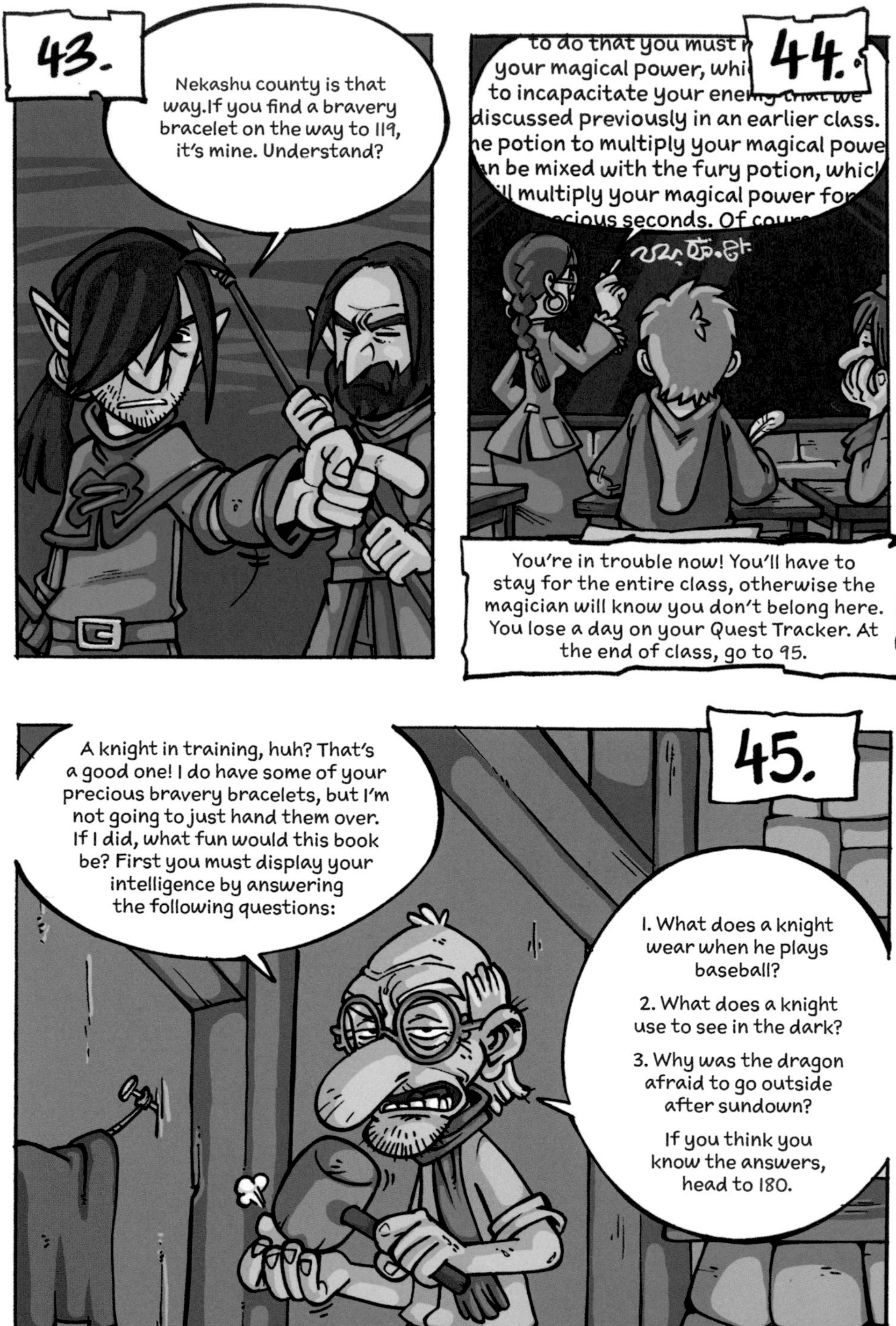

43.
Nekashu county is that way.If you find a bravery bracelet on the way to 119, it's mine. Understand?
44.
to do that you must
your magical power, whi
to incapacitate your enem
discussed previously in an earlier class.
potion to multiply your magical powe
be mixed with the fury potion, whic
multiply your magical power fo
seconds. Of cour
You're in trouble now! You'll have to stay for the entire class, otherwise the magician will know you don't belong here. You lose a day on your Quest Tracker. At the end of class, go to 95.
45.
A knight in training, huh? That's a good one! I do have some of your precious bravery bracelets, but I'm not going to just hand them over. If I did, what fun would this book be? First you must display your intelligence by answering the following questions:
1. What does a knight wear when he plays baseball?
2. What does a knight use to see in the dark?
3. Why was the dragon afraid to go outside after sundown?
If you think you know the answers, head to 180.

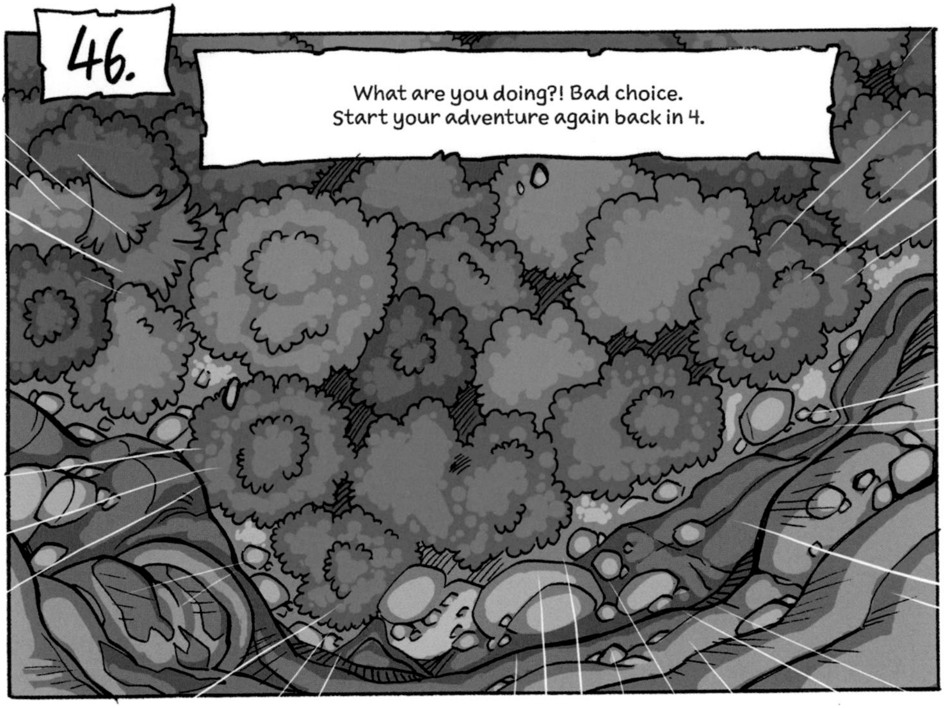
46.
What are you doing?! Bad choice.
Start your adventure again back in 4.

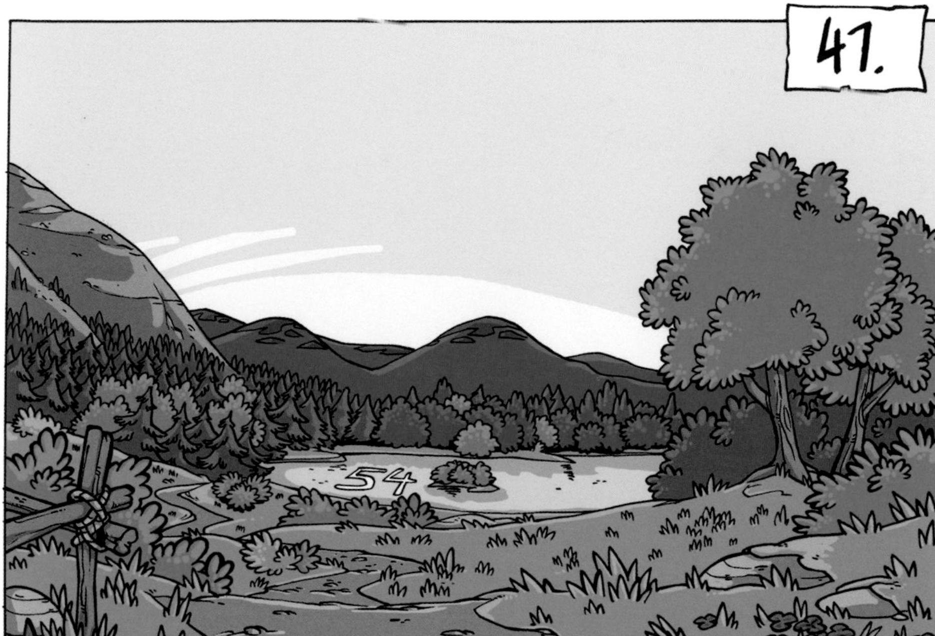
47.
54

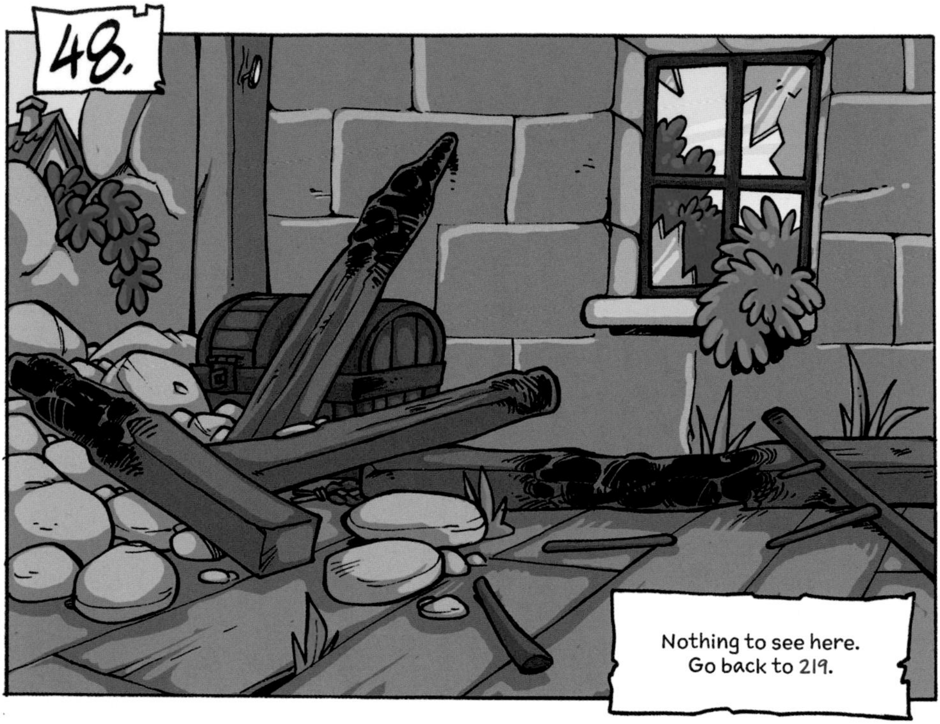
48.
Nothing to see here.
Go back to 219.

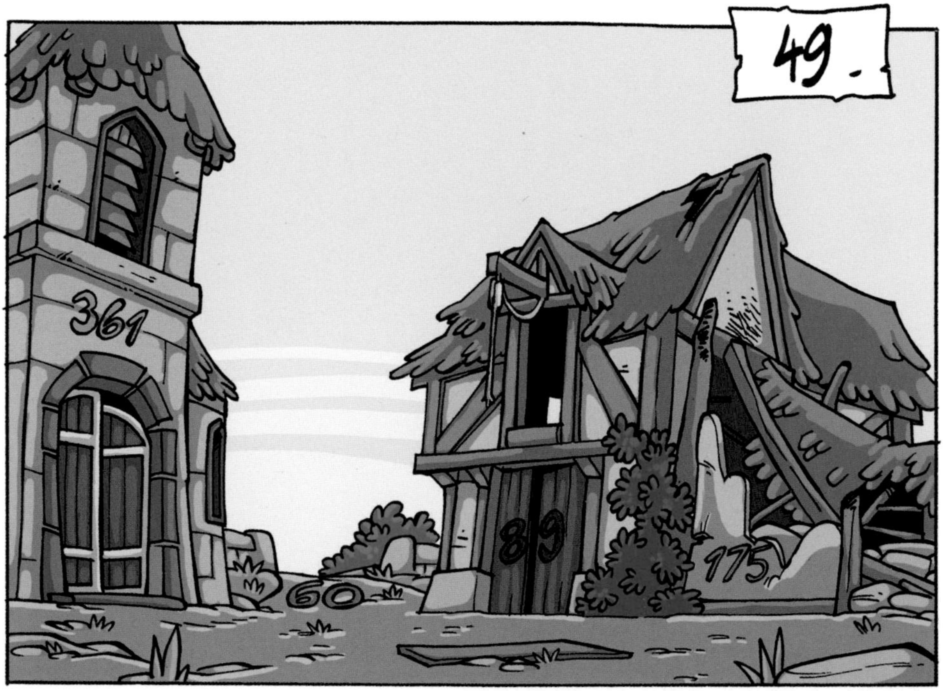
49.
361
60
89
175

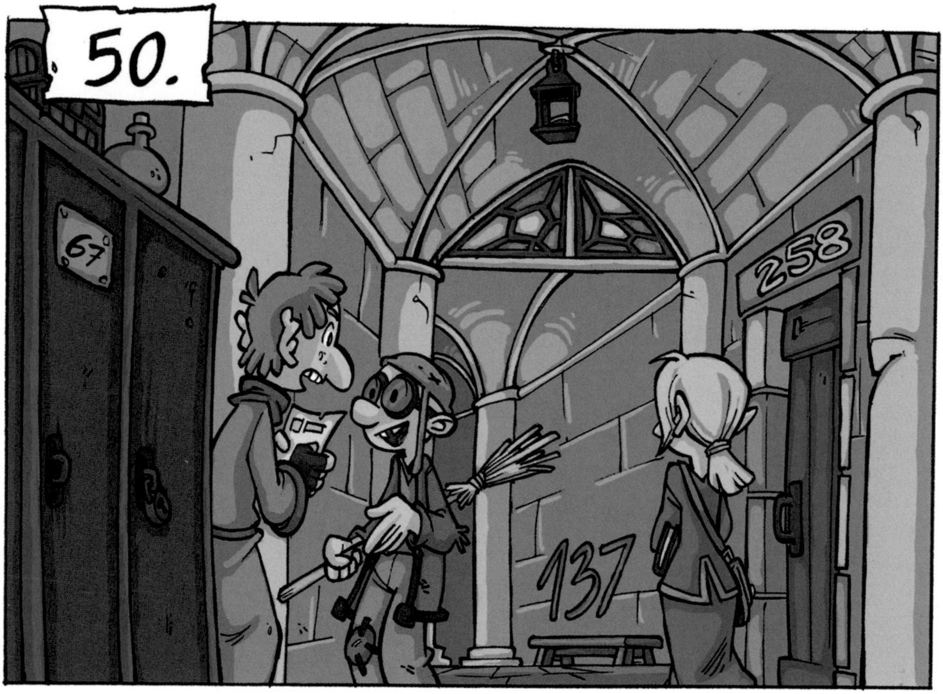
50.
67
258
137

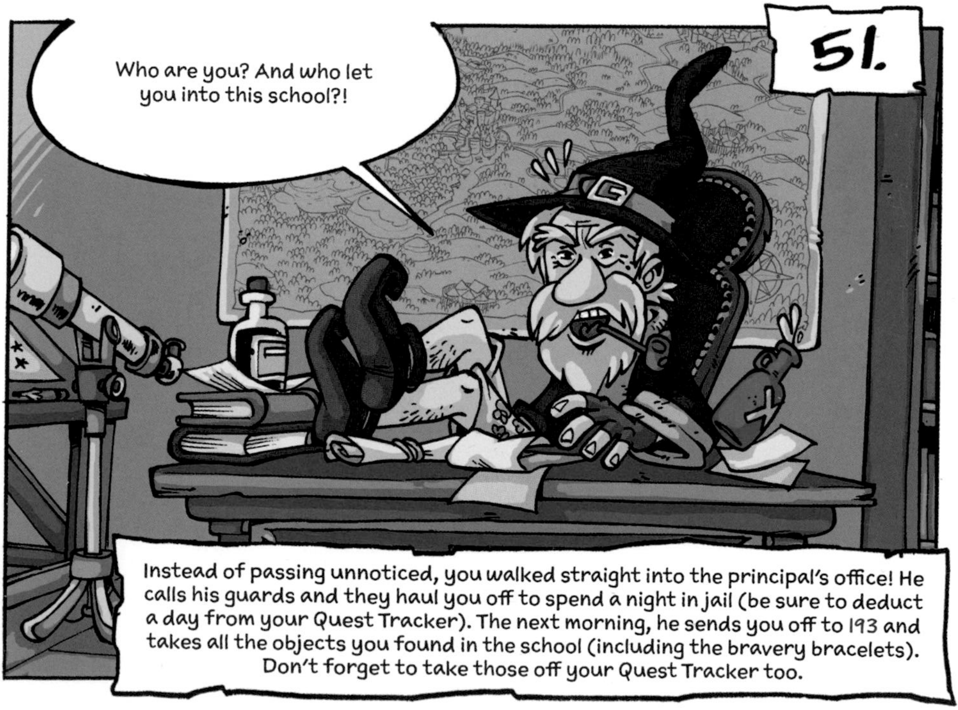
51.
Who are you? And who let you into this school?!
Instead of passing unnoticed, you walked straight into the principal's office! He calls his guards and they haul you off to spend a night in jail (be sure to deduct a day from your Quest Tracker). The next morning, he sends you off to 193 and takes all the objects you found in the school (including the bravery bracelets). Don't forget to take those off your Quest Tracker too.

52.

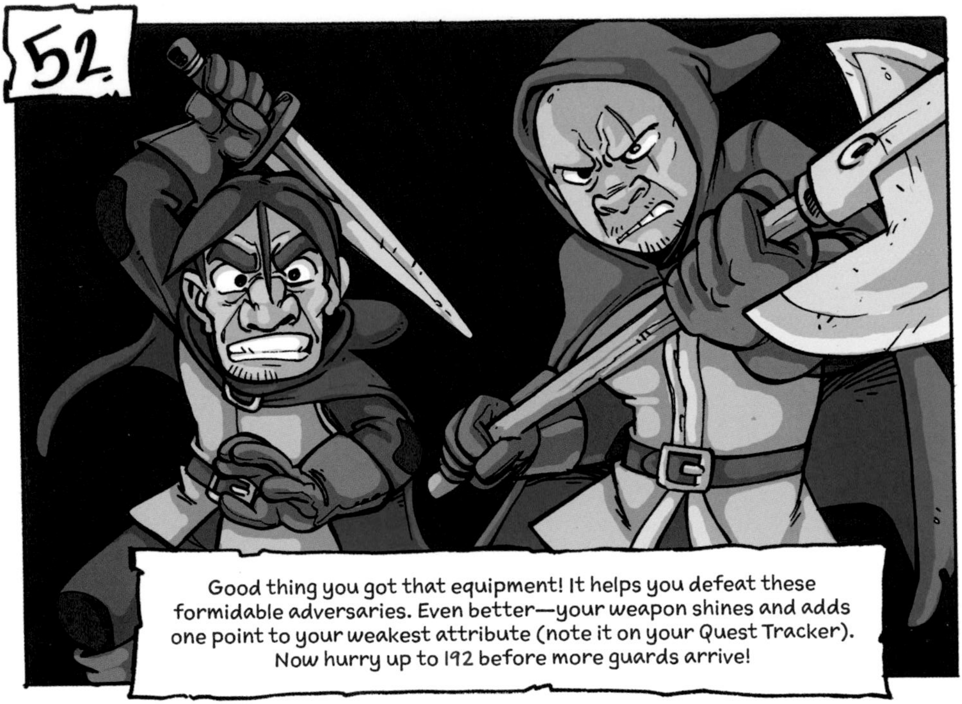
Good thing you got that equipment! It helps you defeat these formidable adversaries. Even better—your weapon shines and adds one point to your weakest attribute (note it on your Quest Tracker). Now hurry up to 192 before more guards arrive!

53.

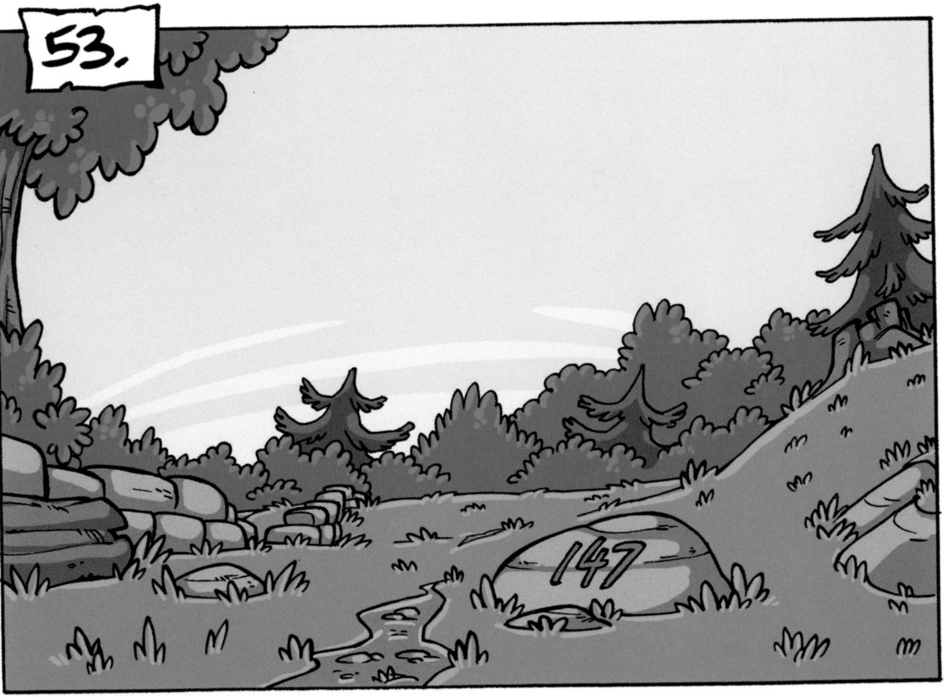
147

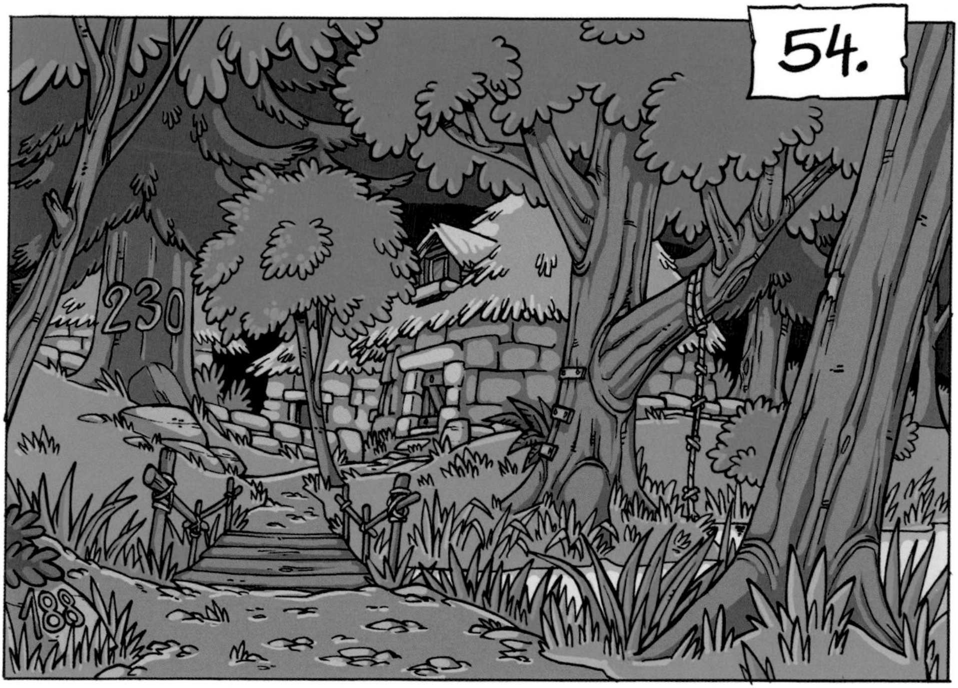
54.
230
188

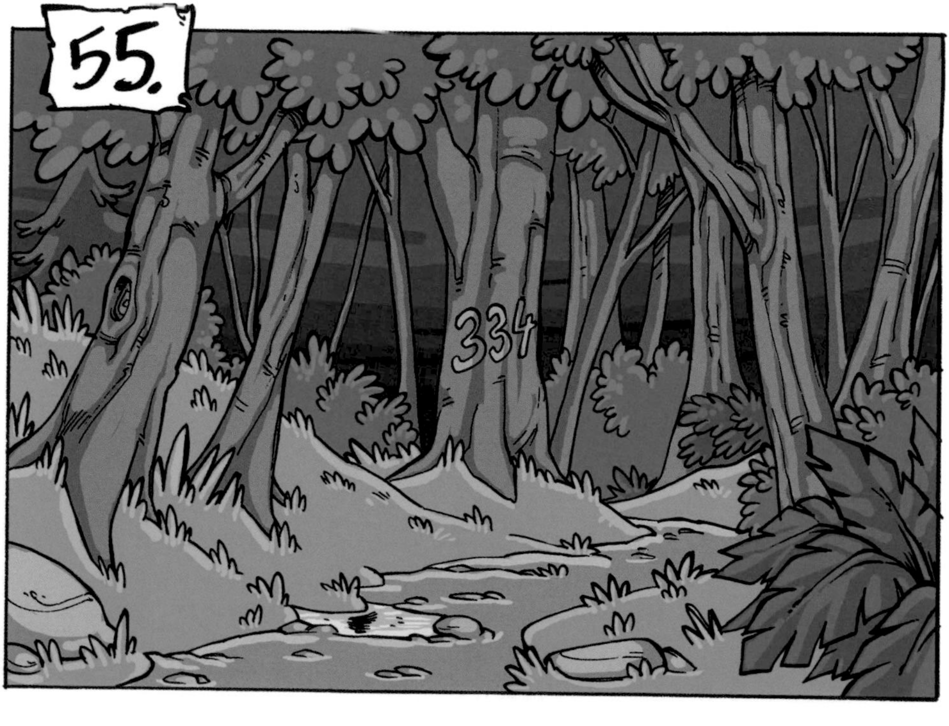
55.
334

56.

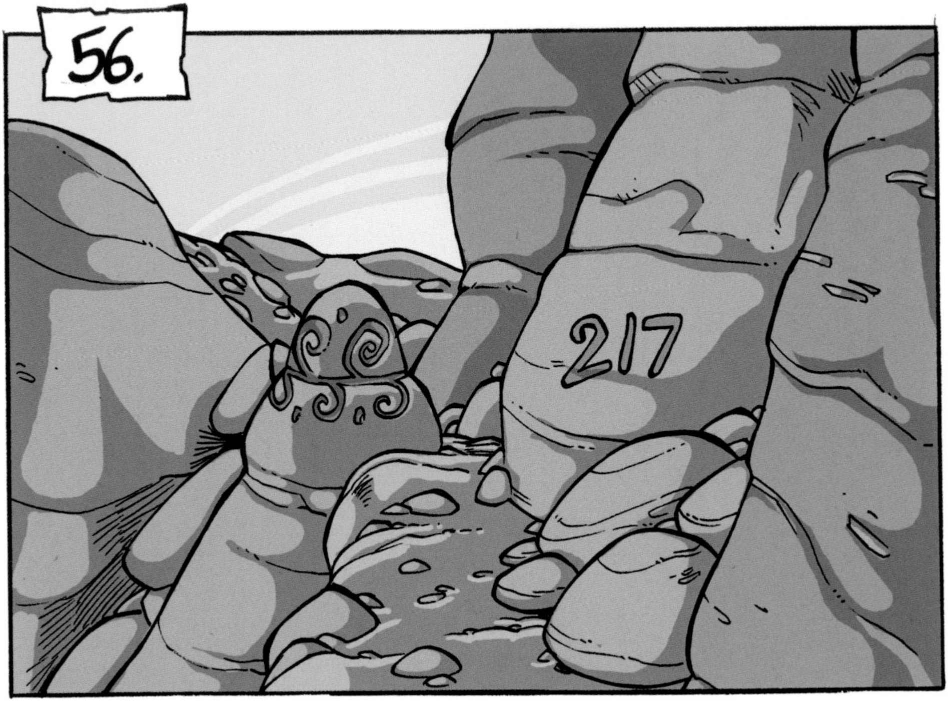
217

57.

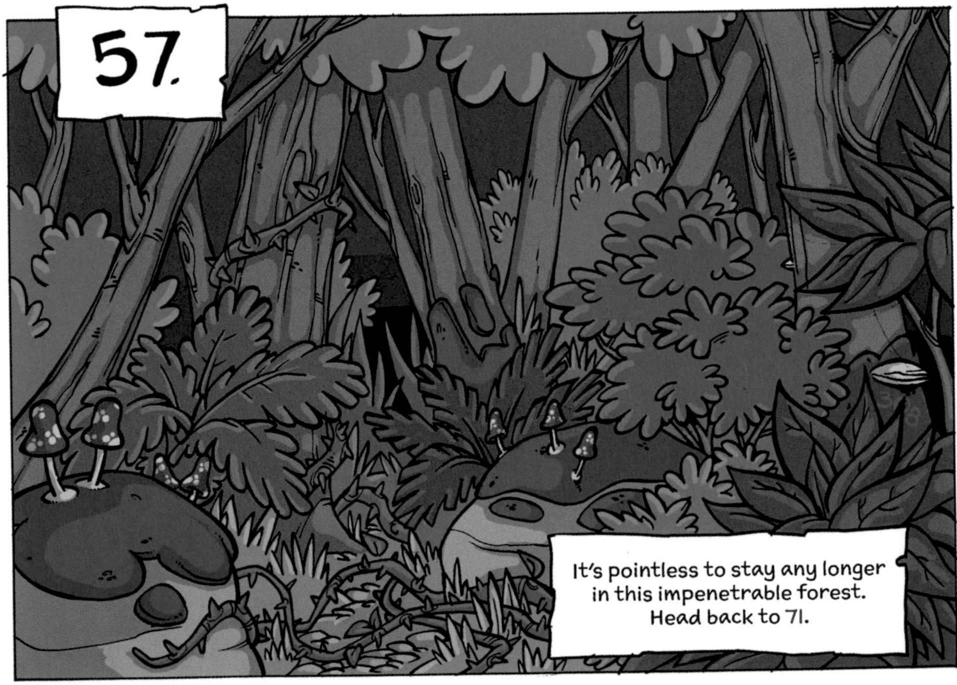
It's pointless to stay any longer in this impenetrable forest. Head back to 71.

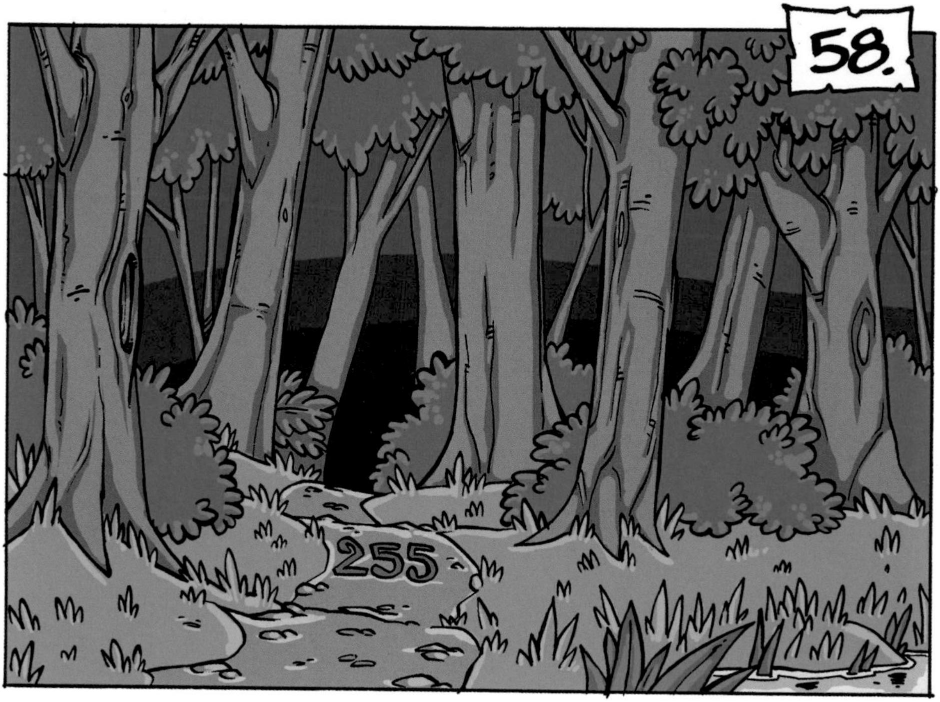
58.
255

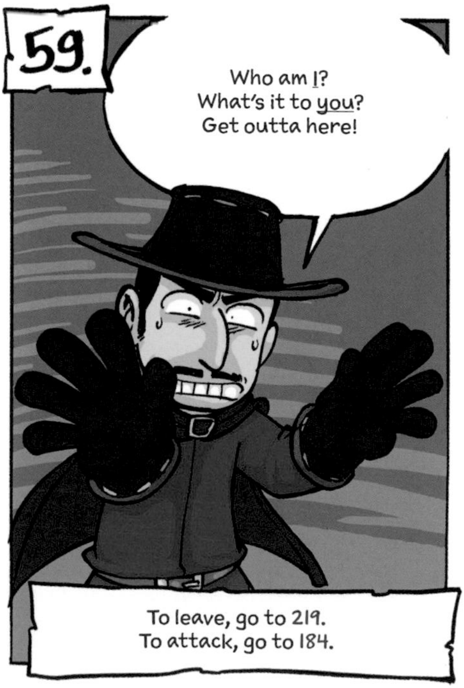
59.
Who am I? What's it to you? Get outta here!
To leave, go to 219. To attack, go to 184.

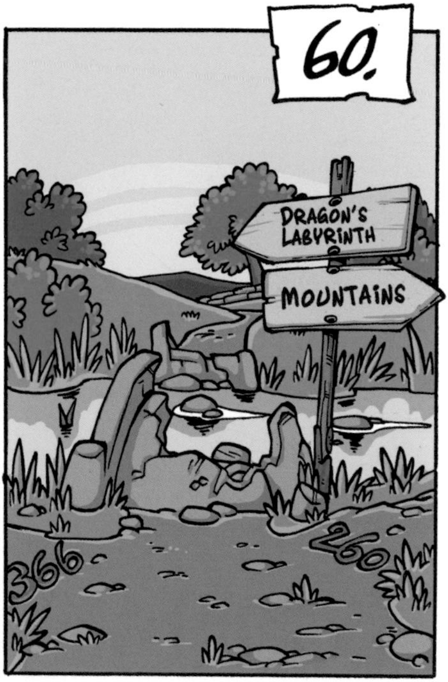
60.
DRAGON'S LABYRINTH
MOUNTAINS
366
260

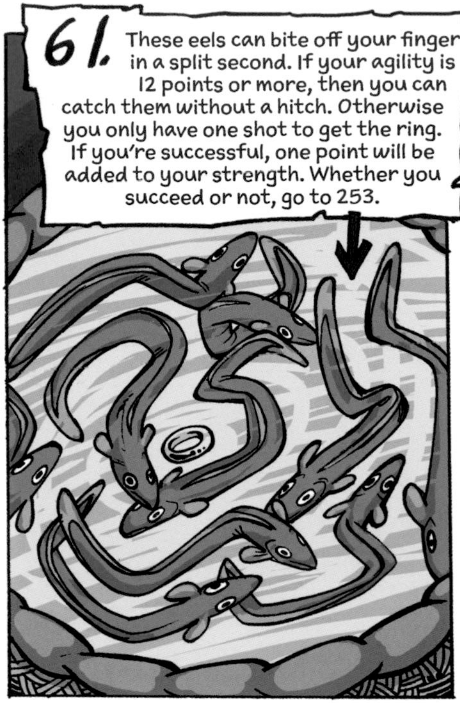
61.
These eels can bite off your finger in a split second. If your agility is 12 points or more, then you can catch them without a hitch. Otherwise you only have one shot to get the ring. If you're successful, one point will be added to your strength. Whether you succeed or not, go to 253.

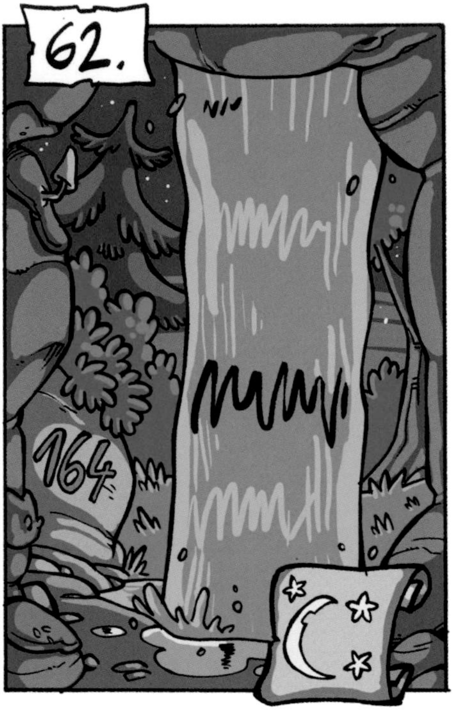
62.
164

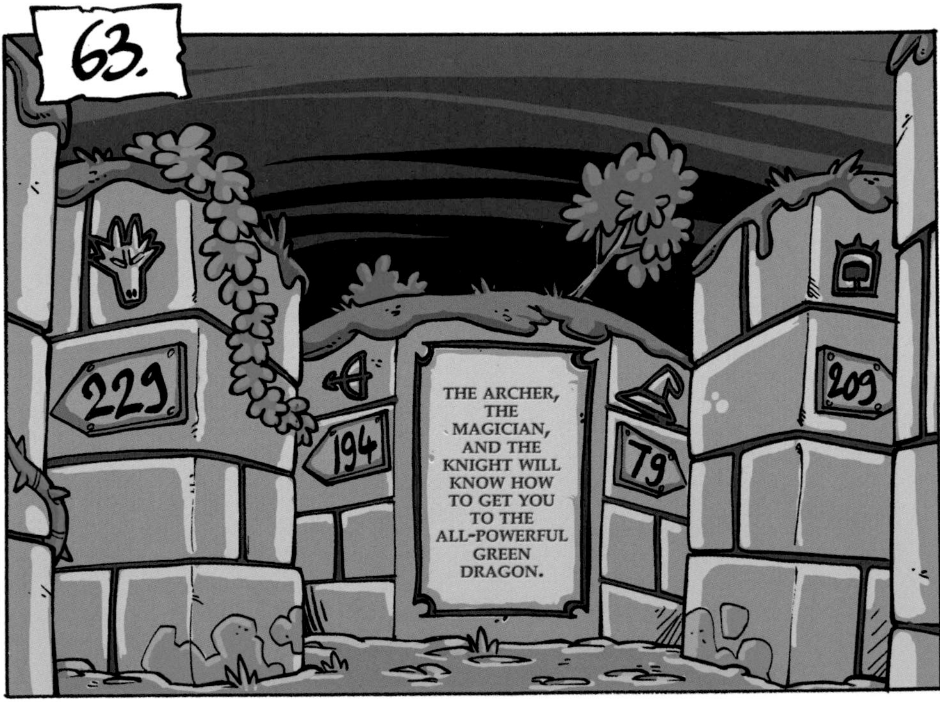
63.
229
194
THE ARCHER, THE MAGICIAN, AND THE KNIGHT WILL KNOW HOW TO GET YOU TO THE ALL-POWERFUL GREEN DRAGON.
79
209

64.

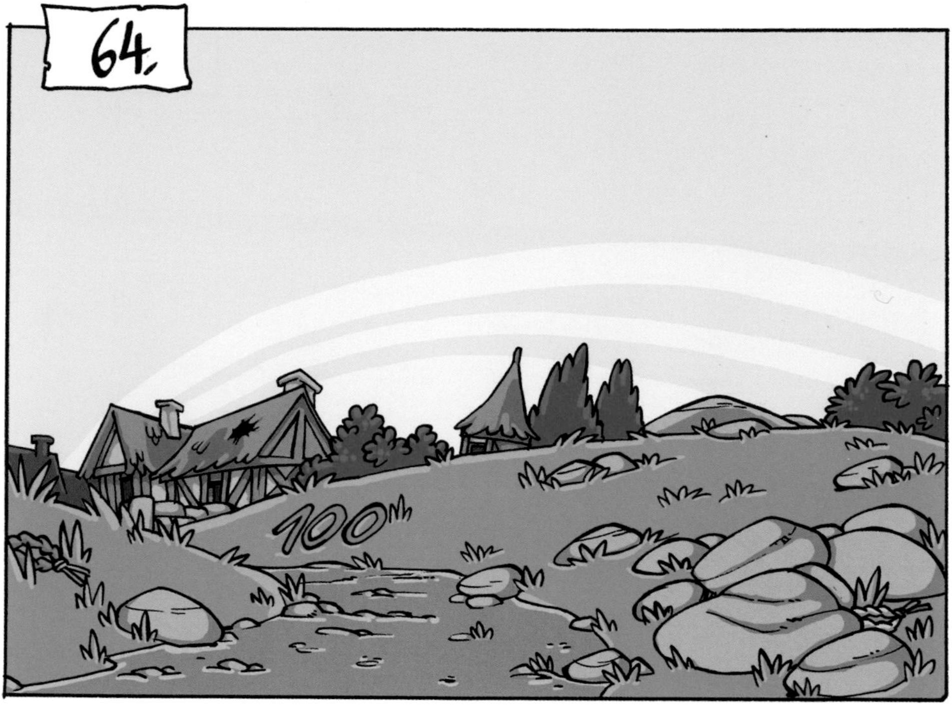
100

65.

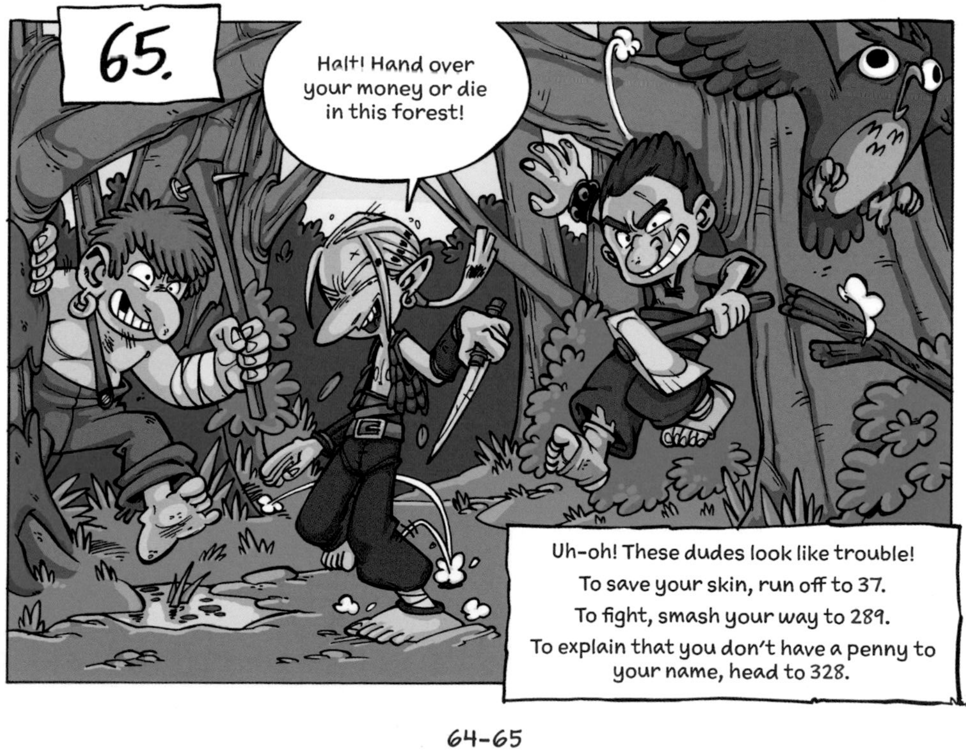
Halt! Hand over your money or die in this forest!
Uh-oh! These dudes look like trouble!
To save your skin, run off to 37.
To fight, smash your way to 289.
To explain that you don't have a penny to your name, head to 328.

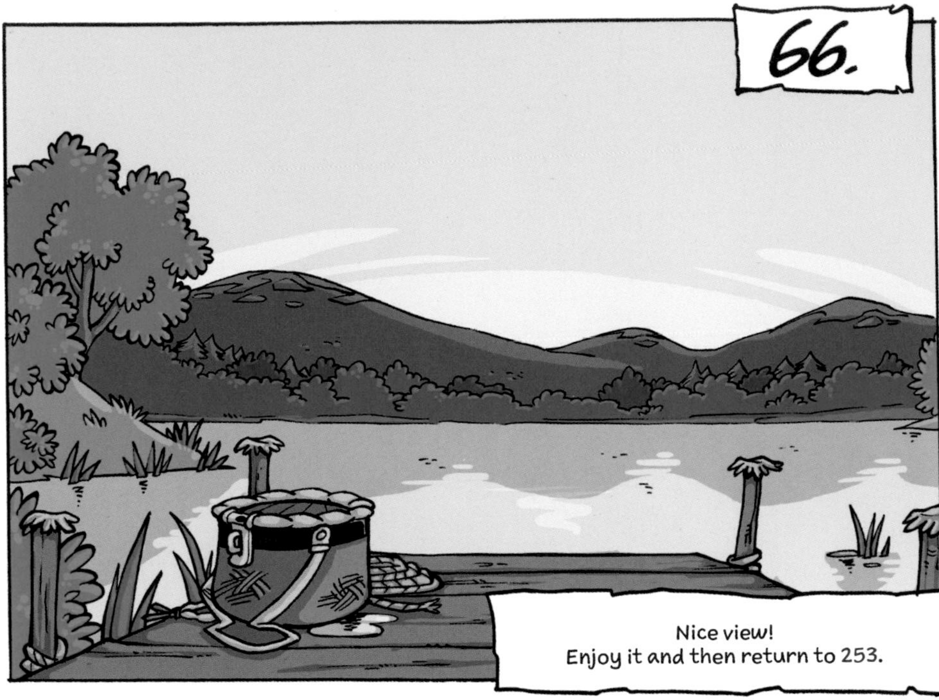
66.
Nice view!
Enjoy it and then return to 253.

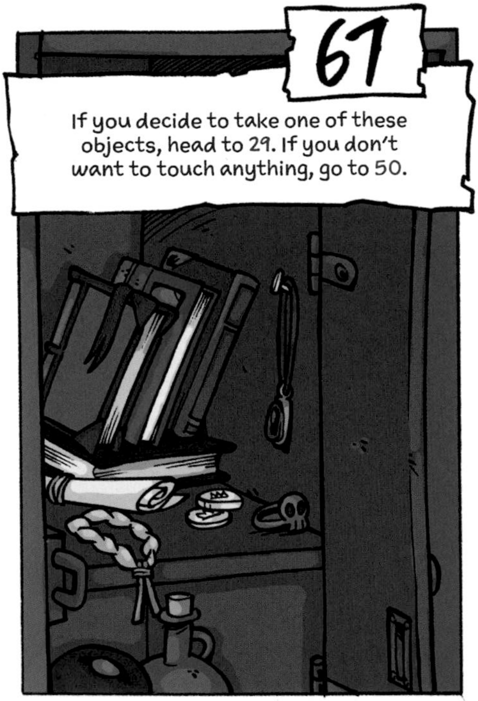
67
If you decide to take one of these objects, head to 29. If you don't want to touch anything, go to 50.

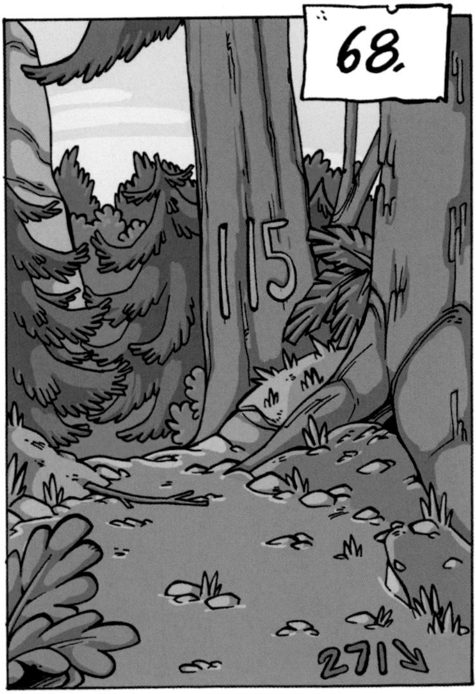
68.
115
271

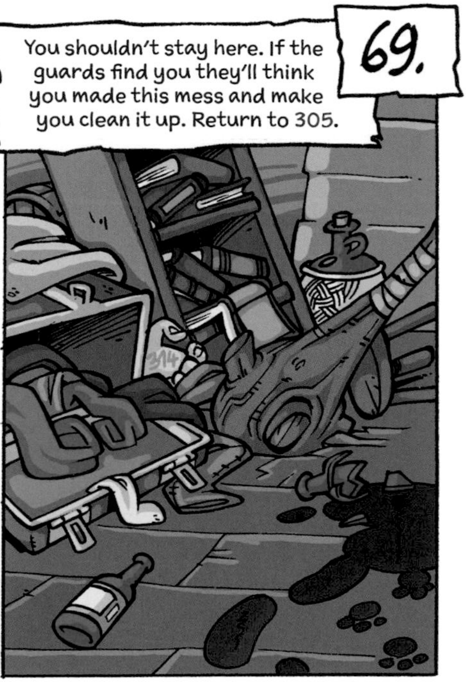
69.
You shouldn't stay here. If the guards find you they'll think you made this mess and make you clean it up. Return to 305.

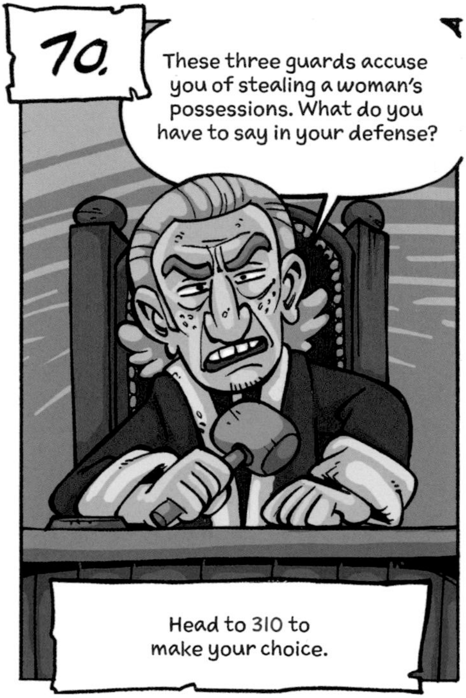
70.
These three guards accuse you of stealing a woman's possessions. What do you have to say in your defense?
Head to 310 to make your choice.

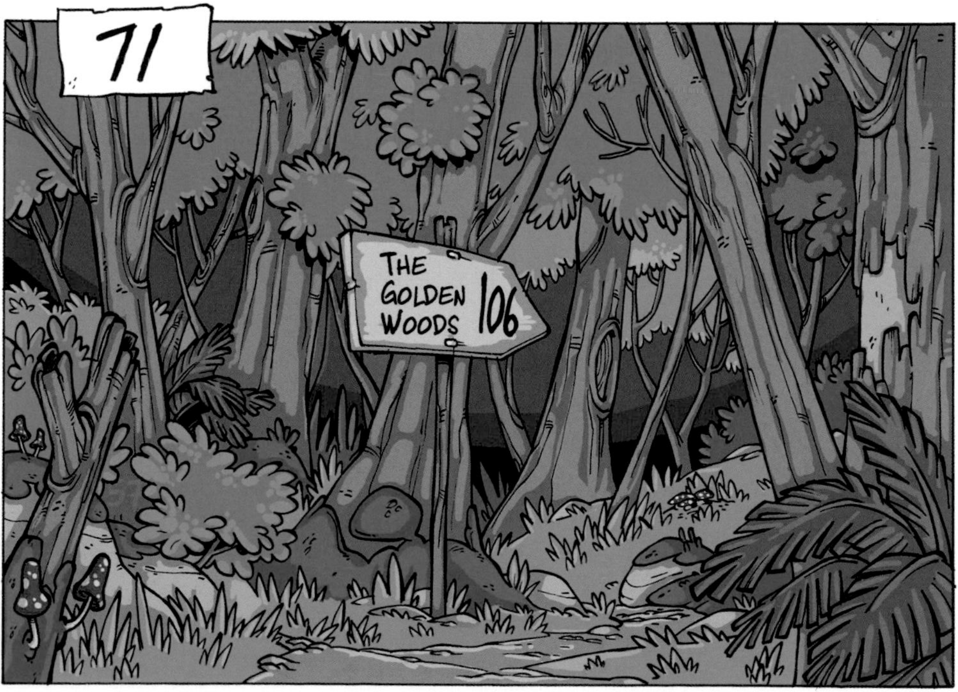
71
THE GOLDEN WOODS
106

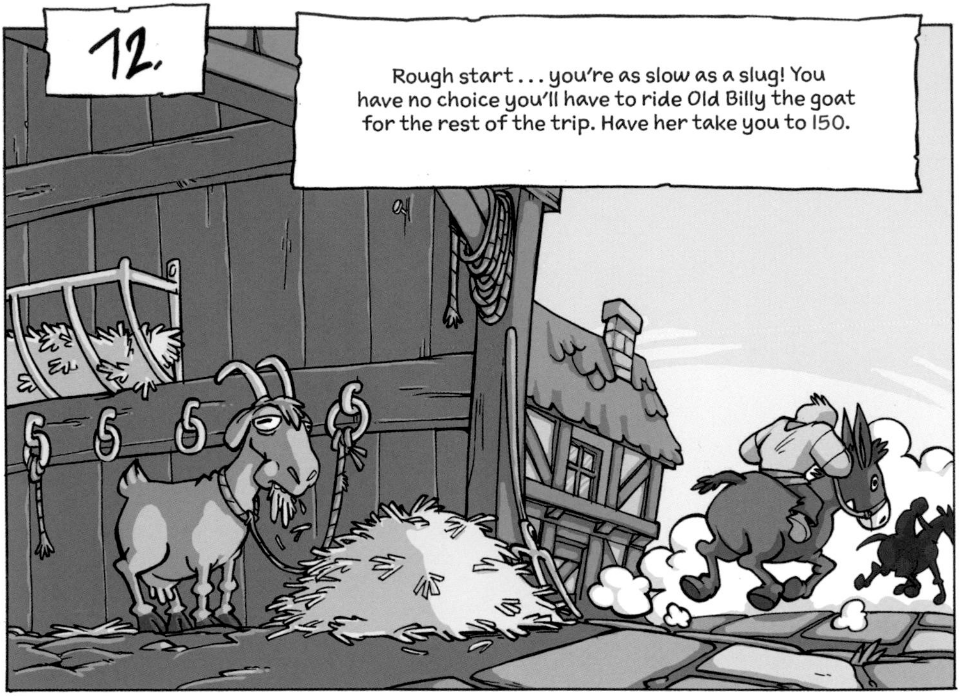
72.
Rough start . . . you're as slow as a slug! You have no choice you'll have to ride Old Billy the goat for the rest of the trip. Have her take you to 150.

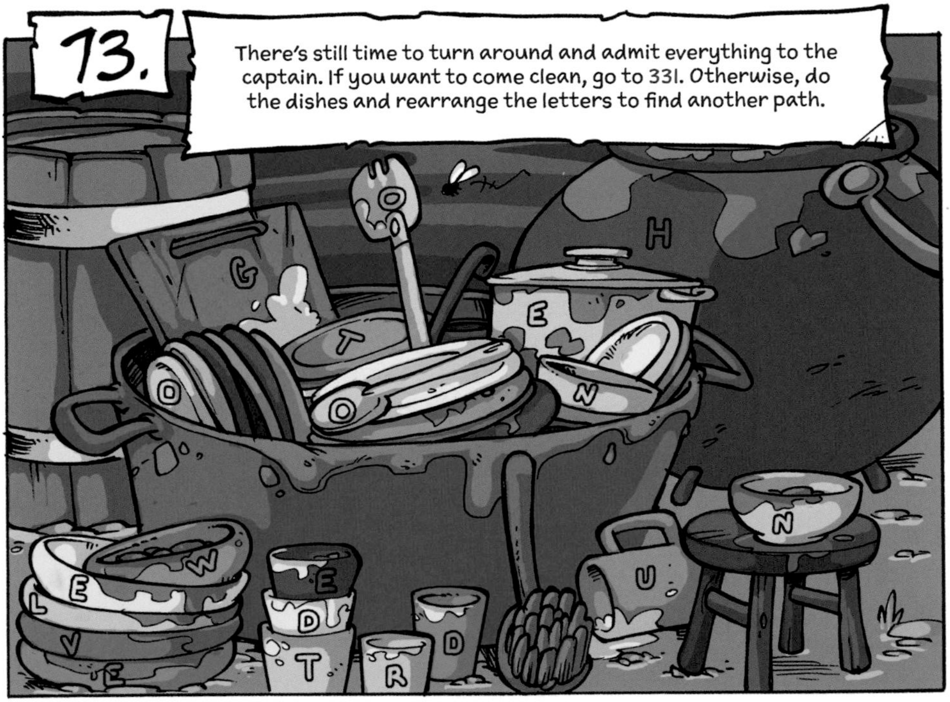
73.
There's still time to turn around and admit everything to the captain. If you want to come clean, go to 331. Otherwise, do the dishes and rearrange the letters to find another path.
O
O
H
G
E
T
D
O
N
W
E
L
E
V
E
D
T
R
D
U
N

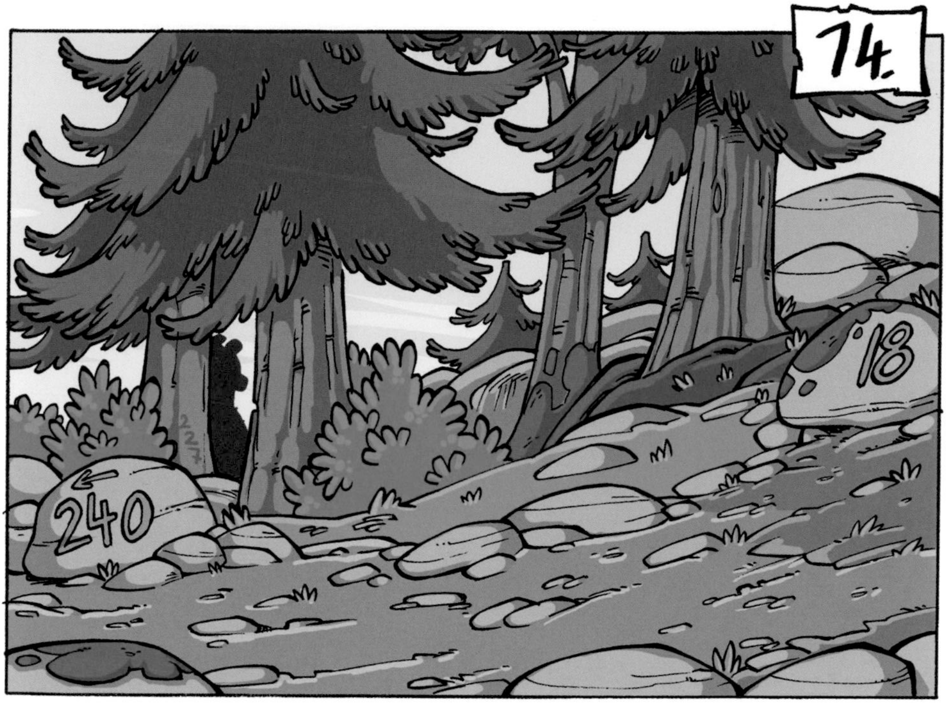
74.
240
227
18

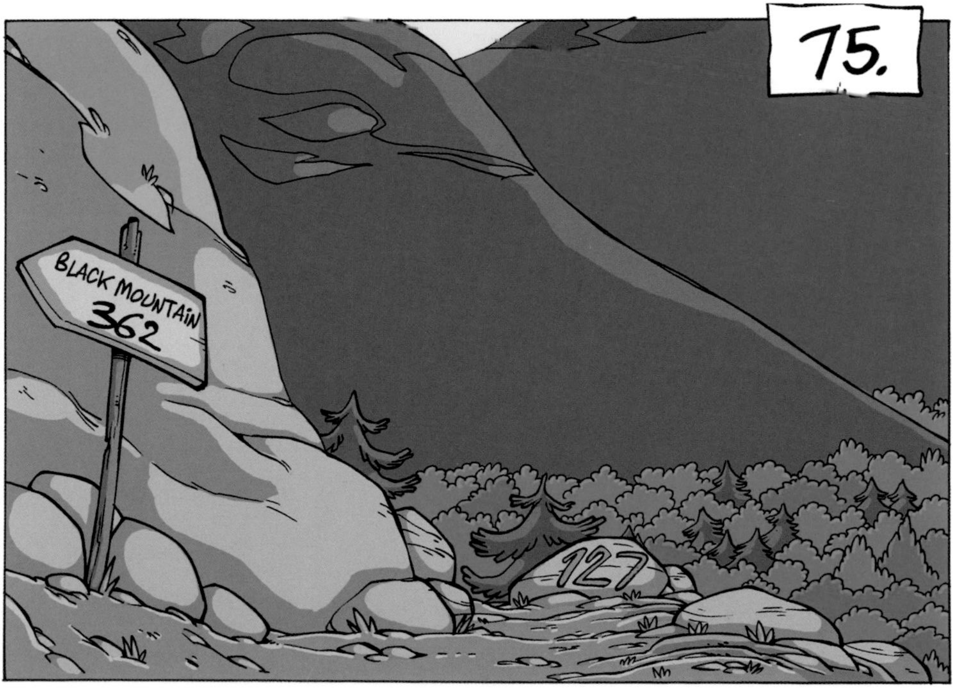
75.
BLACK MOUNTAIN
362
127

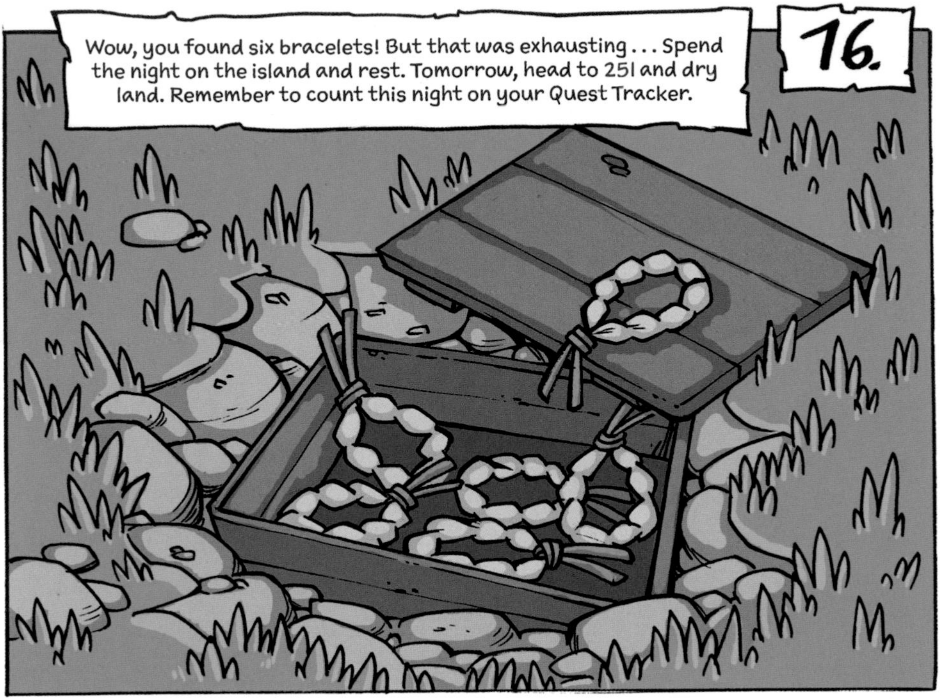
76.
Wow, you found six bracelets! But that was exhausting . . . Spend the night on the island and rest. Tomorrow, head to 251 and dry land. Remember to count this night on your Quest Tracker.

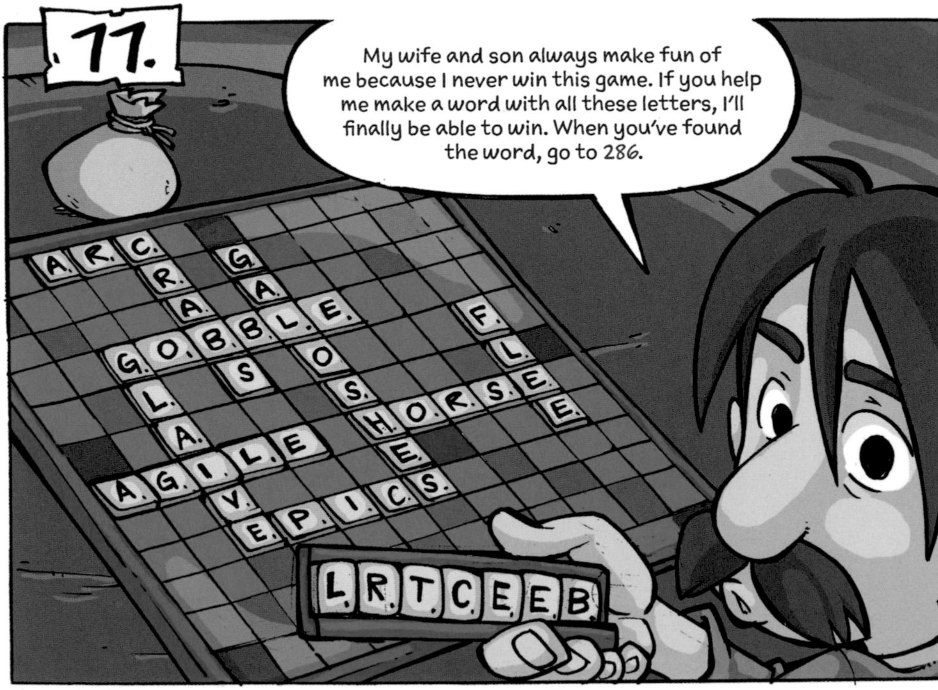
77.
My wife and son always make fun of me because I never win this game. If you help me make a word with all these letters, I'll finally be able to win. When you've found the word, go to 286.
LRTCEEB

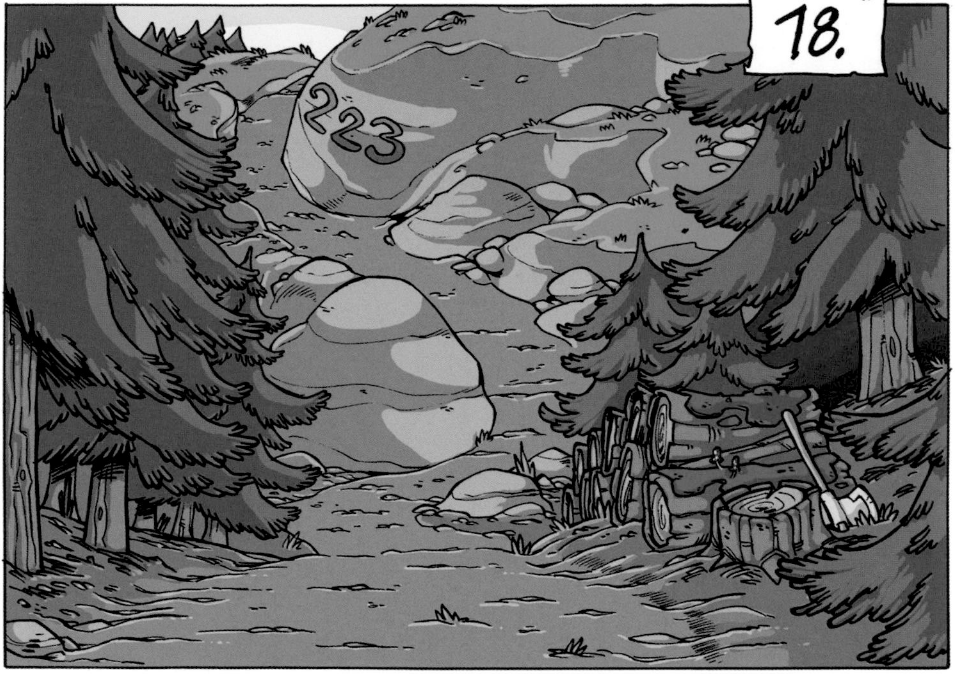
18.
223

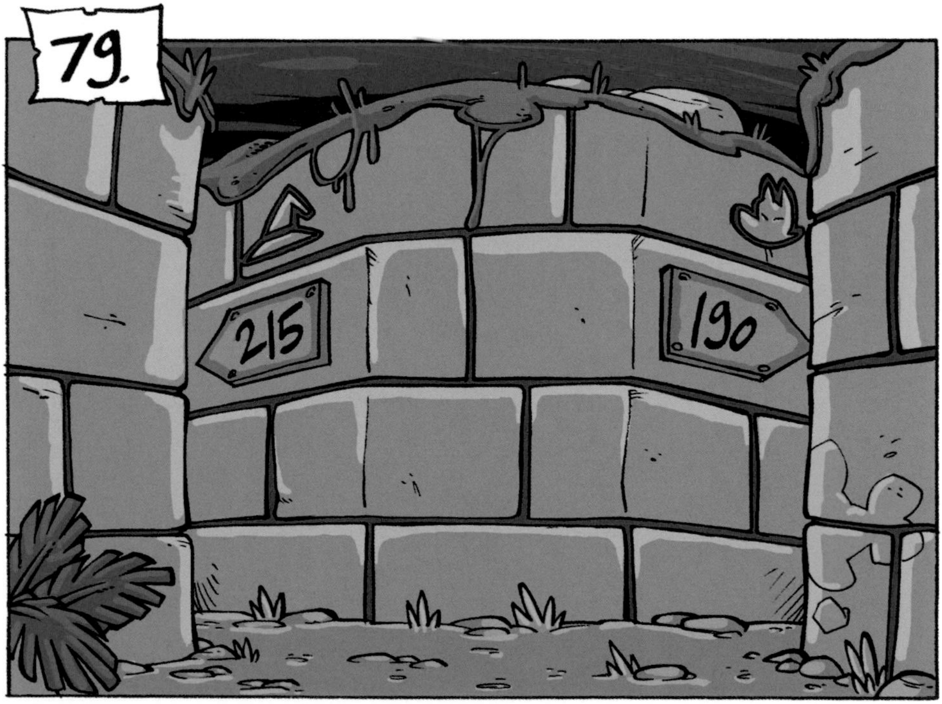
79.
215
190

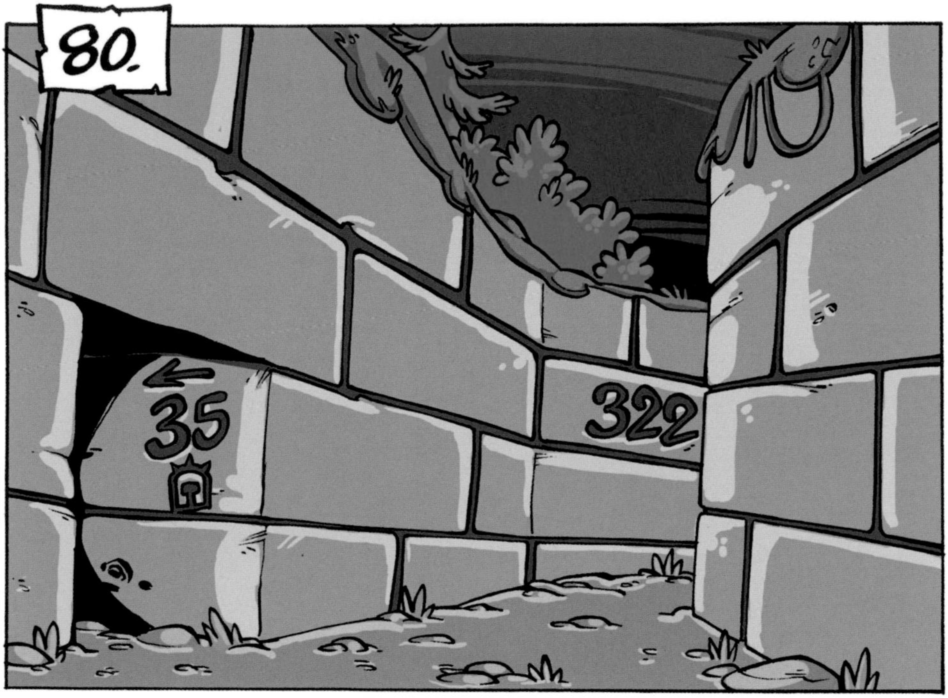
80.
35
322

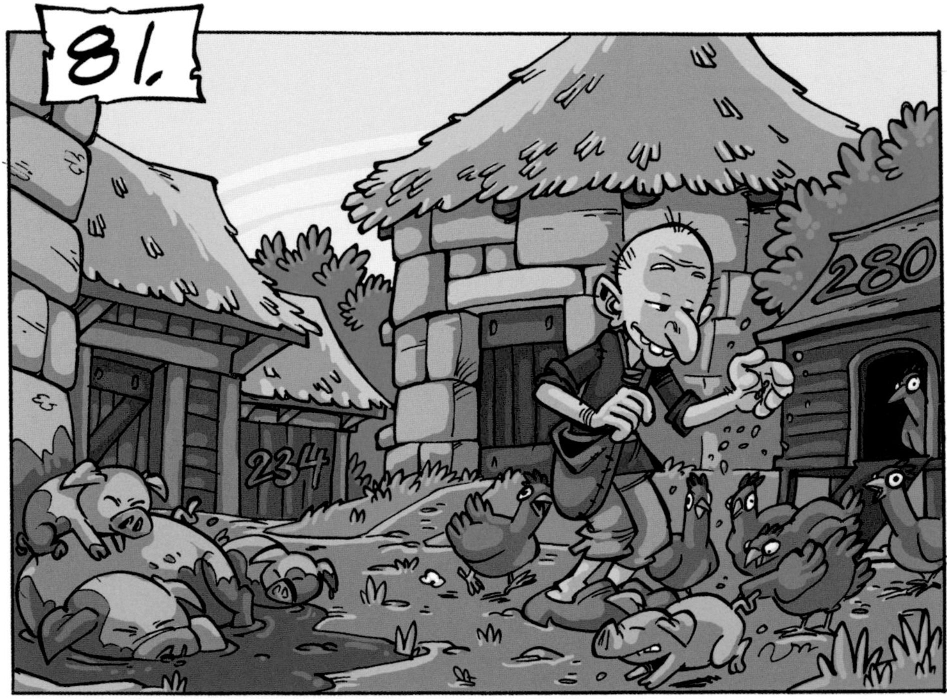
81.
234
280

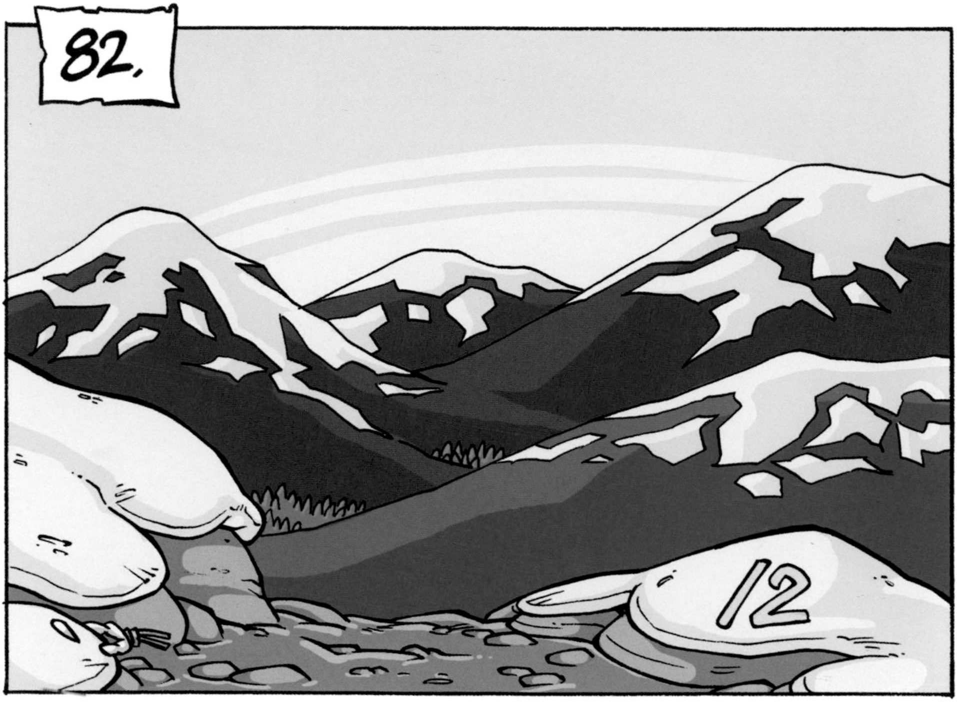
82.
12

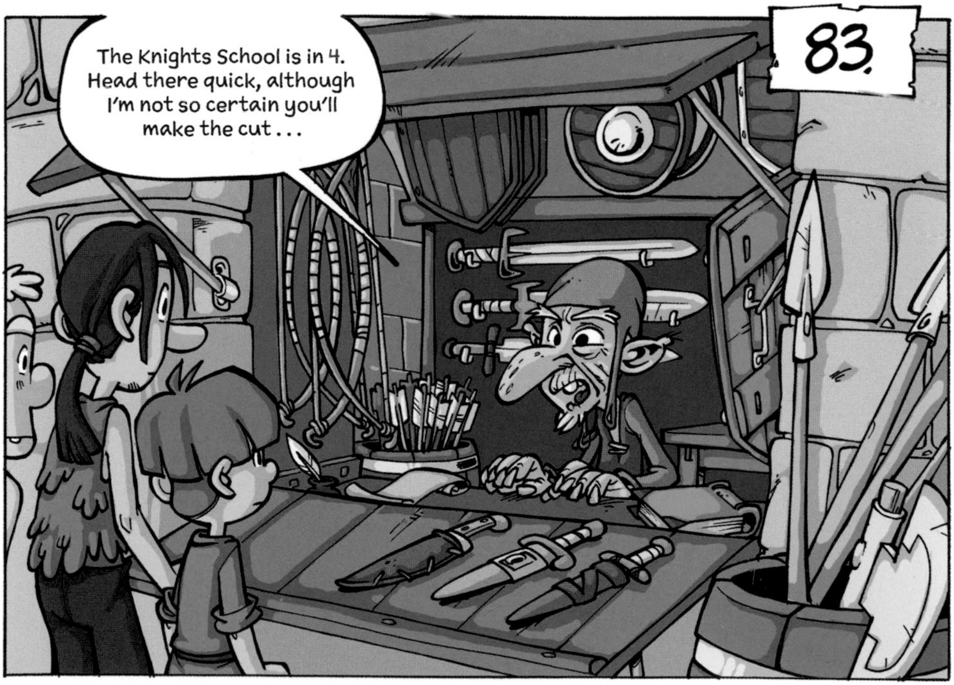
83.
The Knights School is in 4. Head there quick, although I'm not so certain you'll make the cut . . .

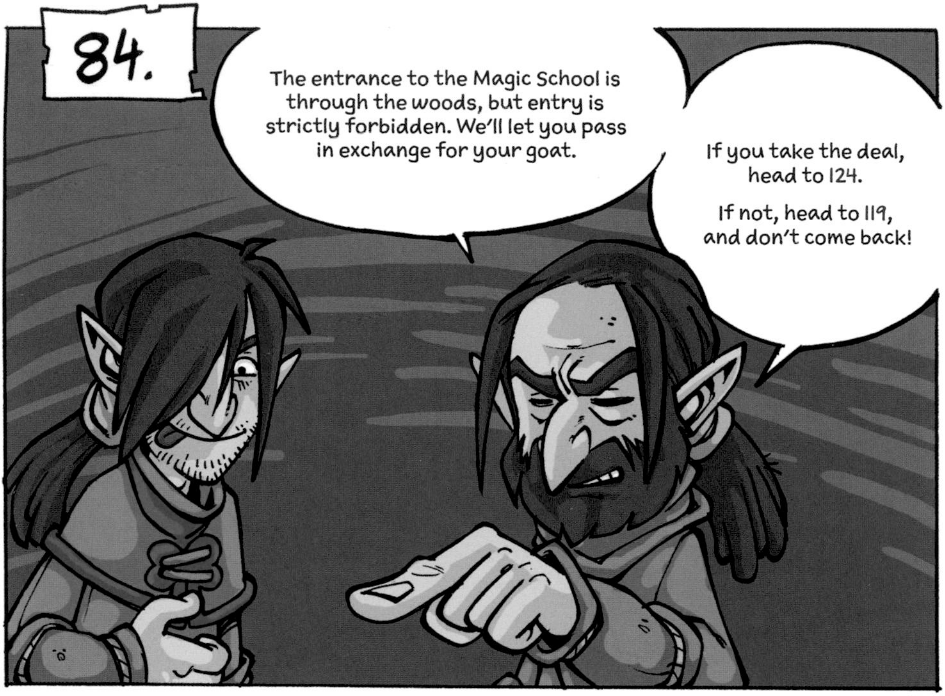
84.
The entrance to the Magic School is through the woods, but entry is strictly forbidden. We'll let you pass in exchange for your goat.
If you take the deal, head to 124.
If not, head to 119, and don't come back!

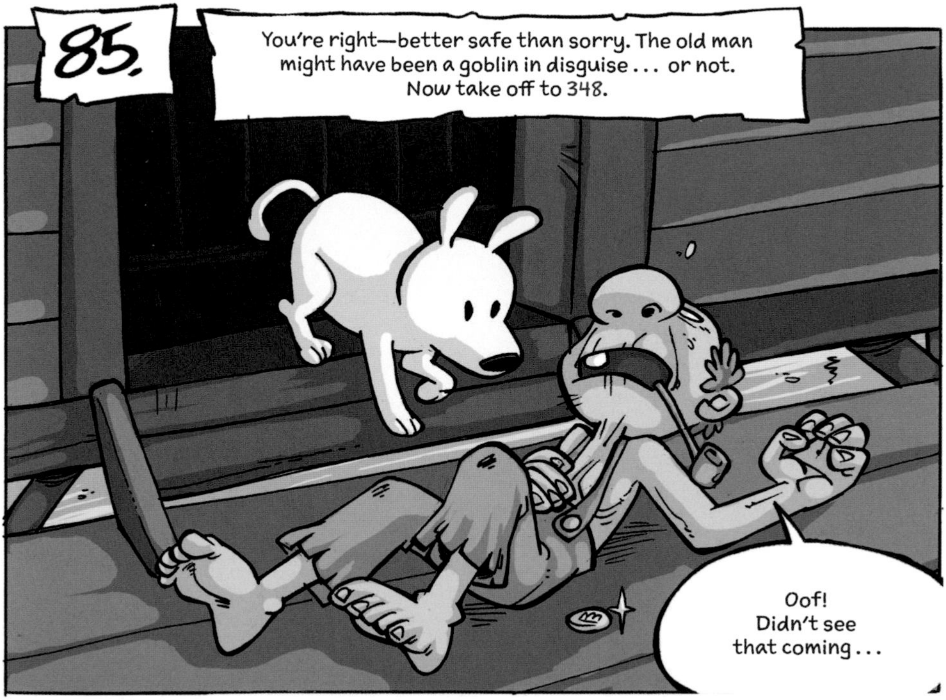
85.
You're right—better safe than sorry. The old man might have been a goblin in disguise . . . or not. Now take off to 348.
Oof! Didn't see that coming . . .

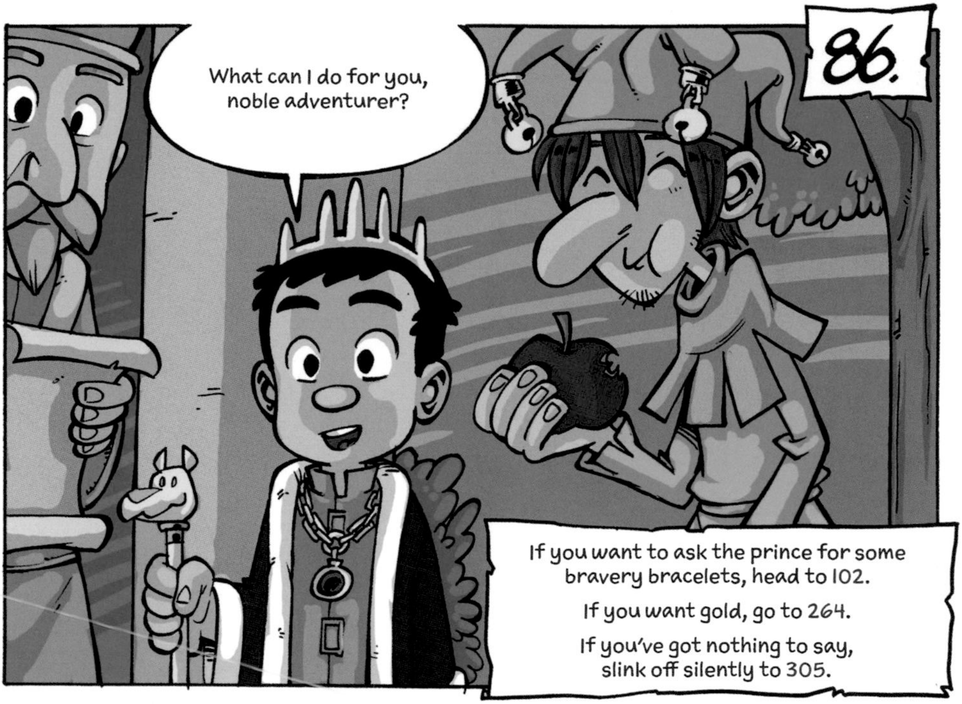
86.
What can I do for you, noble adventurer?
If you want to ask the prince for some bravery bracelets, head to 102.
If you want gold, go to 264.
If you've got nothing to say, slink off silently to 305.

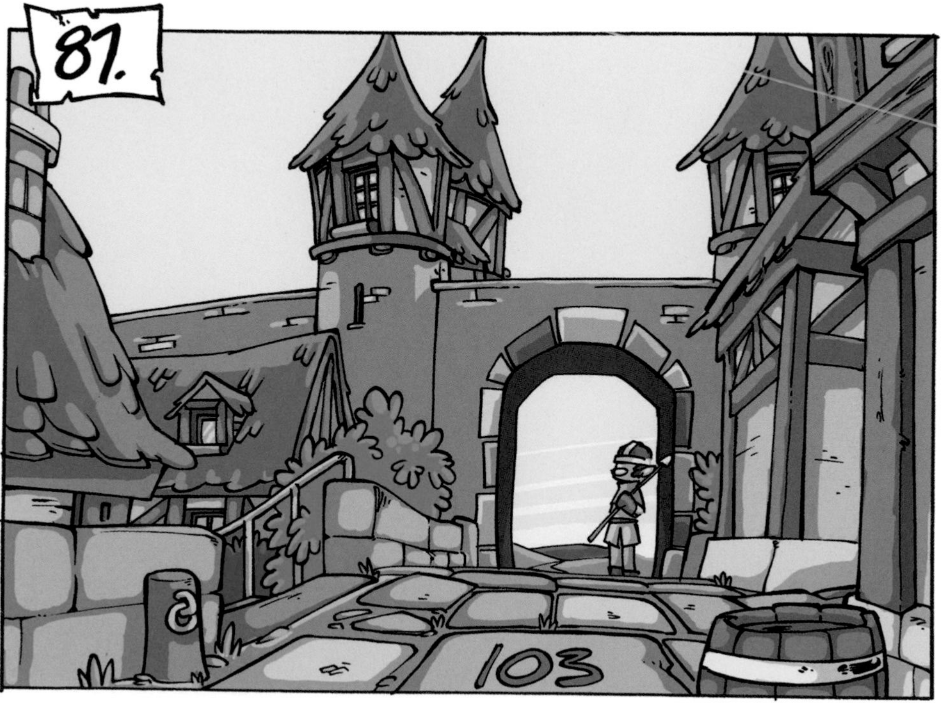
87.
103

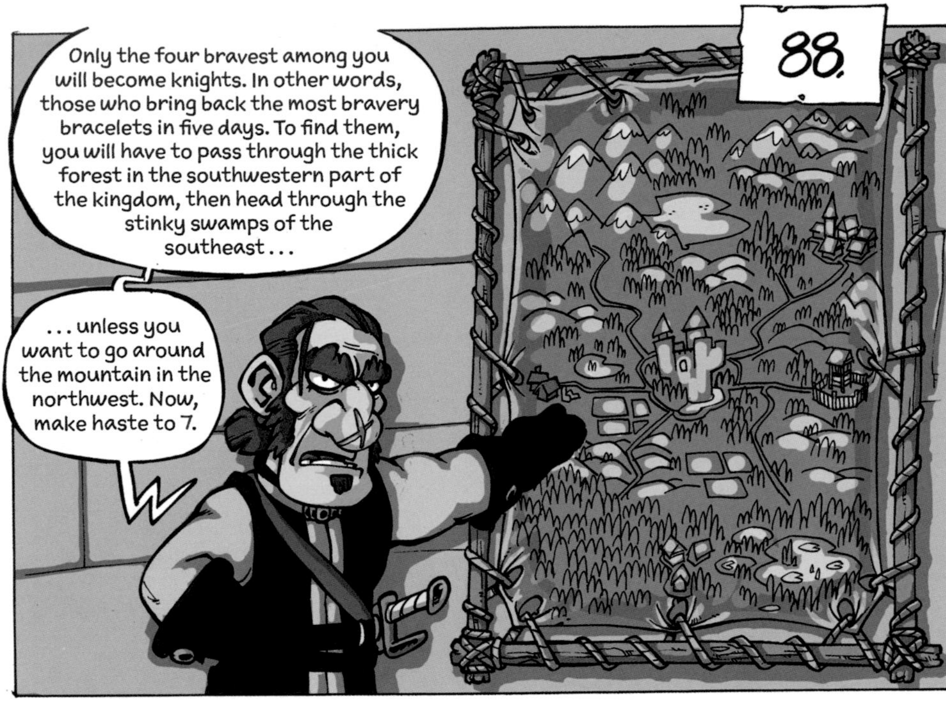
88.
Only the four bravest among you will become knights. In other words, those who bring back the most bravery bracelets in five days. To find them, you will have to pass through the thick forest in the southwestern part of the kingdom, then head through the stinky swamps of the southeast . . .
. . . unless you want to go around the mountain in the northwest. Now, make haste to 7.

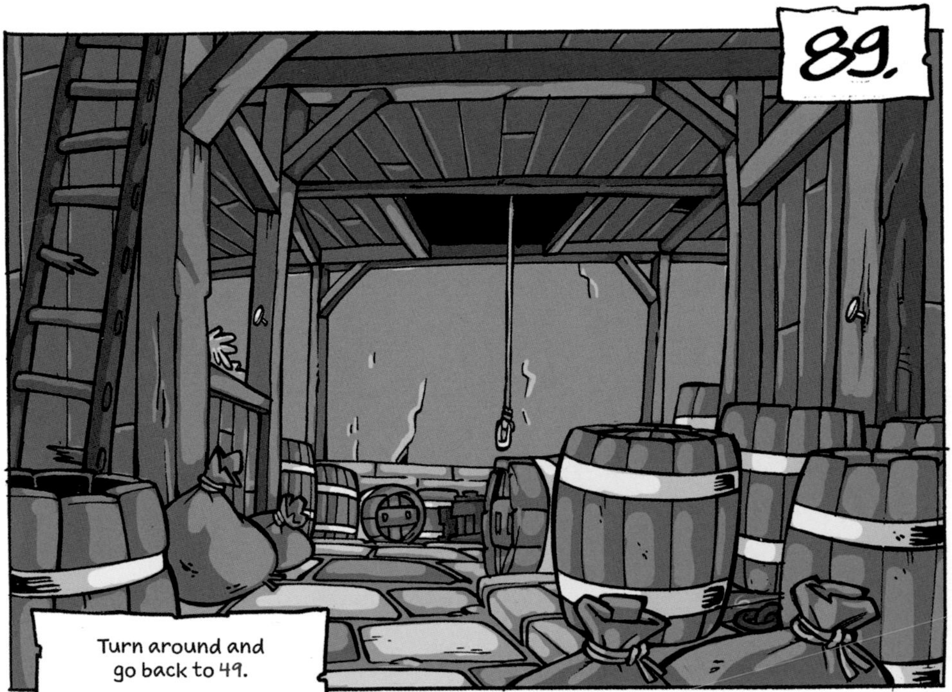
89.
Turn around and go back to 49.

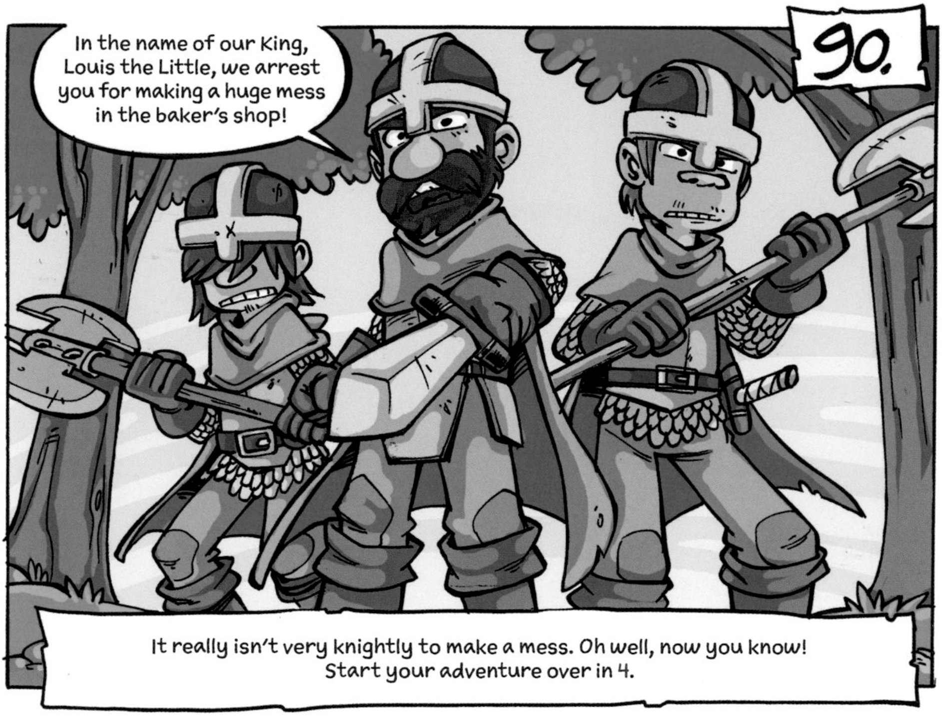
90.
In the name of our King, Louis the Little, we arrest you for making a huge mess in the baker's shop!
It really isn't very knightly to make a mess. Oh well, now you know! Start your adventure over in 4.

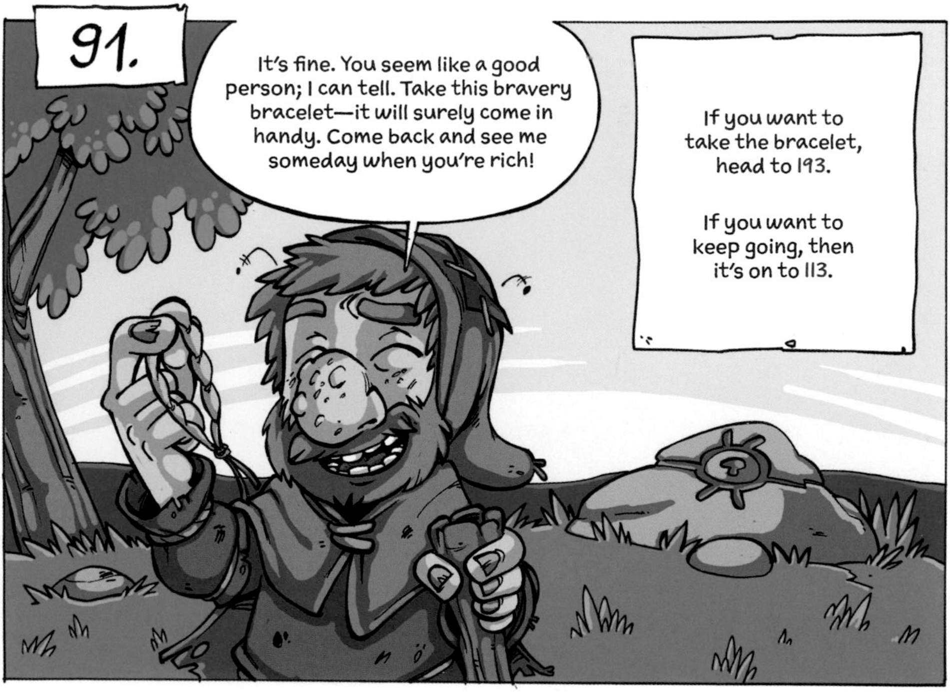
91.
It's fine. You seem like a good person; I can tell. Take this bravery bracelet—it will surely come in handy. Come back and see me someday when you're rich!
If you want to take the bracelet, head to 193.
If you want to keep going, then it's on to 113.

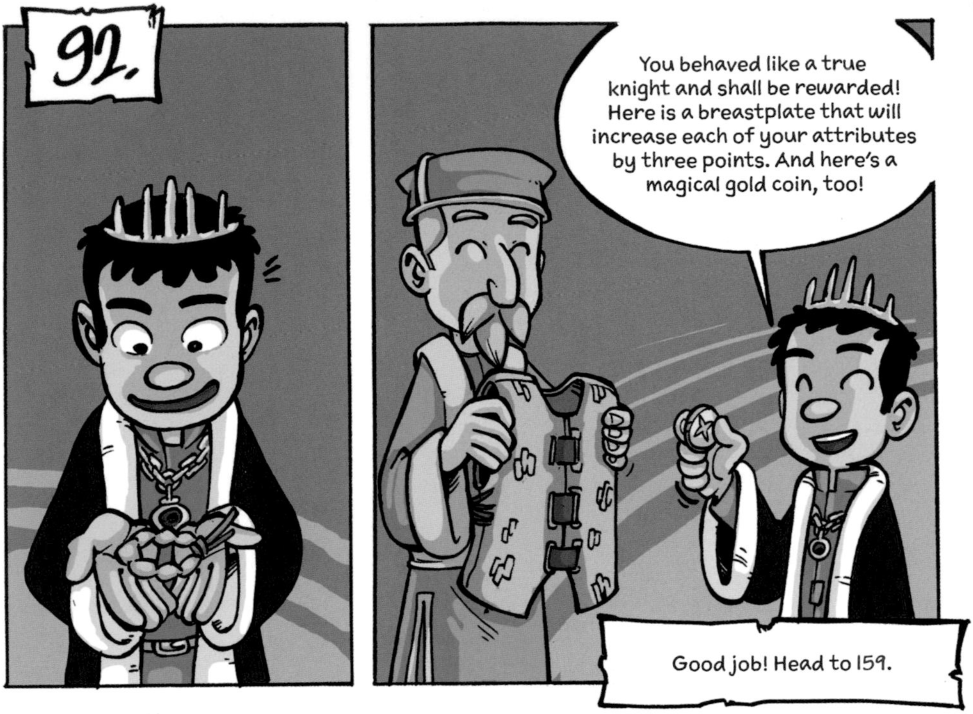
92.
You behaved like a true knight and shall be rewarded! Here is a breastplate that will increase each of your attributes by three points. And here's a magical gold coin, too!
Good job! Head to 159.

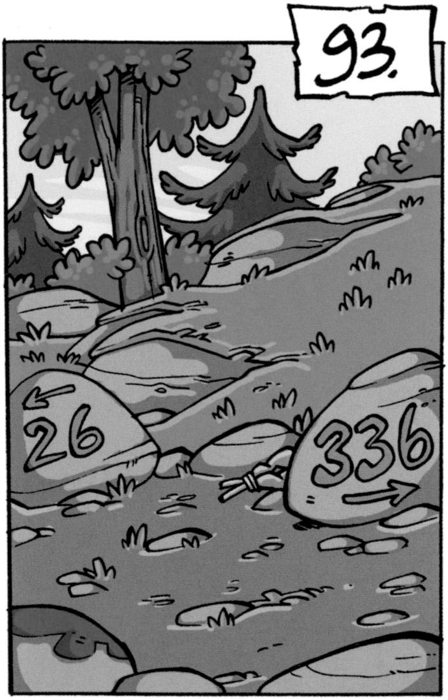
93.
26
336

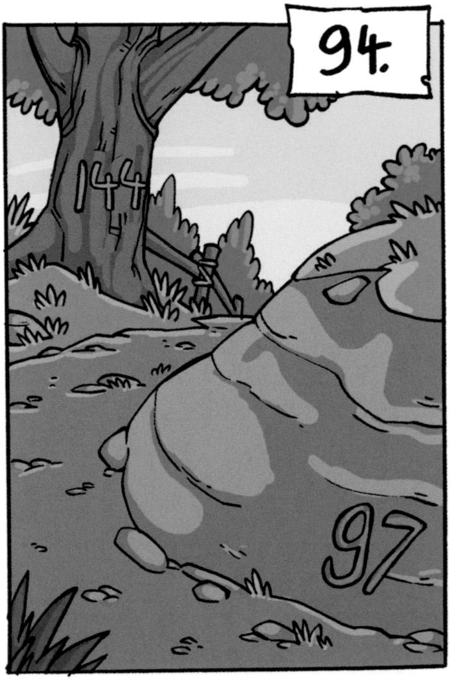
94.
144
97

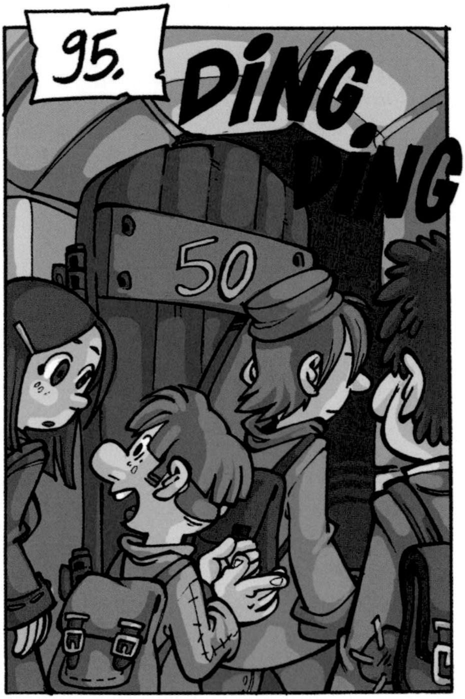
95.
DING DING
50

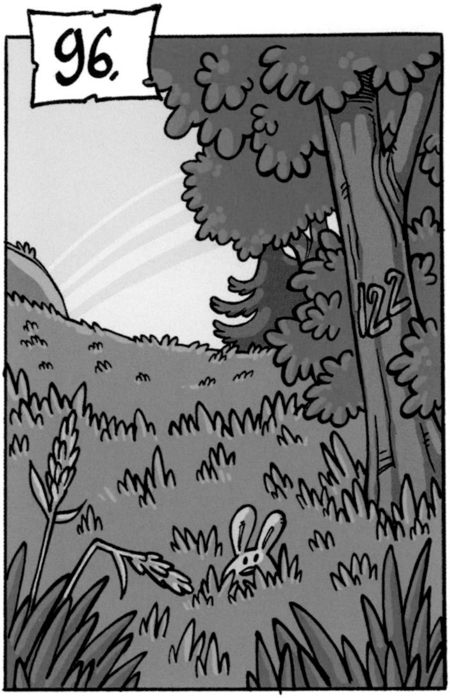
96.
122

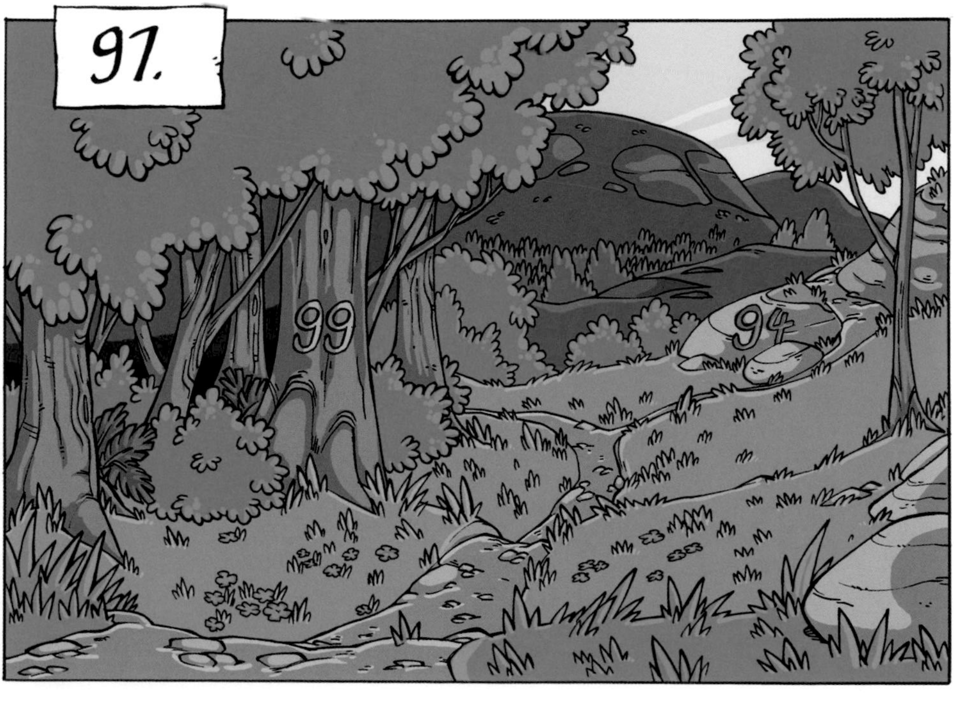
97.
99
94

98.

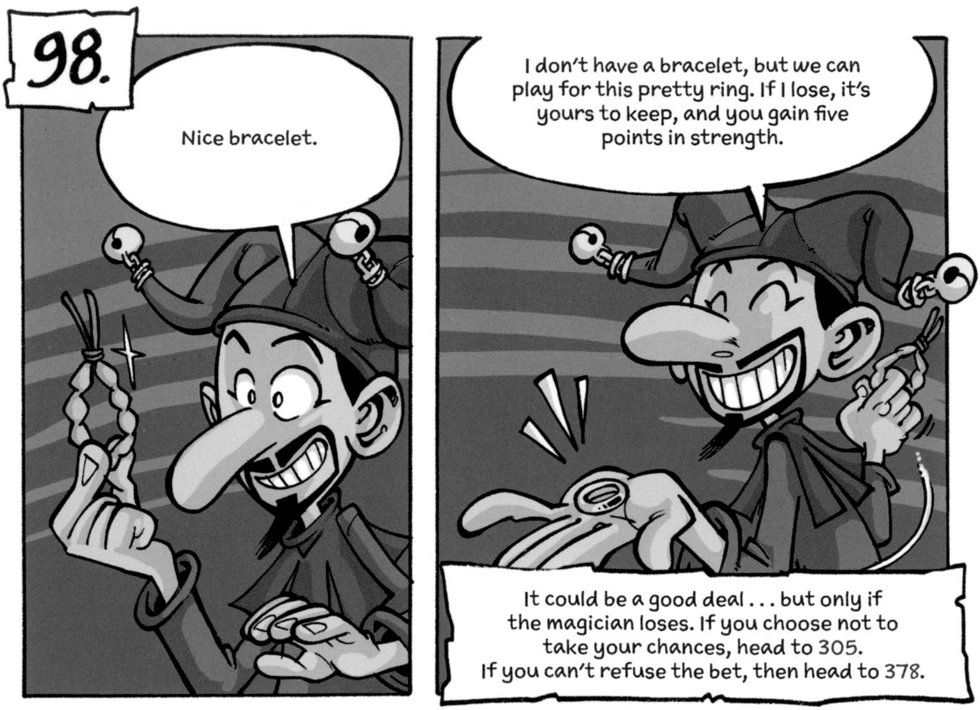
Nice bracelet.
I don't have a bracelet, but we can play for this pretty ring. If I lose, it's yours to keep, and you gain five points in strength.
It could be a good deal . . . but only if the magician loses. If you choose not to take your chances, head to 305.
If you can't refuse the bet, then head to 378.

99.

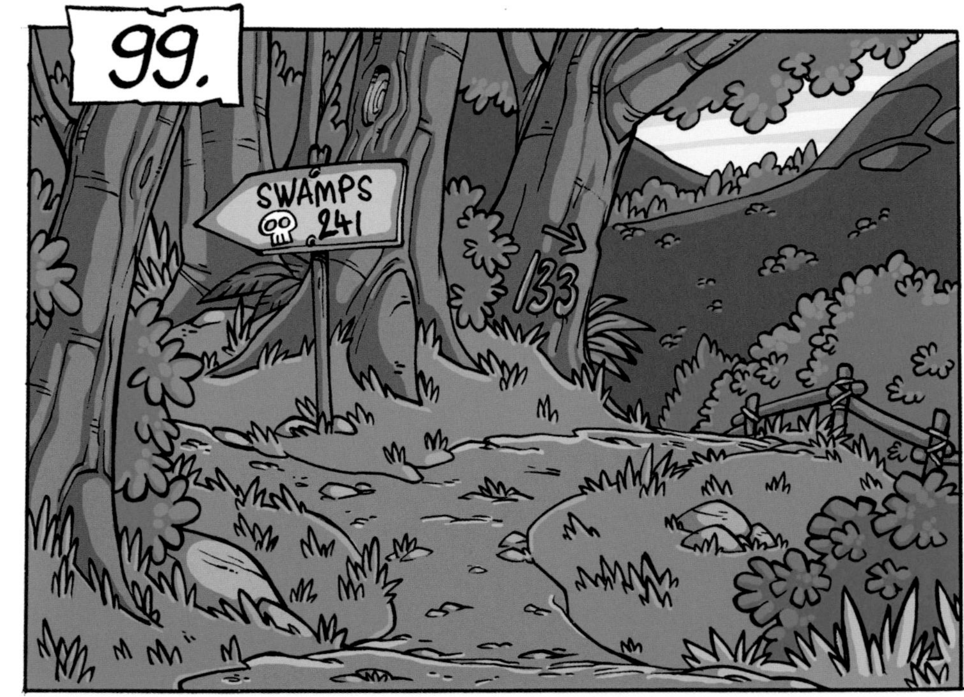
SWAMPS
241
133

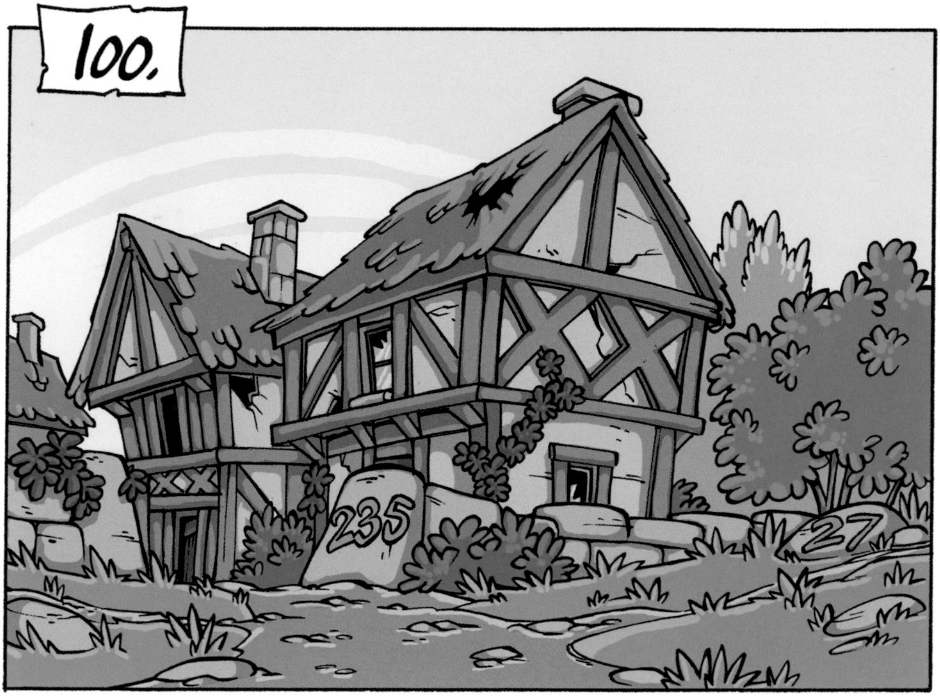
100.
235
27

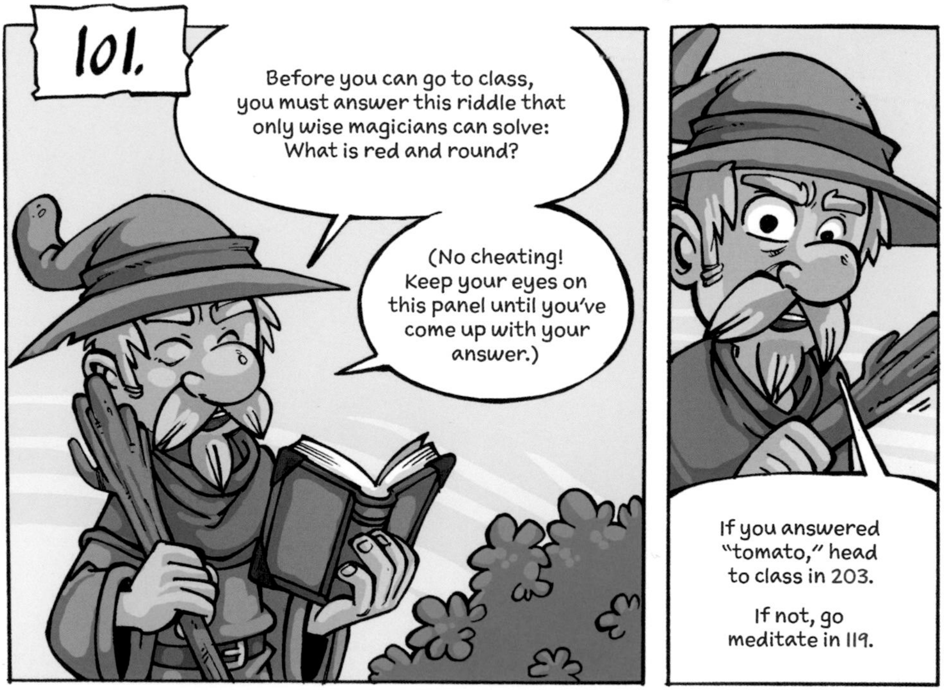
101.
Before you can go to class, you must answer this riddle that only wise magicians can solve: What is red and round?
(No cheating! Keep your eyes on this panel until you've come up with your answer.)
If you answered "tomato," head to class in 203.
If not, go meditate in 119.

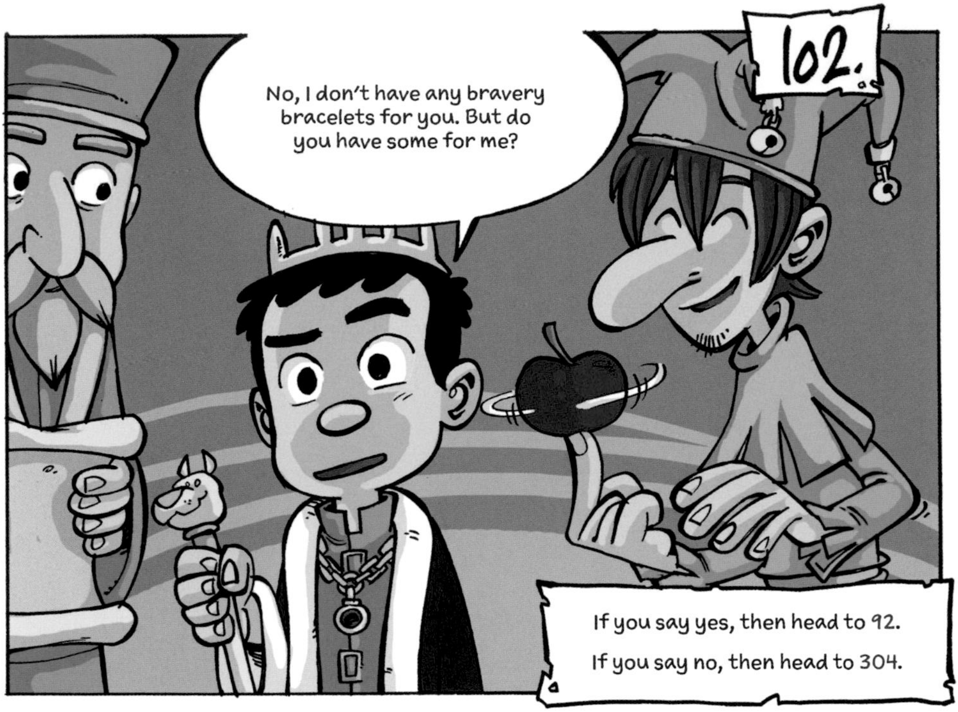
102.
No, I don't have any bravery bracelets for you. But do you have some for me?
If you say yes, then head to 92.
If you say no, then head to 304.

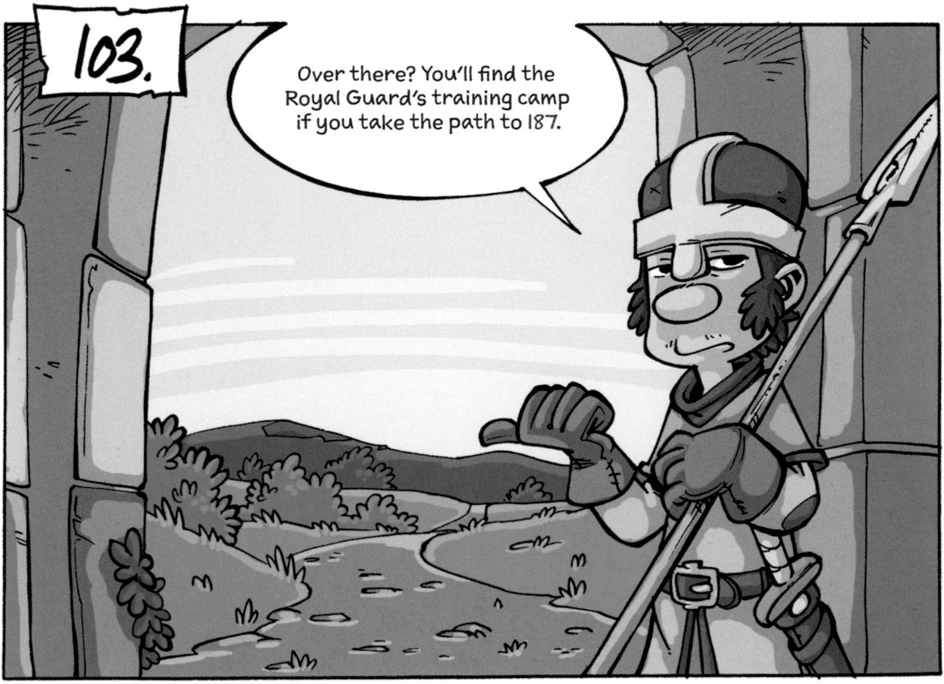
103.
Over there? You'll find the Royal Guard's training camp if you take the path to 187.

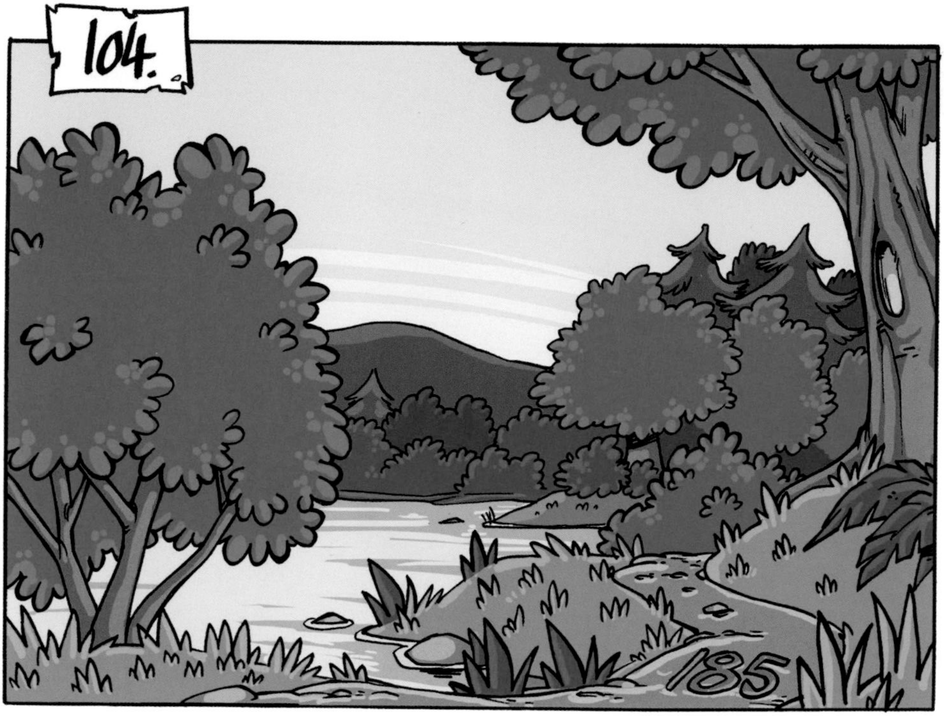
104.
185

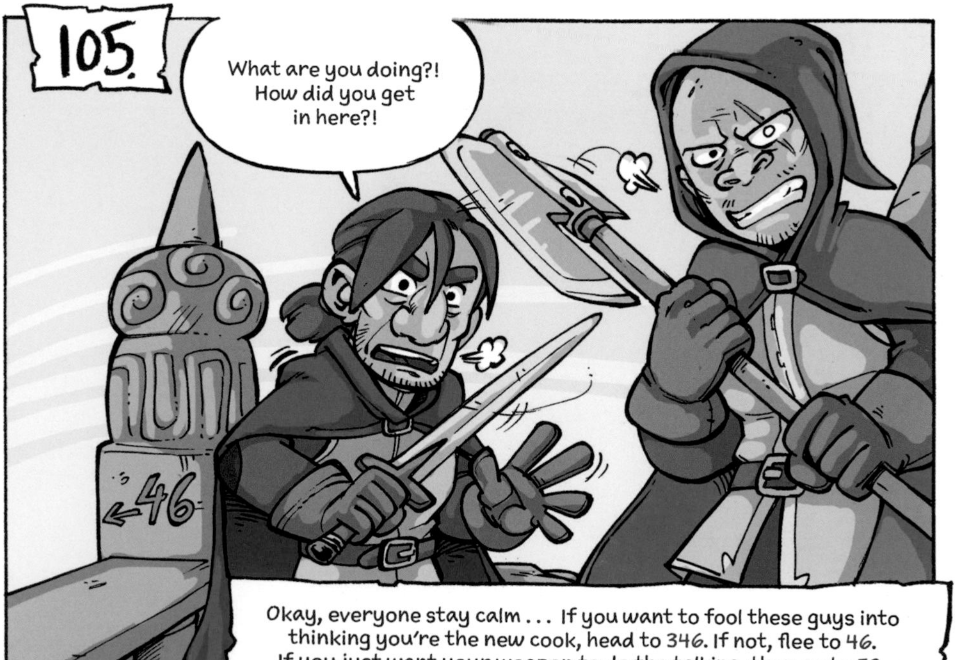
105.
What are you doing?! How did you get in here?!
←46
Okay, everyone stay calm . . . If you want to fool these guys into thinking you're the new cook, head to 346. If not, flee to 46. If you just want your weapon to do the talking, then go to 52.

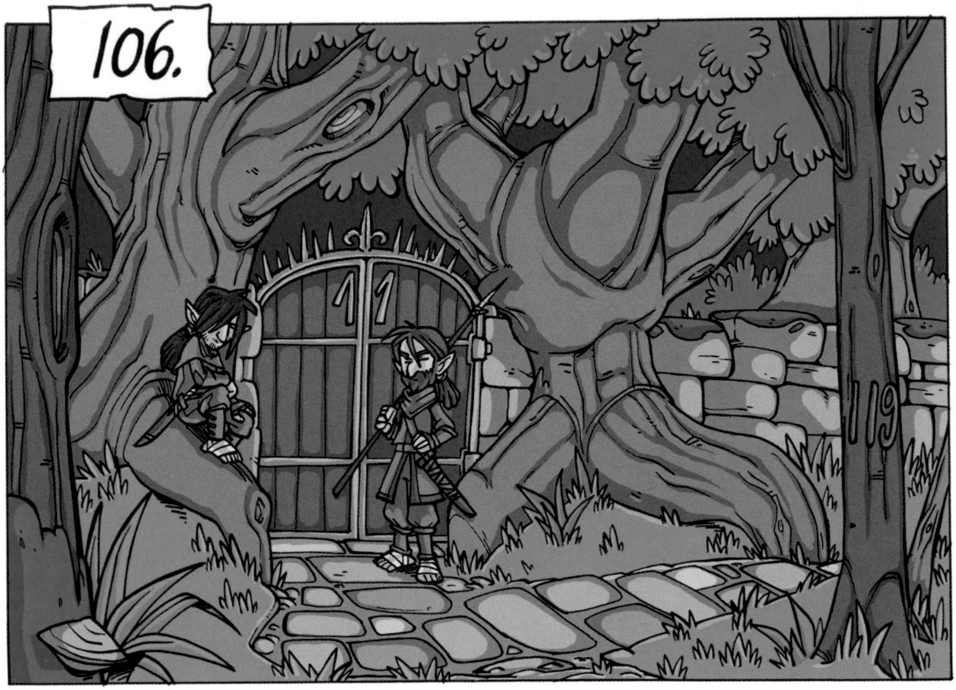
106.
11
119

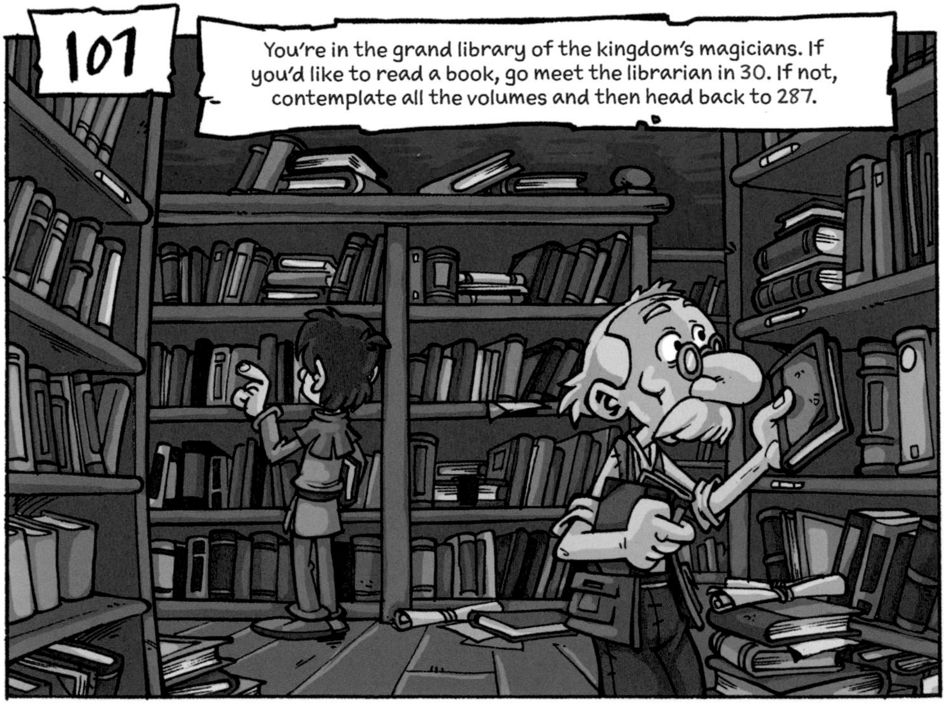
107
You're in the grand library of the kingdom's magicians. If you'd like to read a book, go meet the librarian in 30. If not, contemplate all the volumes and then head back to 287.

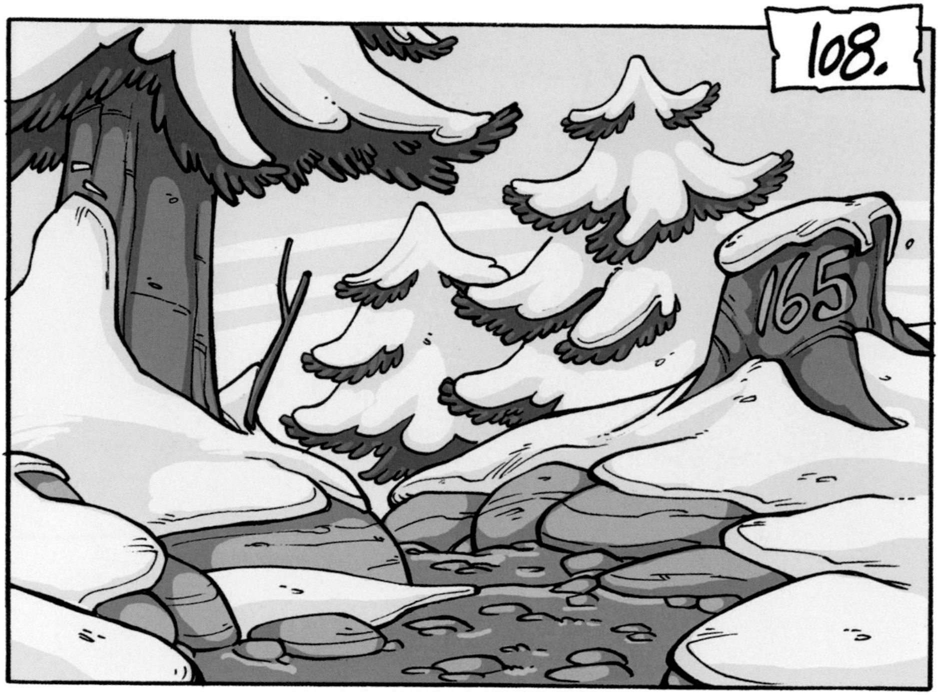
108.
165

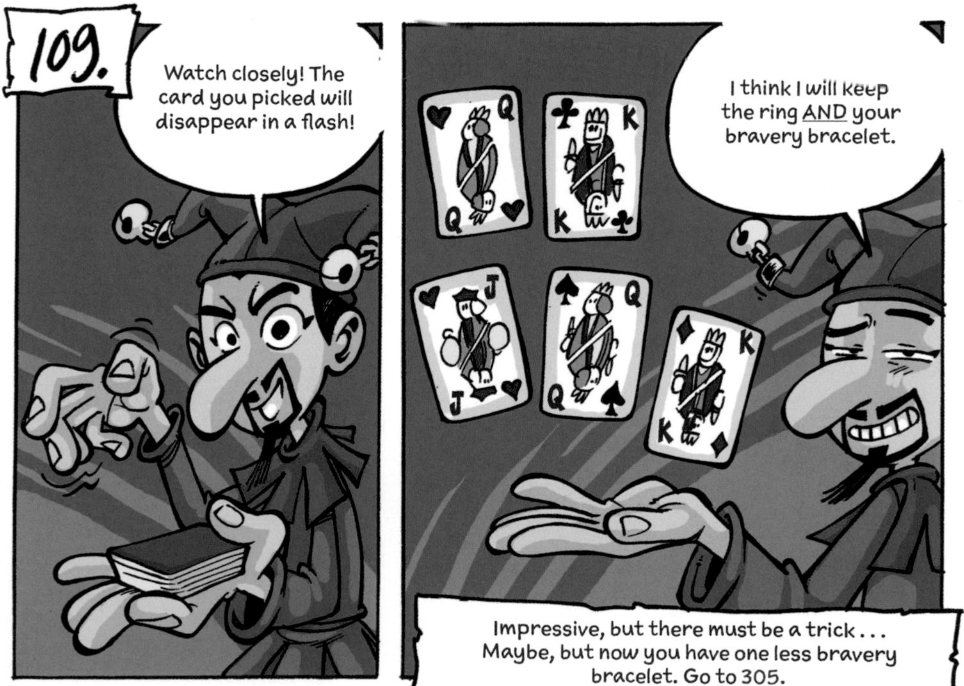
109.
Watch closely! The card you picked will disappear in a flash!
I think I will keep the ring AND your bravery bracelet.
Impressive, but there must be a trick . . . Maybe, but now you have one less bravery bracelet. Go to 305.

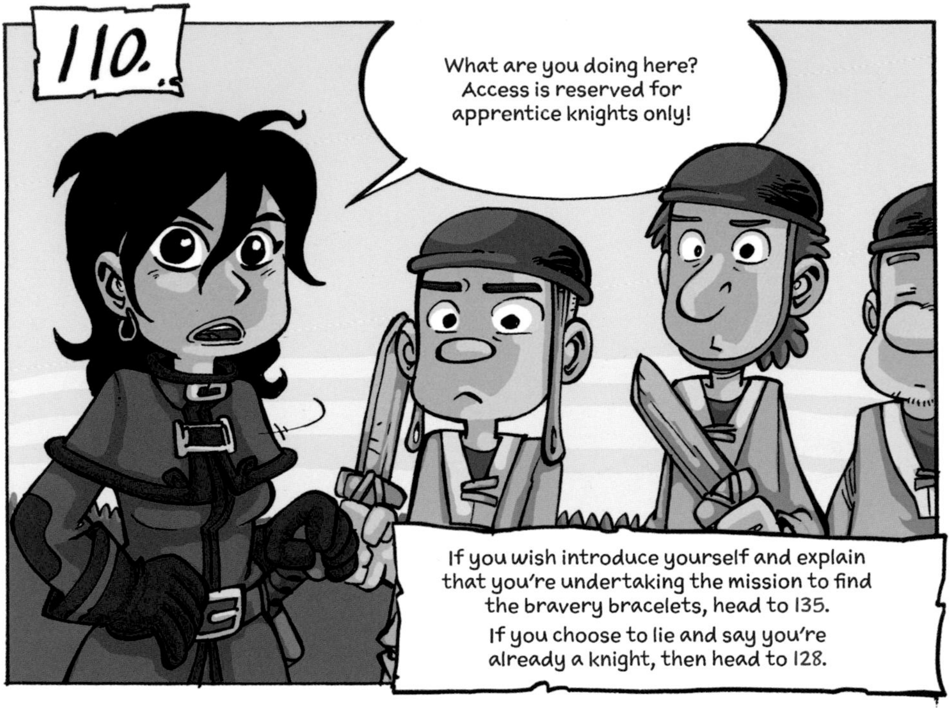
110.
What are you doing here? Access is reserved for apprentice knights only!
If you wish introduce yourself and explain that you're undertaking the mission to find the bravery bracelets, head to 135.
If you choose to lie and say you're already a knight, then head to 128.

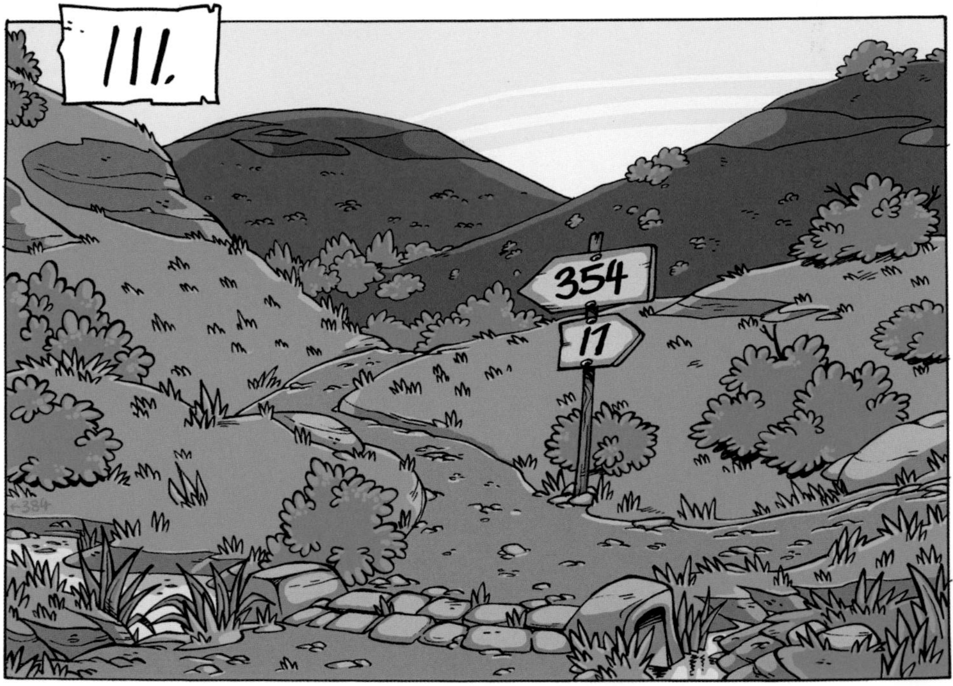
111.
354
17

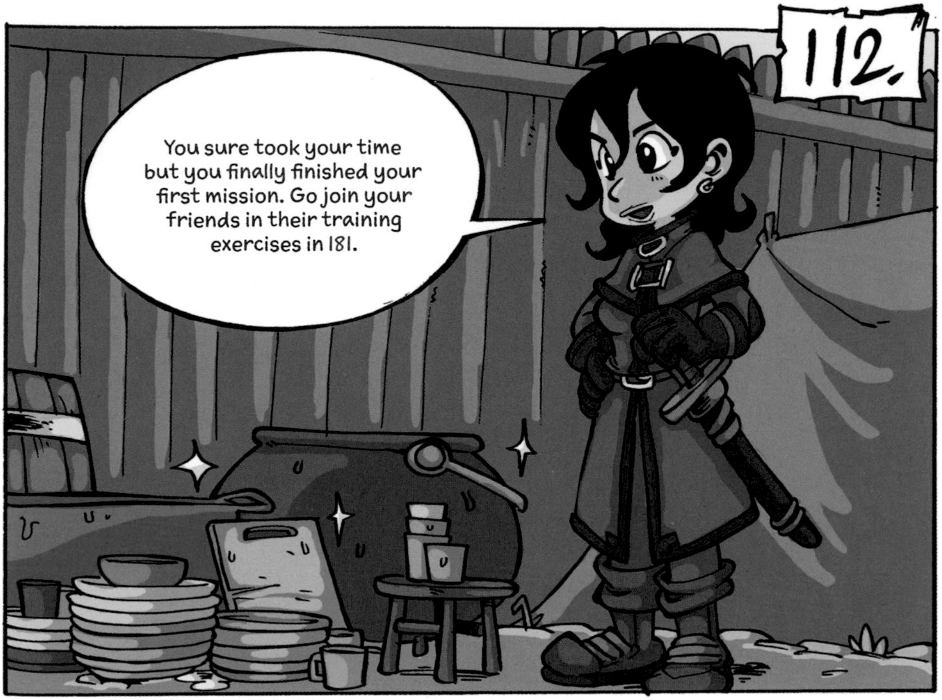
112.
You sure took your time but you finally finished your first mission. Go join your friends in their training exercises in 181.

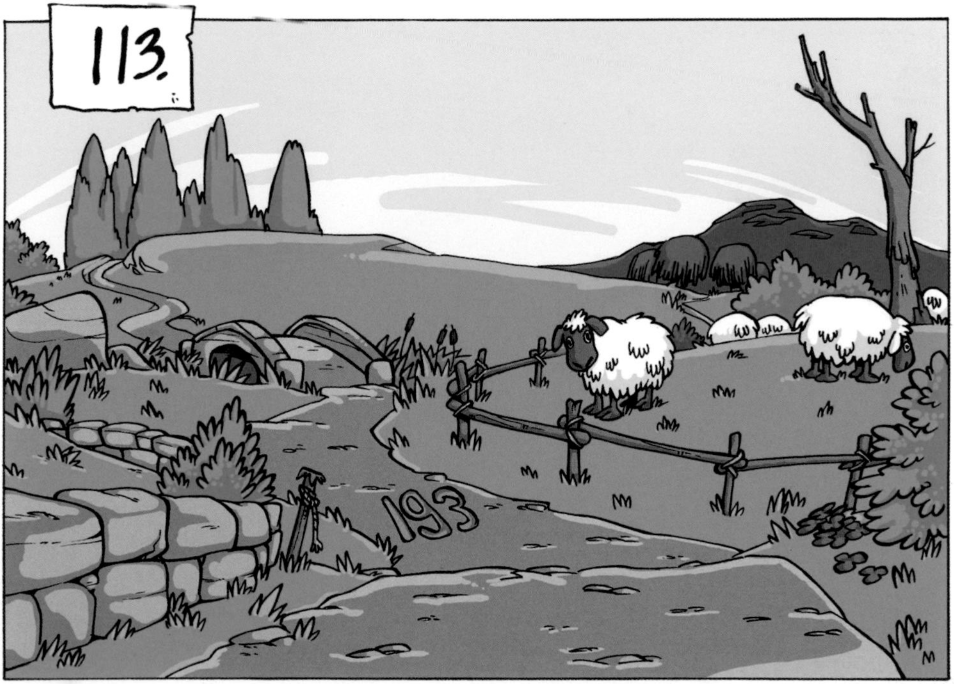
113.
193

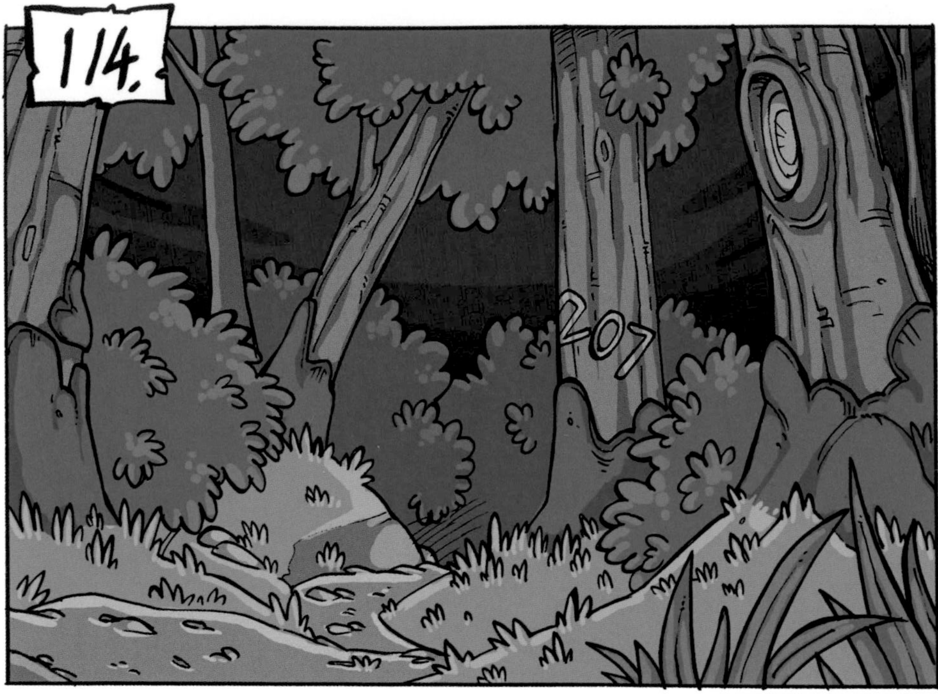
114.
207

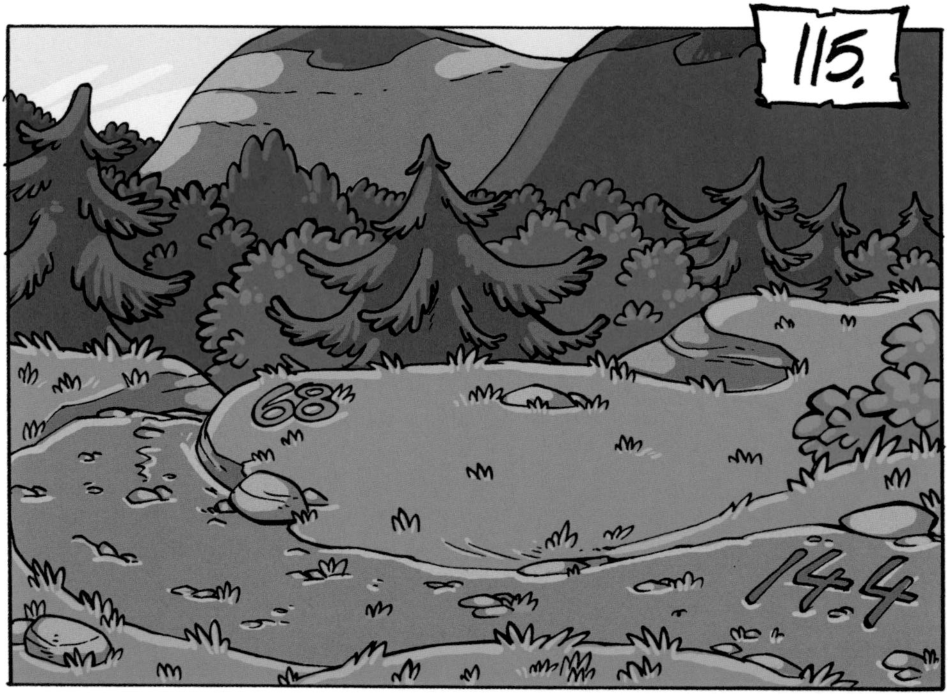
115.
68
144

116.

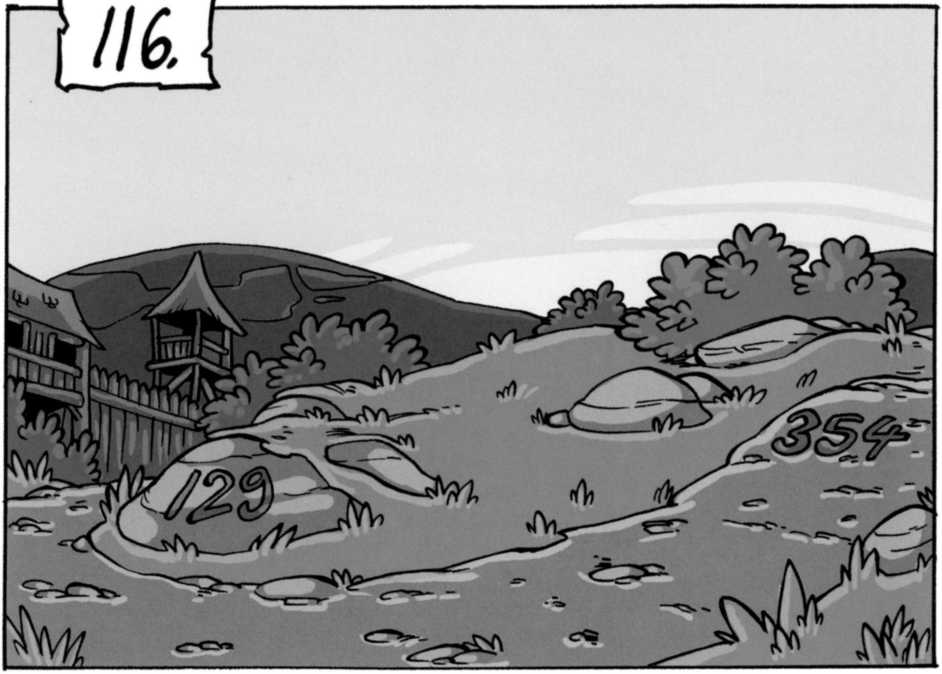
129
354

117.

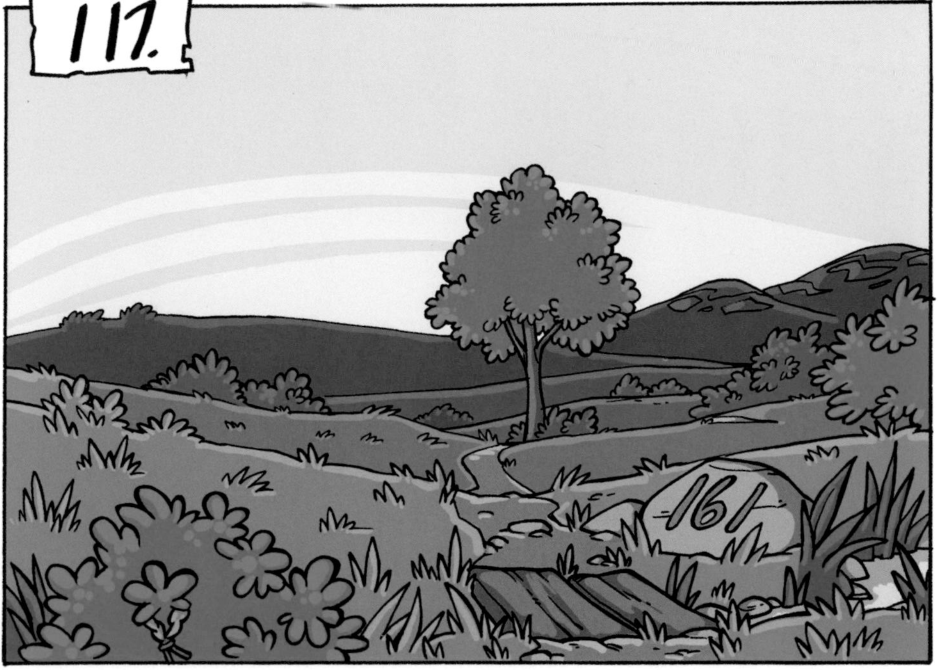
161

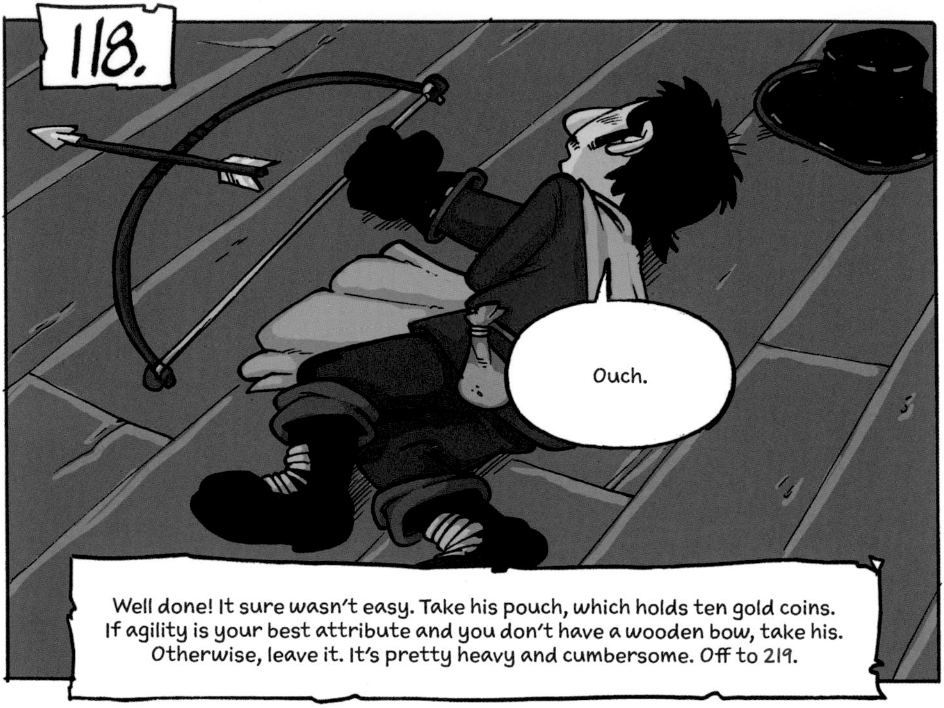
118.
Ouch.
Well done! It sure wasn't easy. Take his pouch, which holds ten gold coins. If agility is your best attribute and you don't have a wooden bow, take his. Otherwise, leave it. It's pretty heavy and cumbersome. Off to 219.

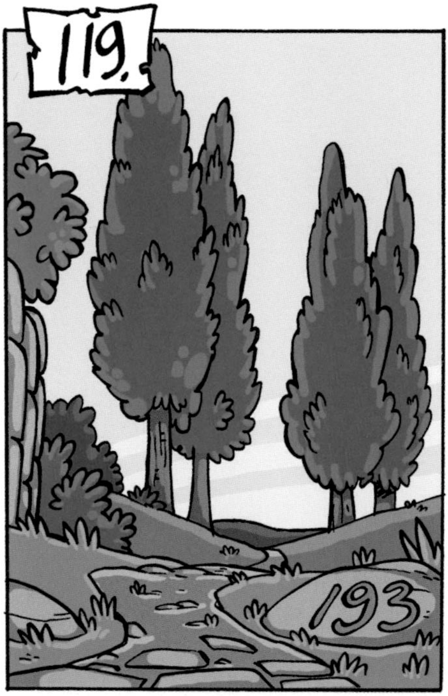
119.
193

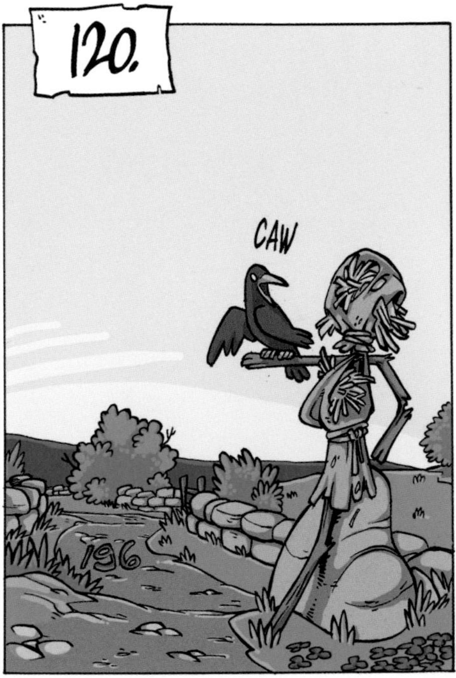
120.
CAW
196

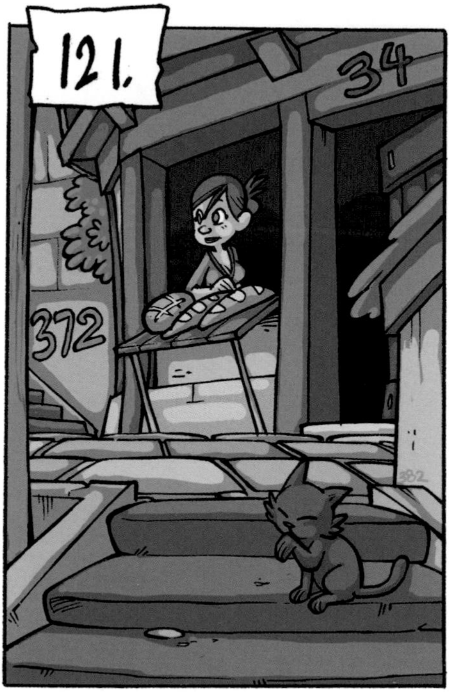
121.
34
372
382

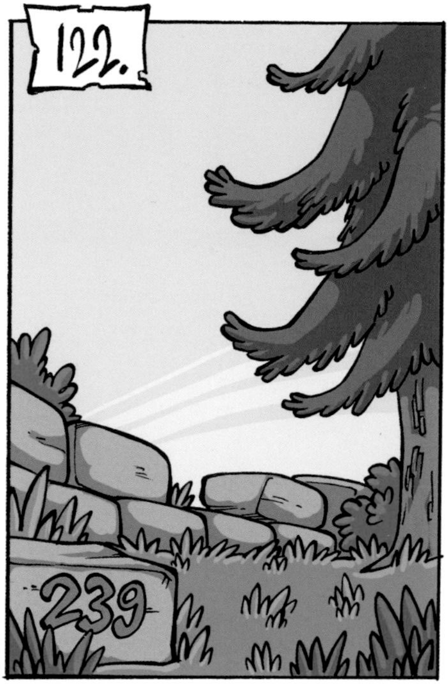
122.
239

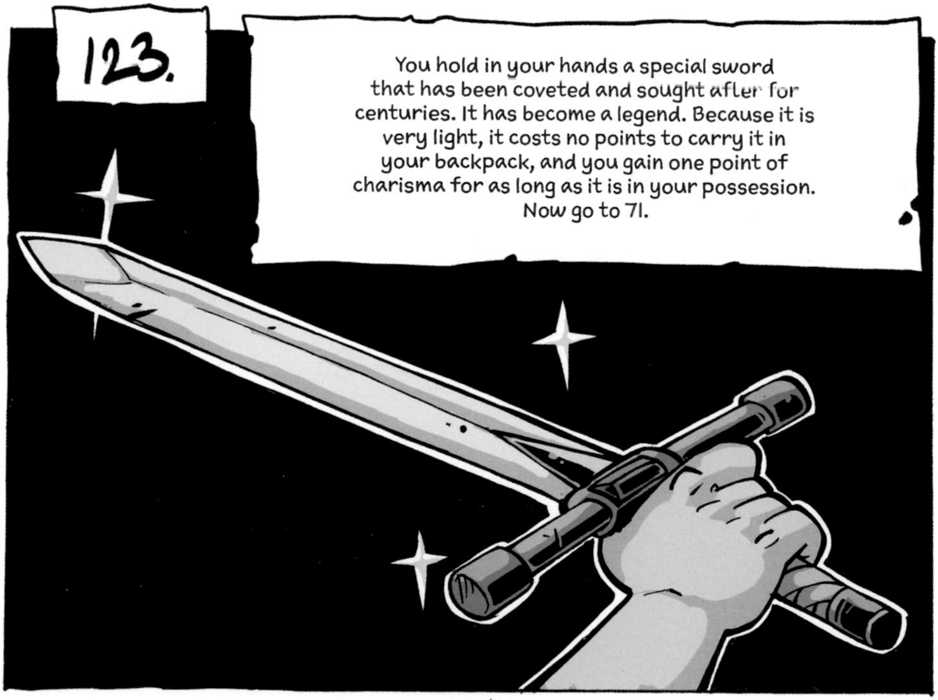
123.
You hold in your hands a special sword that has been coveted and sought after for centuries. It has become a legend. Because it is very light, it costs no points to carry it in your backpack, and you gain one point of charisma for as long as it is in your possession. Now go to 71.

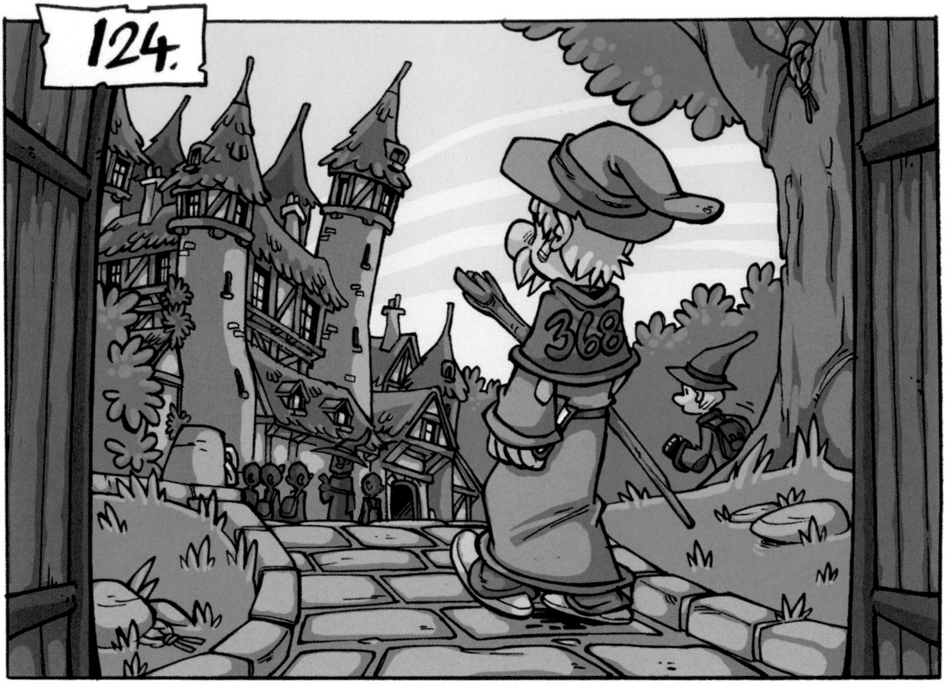
124.
368

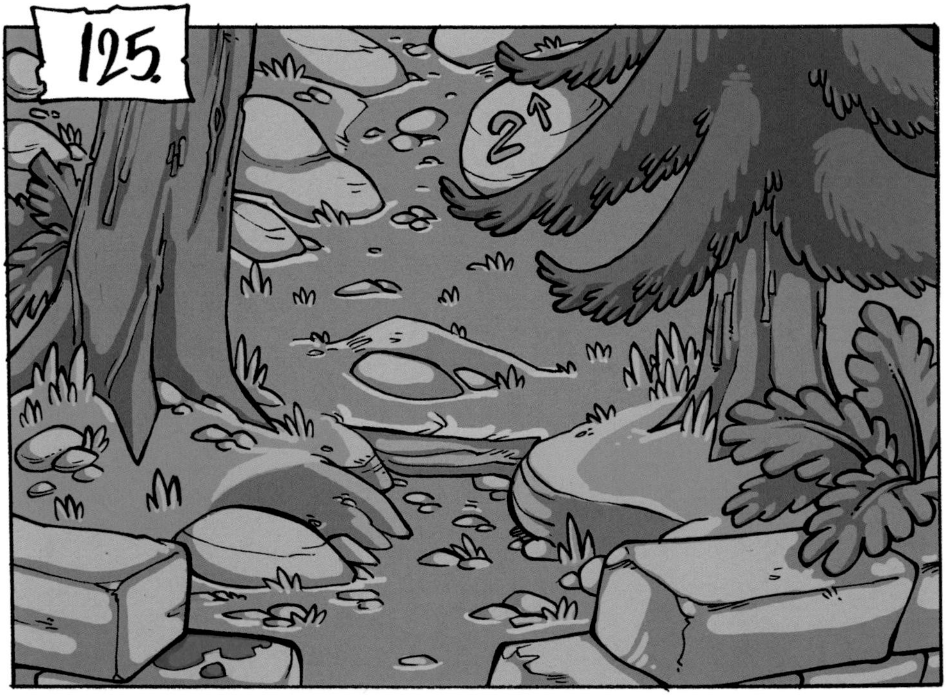
125.
2↑

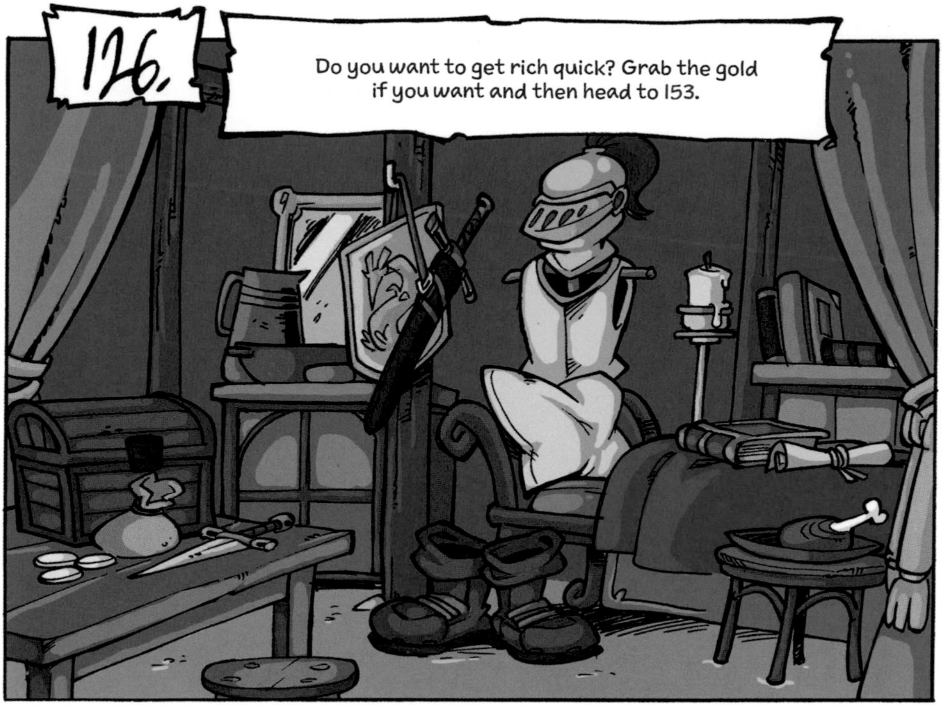
126.
Do you want to get rich quick? Grab the gold if you want and then head to 153.

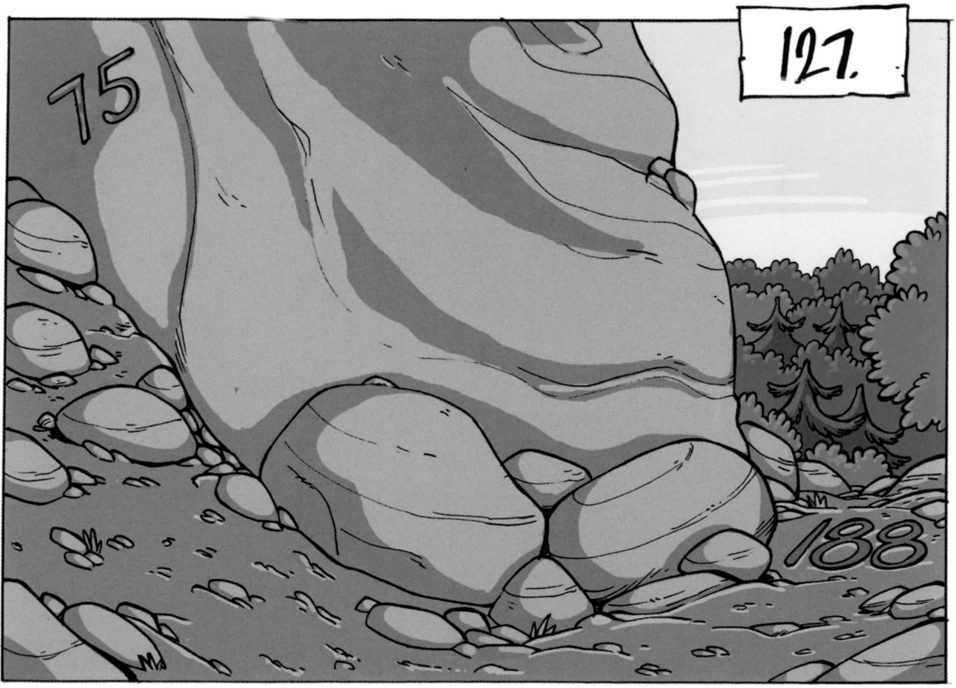
127.
75
188

128.

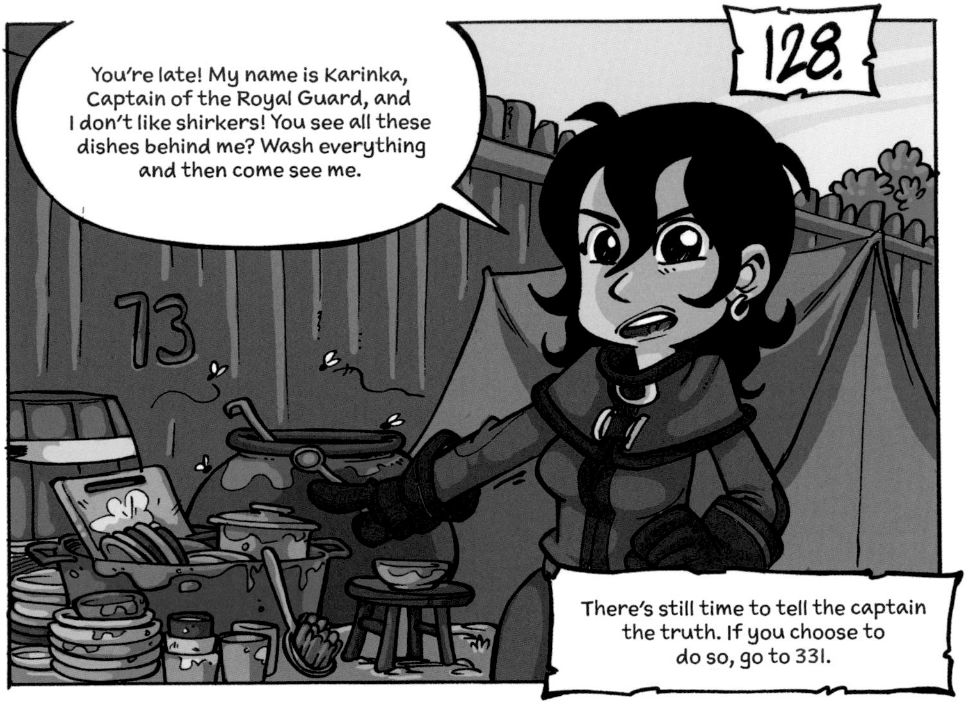
You're late! My name is Karinka, Captain of the Royal Guard, and I don't like shirkers! You see all these dishes behind me? Wash everything and then come see me.
73
There's still time to tell the captain the truth. If you choose to do so, go to 331.

129.

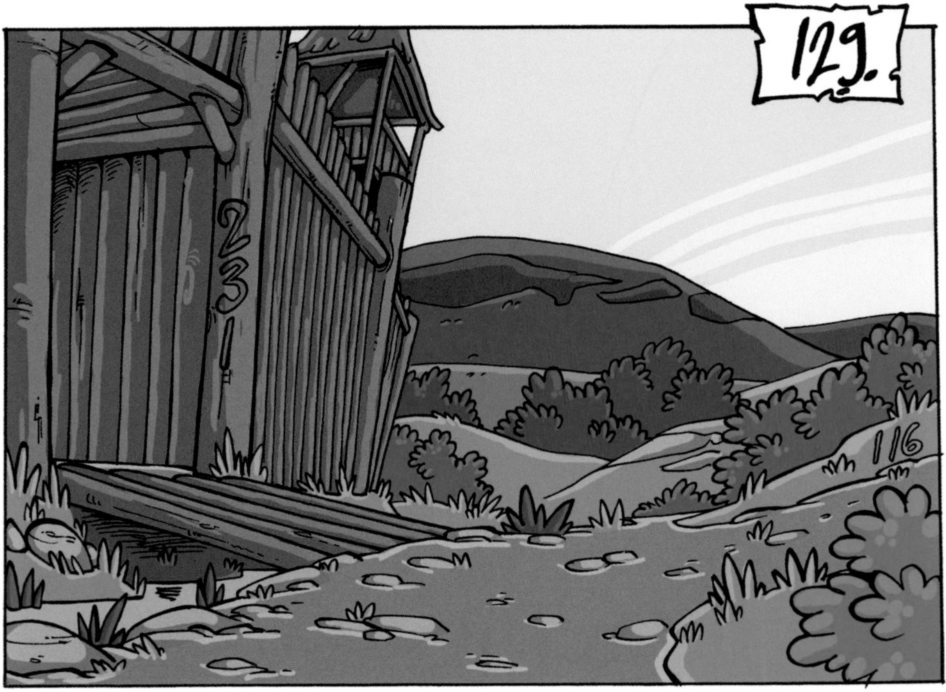
231
116

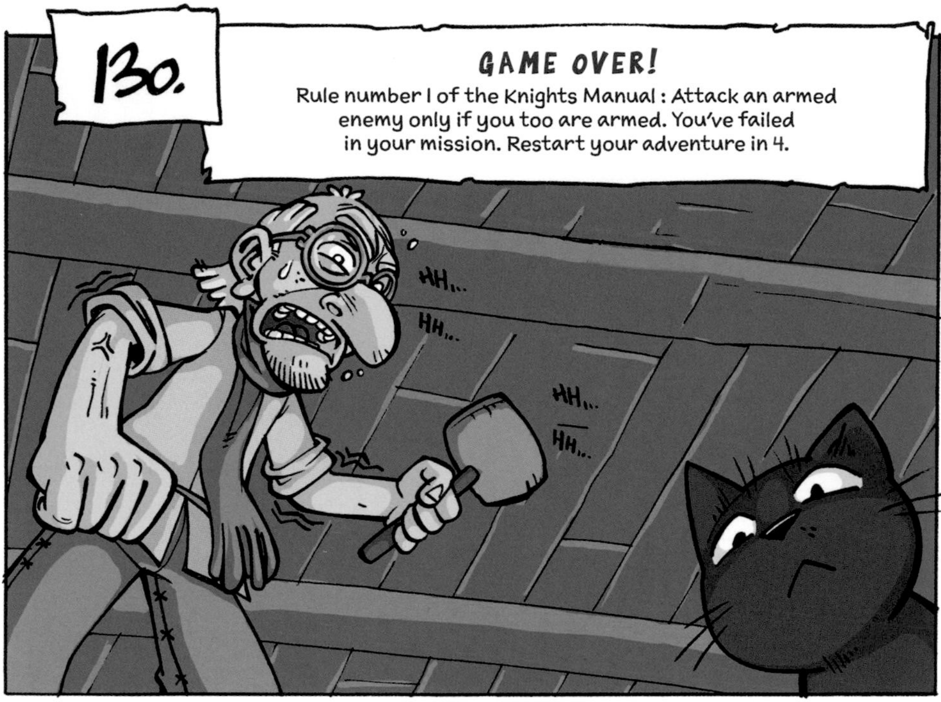
130.
GAME OVER!
Rule number 1 of the Knights Manual : Attack an armed enemy only if you too are armed. You've failed in your mission. Restart your adventure in 4.
HH...
HH...
HH...
HH...

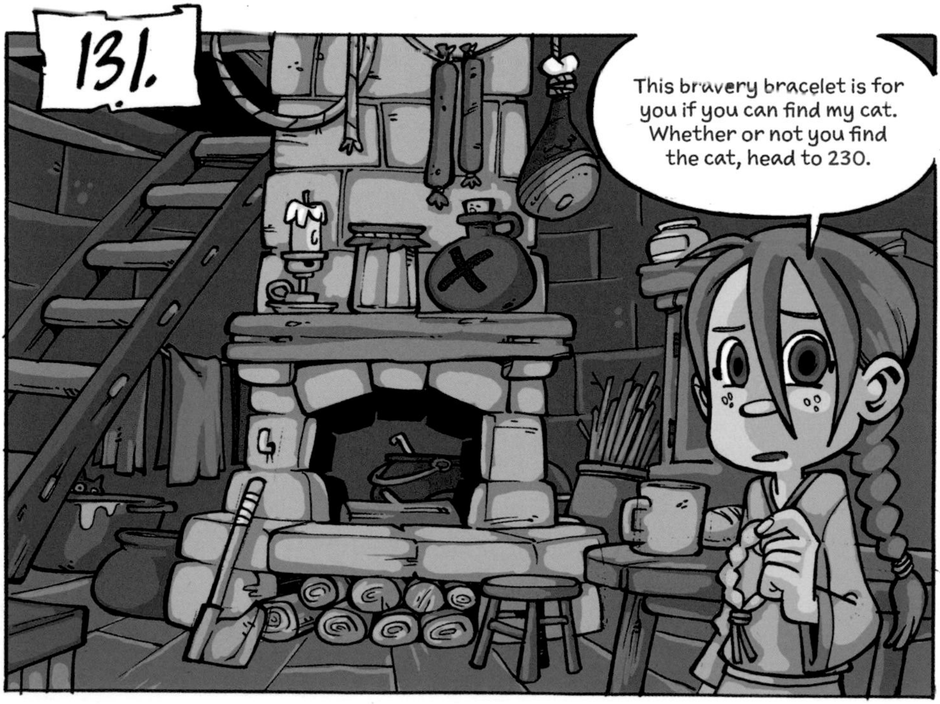
131.
This bravery bracelet is for you if you can find my cat. Whether or not you find the cat, head to 230.

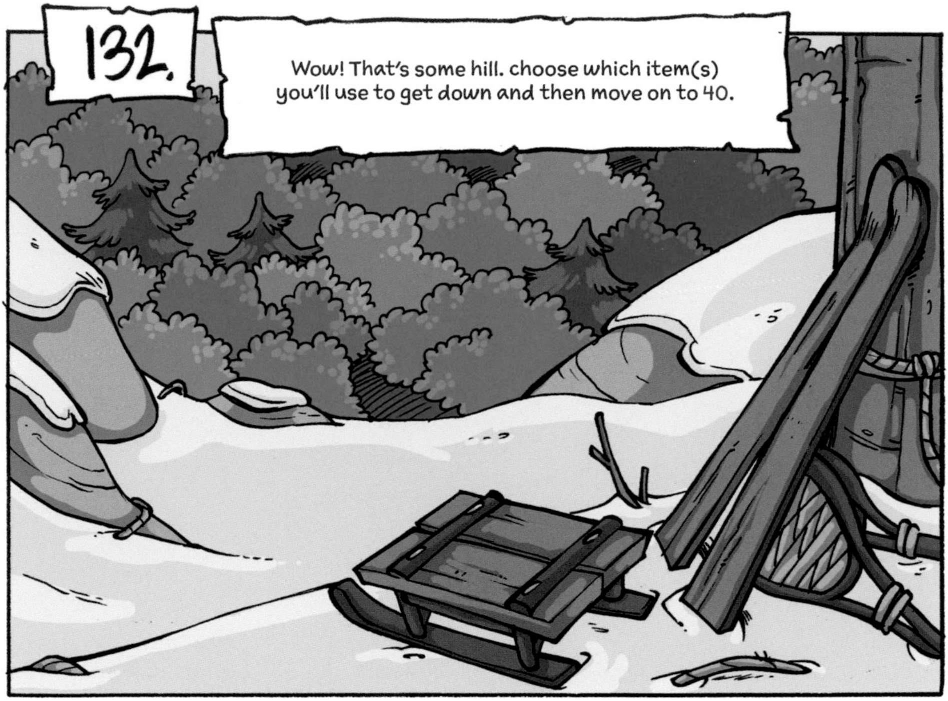
132.
Wow! That's some hill. choose which item(s) you'll use to get down and then move on to 40.

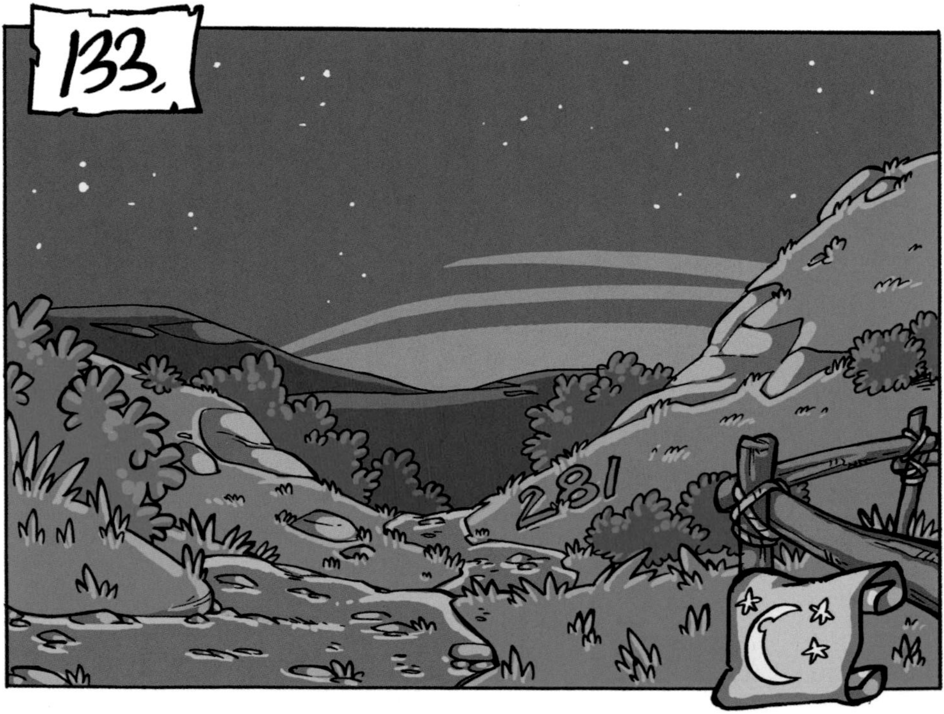
133.
281

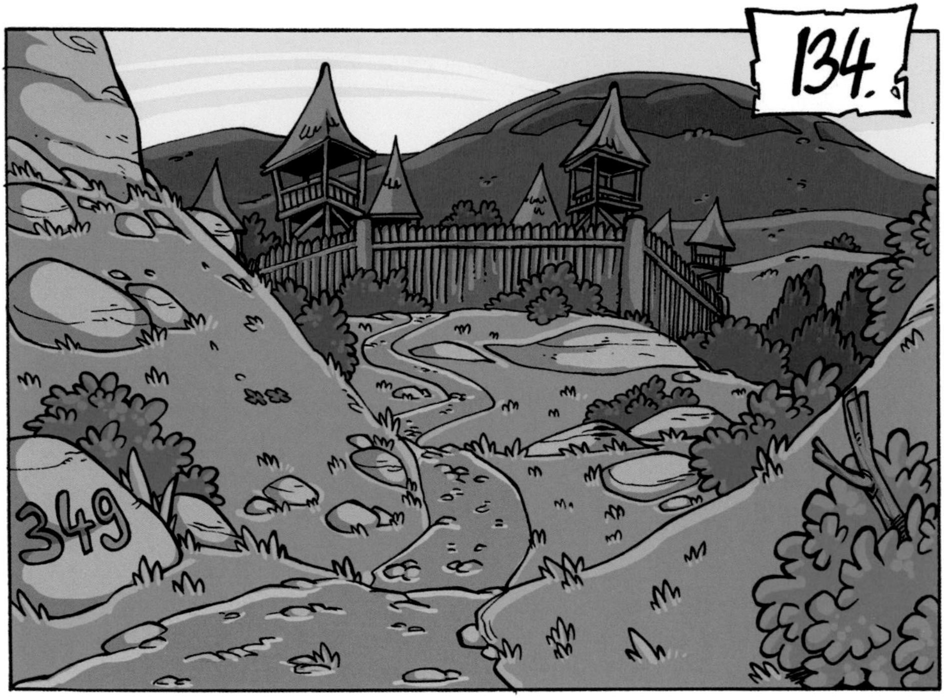
134.
349

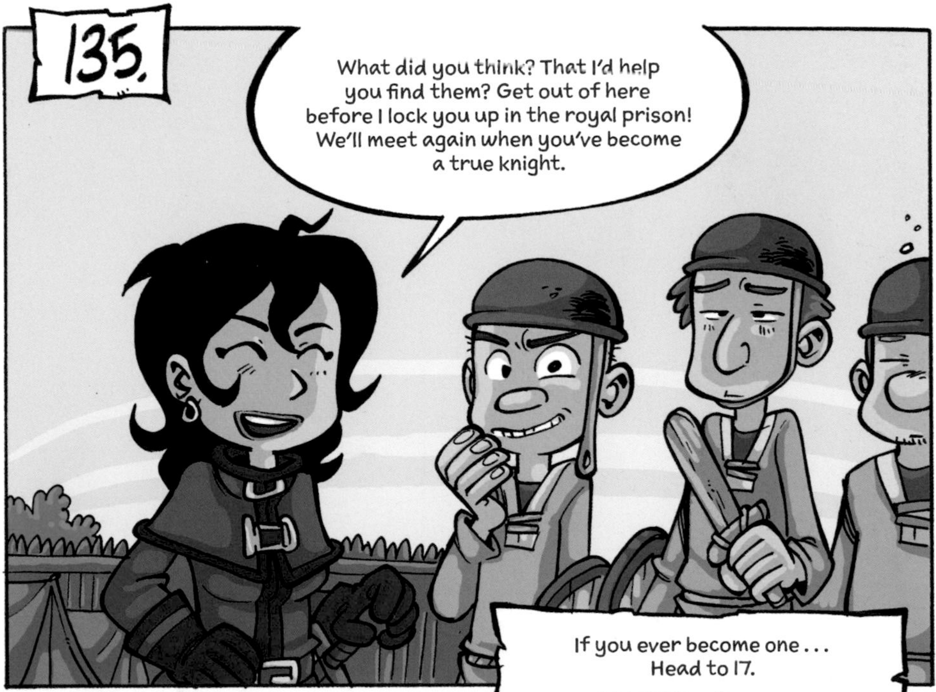
135.
What did you think? That I'd help you find them? Get out of here before I lock you up in the royal prison! We'll meet again when you've become a true knight.
If you ever become one . . . Head to 17.

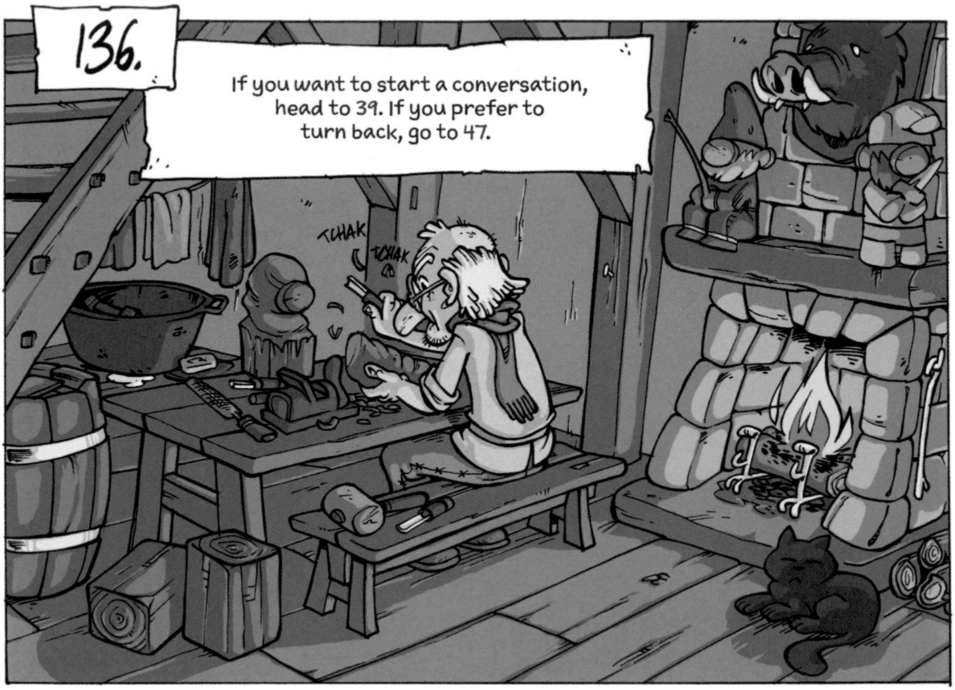
136.
If you want to start a conversation, head to 39. If you prefer to turn back, go to 47.
TCHAK
TCHAK

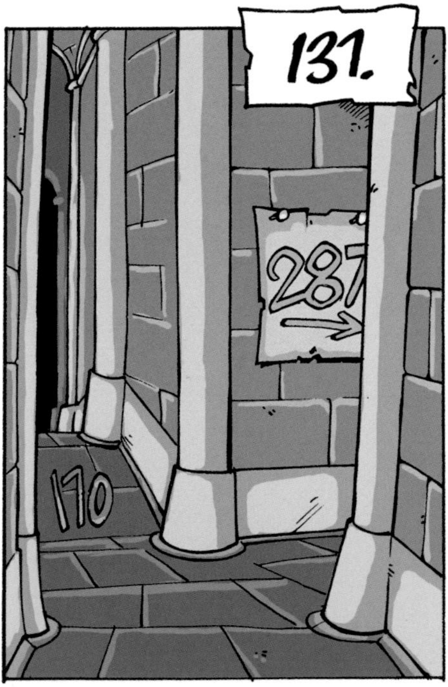
137.
287
170

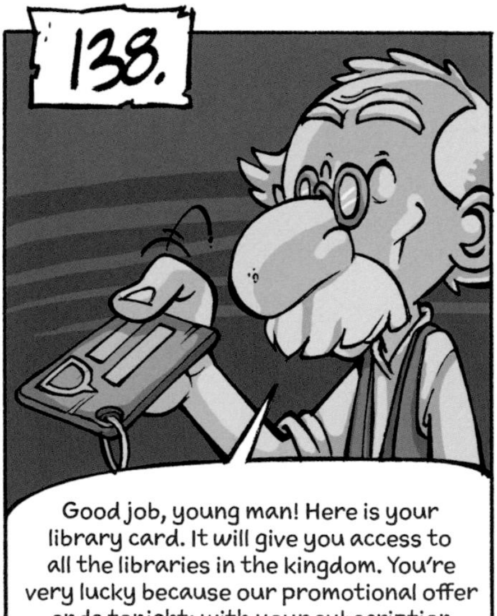
138.
Good job, young man! Here is your library card. It will give you access to all the libraries in the kingdom. You're very lucky because our promotional offer ends tonight: with your subscription comes a bravery bracelet or a wooden toy. Choose whichever gift you prefer. All right, I have to close now. Return to 287 and come back another day.

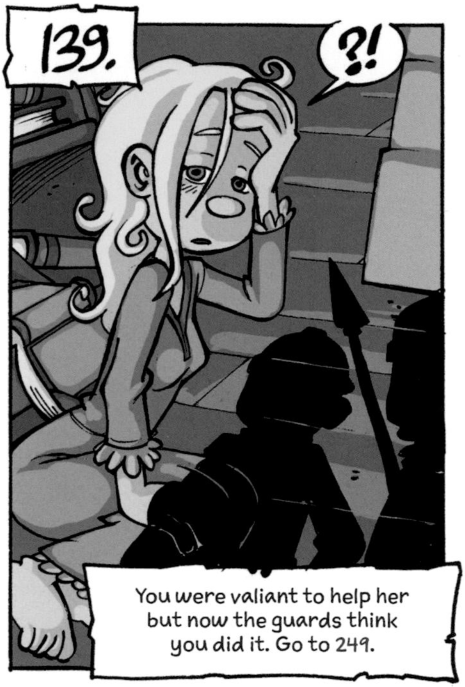
139.
?!
You were valiant to help her but now the guards think you did it. Go to 249.

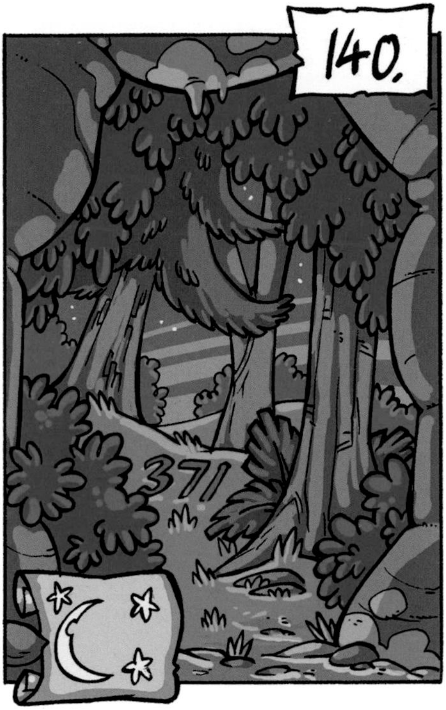
140.
371

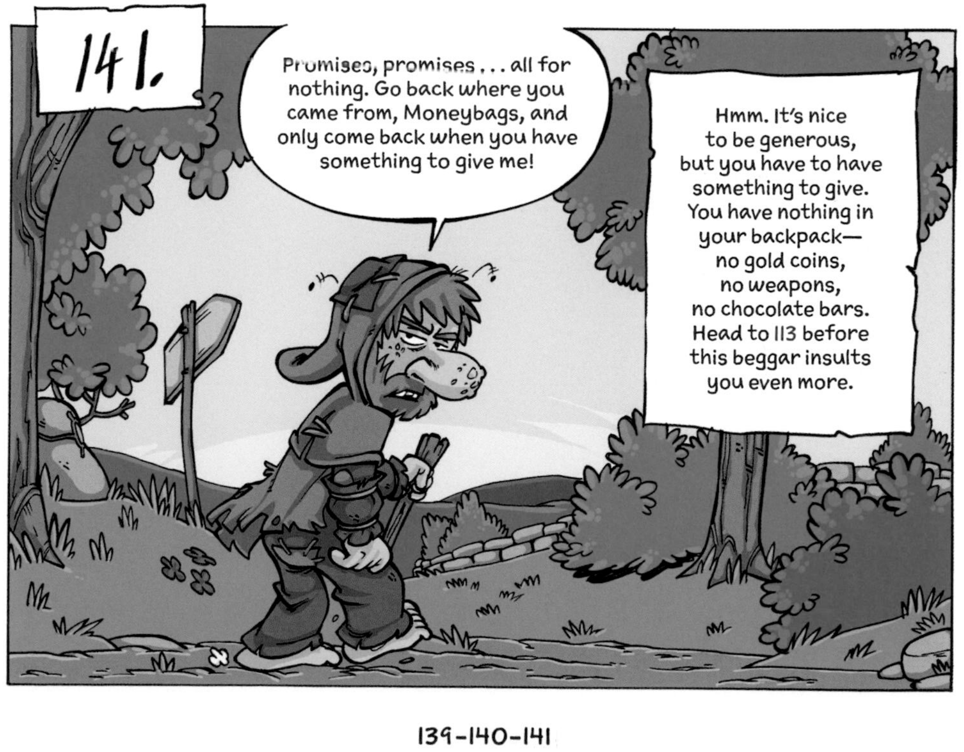
141.
Promises, promises . . . all for nothing. Go back where you came from, Moneybags, and only come back when you have something to give me!
Hmm. It's nice to be generous, but you have to have something to give. You have nothing in your backpack— no gold coins, no weapons, no chocolate bars. Head to 113 before this beggar insults you even more.

142.

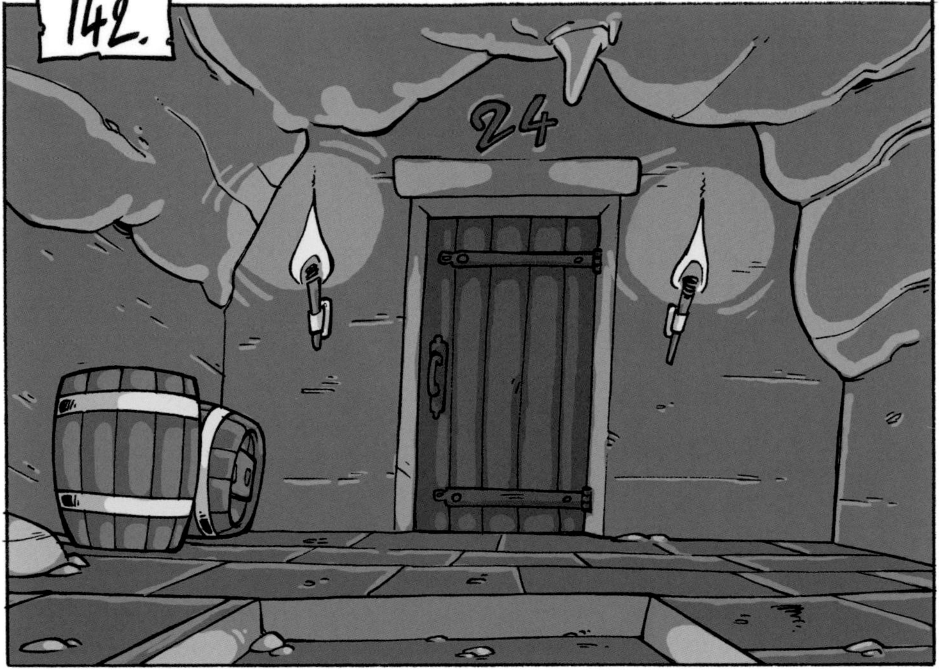
24

143.

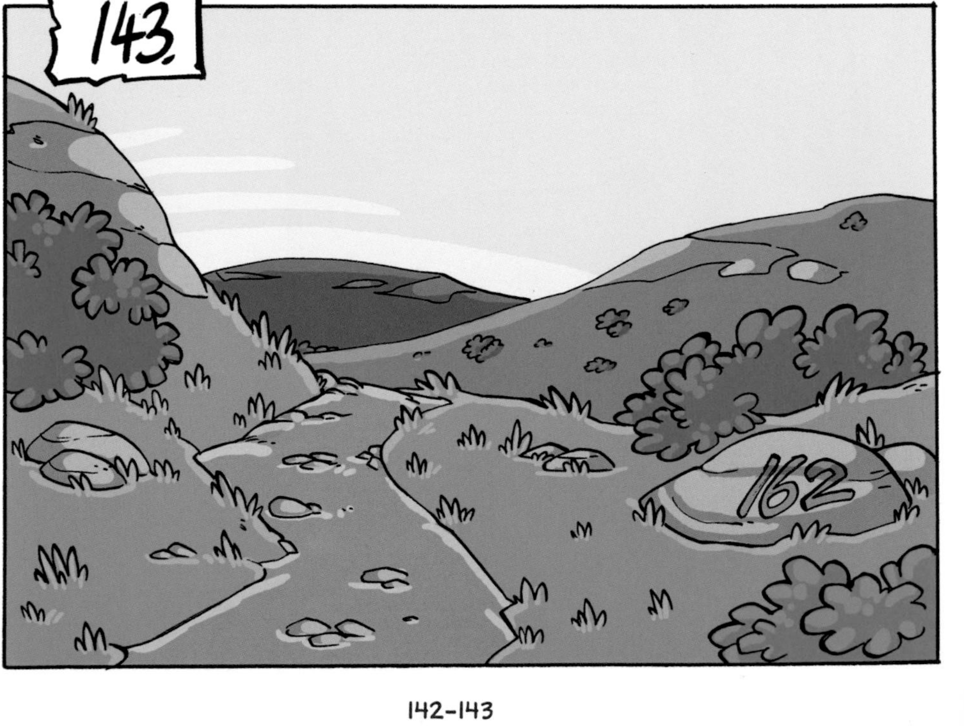
162

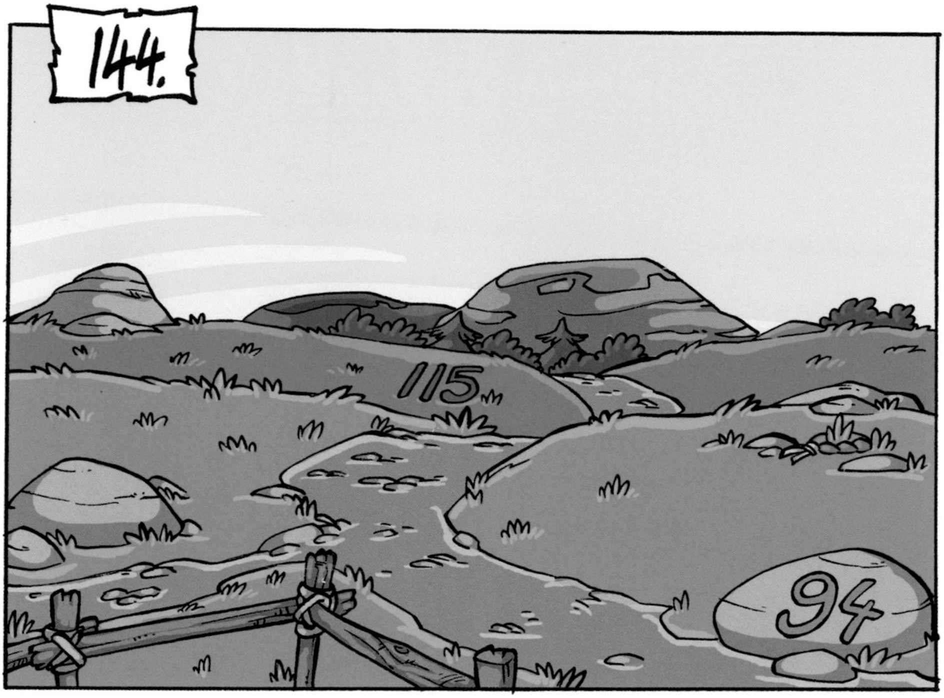
144.
115
94

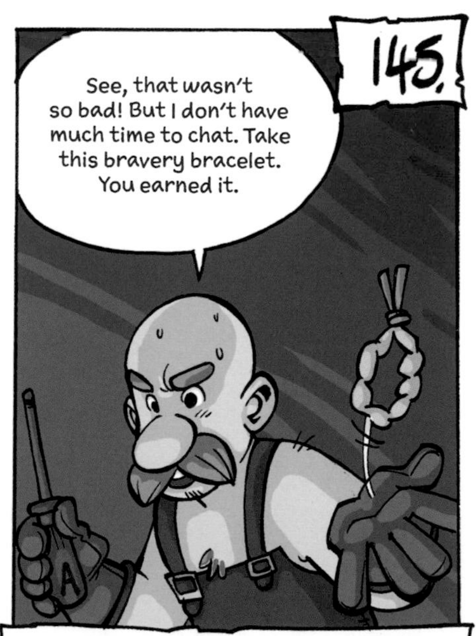
145.
See, that wasn't so bad! But I don't have much time to chat. Take this bravery bracelet. You earned it.
You can take it only if you got the right answer. Now head back to 305.

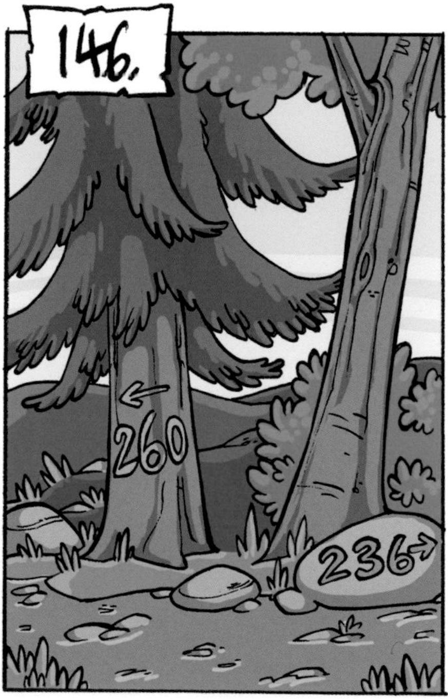
146.
260
236

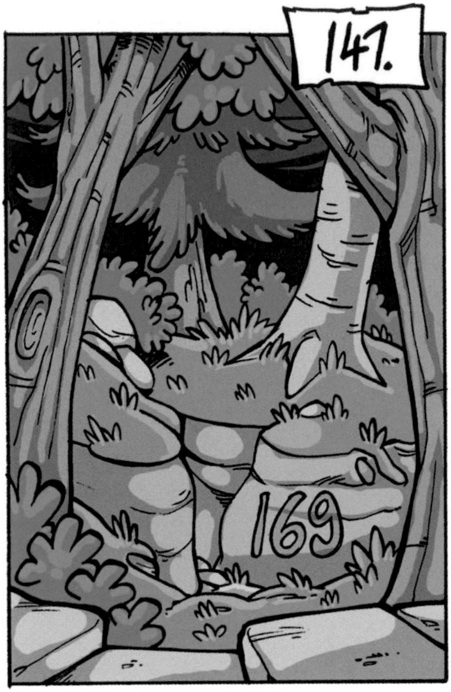
147.
169

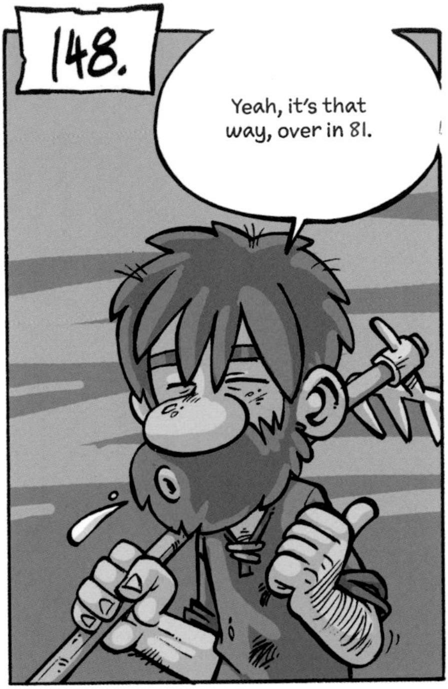
148.
Yeah, it's that way, over in 81.

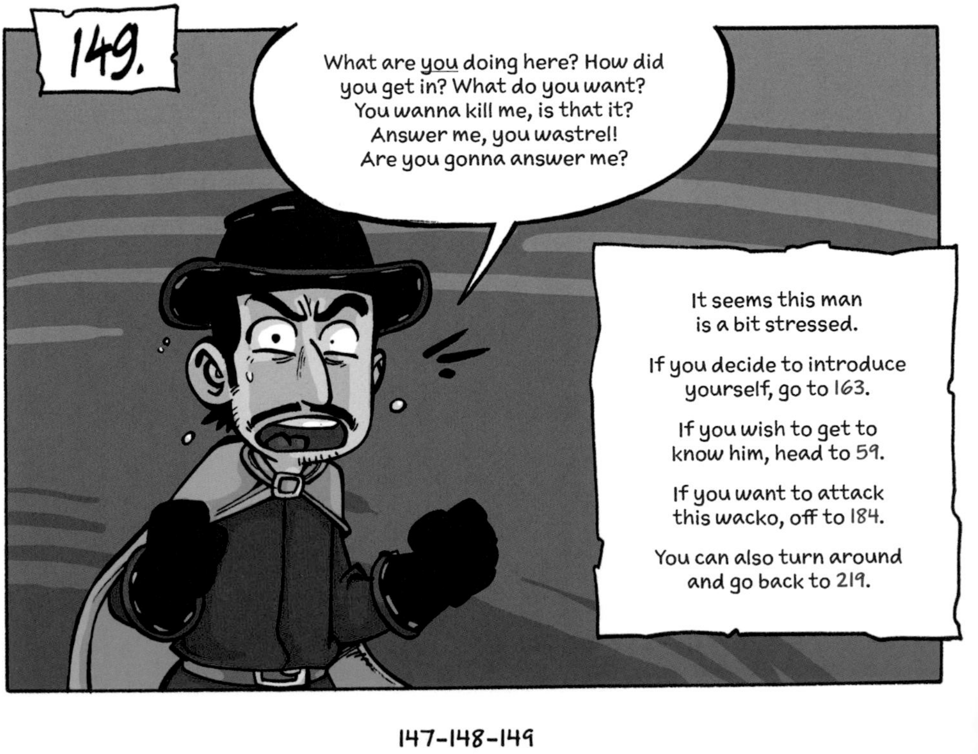
149.
What are you doing here? How did you get in? What do you want? You wanna kill me, is that it? Answer me, you wastrel! Are you gonna answer me?
It seems this man is a bit stressed.
If you decide to introduce yourself, go to 163.
If you wish to get to know him, head to 59.
If you want to attack this wacko, off to 184.
You can also turn around and go back to 219.

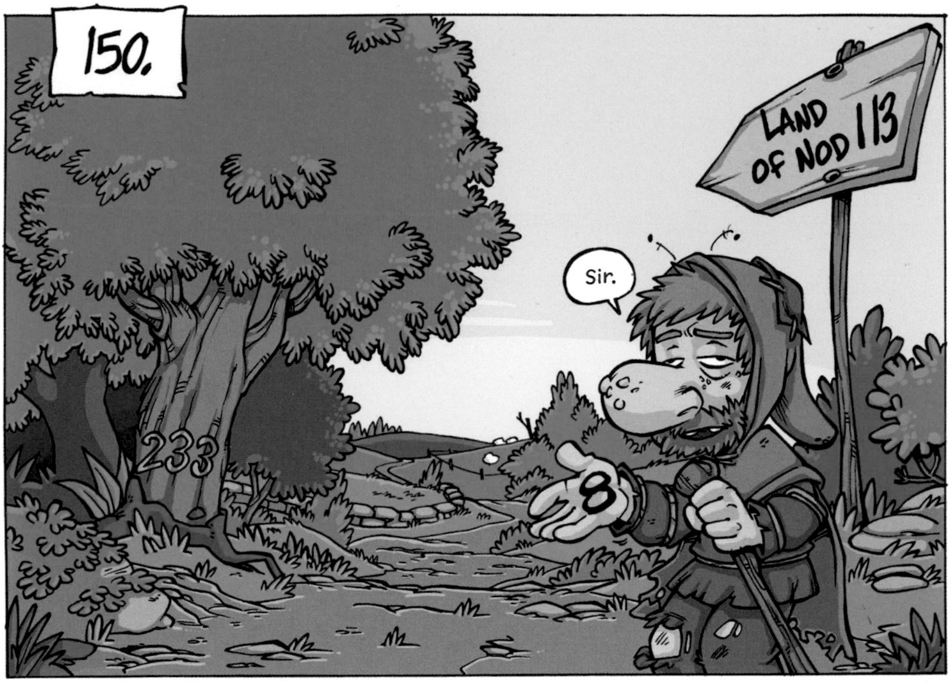
150.
LAND OF NOD 113
Sir.
233
8

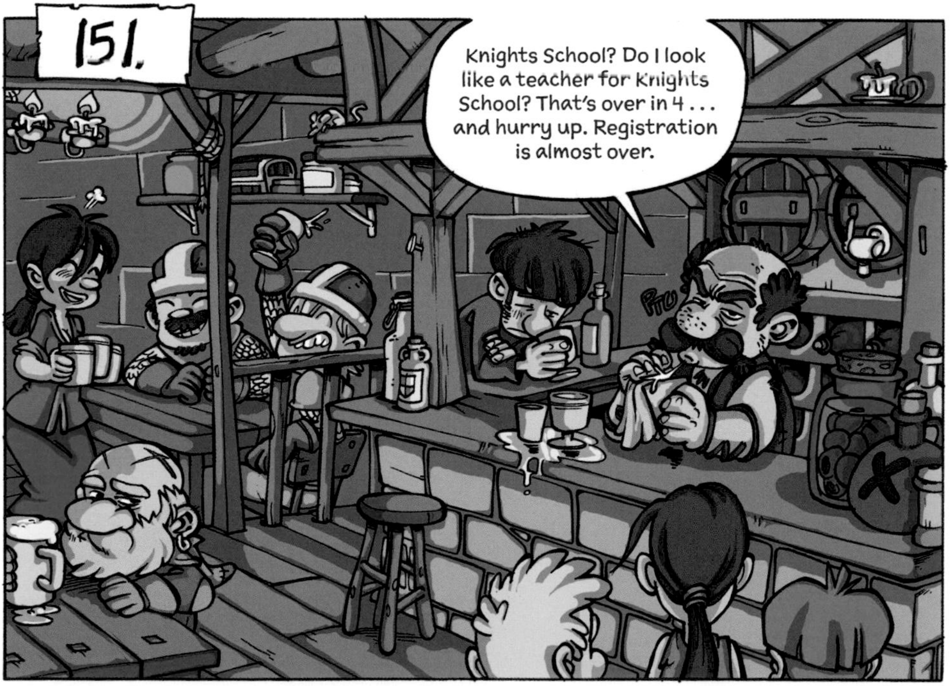
151.
Knights School? Do I look like a teacher for Knights School? That's over in 4 . . . and hurry up. Registration is almost over.
PTU

152

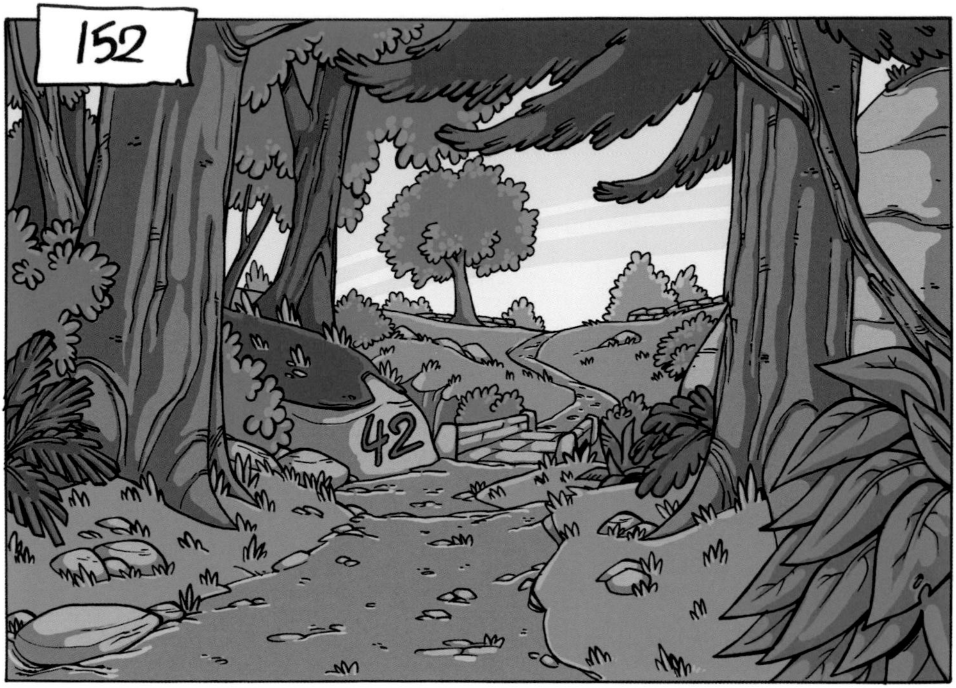
42

153.

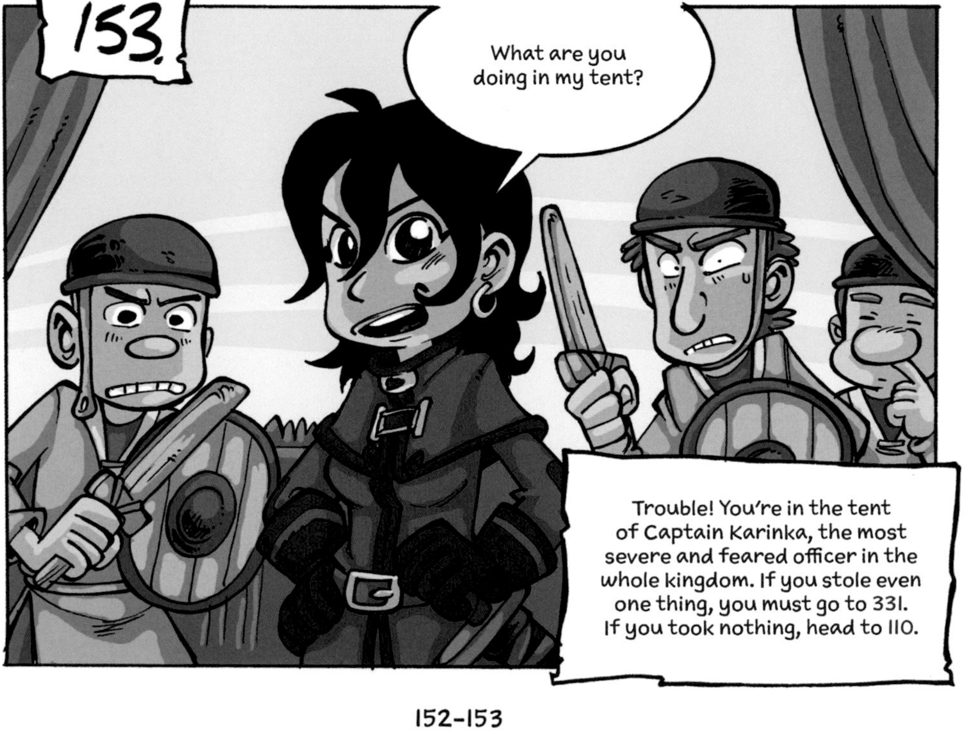
What are you doing in my tent?
Trouble! You're in the tent of Captain Karinka, the most severe and feared officer in the whole kingdom. If you stole even one thing, you must go to 331. If you took nothing, head to 110.

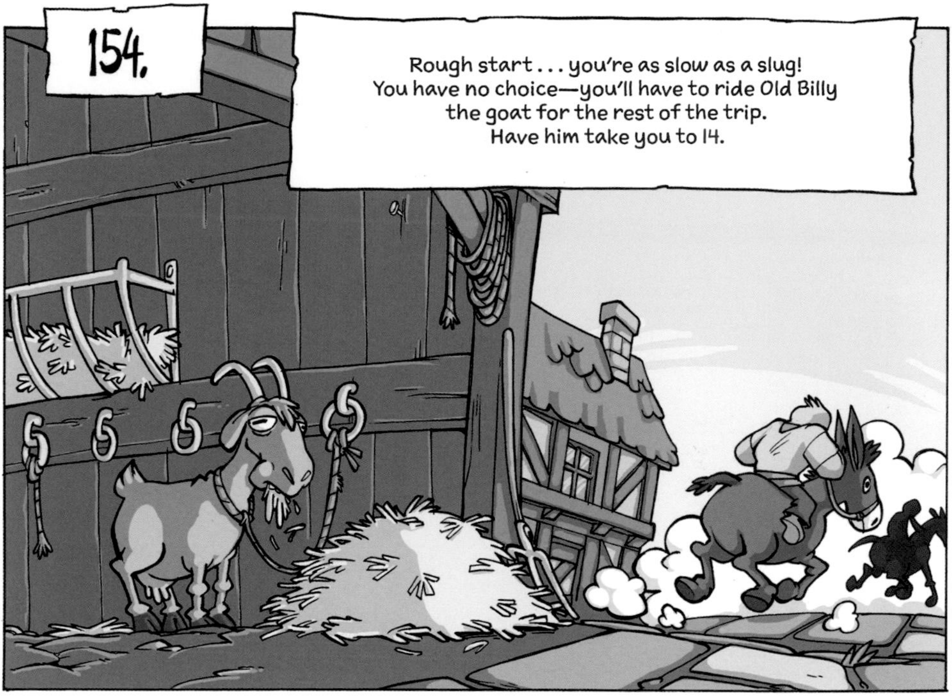
154.
Rough start . . . you're as slow as a slug! You have no choice—you'll have to ride Old Billy the goat for the rest of the trip. Have him take you to 14.

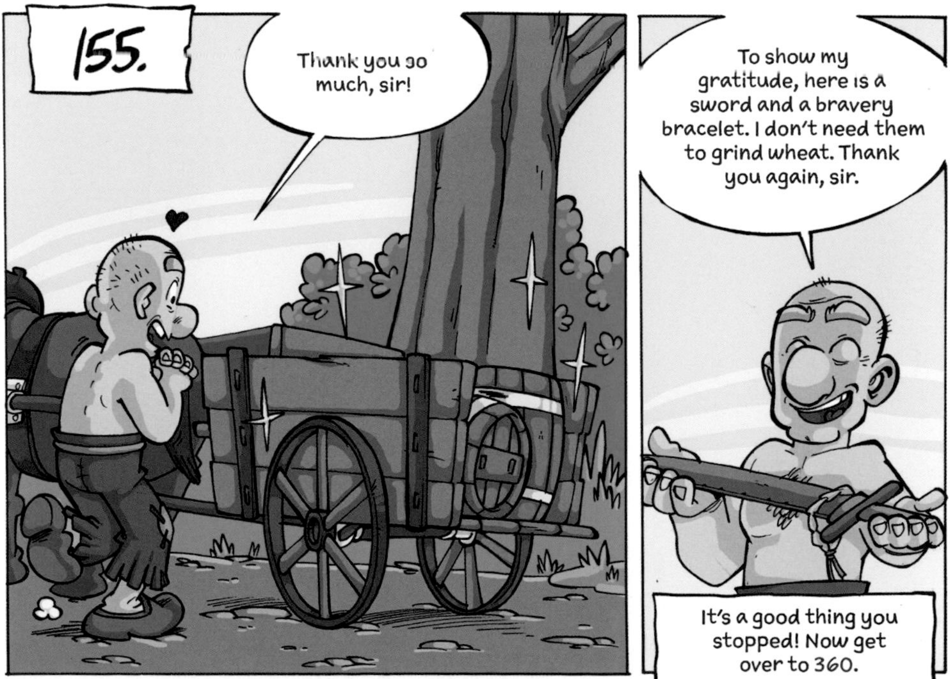
155.
Thank you so much, sir!
To show my gratitude, here is a sword and a bravery bracelet. I don't need them to grind wheat. Thank you again, sir.
It's a good thing you stopped! Now get over to 360.

156.

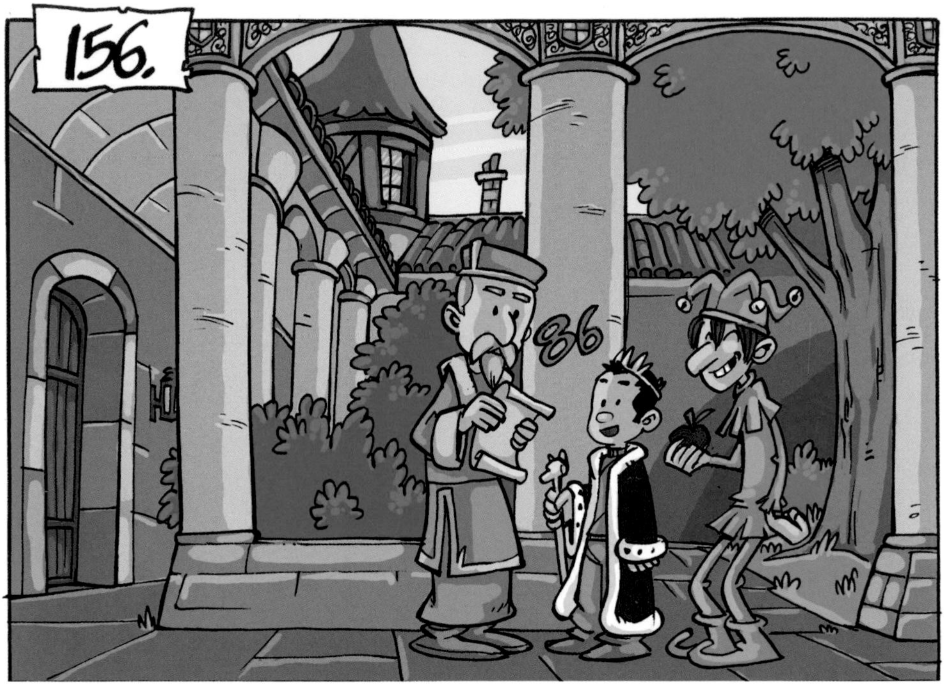
86

157.

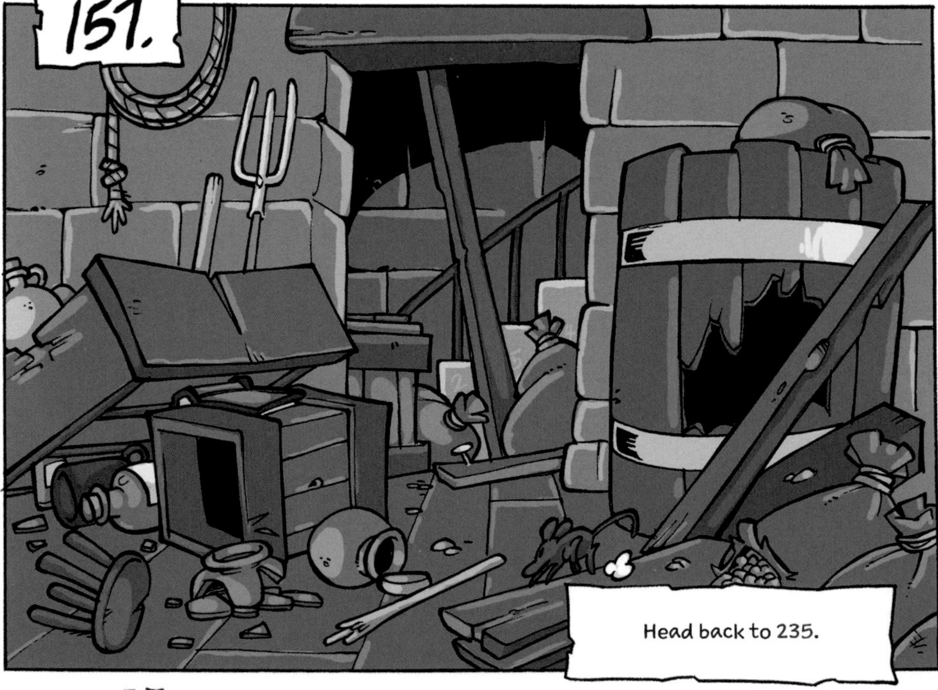
Head back to 235.

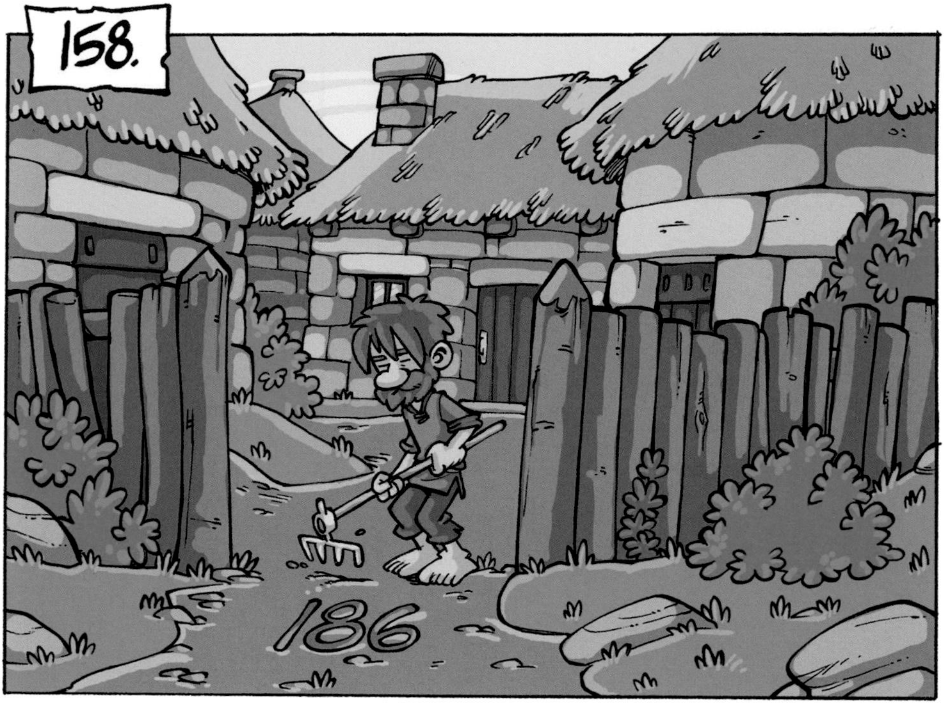
158.
186

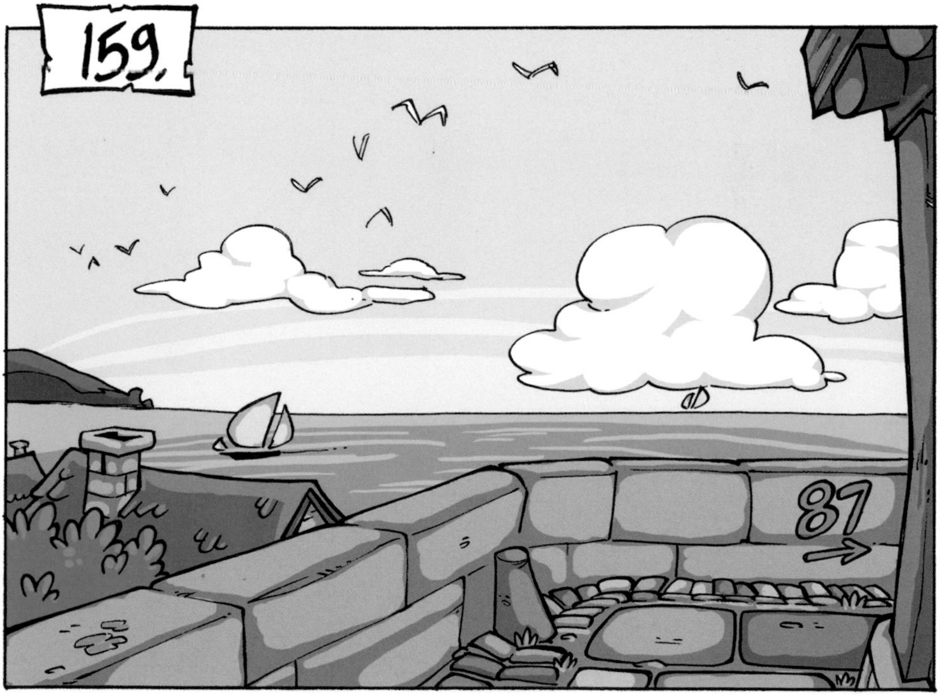
159.
87

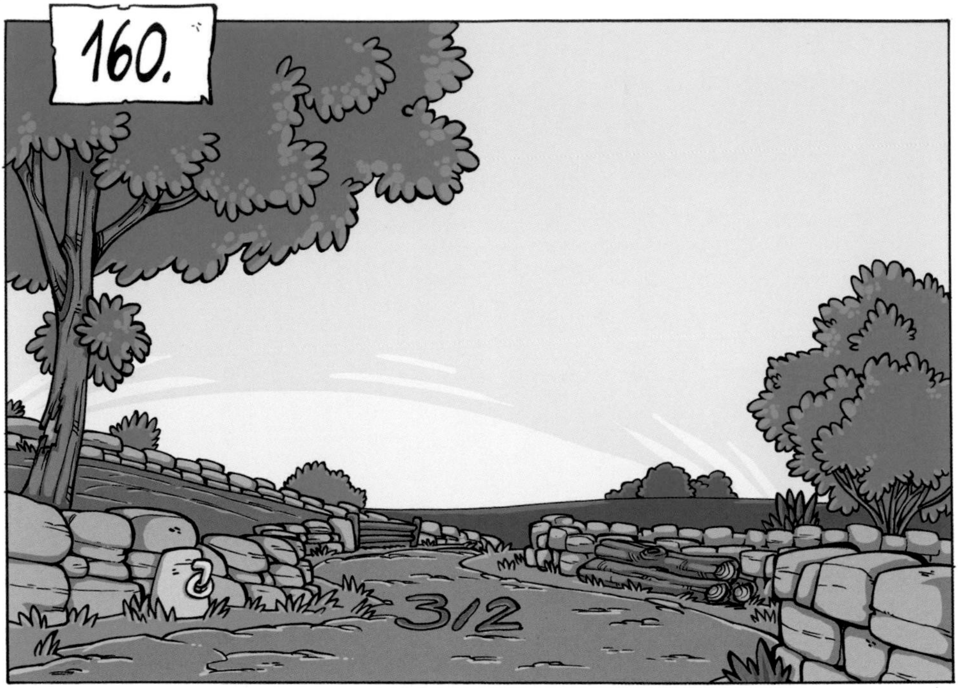
160.
2
3/2

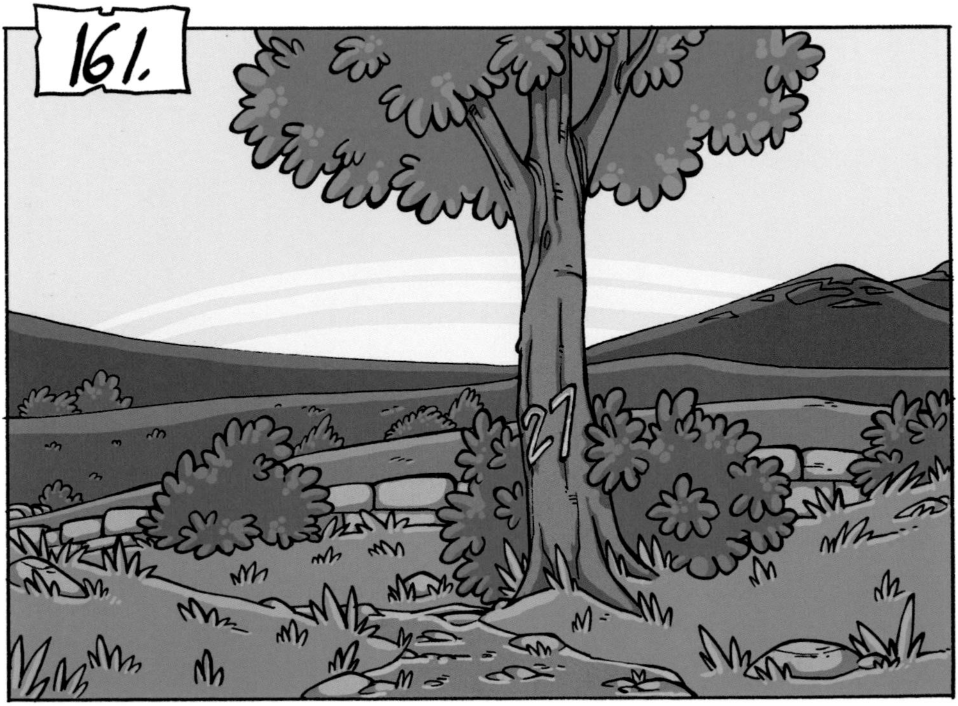
161.
27

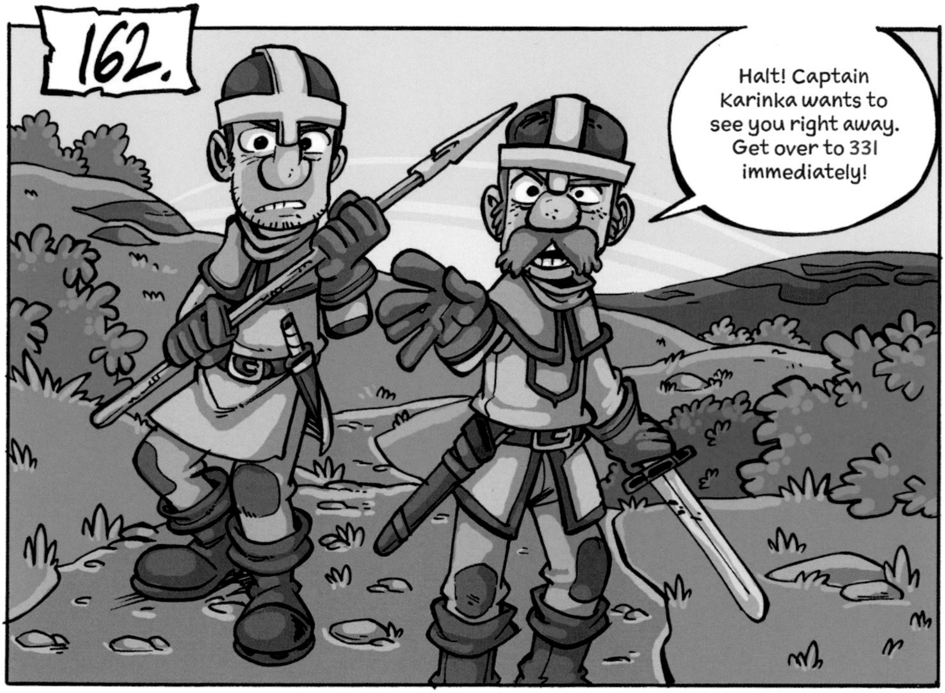
162.
Halt! Captain Karinka wants to see you right away. Get over to 331 immediately!

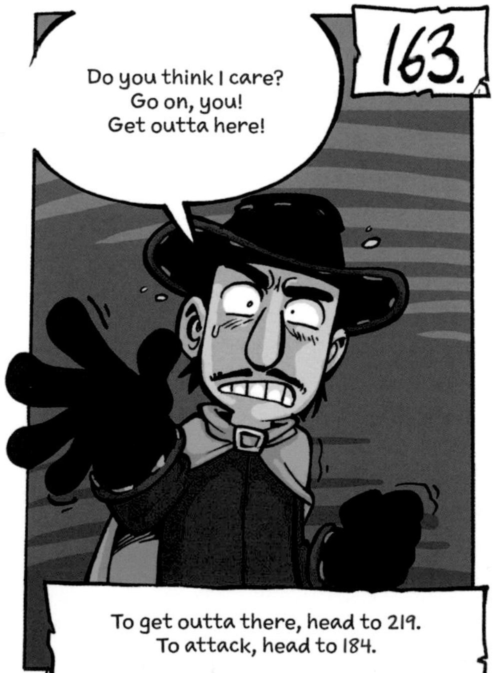
163.
Do you think I care? Go on, you! Get outta here!
To get outta there, head to 219. To attack, head to 184.

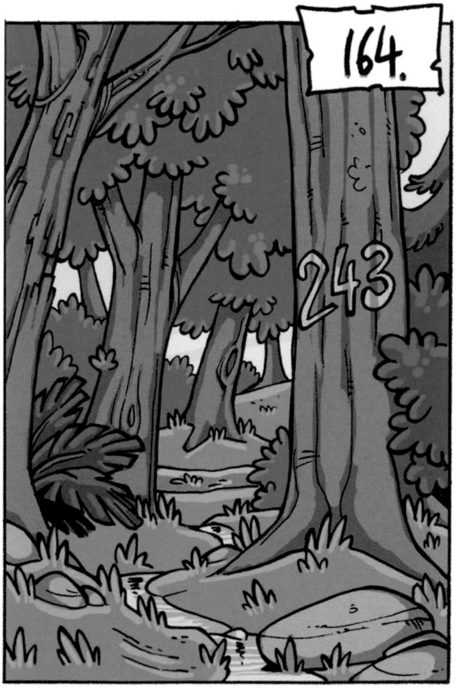
164.
243

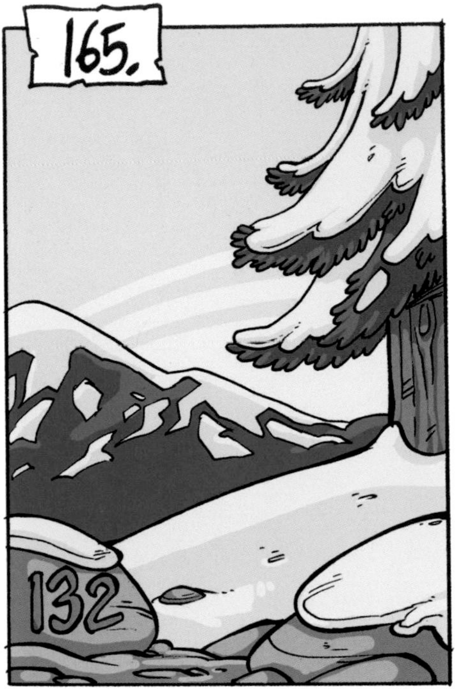
165.
132

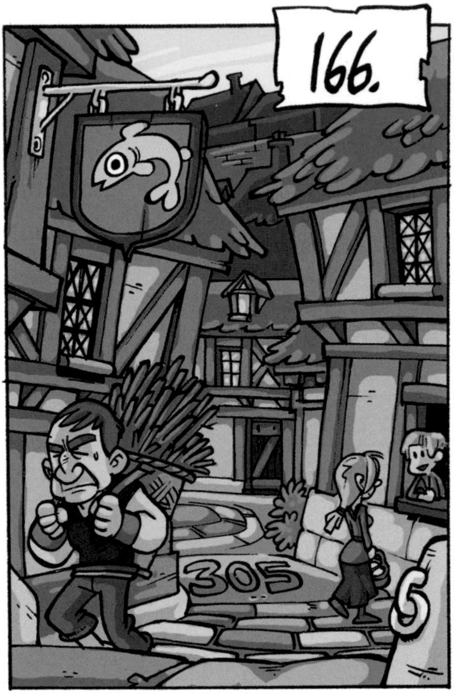
166.
305
6

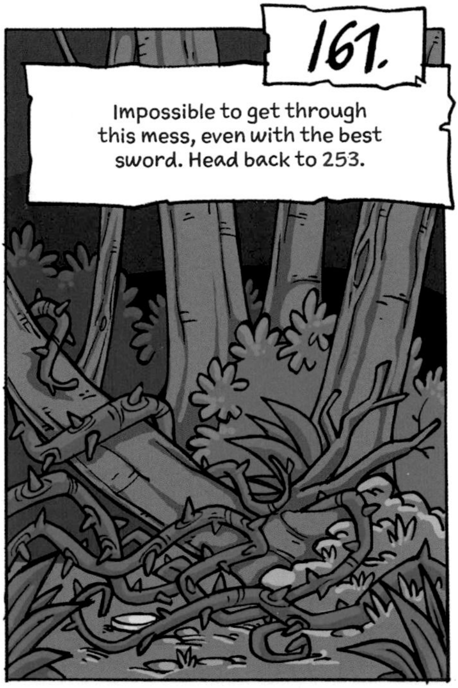
167.
Impossible to get through this mess, even with the best sword. Head back to 253.

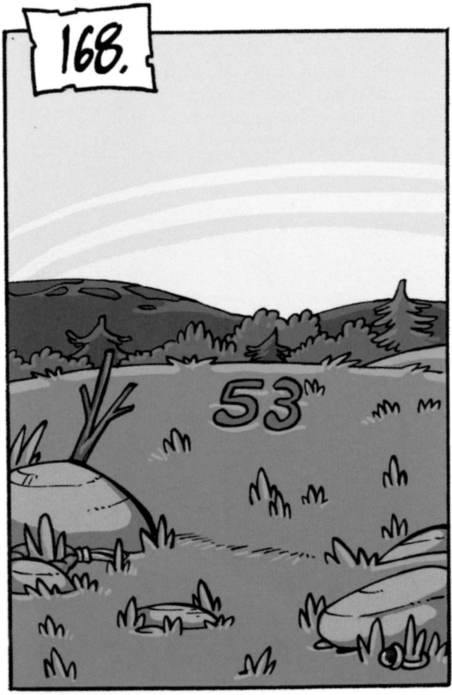
168.
53

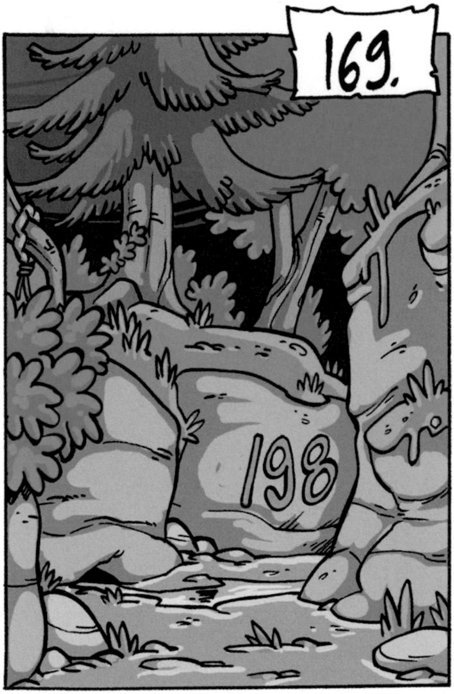
169.
198

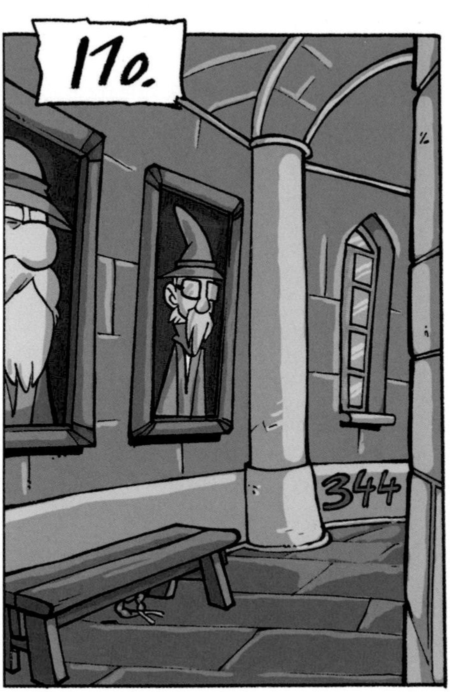
170.
344

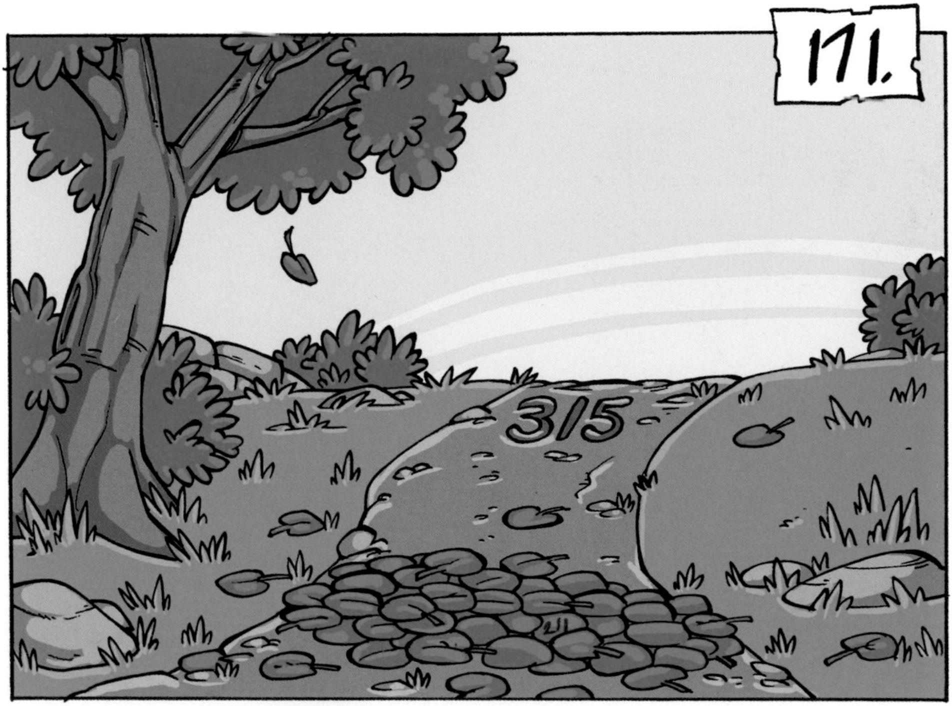
171.
315
211

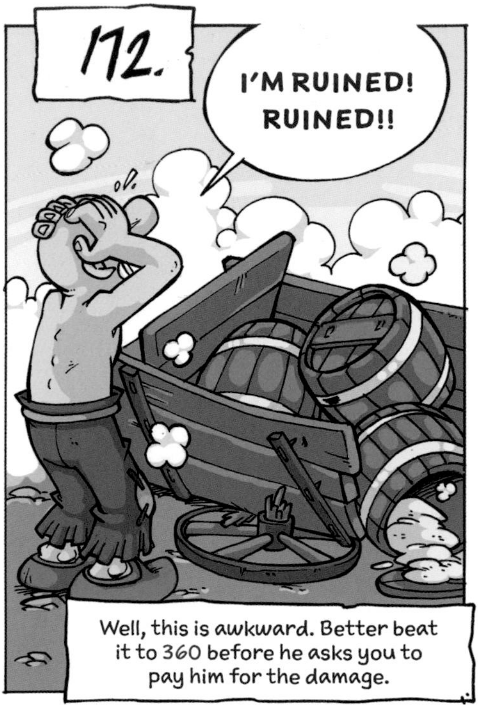
172.
I'M RUINED! RUINED!!
Well, this is awkward. Better beat it to 360 before he asks you to pay him for the damage.

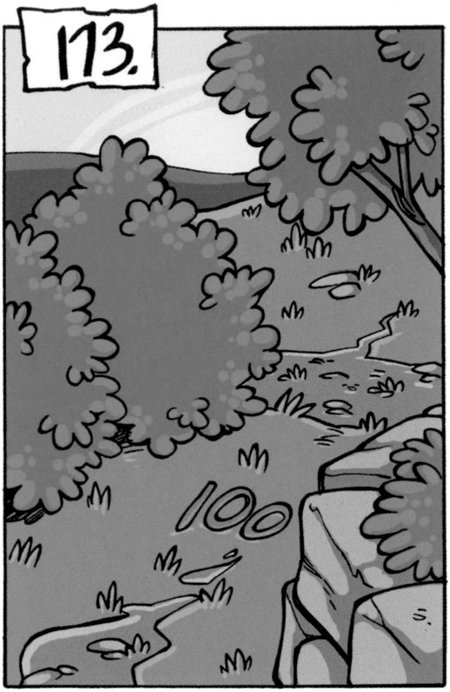
173.
100

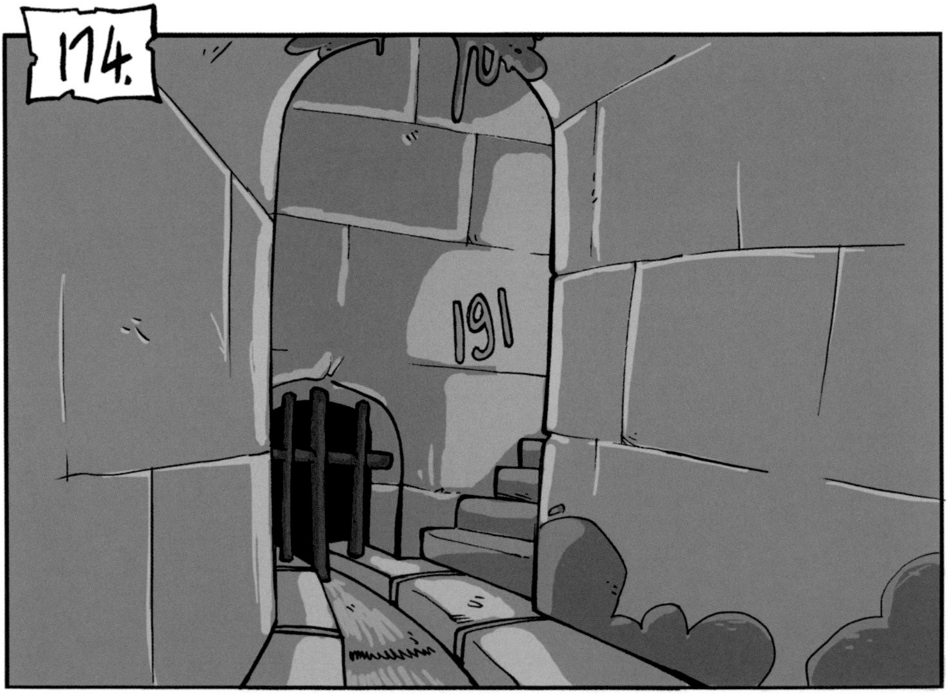
174.
191

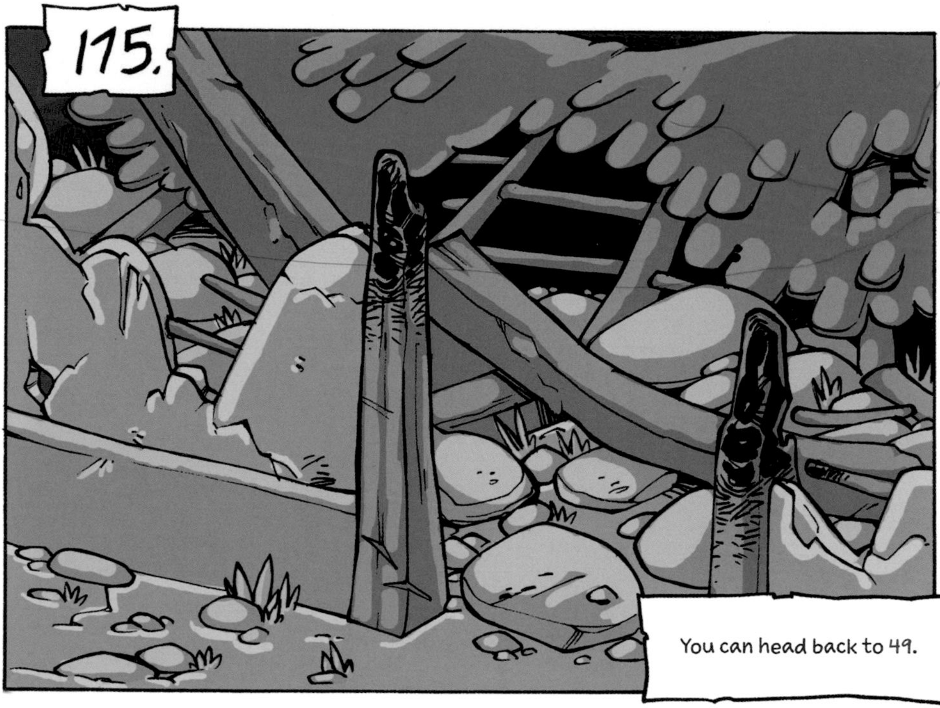
175.
You can head back to 49.

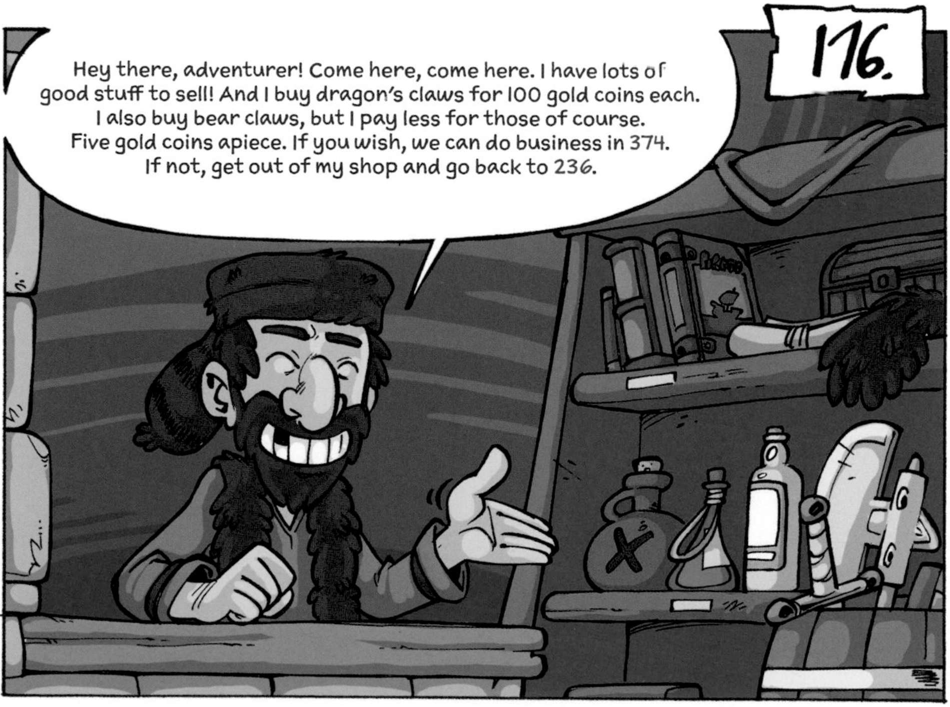
176.
Hey there, adventurer! Come here, come here. I have lots of good stuff to sell! And I buy dragon's claws for 100 gold coins each. I also buy bear claws, but I pay less for those of course. Five gold coins apiece. If you wish, we can do business in 374. If not, get out of my shop and go back to 236.

177.

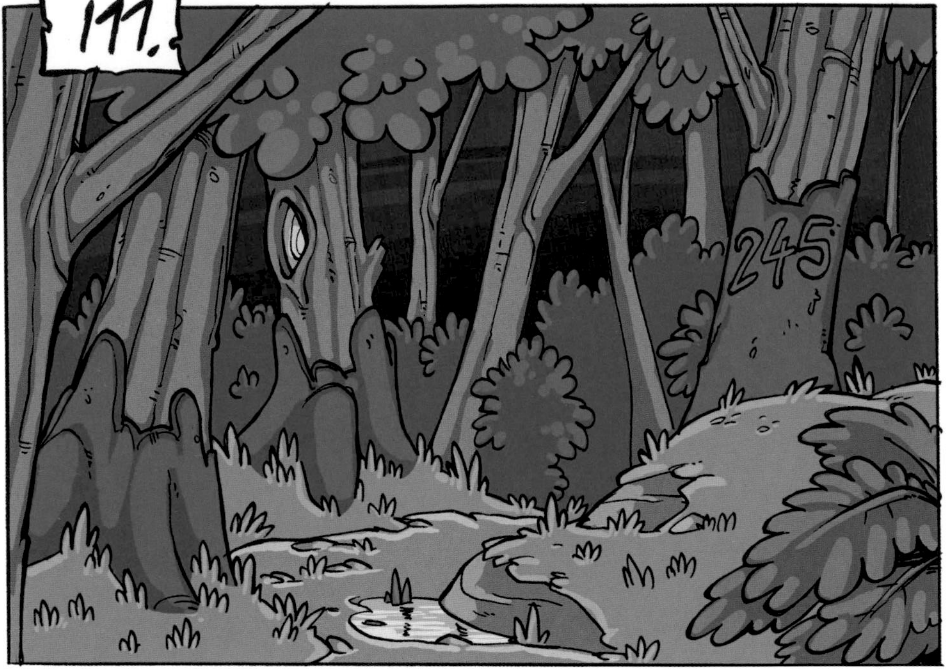
245

178.

If you want to help this poor man, go to 248.

If not, continue on your path to 360.

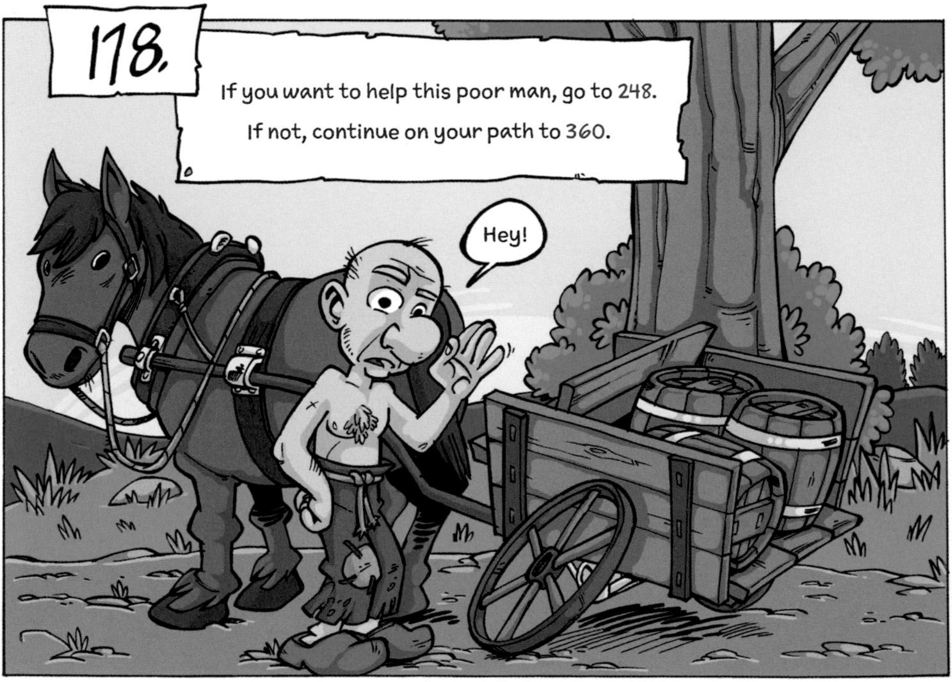
Hey!

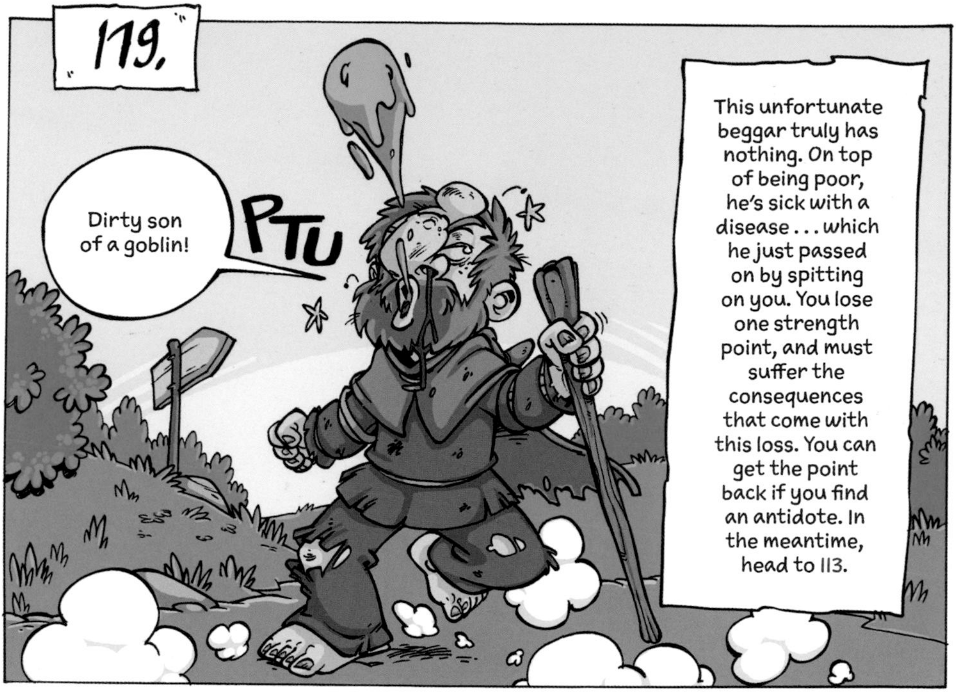
179.
This unfortunate beggar truly has nothing. On top of being poor, he's sick with a disease . . . which he just passed on by spitting on you. You lose one strength point, and must suffer the consequences that come with this loss. You can get the point back if you find an antidote. In the meantime, head to 113.
Dirty son of a goblin!
PTU

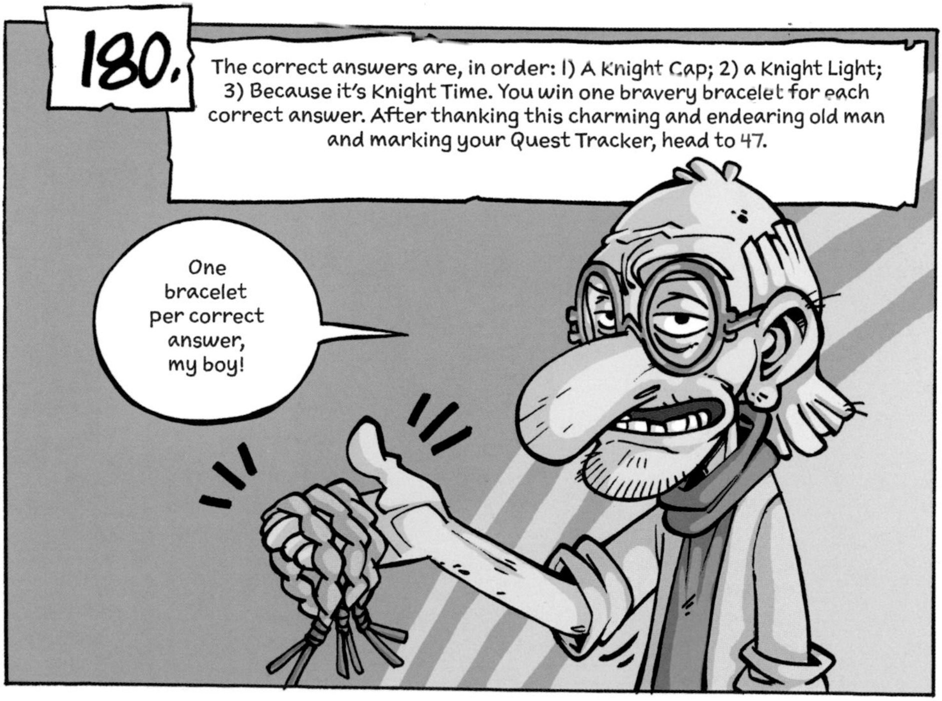
180.
The correct answers are, in order: 1) A Knight Cap; 2) a Knight Light; 3) Because it's Knight Time. You win one bravery bracelet for each correct answer. After thanking this charming and endearing old man and marking your Quest Tracker, head to 47.
One bracelet per correct answer, my boy!

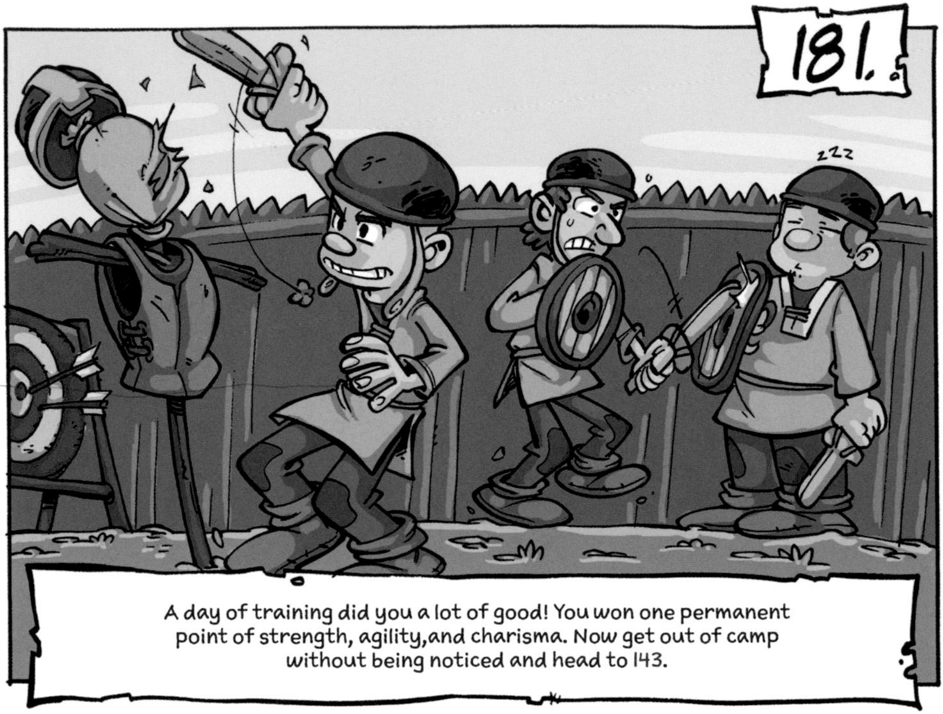
181.
ZZZ

A day of training did you a lot of good! You won one permanent point of strength, agility,and charisma. Now get out of camp without being noticed and head to 143.

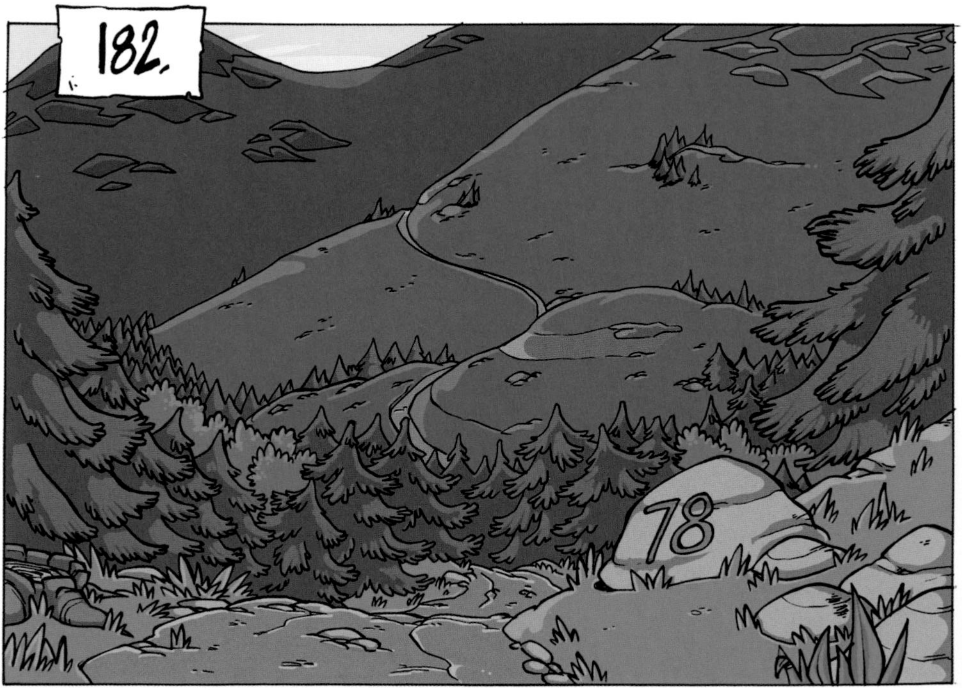
182.
78

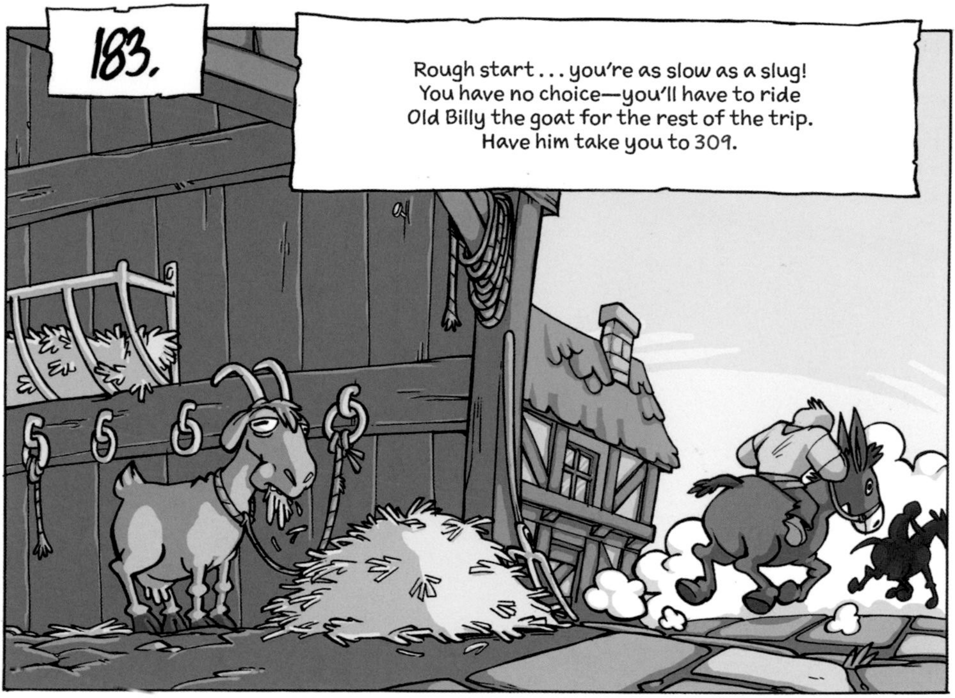
183.
Rough start . . . you're as slow as a slug! You have no choice—you'll have to ride Old Billy the goat for the rest of the trip. Have him take you to 309.

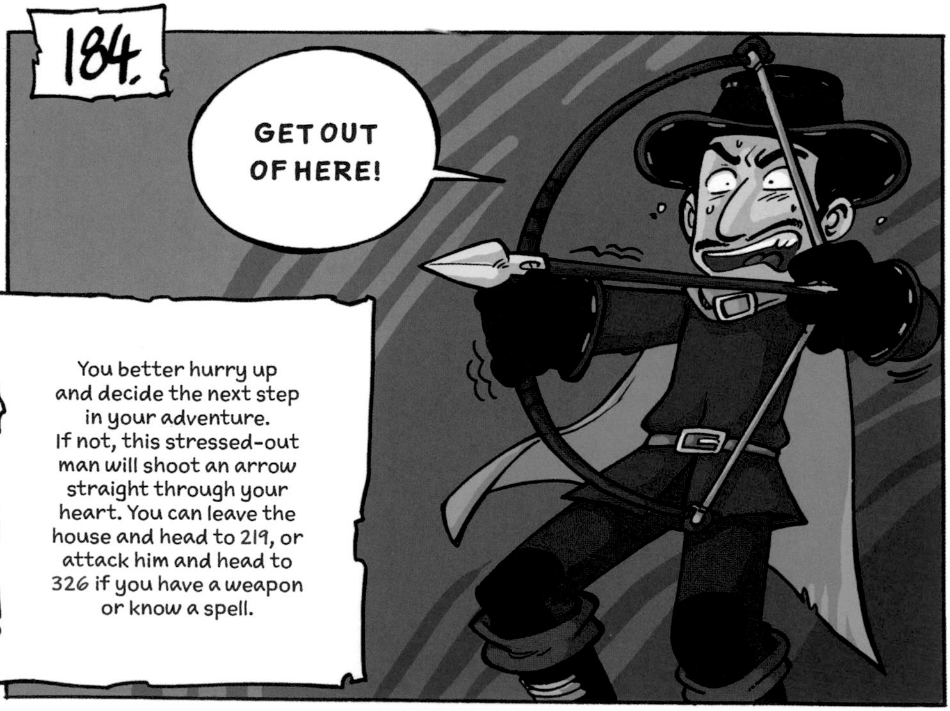
184.
GET OUT OF HERE!
You better hurry up and decide the next step in your adventure. If not, this stressed-out man will shoot an arrow straight through your heart. You can leave the house and head to 219, or attack him and head to 326 if you have a weapon or know a spell.

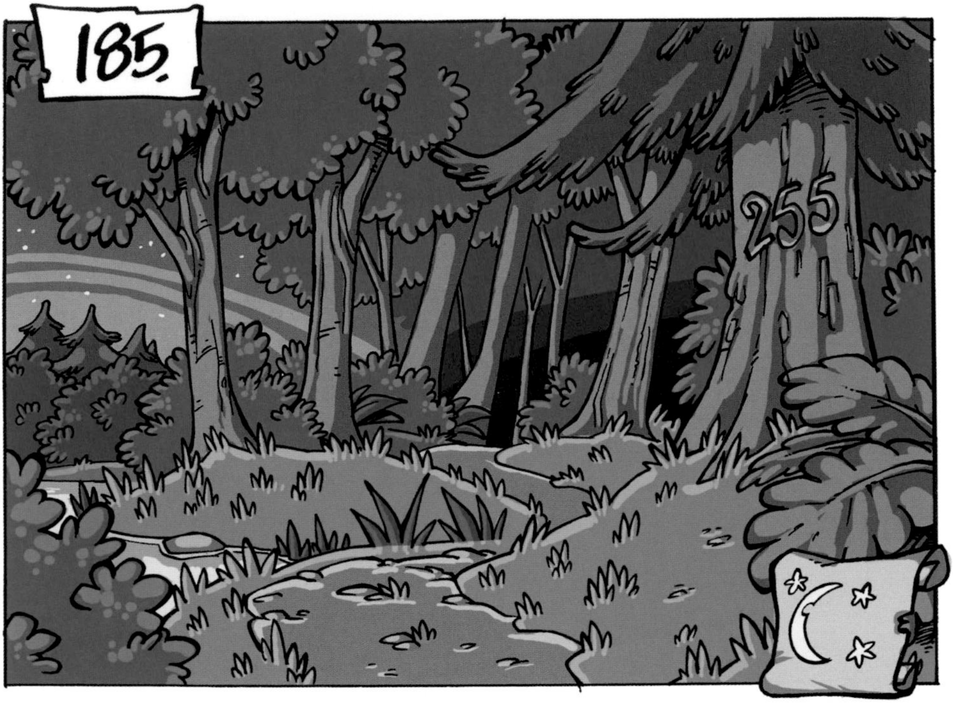
185.
255

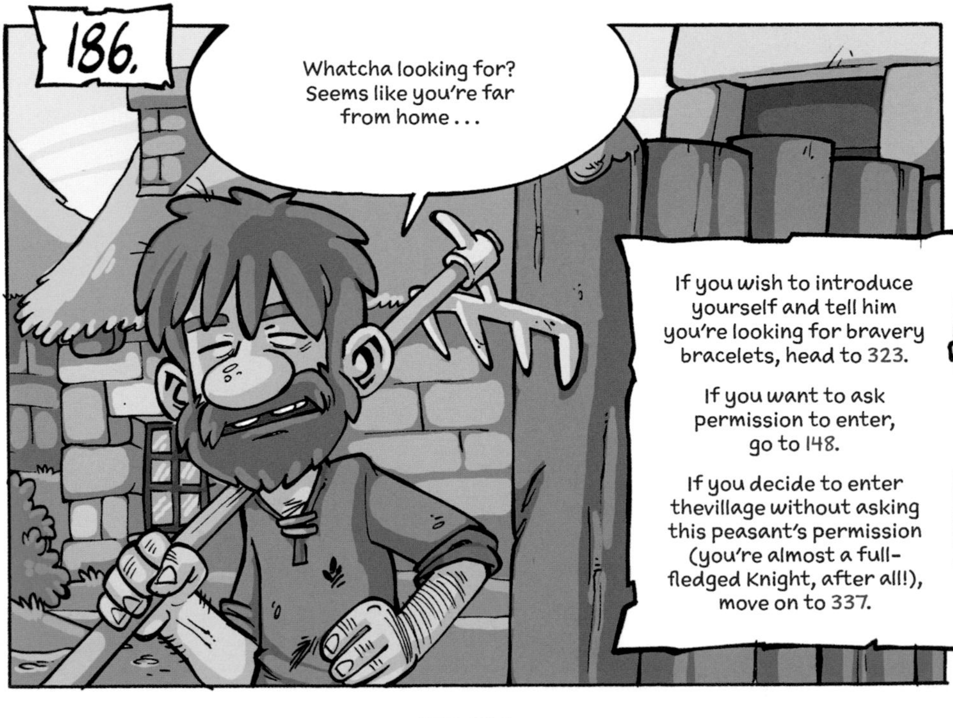
186.
Whatcha looking for? Seems like you're far from home . . .
If you wish to introduce yourself and tell him you're looking for bravery bracelets, head to 323.
If you want to ask permission to enter, go to 148.
If you decide to enter thevillage without asking this peasant's permission (you're almost a full-fledged Knight, after all!), move on to 337.

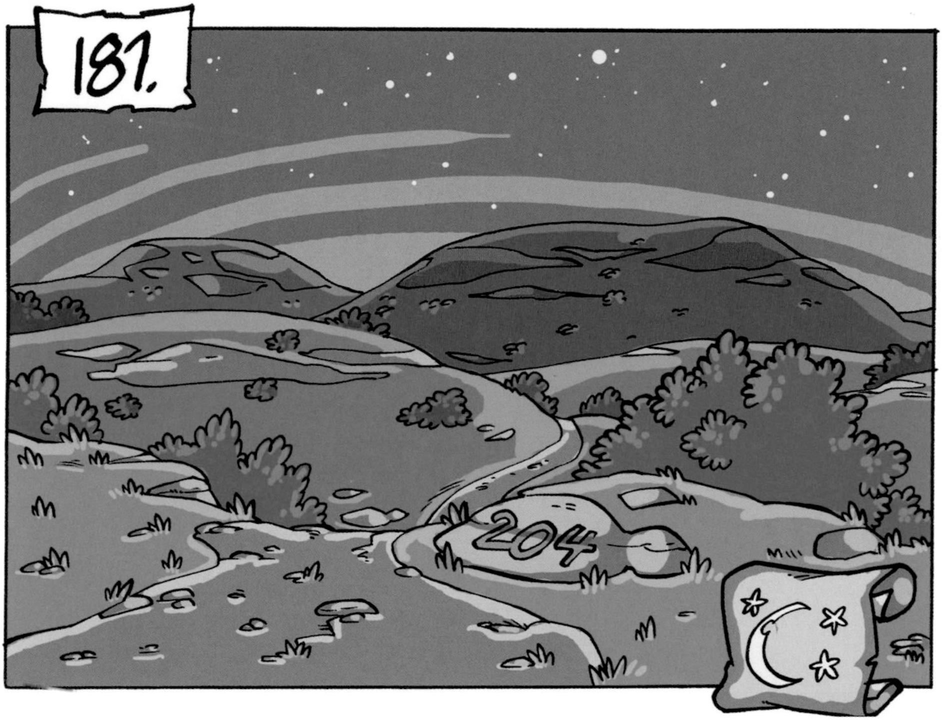
187.
204

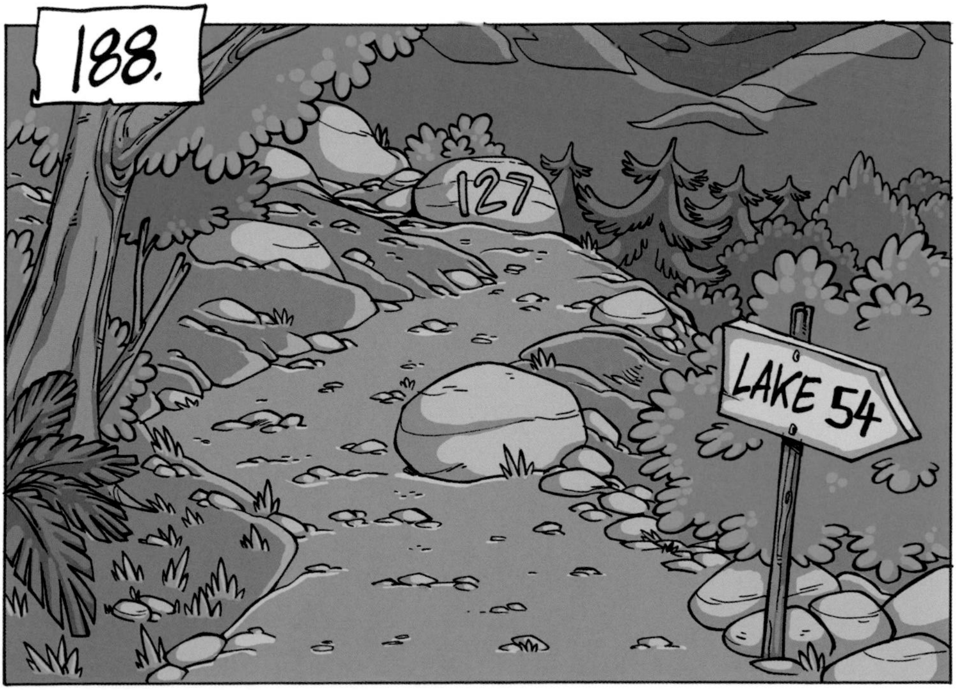
188.
127
LAKE 54

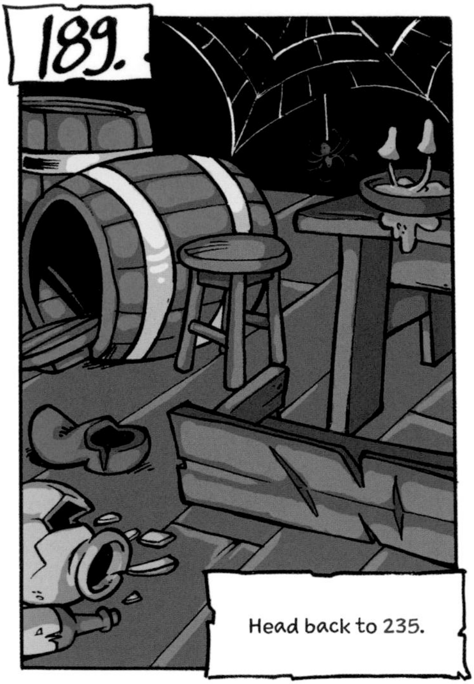
189.
Head back to 235.

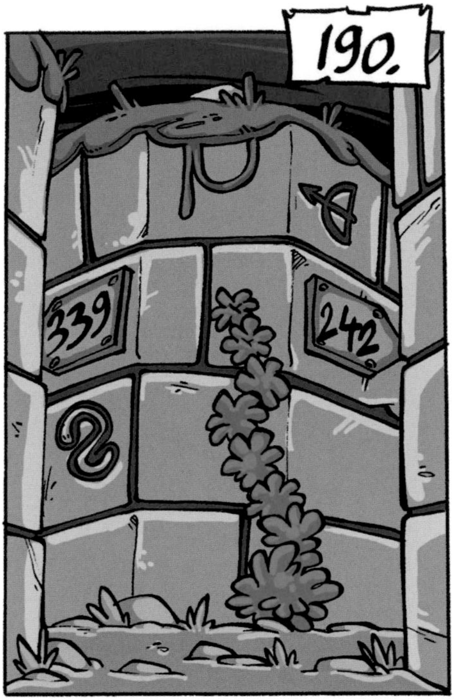
190.
339
242

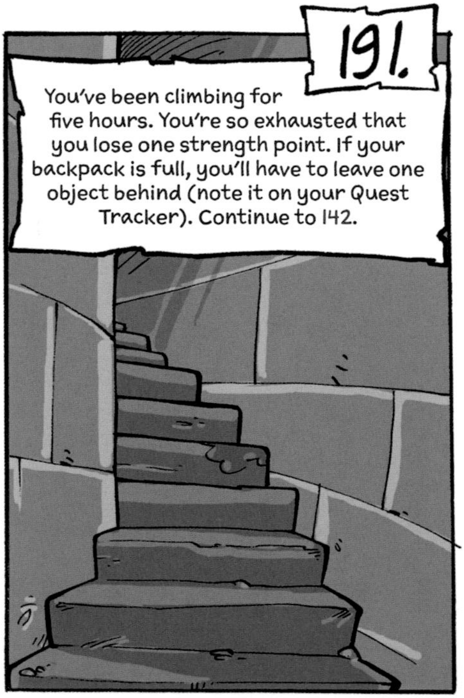
191.
You've been climbing for five hours. You're so exhausted that you lose one strength point. If your backpack is full, you'll have to leave one object behind (note it on your Quest Tracker). Continue to 142.

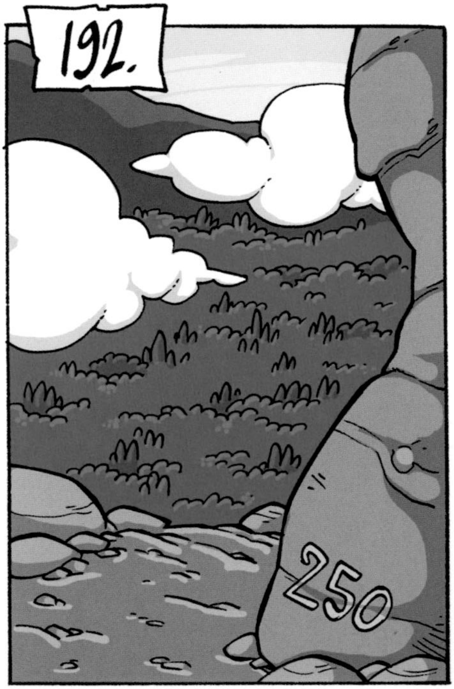
192.
250

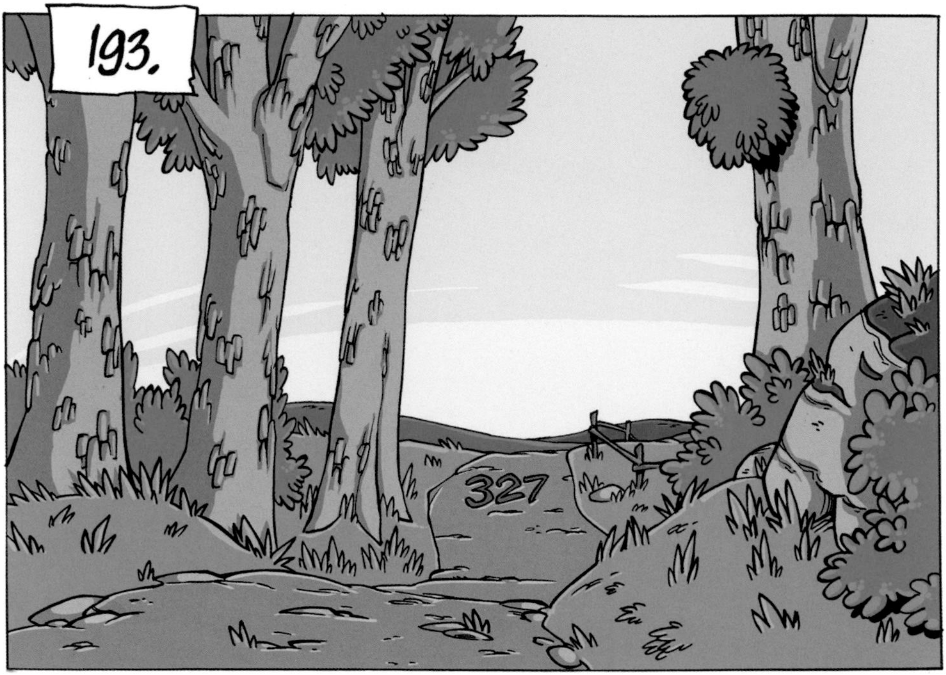
193.
327

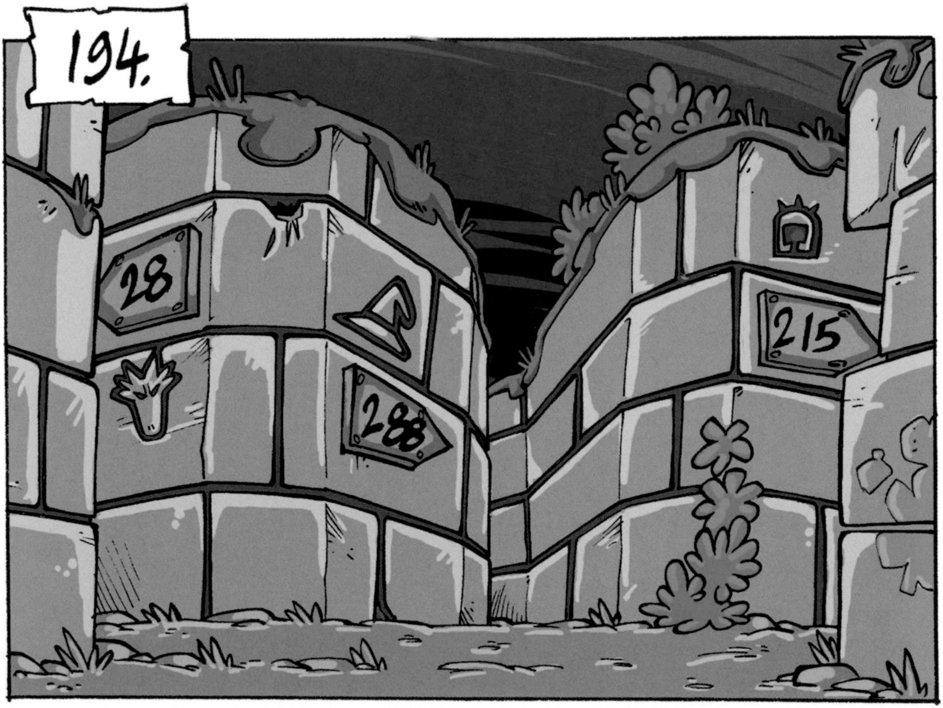
194.
28
215
288

195.

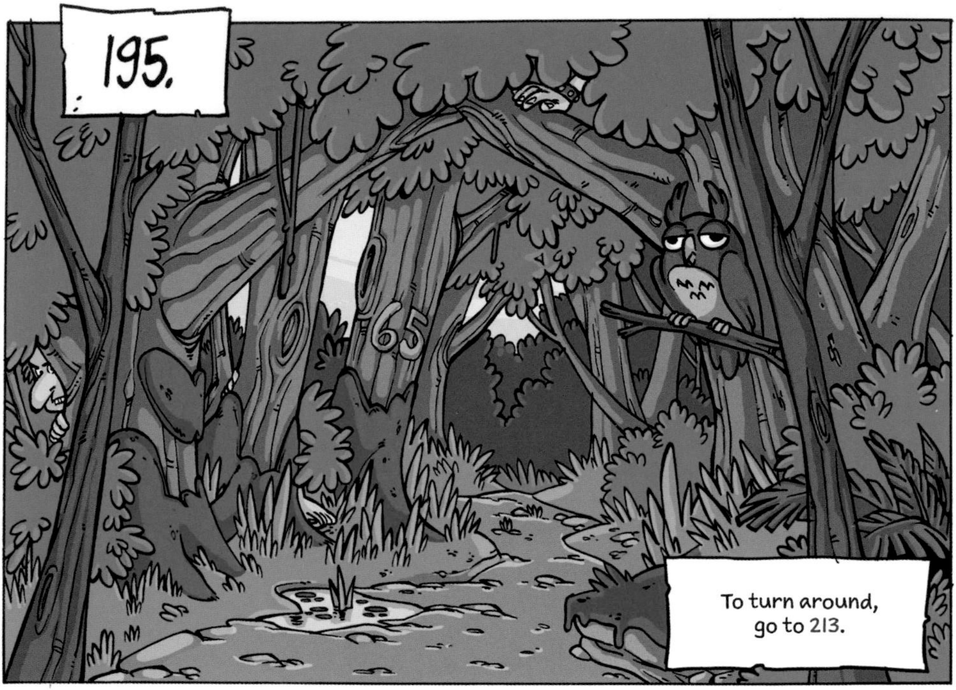
65
To turn around, go to 213.

196.

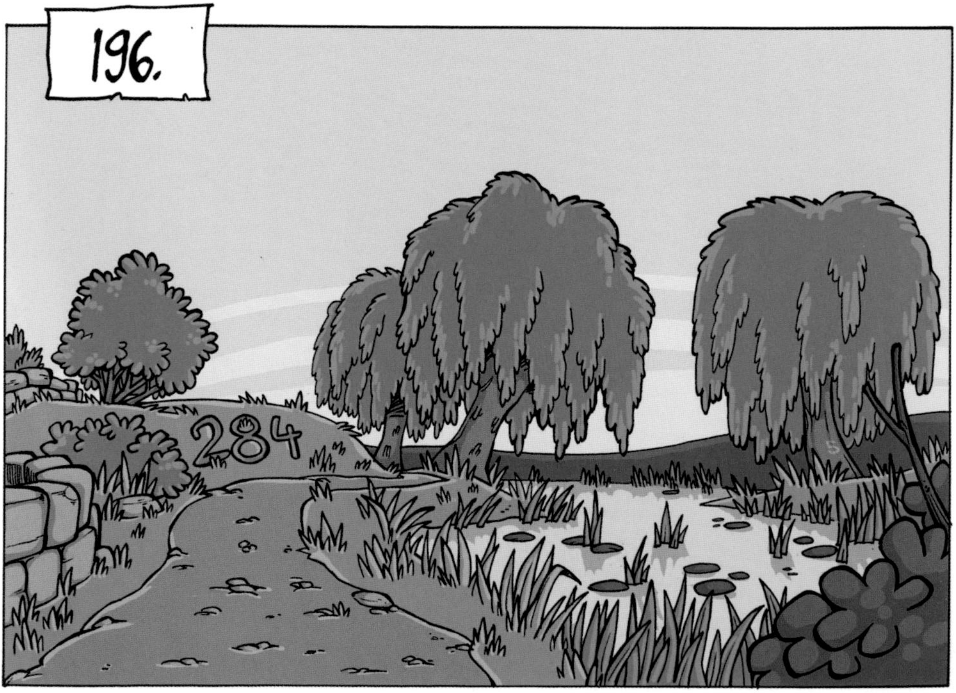
284

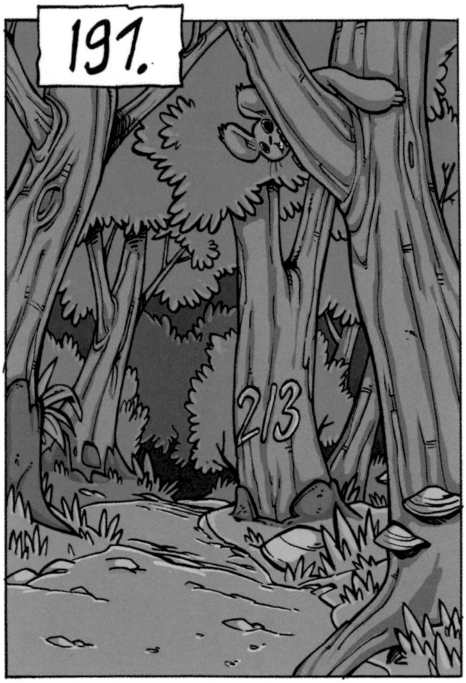
197.
213

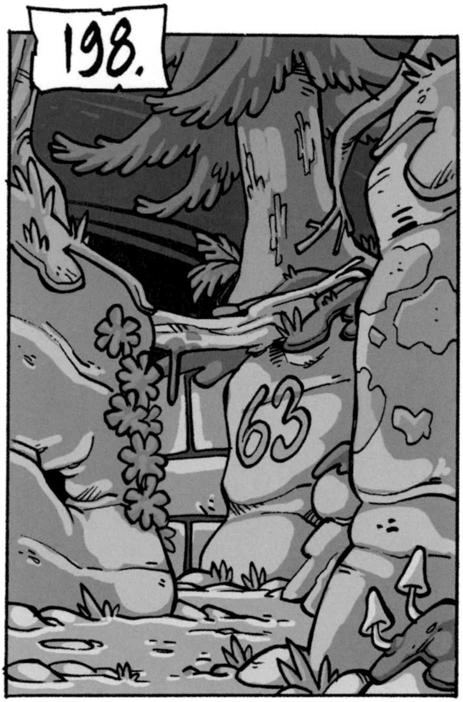
198.
63

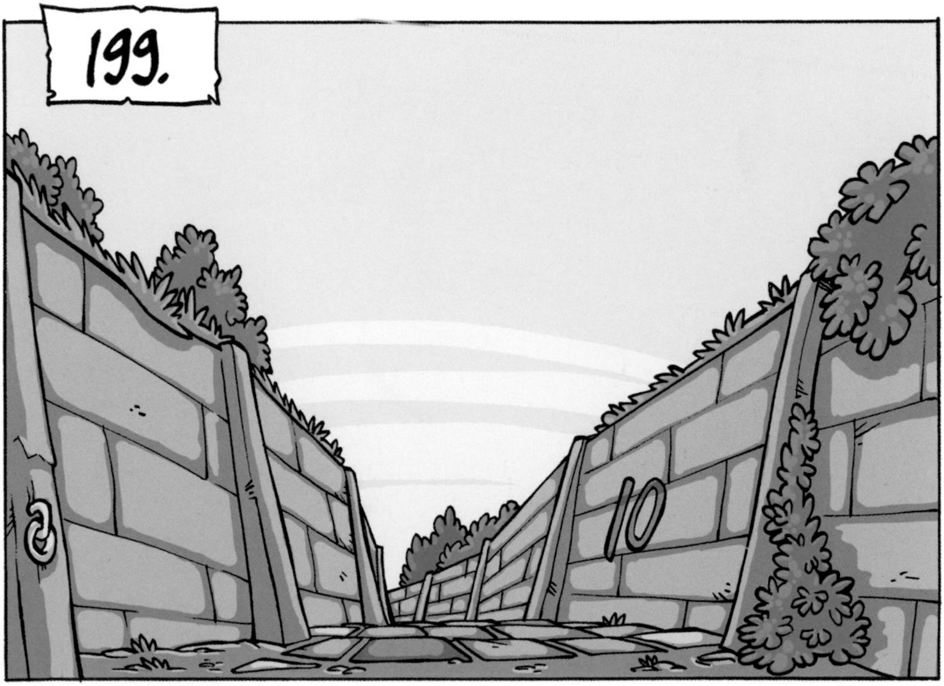
199.
8
10

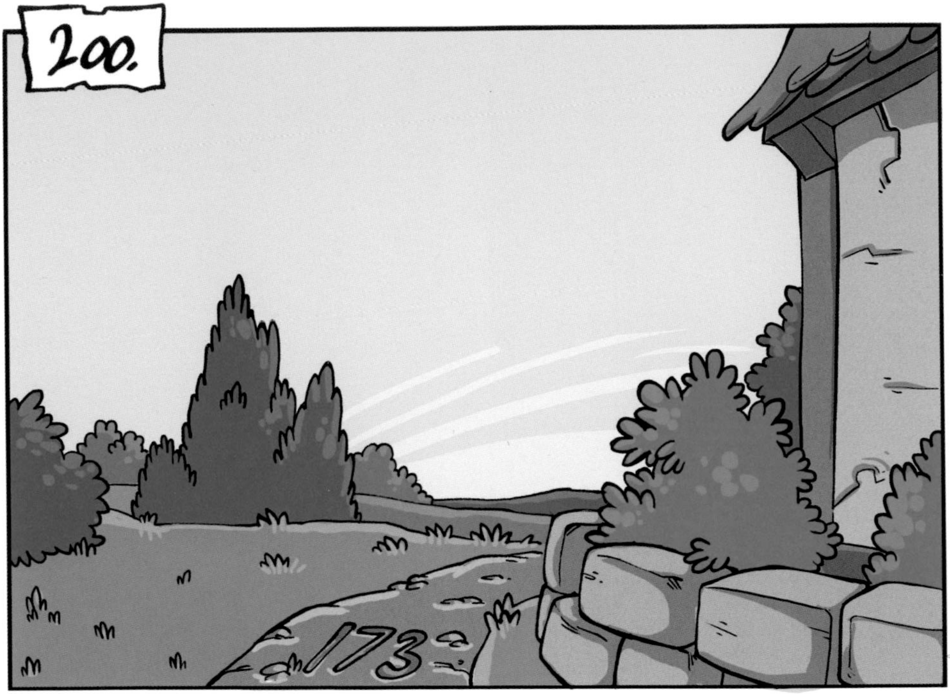
200.
173

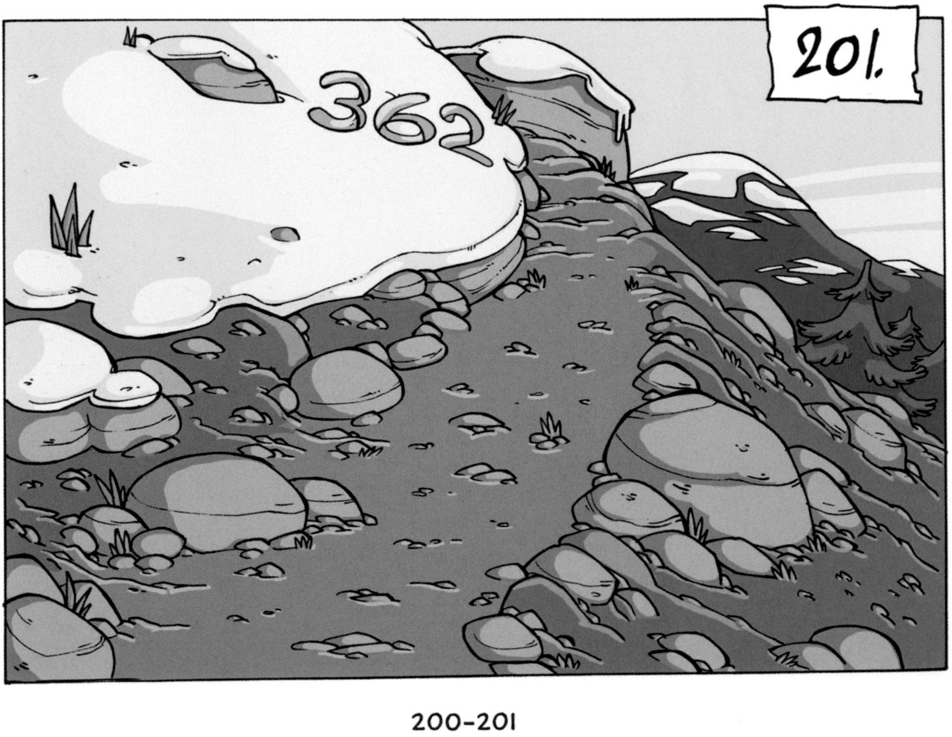
201.
362

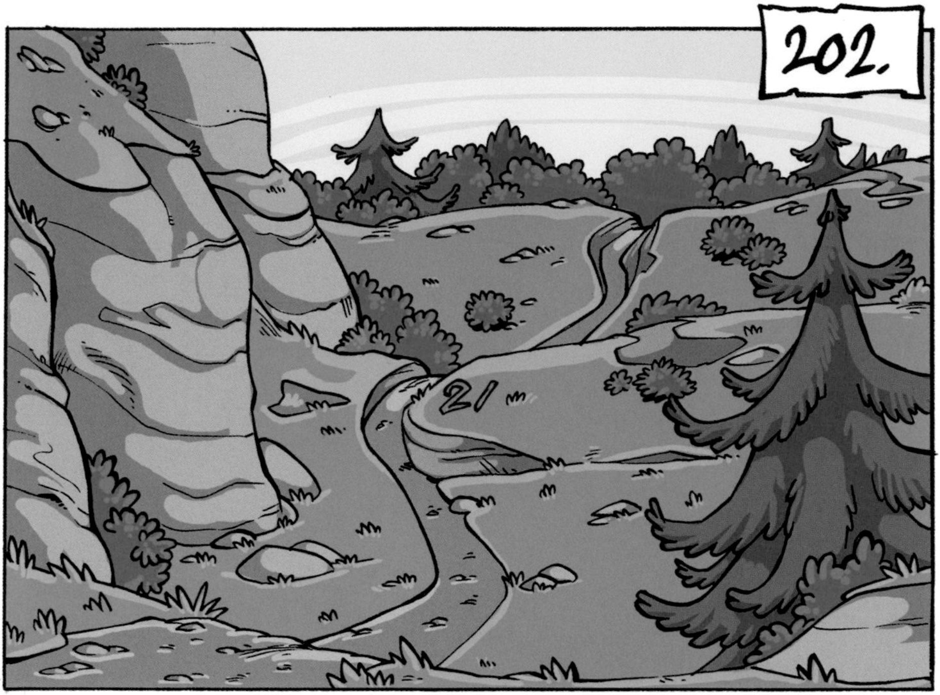
202.
21

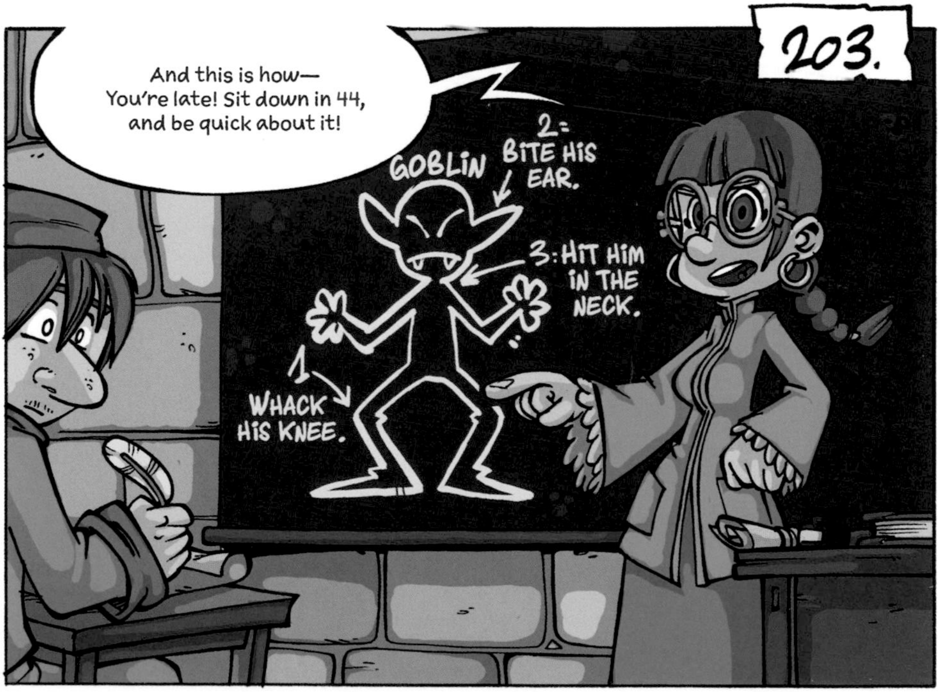
203.
And this is how— You're late! Sit down in 44, and be quick about it!
GOBLIN
2= BITE HIS EAR.
3: HIT HIM IN THE NECK.
1 WHACK HIS KNEE.

204.

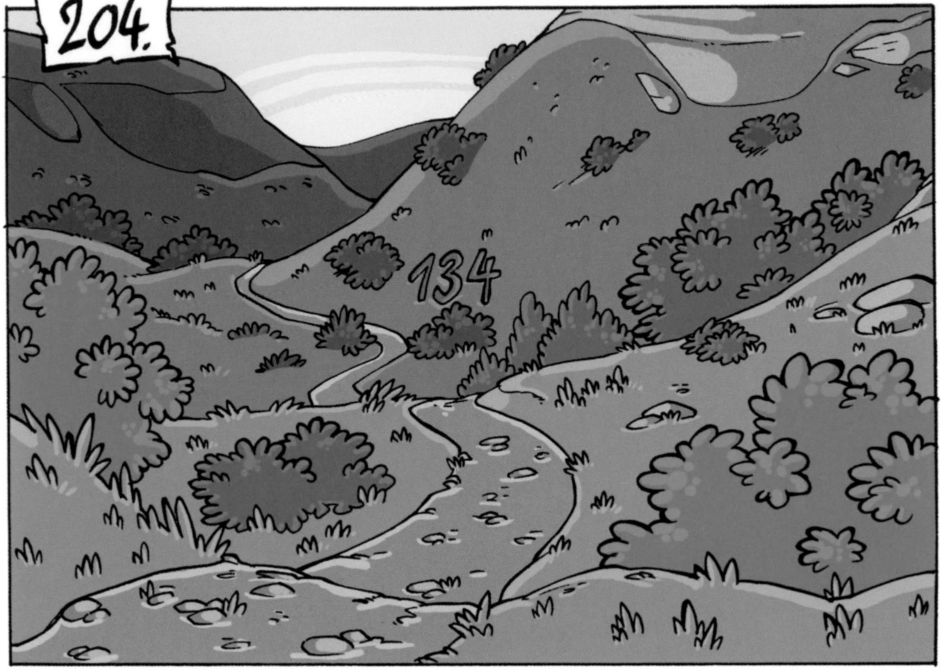
134

205.

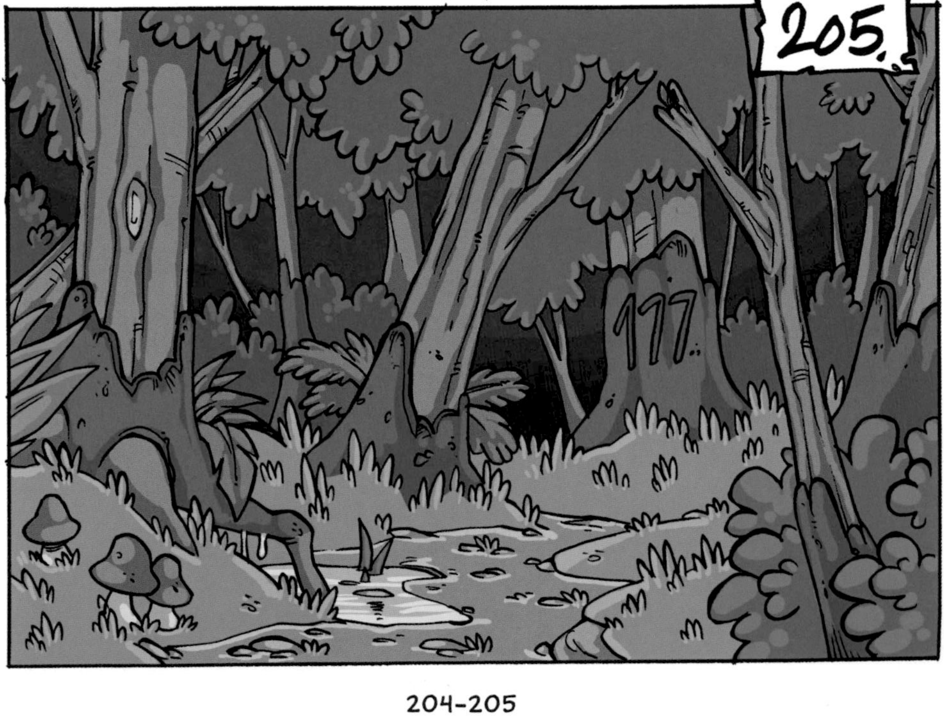
177

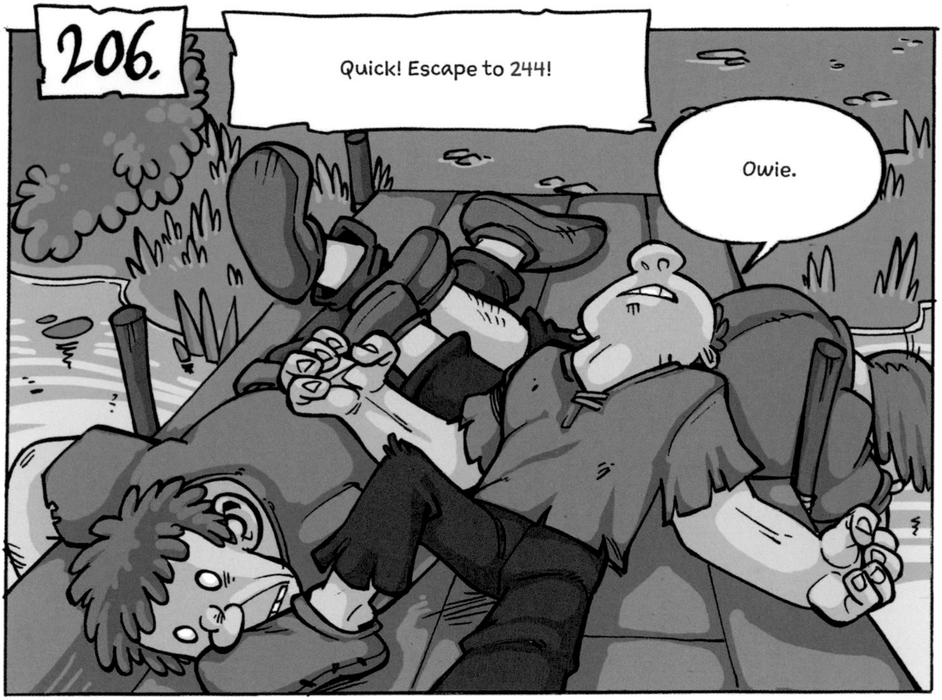
206.
Quick! Escape to 244!
Owie.

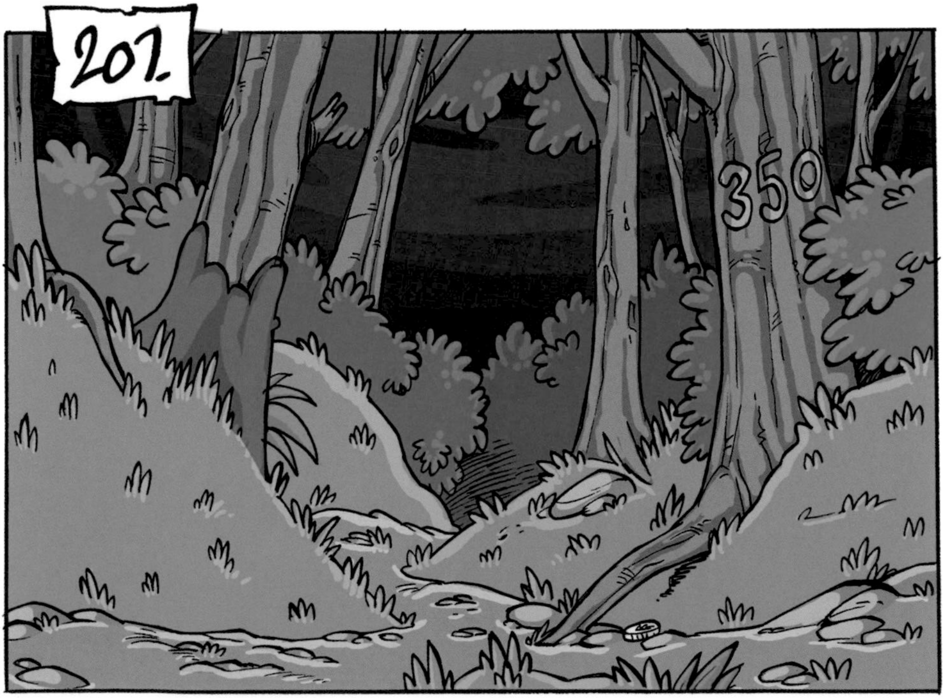
207.
350

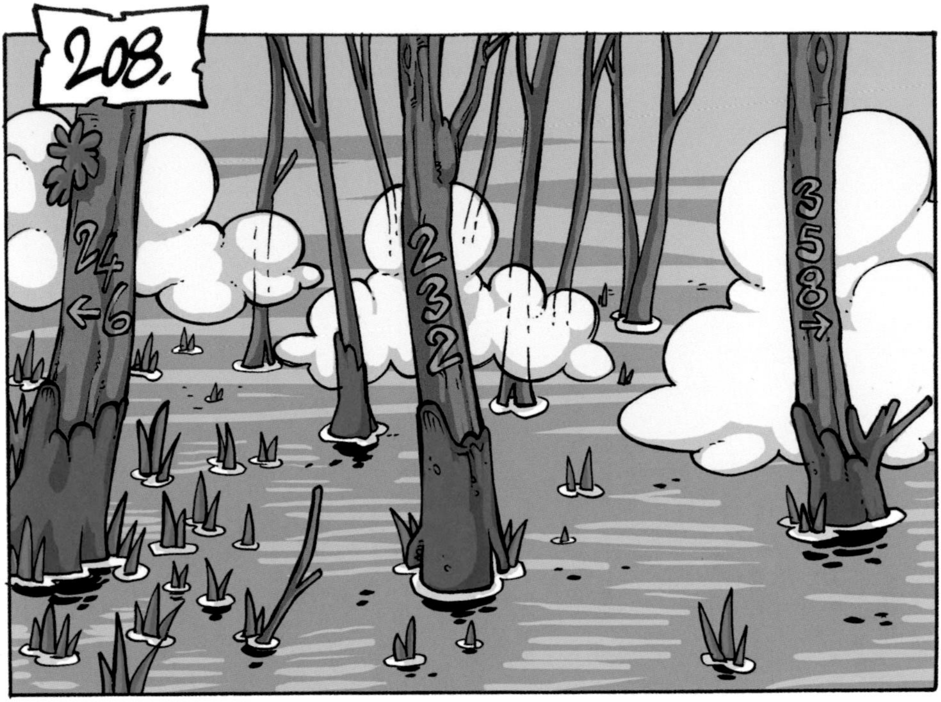
208.
246
232
358

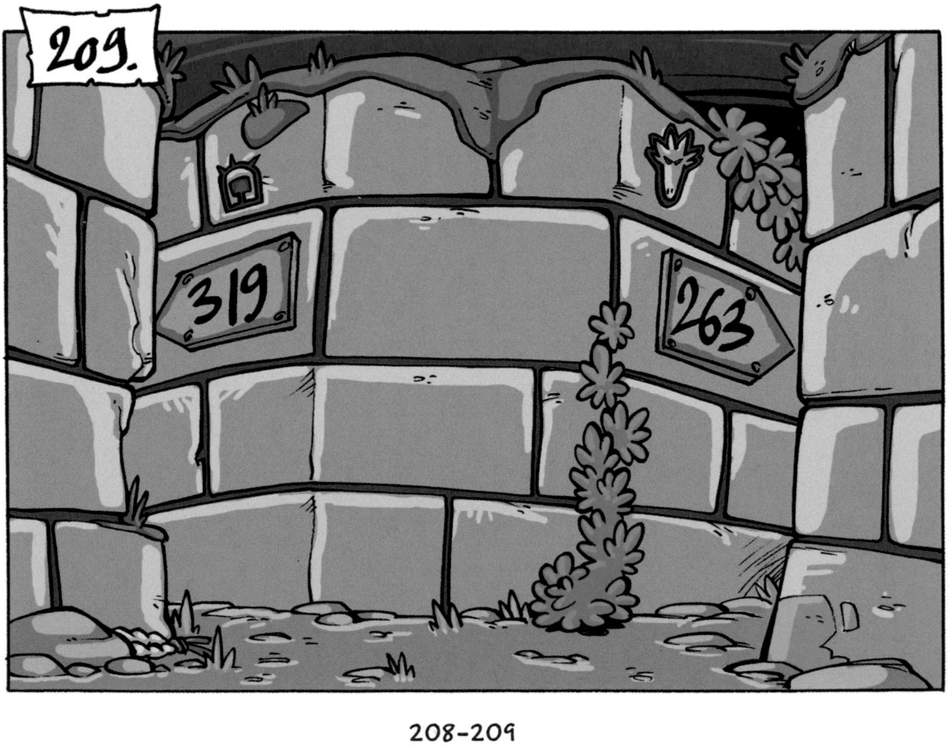
209.
319
263

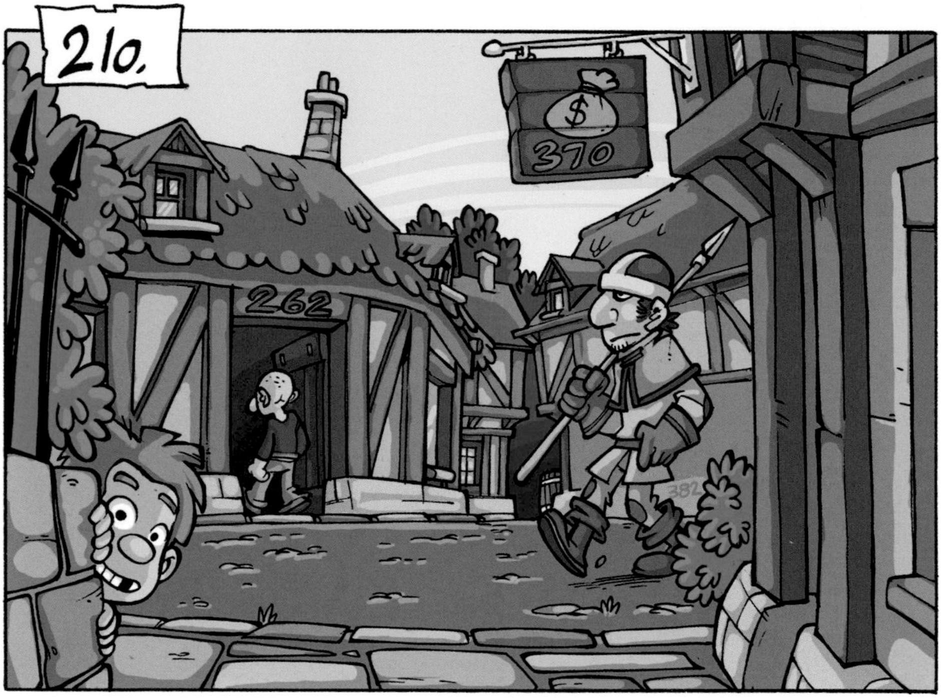
210.
370
262
382

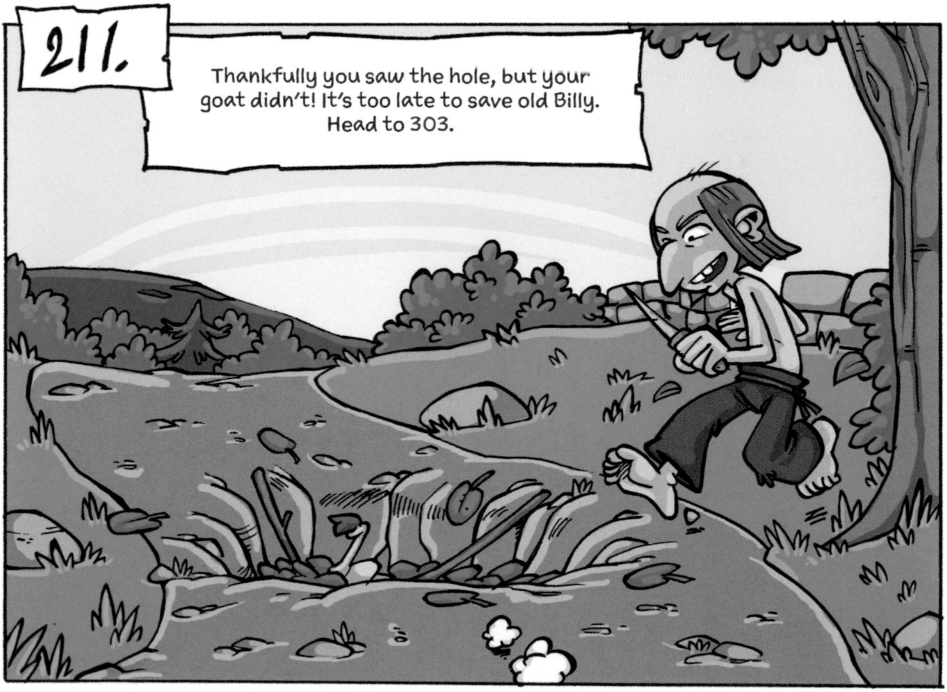
211.
Thankfully you saw the hole, but your goat didn't! It's too late to save old Billy. Head to 303.

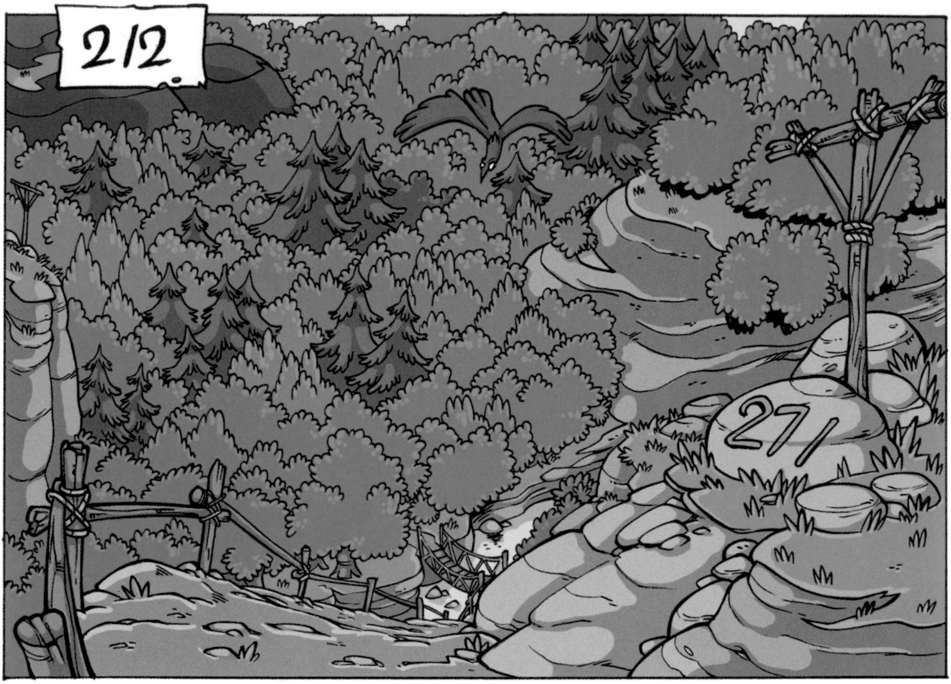
212.
271

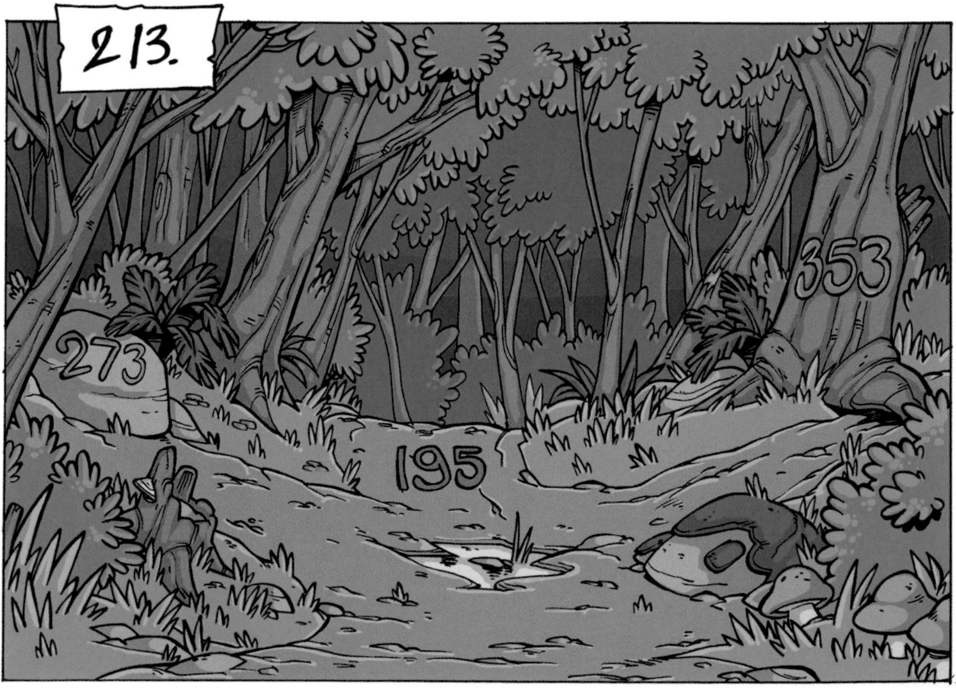
213.
353
273
195

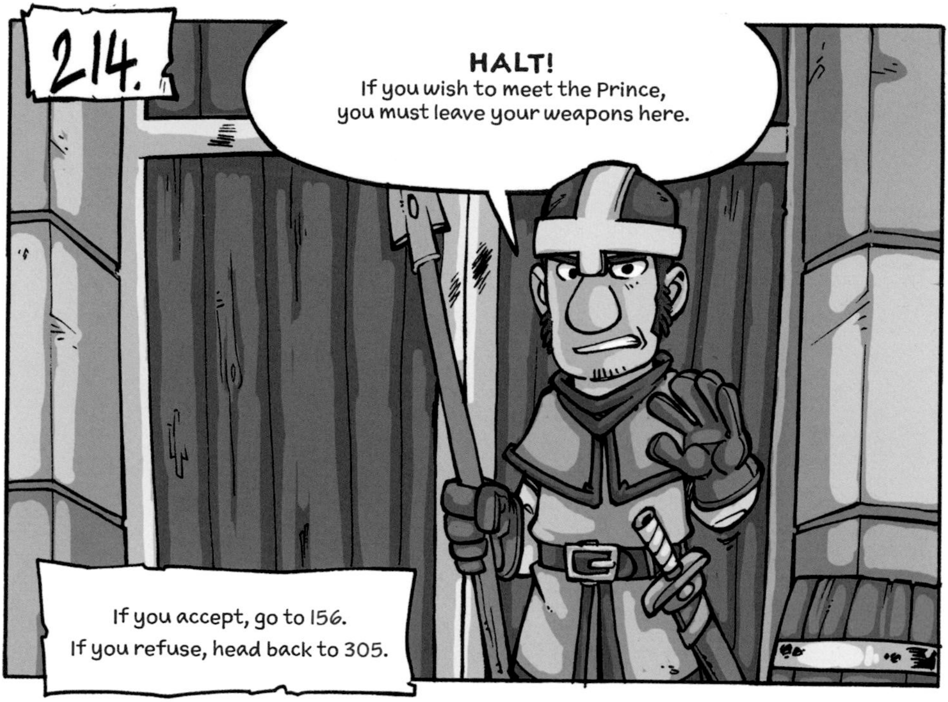
214.
HALT!
If you wish to meet the Prince, you must leave your weapons here.
If you accept, go to 156.
If you refuse, head back to 305.

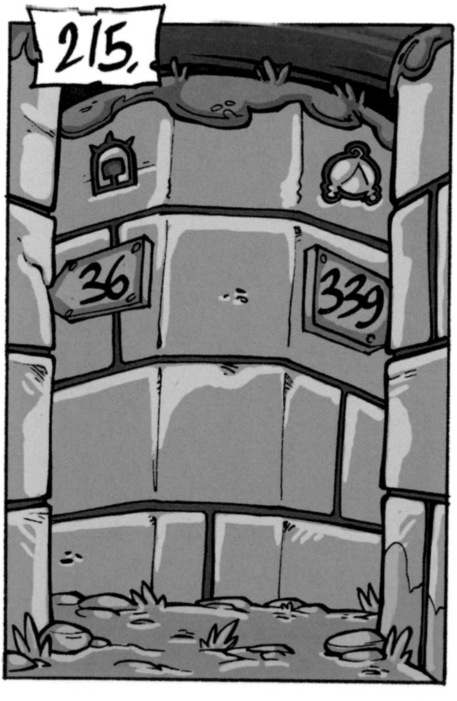
215.
36
339

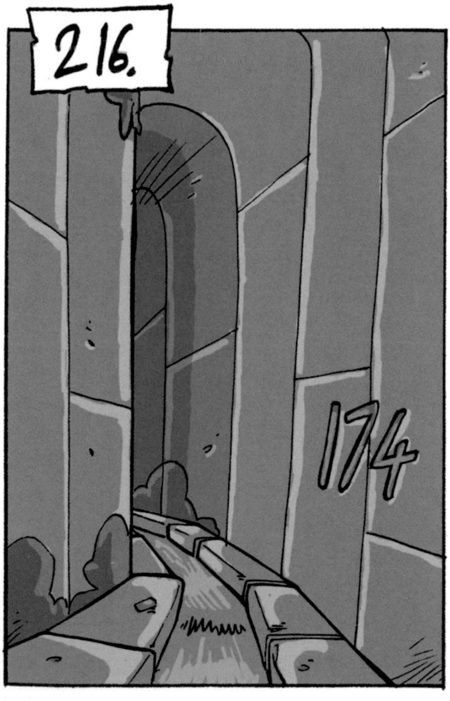
216.
174

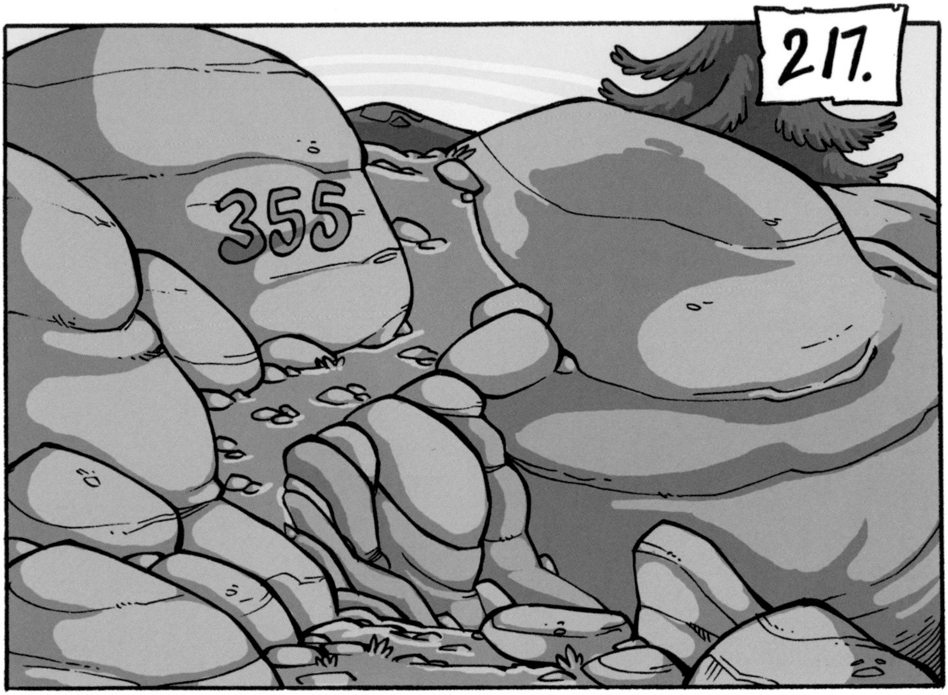
217.
355

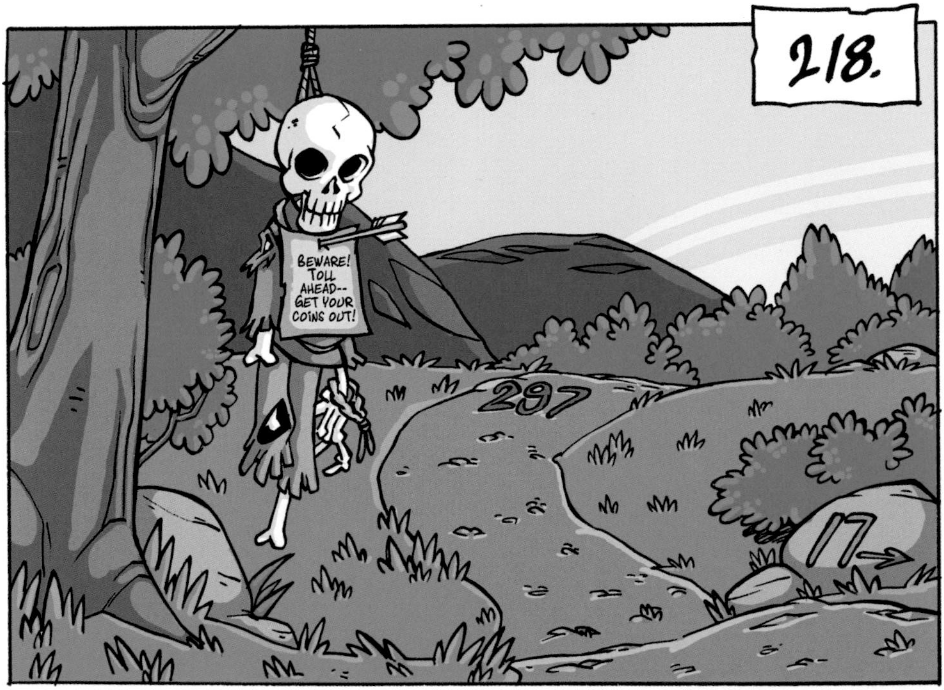
218.
BEWARE! TOLL AHEAD-- GET YOUR COINS OUT!
297
17

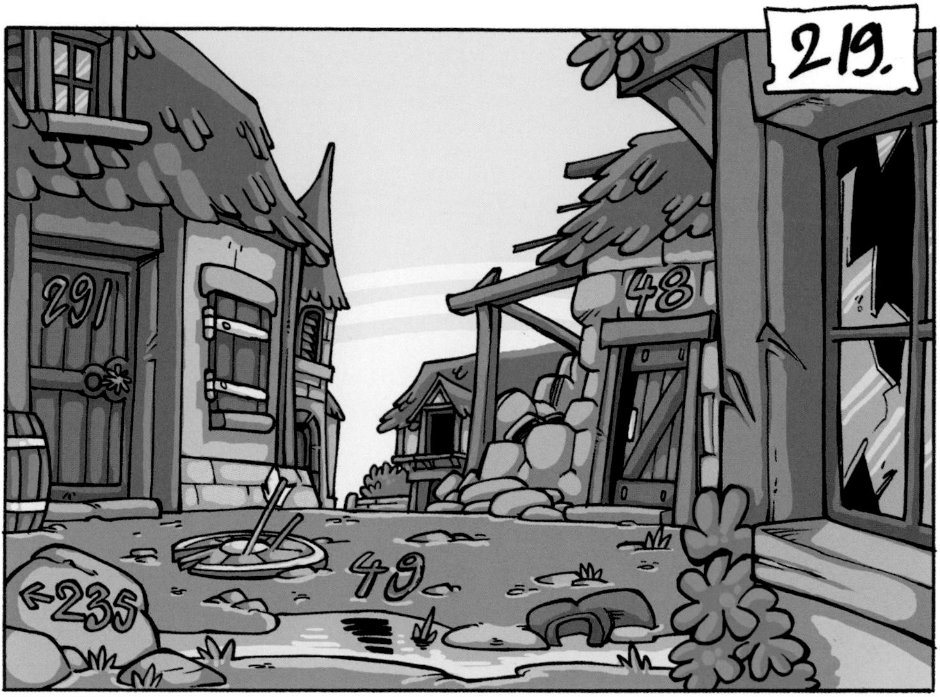
219.
291
48
49
←235

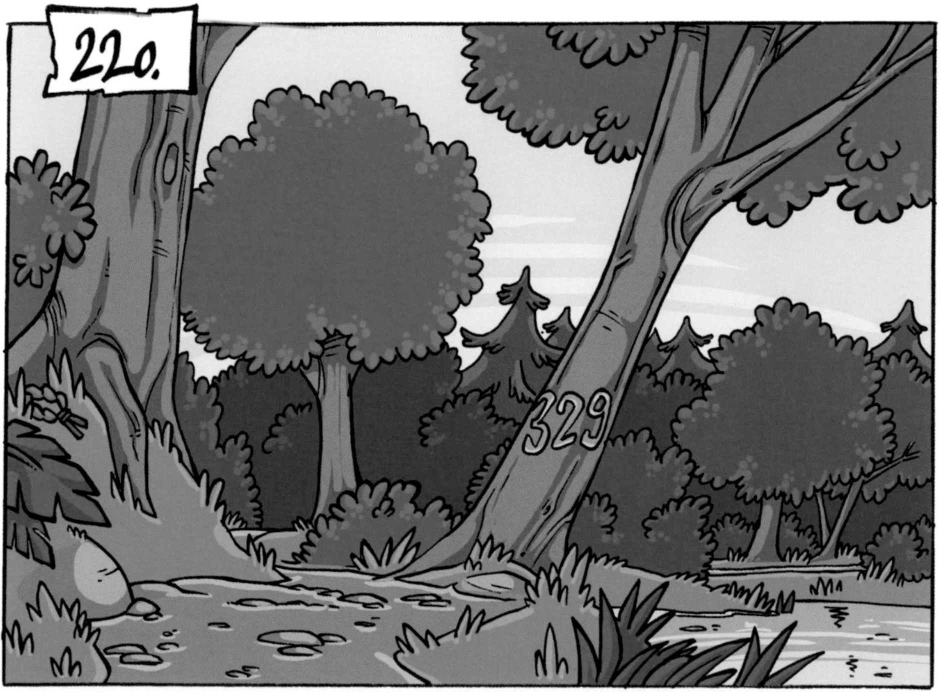
220.
329

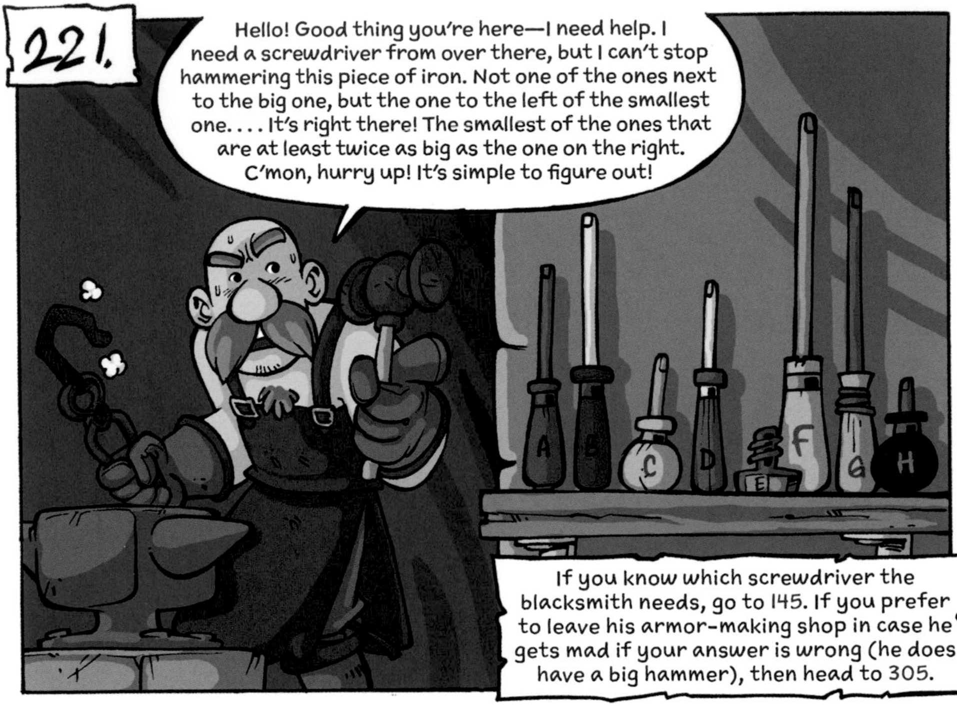
221.
Hello! Good thing you're here—I need help. I need a screwdriver from over there, but I can't stop hammering this piece of iron. Not one of the ones next to the big one, but the one to the left of the smallest one. . . . It's right there! The smallest of the ones that are at least twice as big as the one on the right. C'mon, hurry up! It's simple to figure out!
A
B
C
D
E
F
G
H
If you know which screwdriver the blacksmith needs, go to 145. If you prefer to leave his armor-making shop in case he gets mad if your answer is wrong (he does have a big hammer), then head to 305.

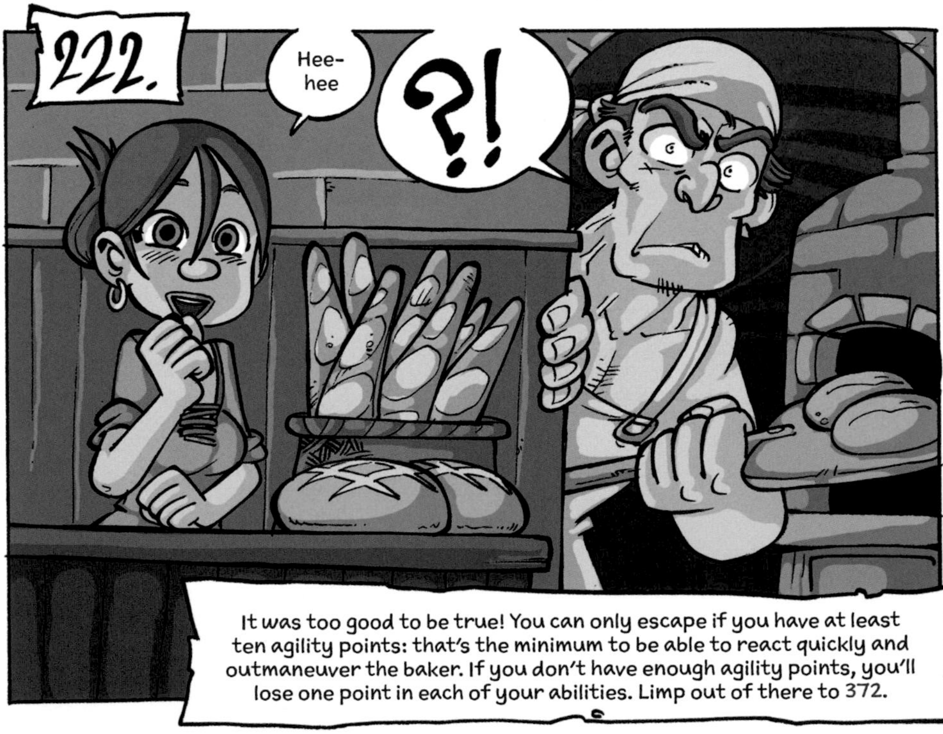
222.
Hee-hee
?!
It was too good to be true! You can only escape if you have at least ten agility points: that's the minimum to be able to react quickly and outmaneuver the baker. If you don't have enough agility points, you'll lose one point in each of your abilities. Limp out of there to 372.

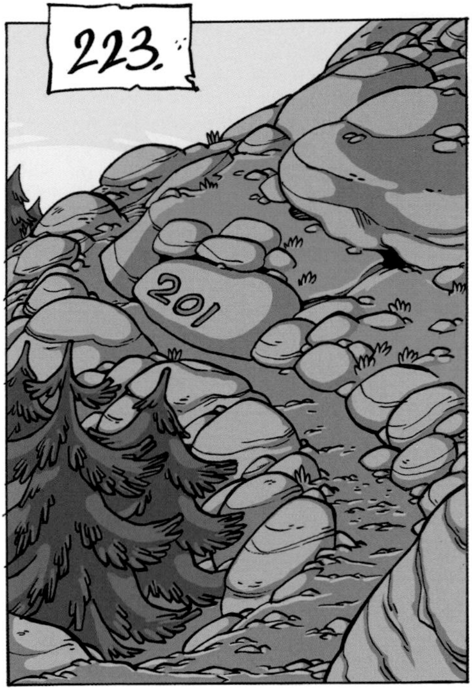
223.
201

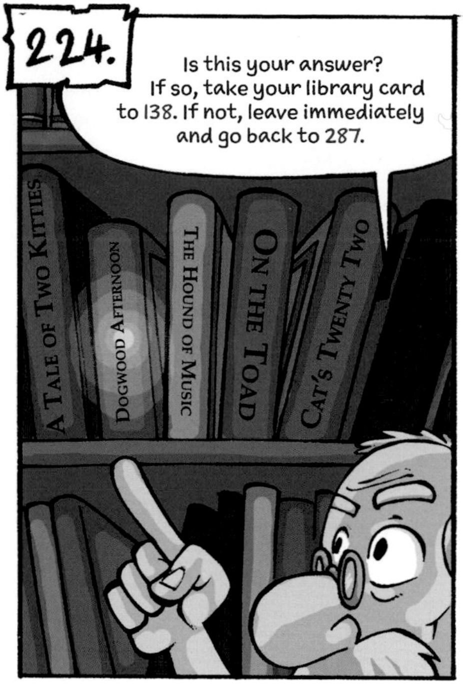
224.
Is this your answer? If so, take your library card to 138. If not, leave immediately and go back to 287.
A Tale of Two Kitties
Dogwood Afternoon
The Hound of Music
On the Toad
Cat's Twenty Two

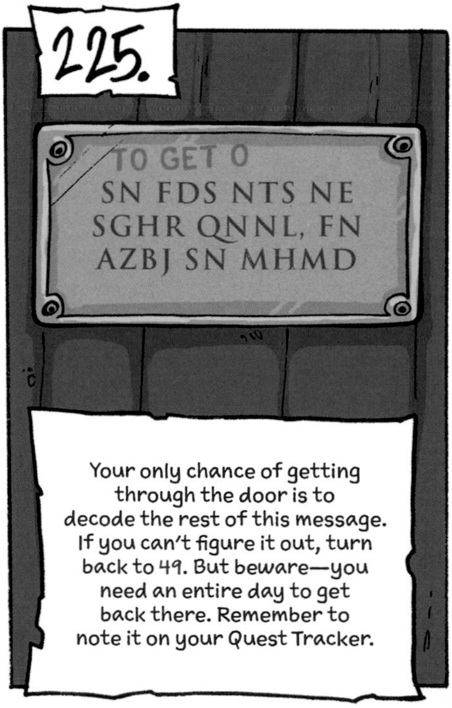
225.
TO GET O
SN FDS NTS NE
SGHR QNNL, FN
AZBJ SN MHMD
Your only chance of getting through the door is to decode the rest of this message. If you can't figure it out, turn back to 49. But beware—you need an entire day to get back there. Remember to note it on your Quest Tracker.

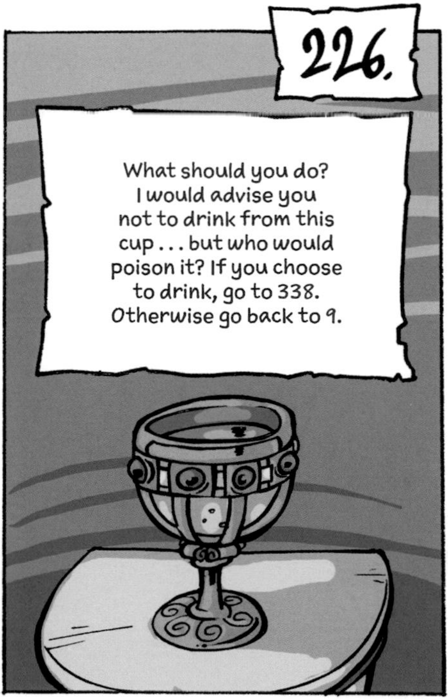
226.
What should you do? I would advise you not to drink from this cup . . . but who would poison it? If you choose to drink, go to 338. Otherwise go back to 9.

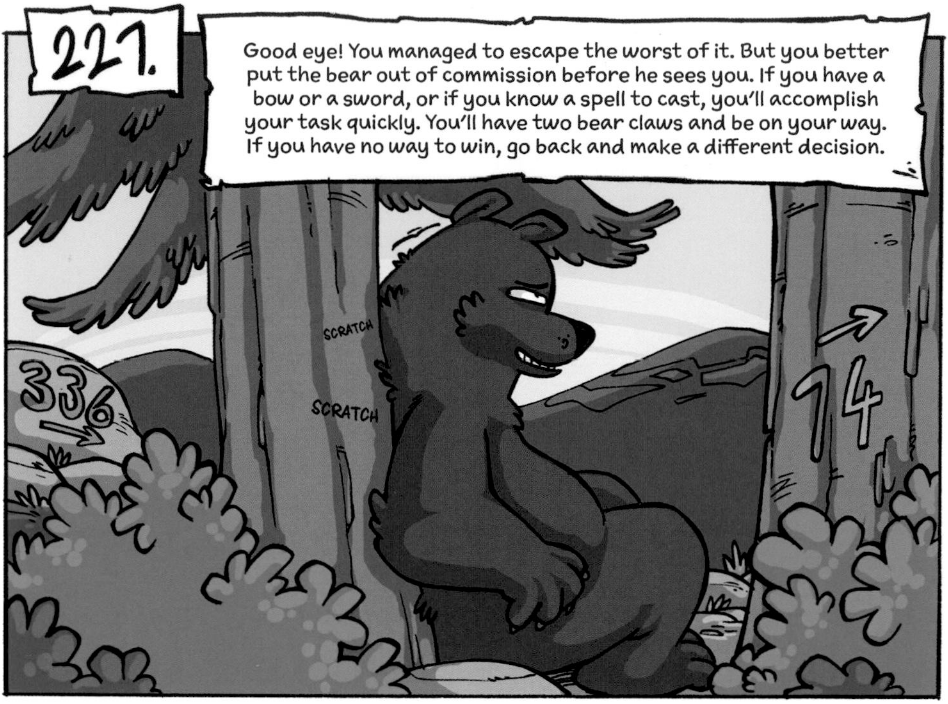
227.
Good eye! You managed to escape the worst of it. But you better put the bear out of commission before he sees you. If you have a bow or a sword, or if you know a spell to cast, you'll accomplish your task quickly. You'll have two bear claws and be on your way. If you have no way to win, go back and make a different decision.
SCRATCH
SCRATCH
336
74

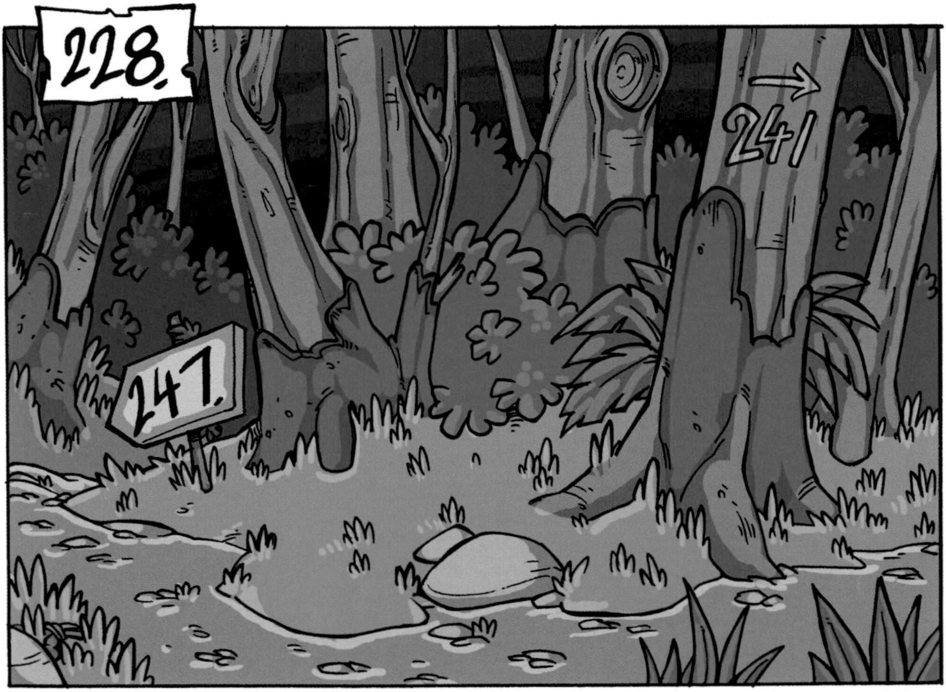
228.
241
247.

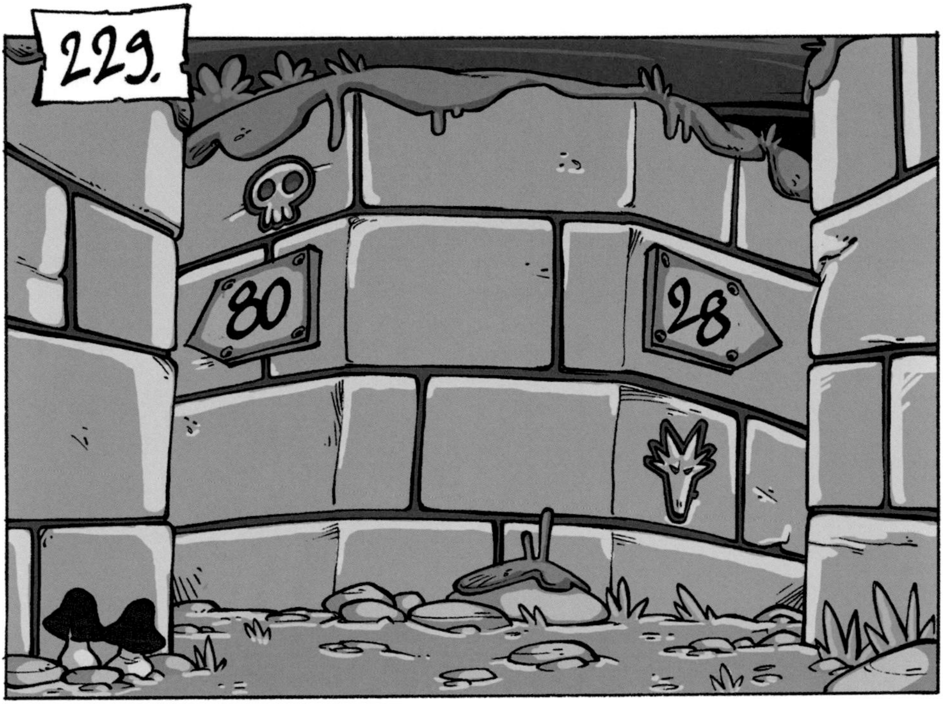
229.
80
28

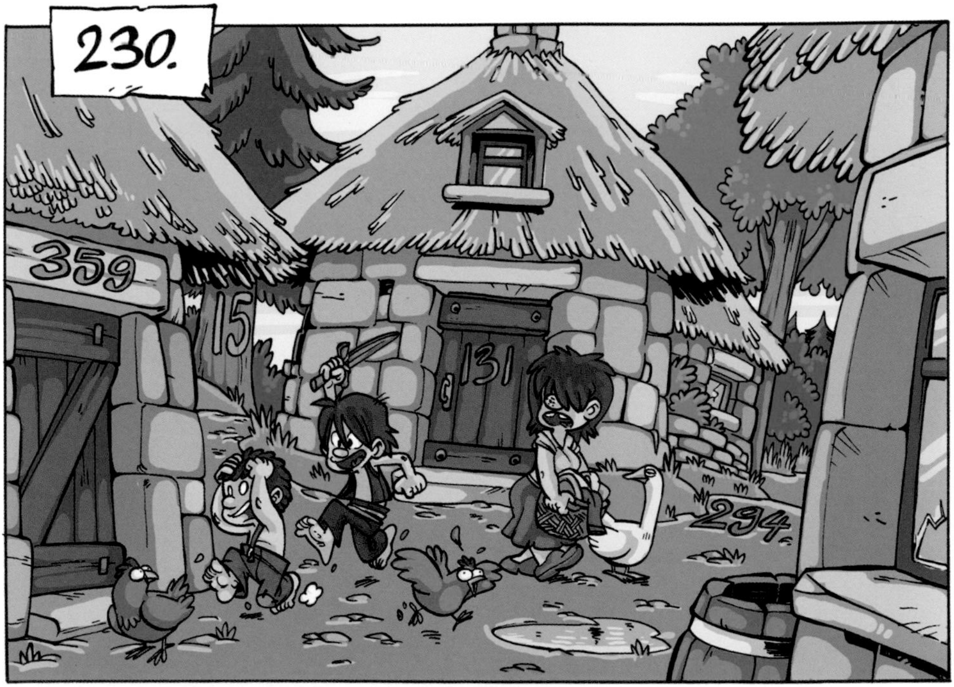
230.
359
15
131
294

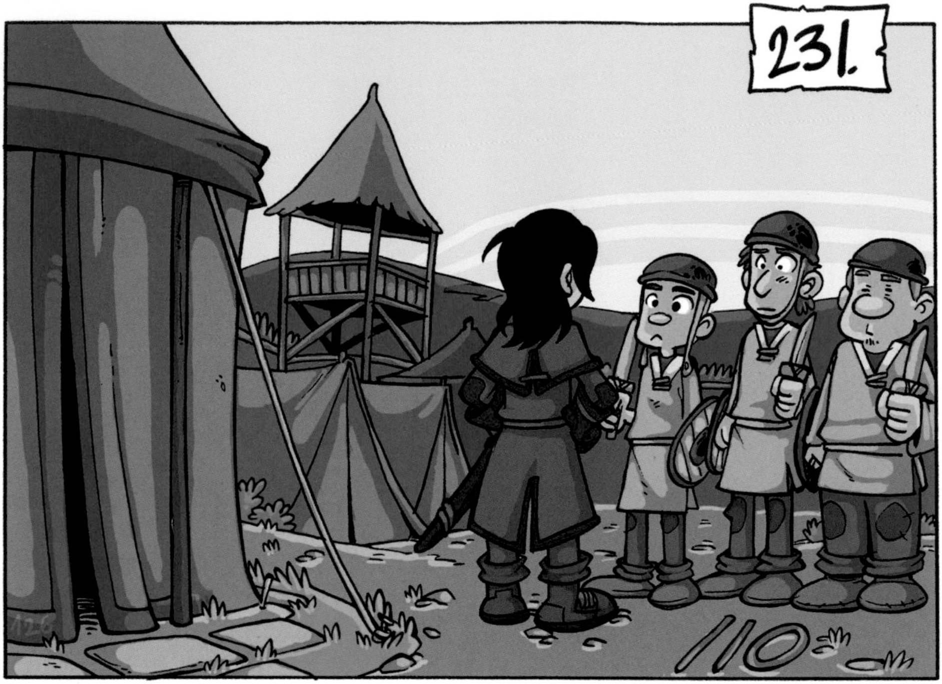
231.
110

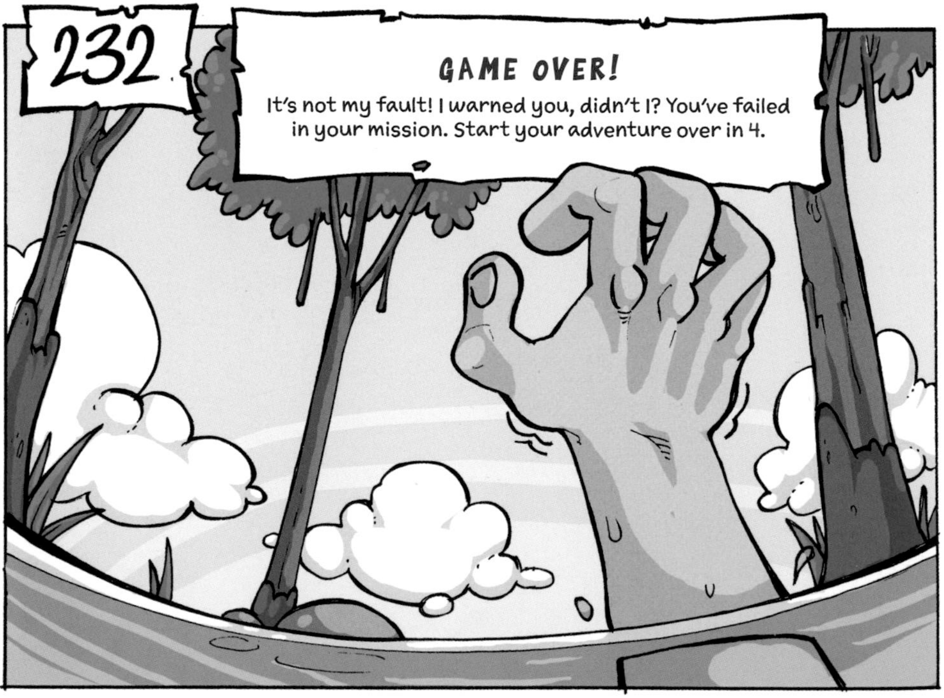
232
GAME OVER!
It's not my fault! I warned you, didn't I? You've failed in your mission. Start your adventure over in 4.

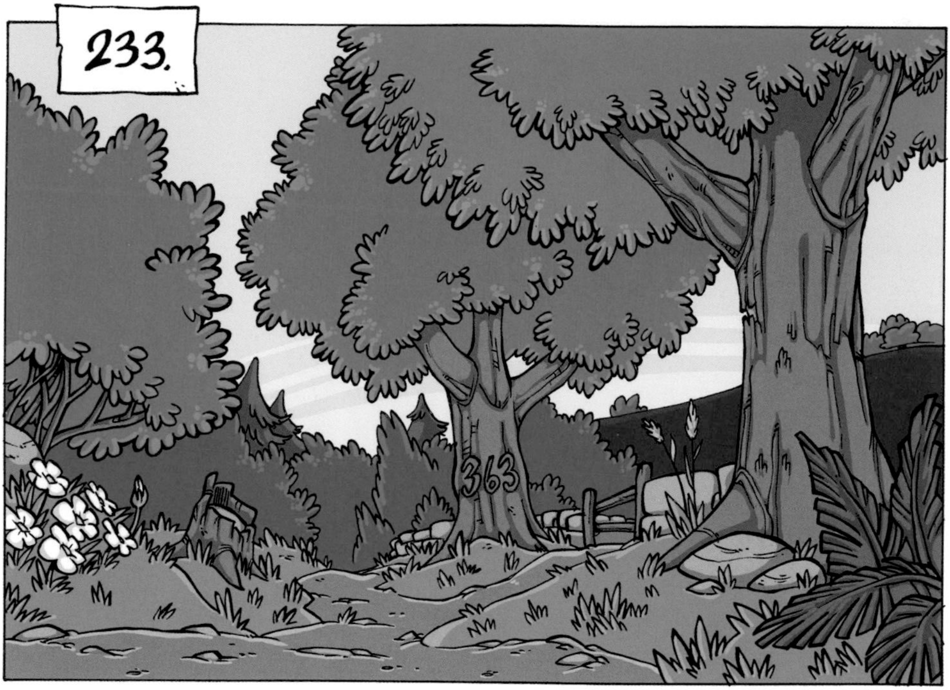
233.
363

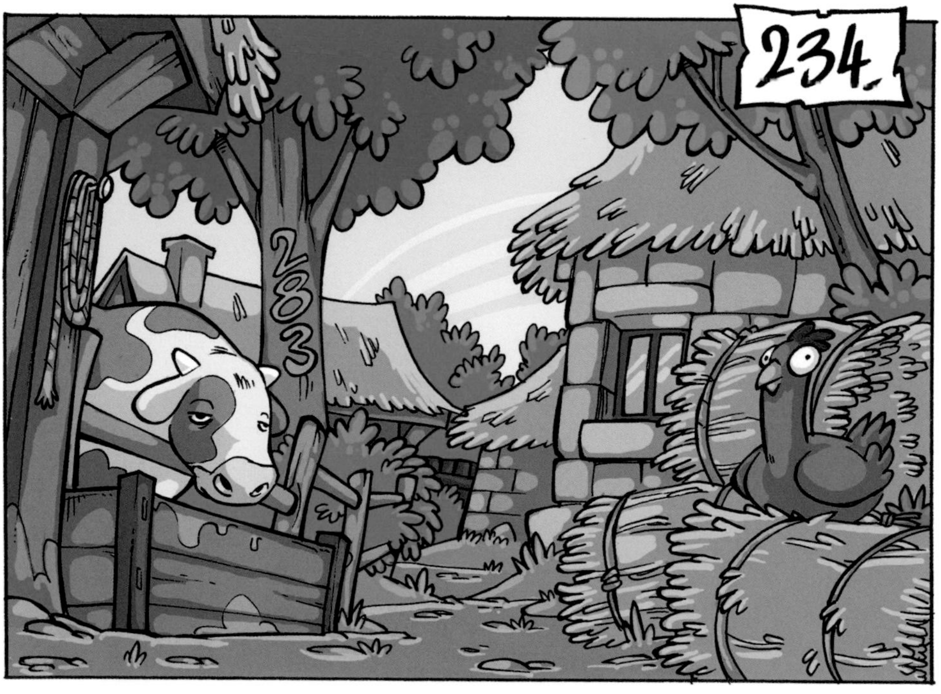
234.
283

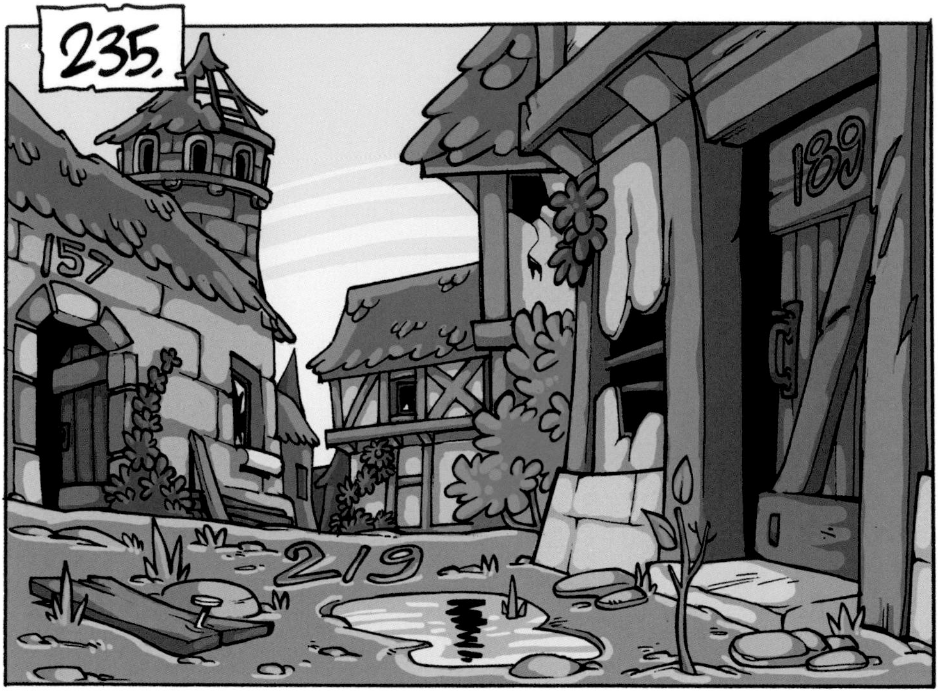
235.
157
189
219

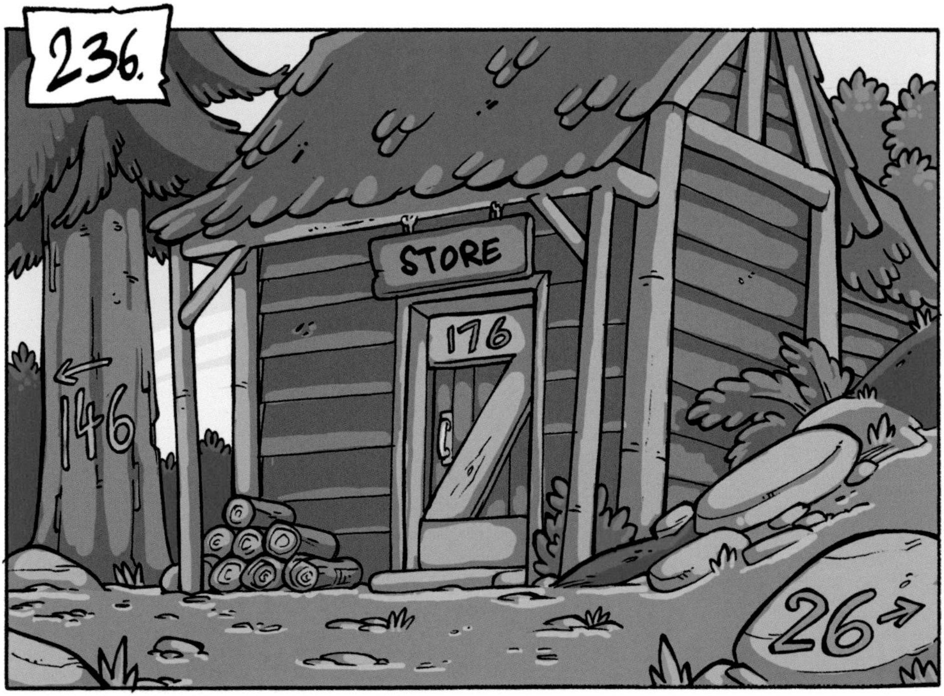
236.
STORE
176
146
26

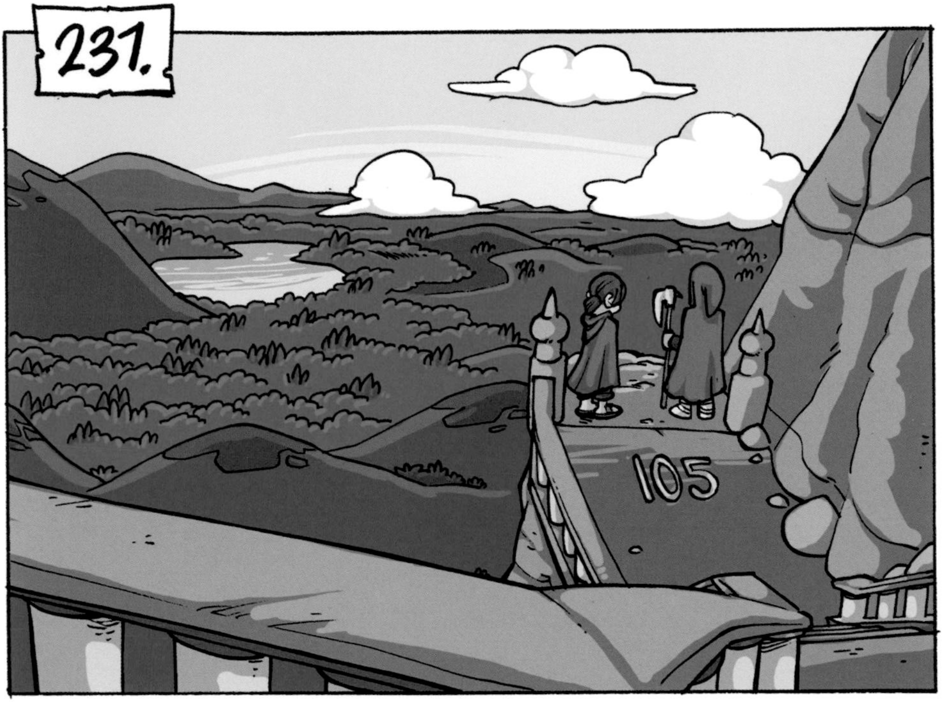
231.
105

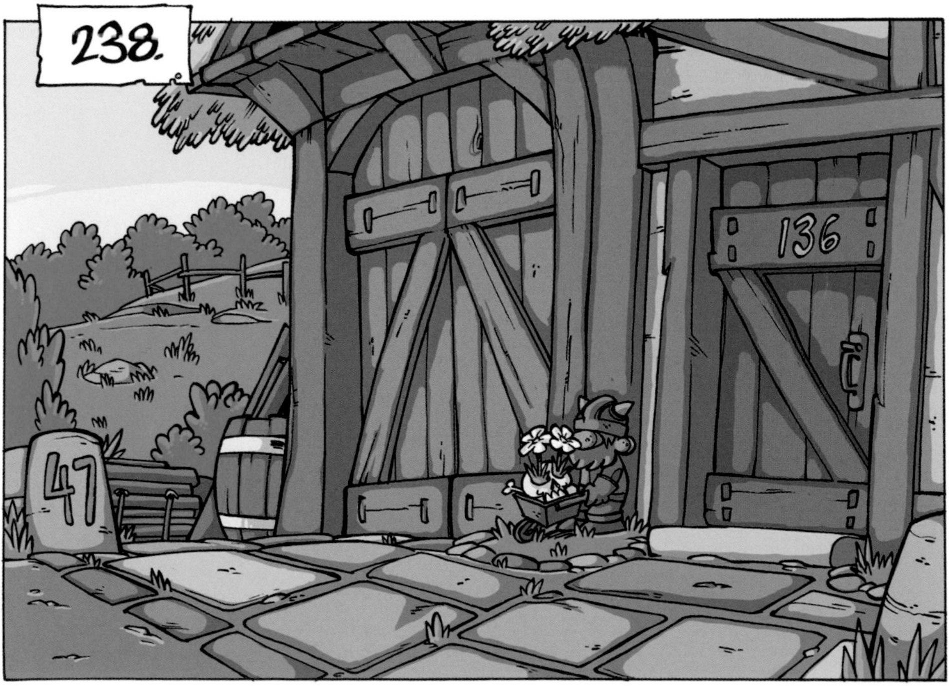
238.
136
47

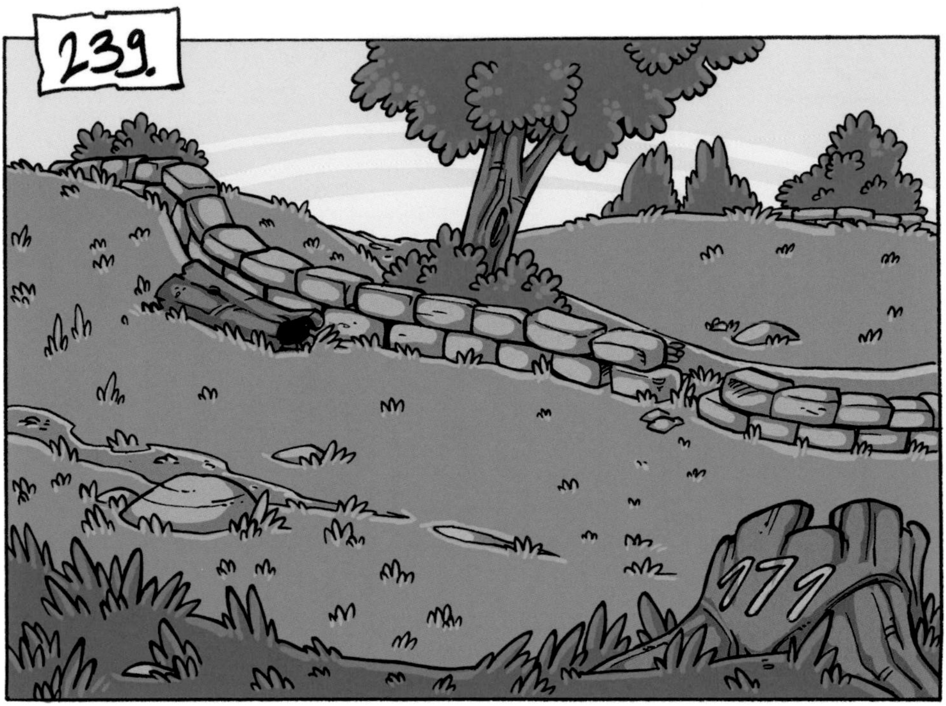
239.
171

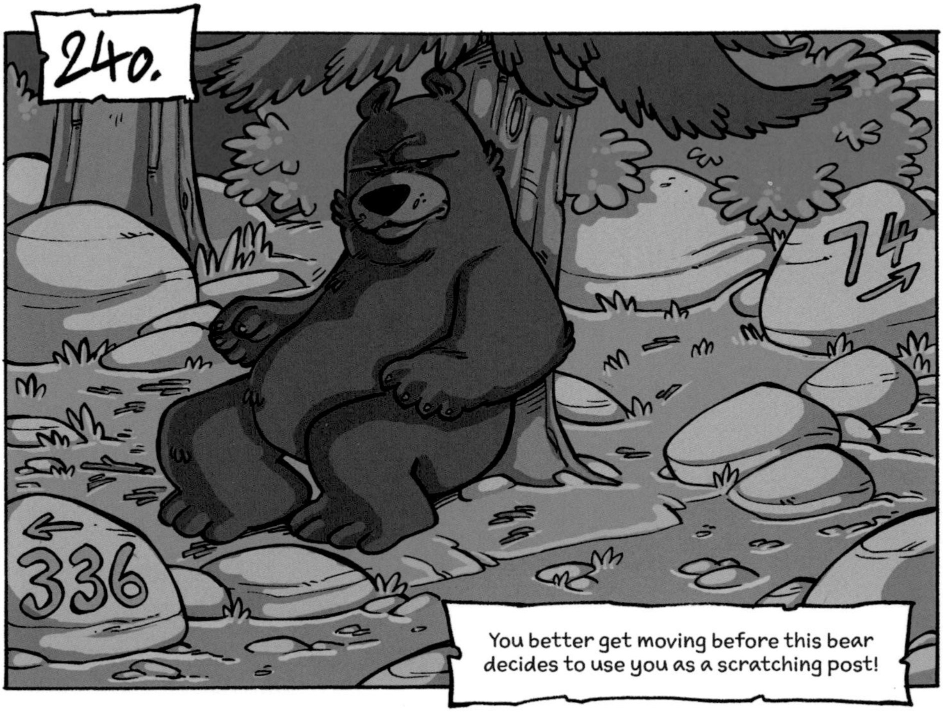
240.
74
336
You better get moving before this bear decides to use you as a scratching post!

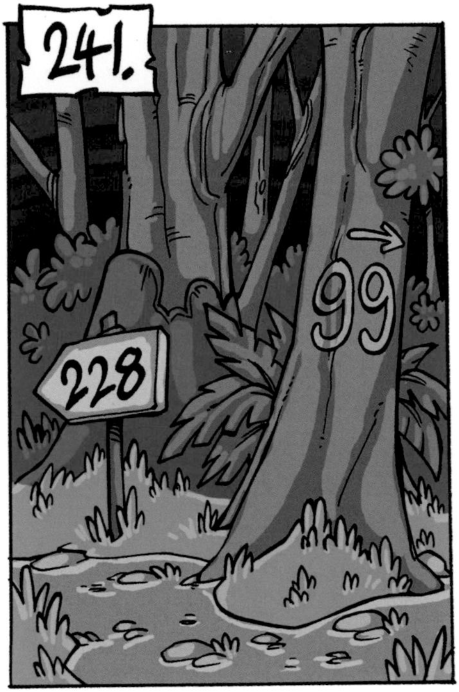
241.
228
99

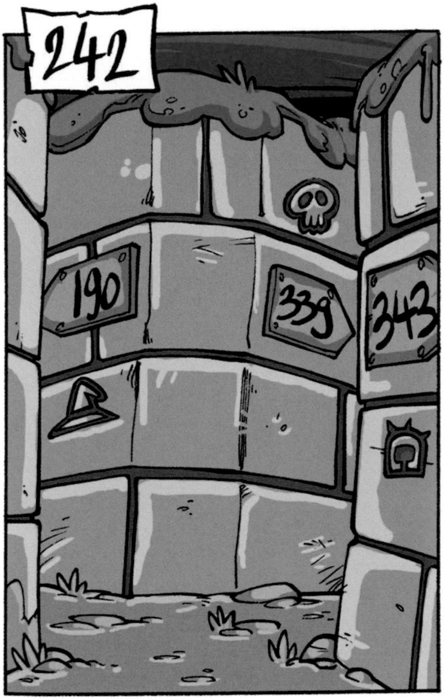
242
190
339
343

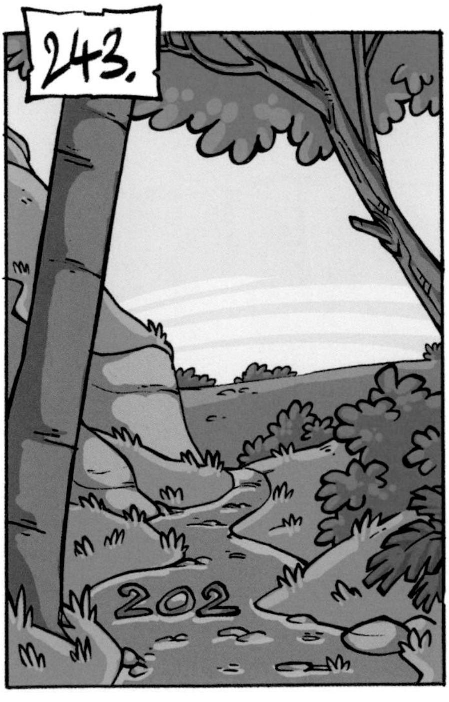
243.
202

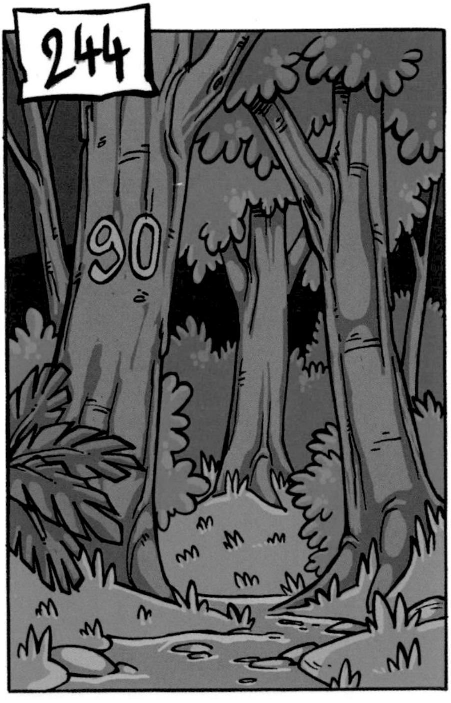
244
90

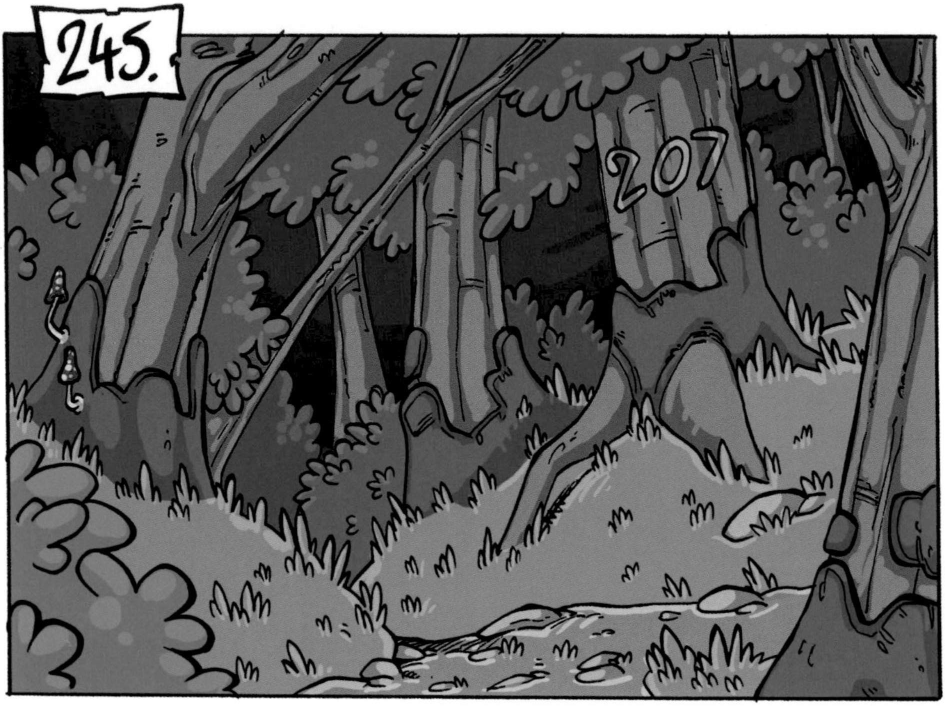
245.
207

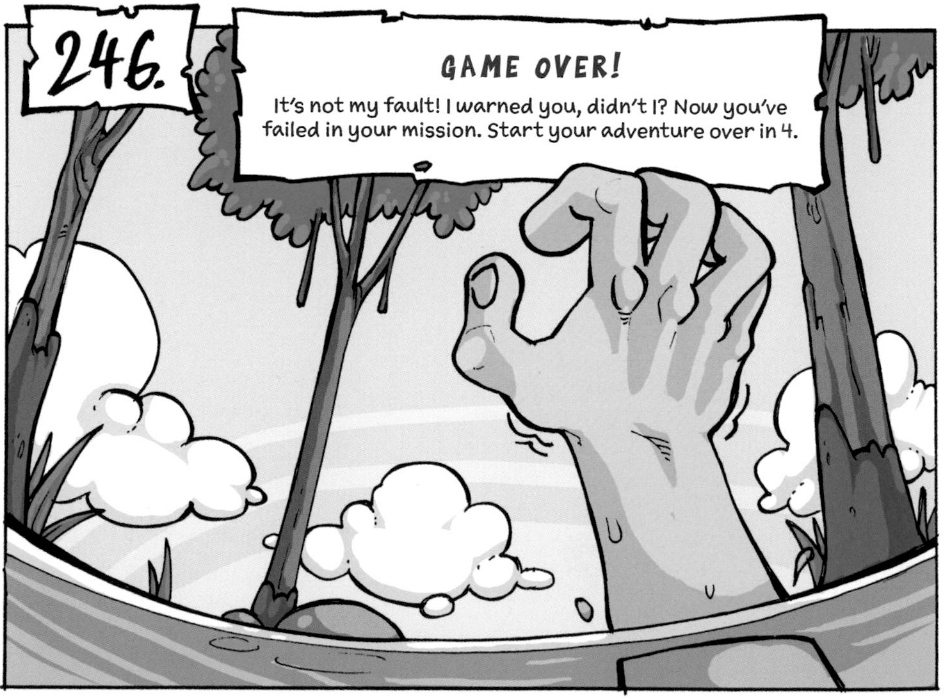
246.
GAME OVER!
It's not my fault! I warned you, didn't I? Now you've failed in your mission. Start your adventure over in 4.

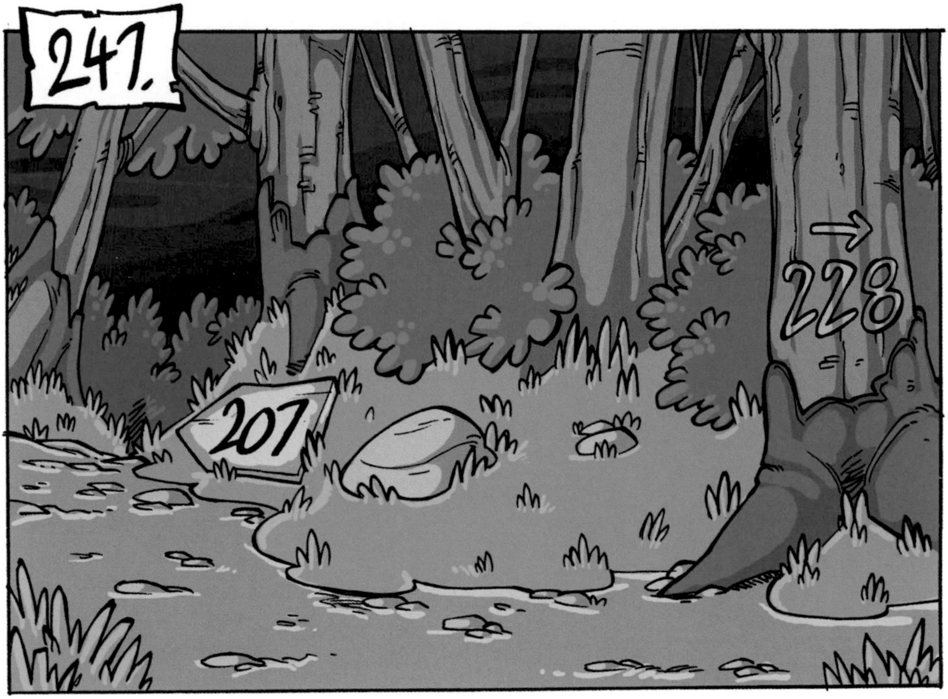
247.
207
→ 228

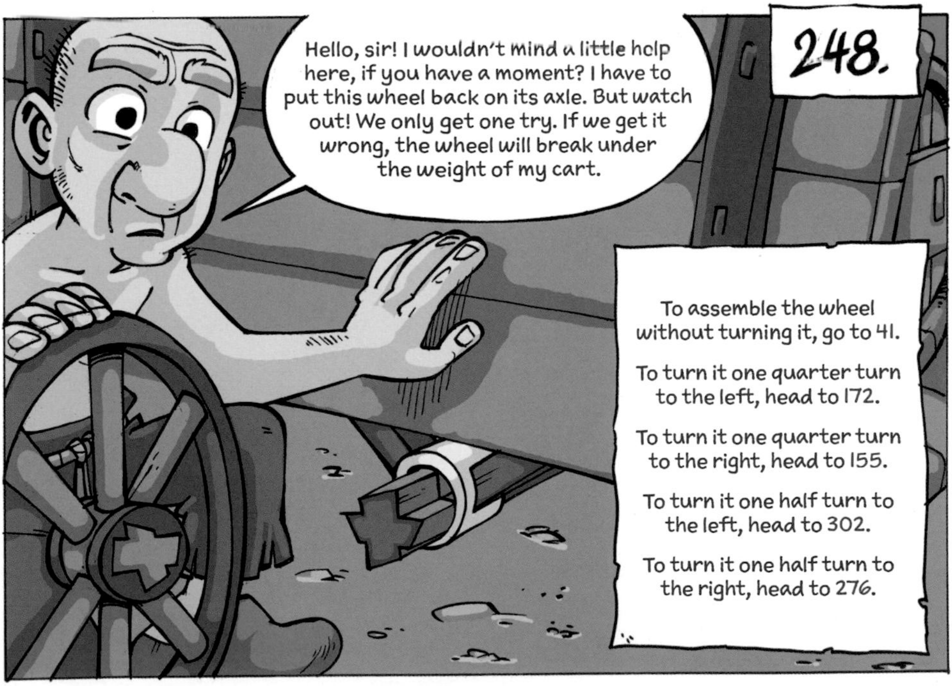
248.
Hello, sir! I wouldn't mind a little help here, if you have a moment? I have to put this wheel back on its axle. But watch out! We only get one try. If we get it wrong, the wheel will break under the weight of my cart.
To assemble the wheel without turning it, go to 41.
To turn it one quarter turn to the left, head to 172.
To turn it one quarter turn to the right, head to 155.
To turn it one half turn to the left, head to 302.
To turn it one half turn to the right, head to 276.

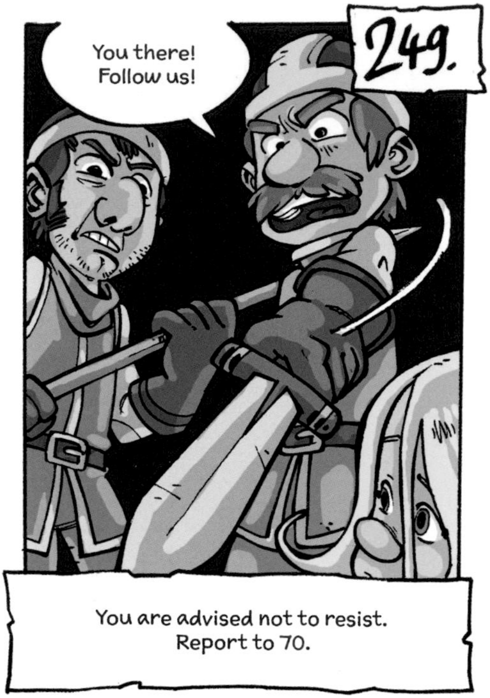
249.
You there! Follow us!
You are advised not to resist. Report to 70.

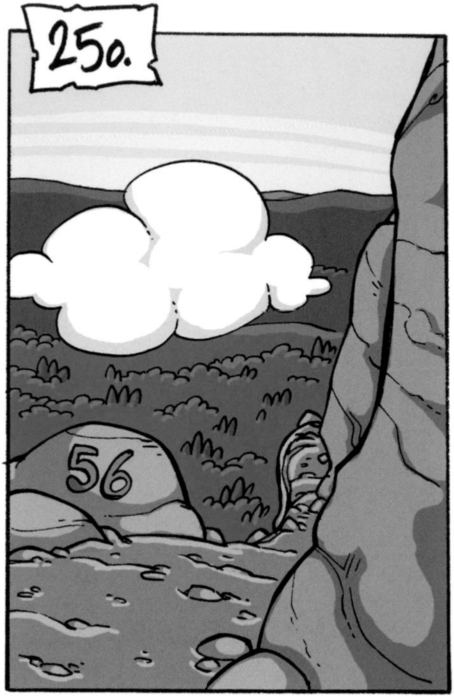
250.
56

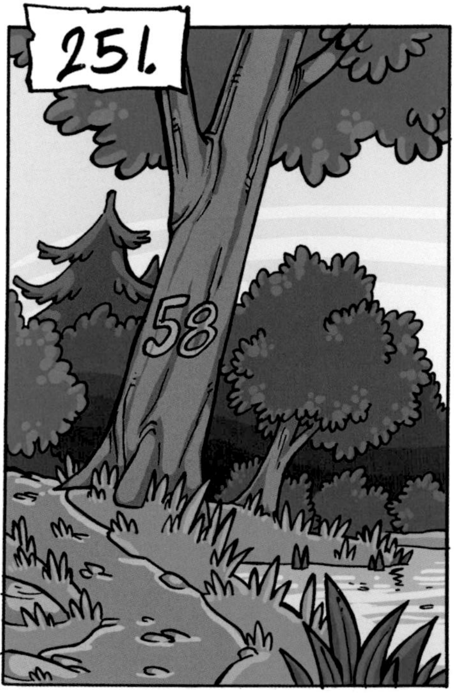
251.
58

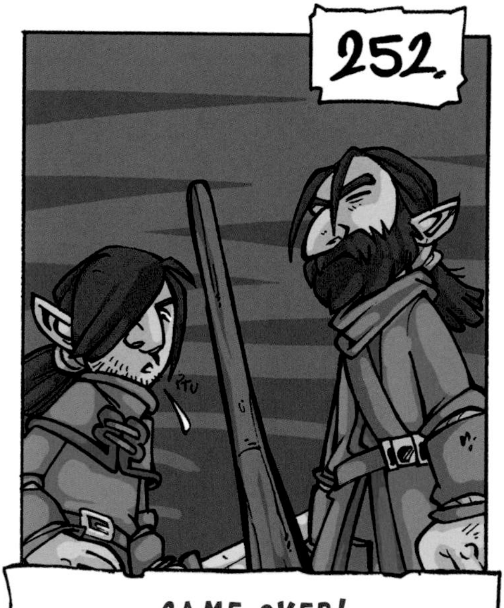
252.
PTU
GAME OVER!
I agree with you: these guards have no sense of humor. But you've failed in your mission, so start your adventure over in 4.

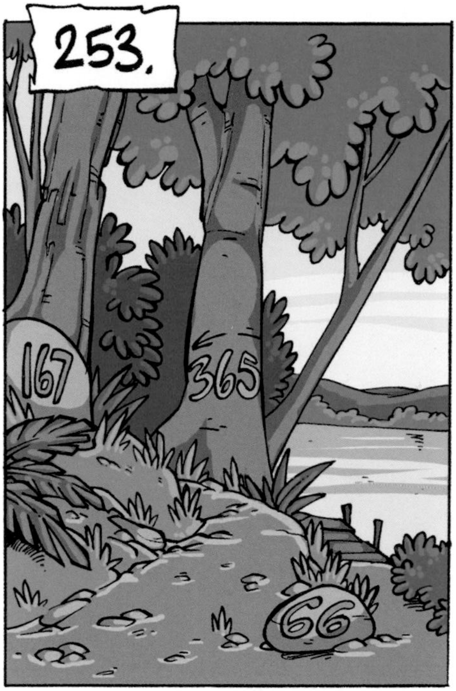
253.
167
365
66

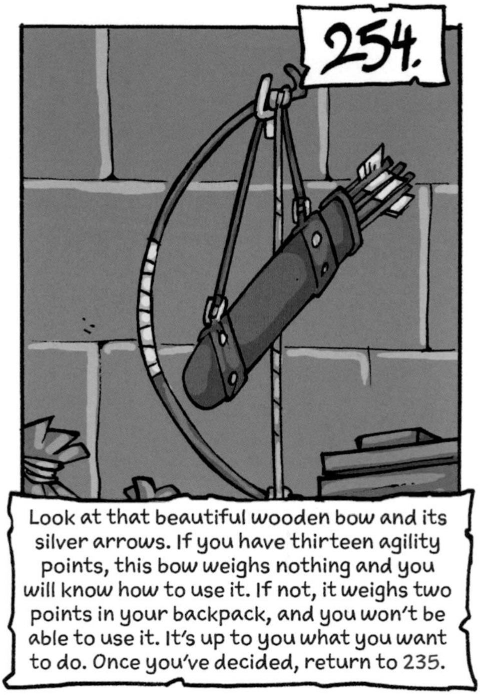
254.
Look at that beautiful wooden bow and its silver arrows. If you have thirteen agility points, this bow weighs nothing and you will know how to use it. If not, it weighs two points in your backpack, and you won't be able to use it. It's up to you what you want to do. Once you've decided, return to 235.

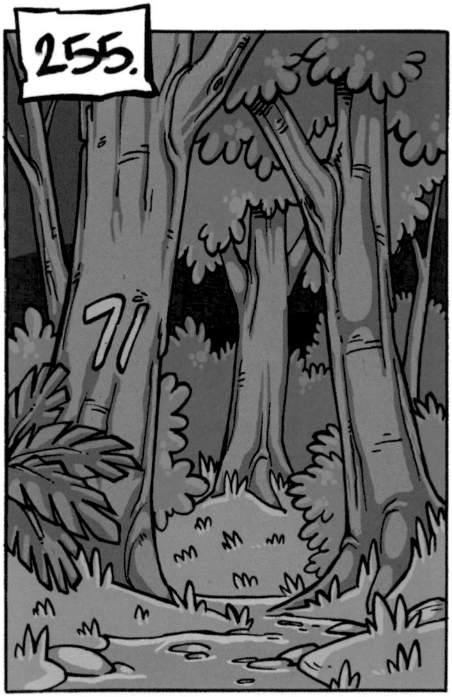
255.
71

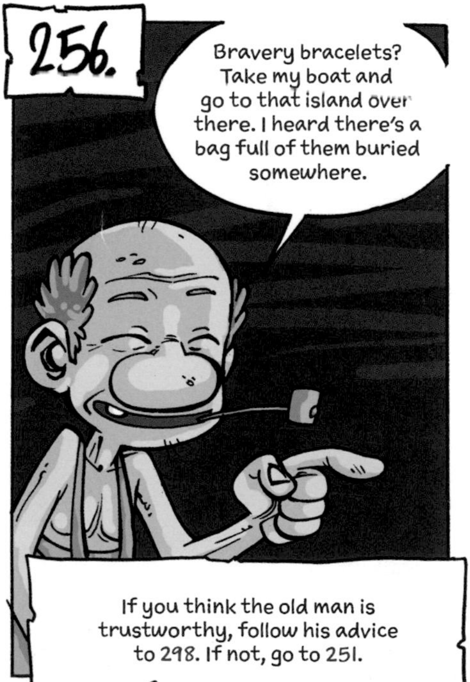
256.
Bravery bracelets? Take my boat and go to that island over there. I heard there's a bag full of them buried somewhere.
If you think the old man is trustworthy, follow his advice to 298. If not, go to 251.

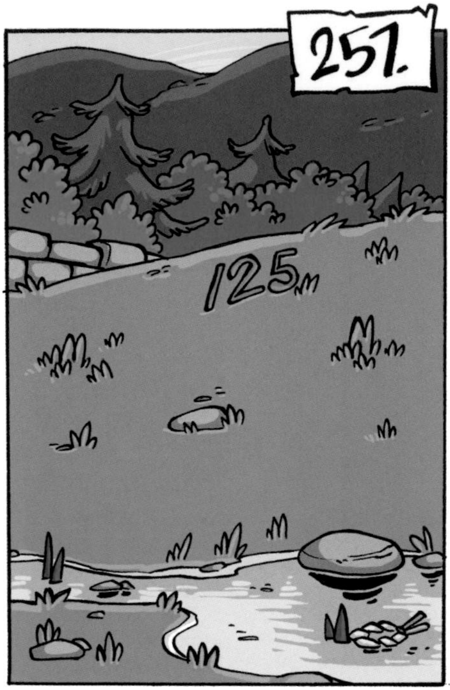
257.
125

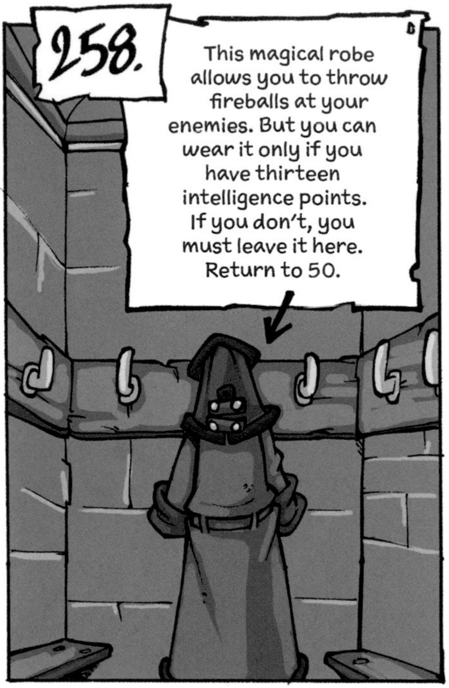
258.
This magical robe allows you to throw fireballs at your enemies. But you can wear it only if you have thirteen intelligence points. If you don't, you must leave it here. Return to 50.

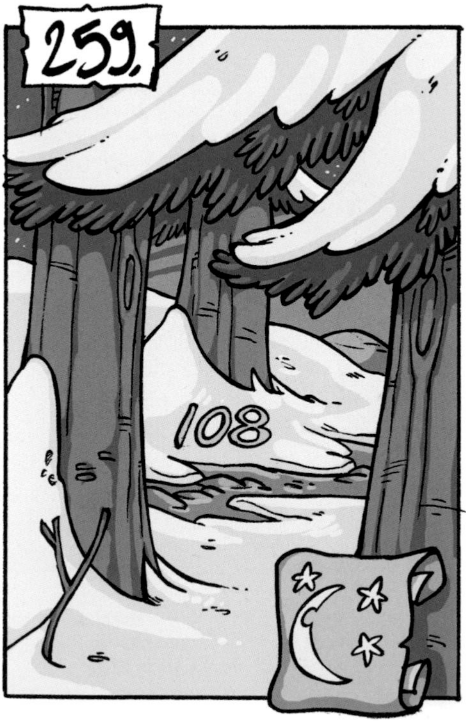
259.
108

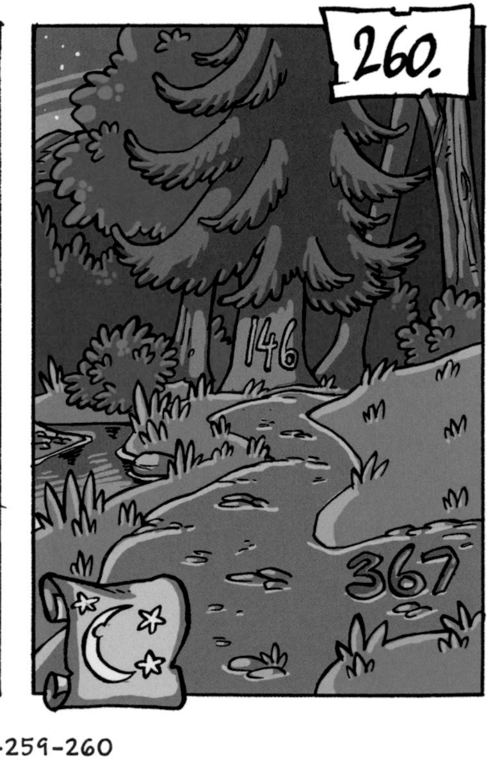
260.
146
367

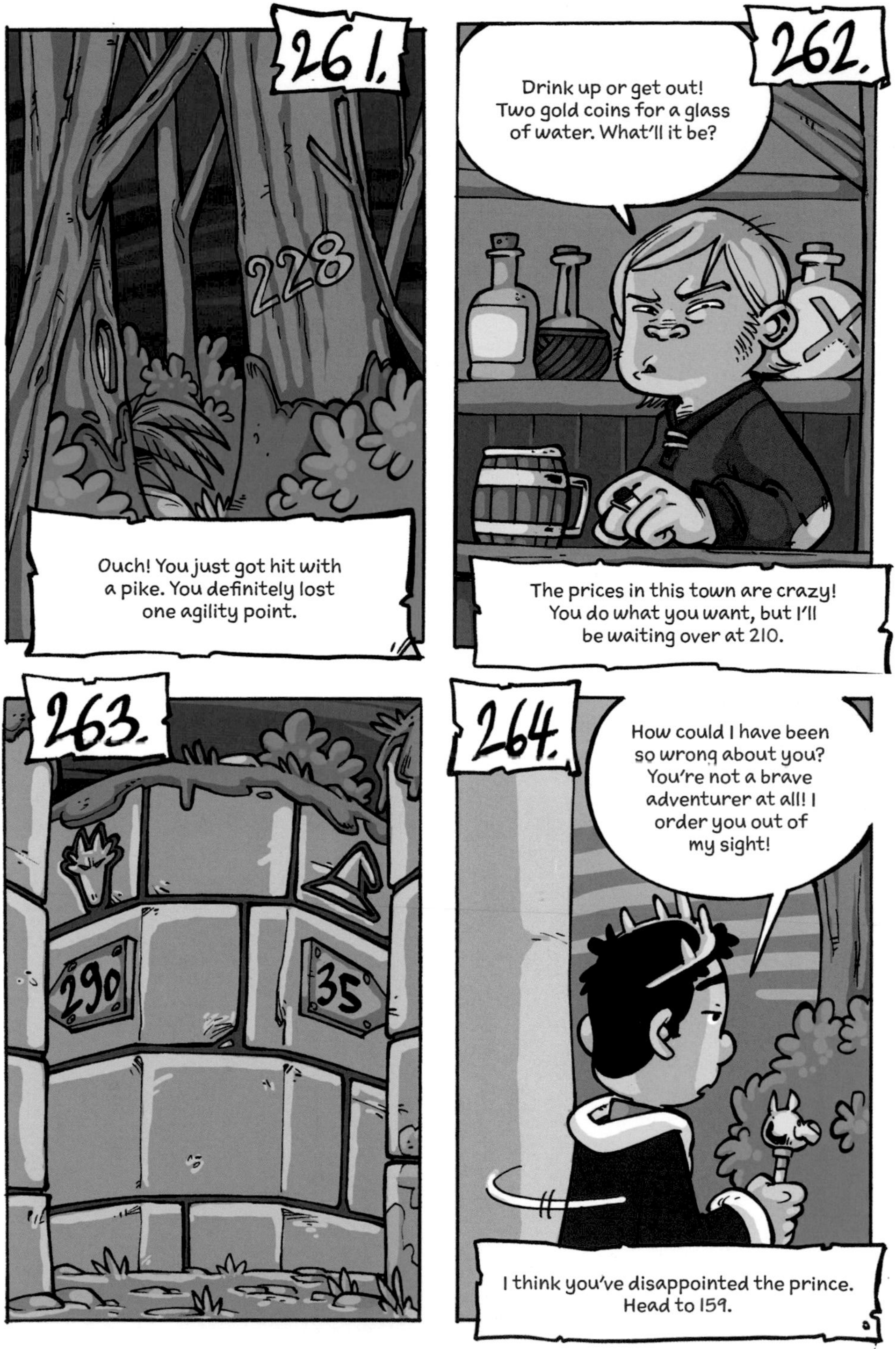
261.
228
Ouch! You just got hit with a pike. You definitely lost one agility point.
262.
Drink up or get out! Two gold coins for a glass of water. What'll it be?
The prices in this town are crazy! You do what you want, but I'll be waiting over at 210.
263.
290
35
264.
How could I have been so wrong about you? You're not a brave adventurer at all! I order you out of my sight!
I think you've disappointed the prince. Head to 159.

265.

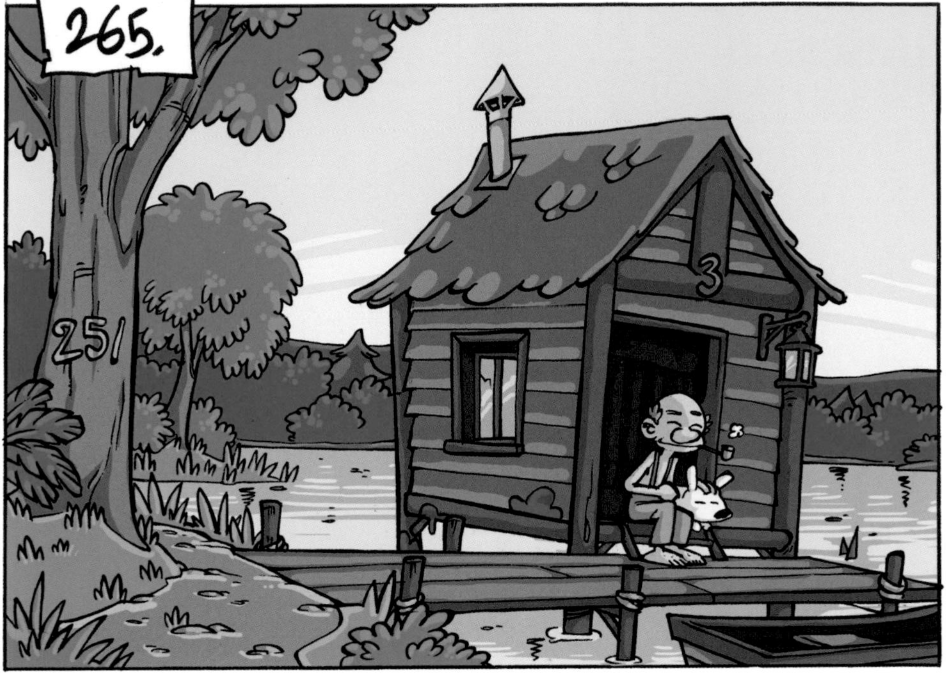
251
3

266.

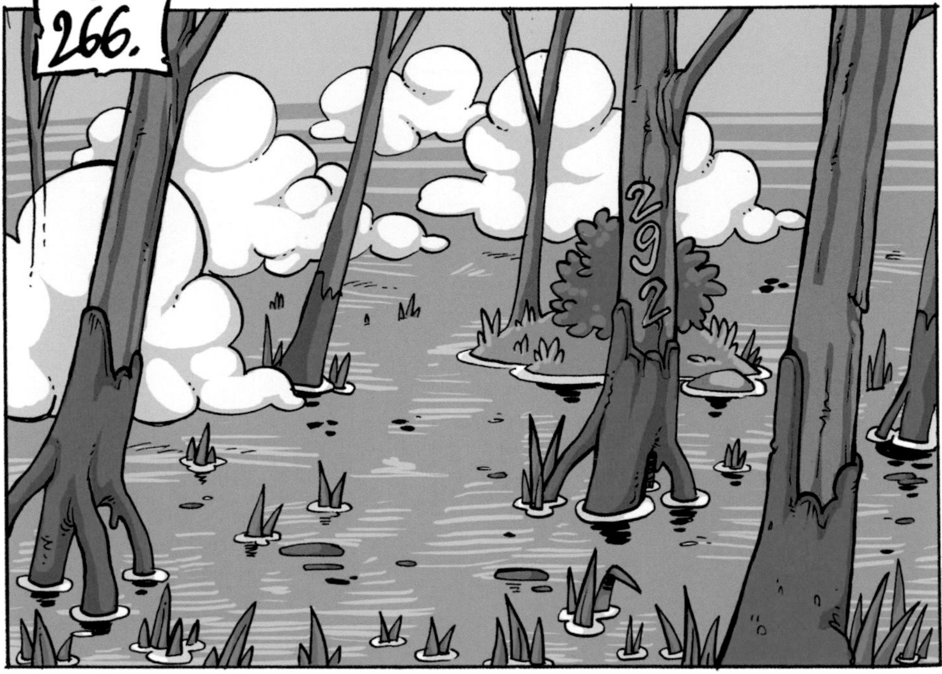
292

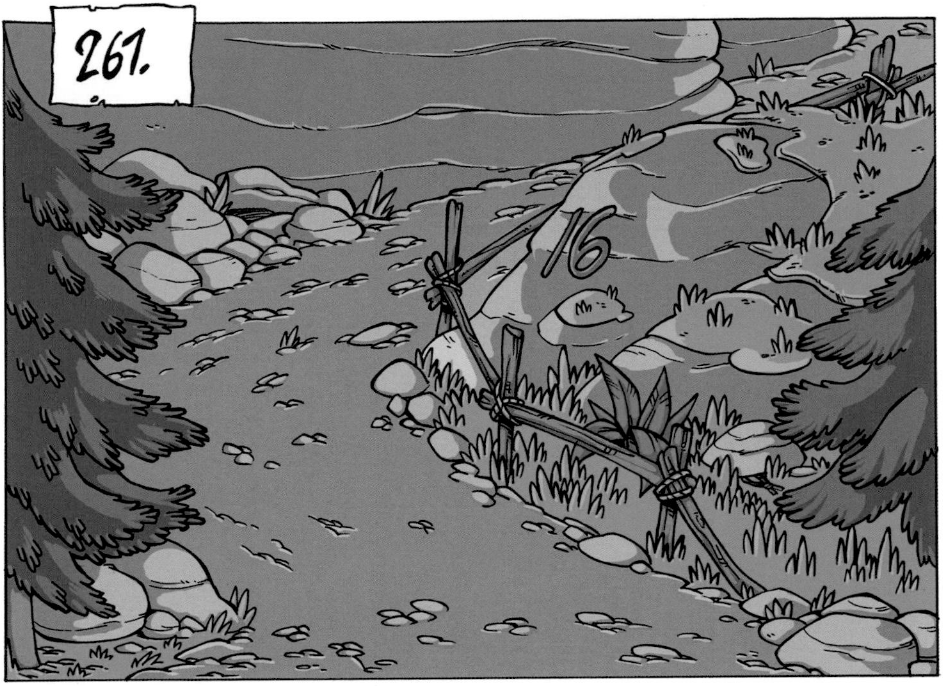
267.
16

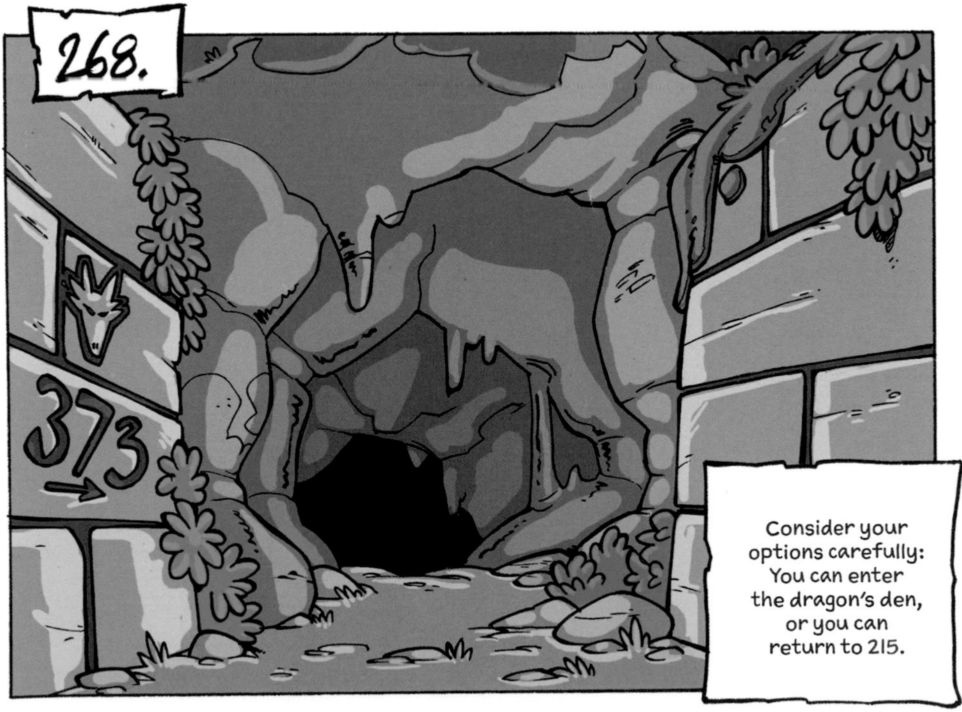
268.
373
Consider your options carefully: You can enter the dragon's den, or you can return to 215.

269.

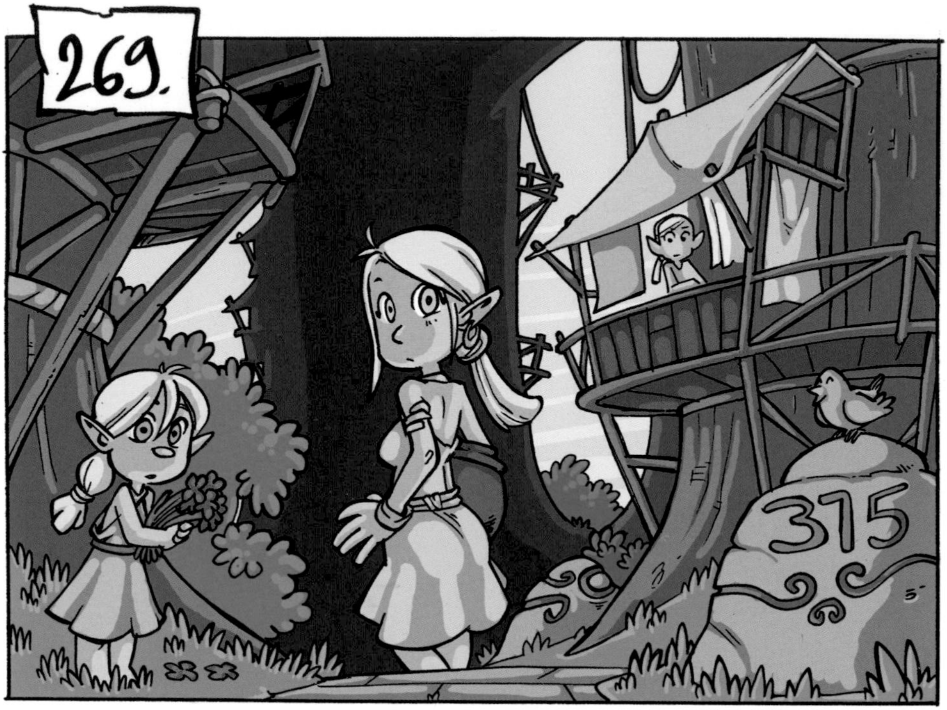
375

270.

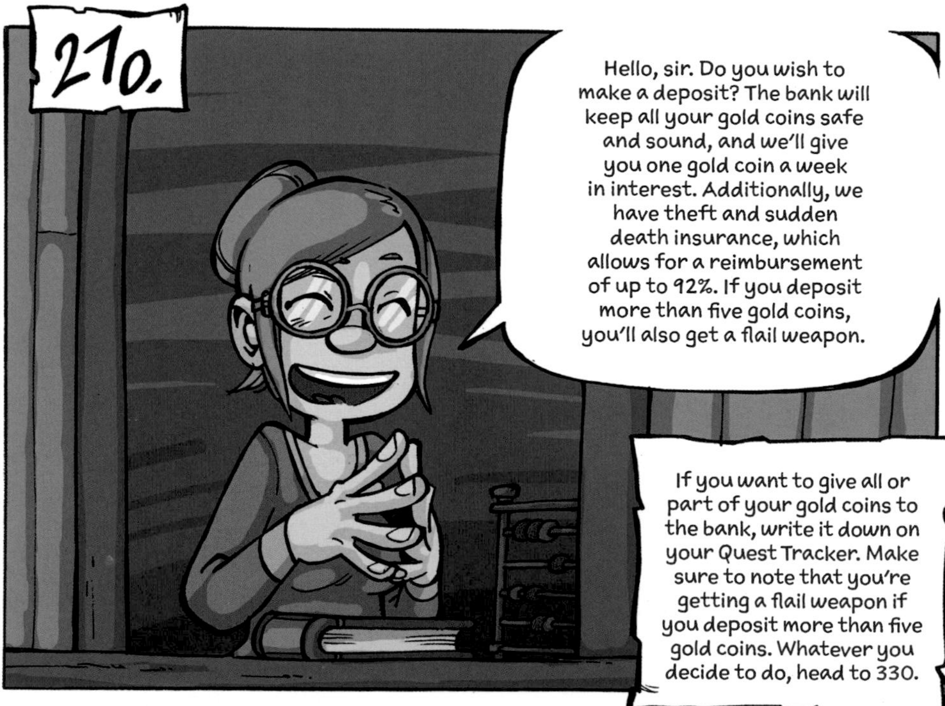
Hello, sir. Do you wish to make a deposit? The bank will keep all your gold coins safe and sound, and we'll give you one gold coin a week in interest. Additionally, we have theft and sudden death insurance, which allows for a reimbursement of up to 92%. If you deposit more than five gold coins, you'll also get a flail weapon.
If you want to give all or part of your gold coins to the bank, write it down on your Quest Tracker. Make sure to note that you're getting a flail weapon if you deposit more than five gold coins. Whatever you decide to do, head to 330.

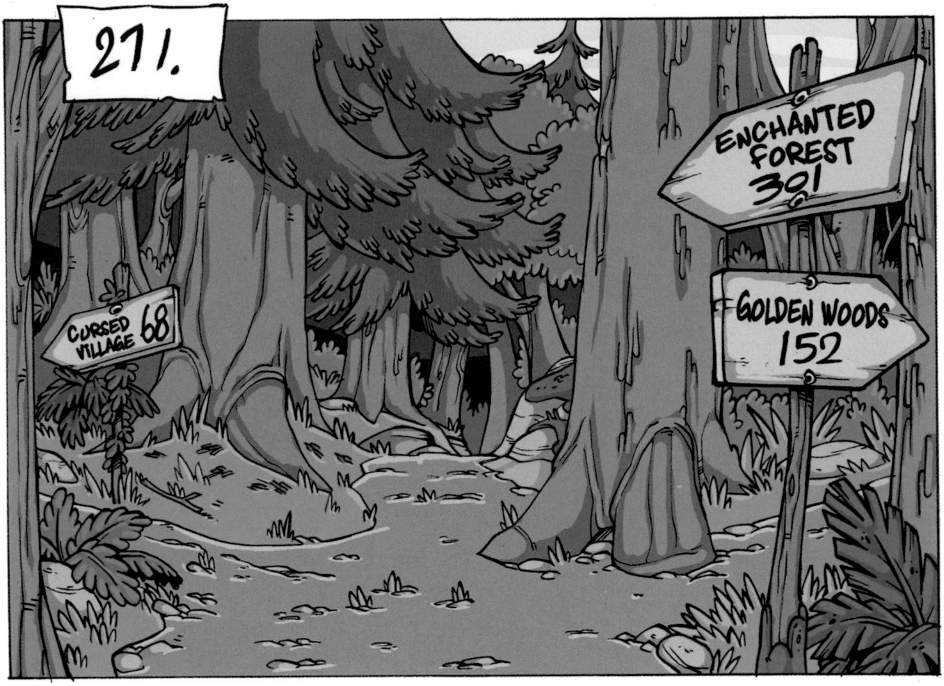
271.
ENCHANTED FOREST 301
GOLDEN WOODS 152
CURSED VILLAGE 68

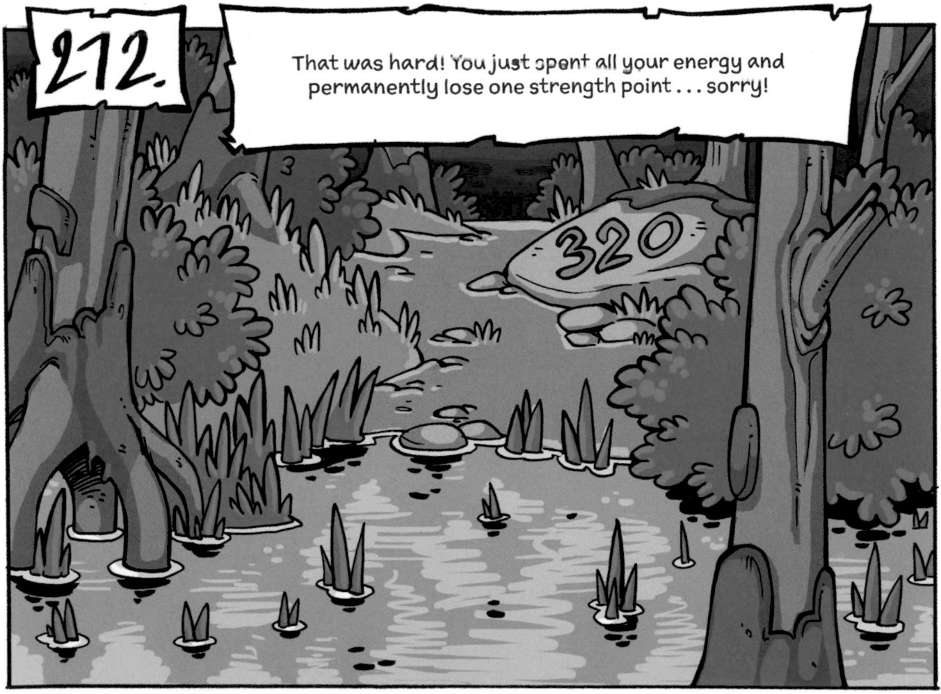
272.
That was hard! You just spent all your energy and permanently lose one strength point . . . sorry!
320

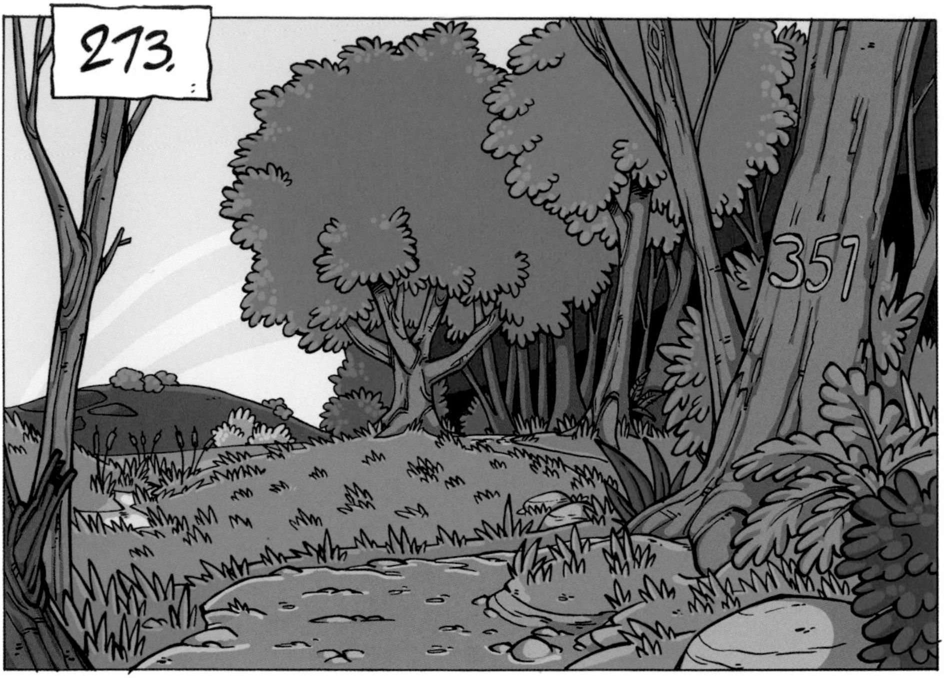
273.
351

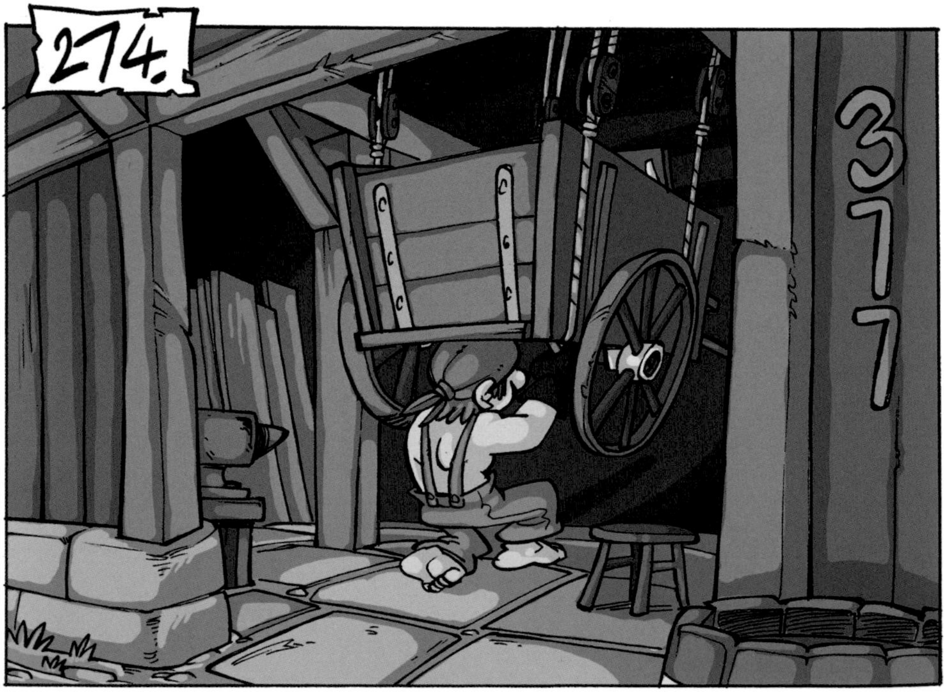
274.
377

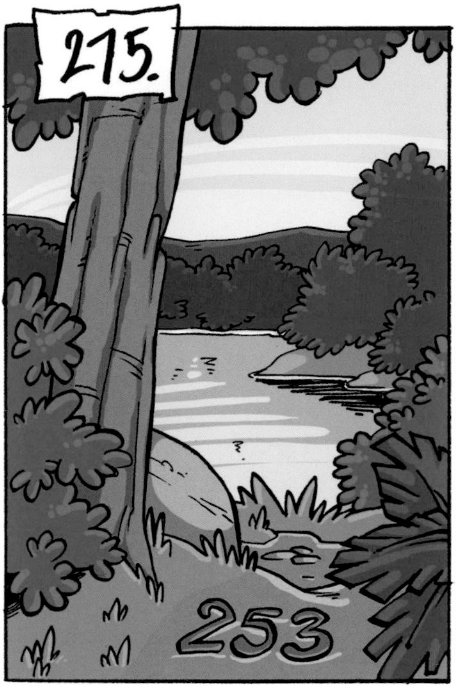
275.
253

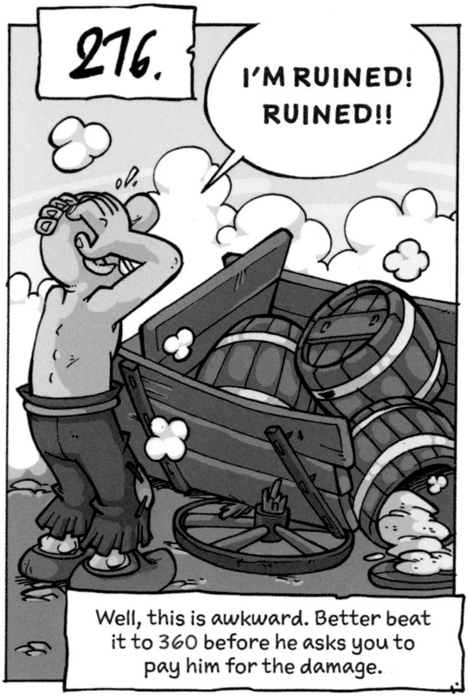
276.
I'M RUINED! RUINED!!
Well, this is awkward. Better beat it to 360 before he asks you to pay him for the damage.

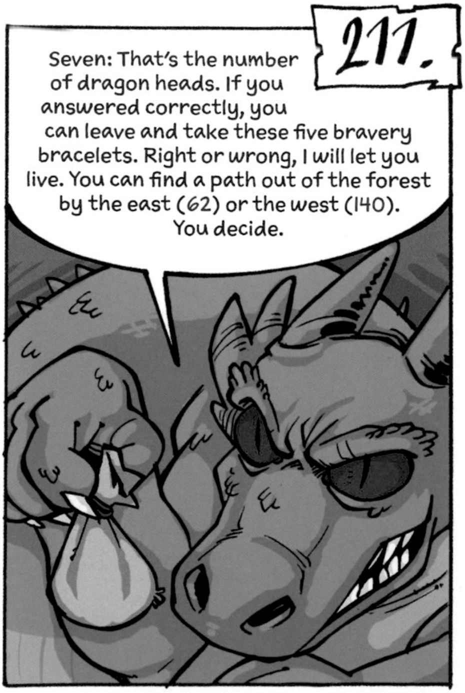
277.
Seven: That's the number of dragon heads. If you answered correctly, you can leave and take these five bravery bracelets. Right or wrong, I will let you live. You can find a path out of the forest by the east (62) or the west (140). You decide.

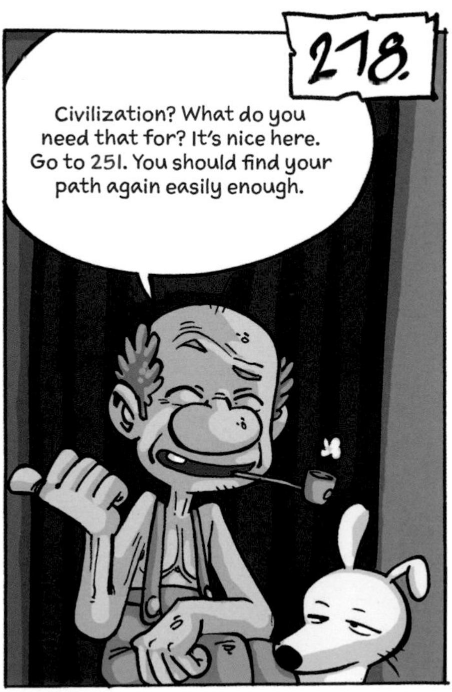
278.
Civilization? What do you need that for? It's nice here. Go to 251. You should find your path again easily enough.

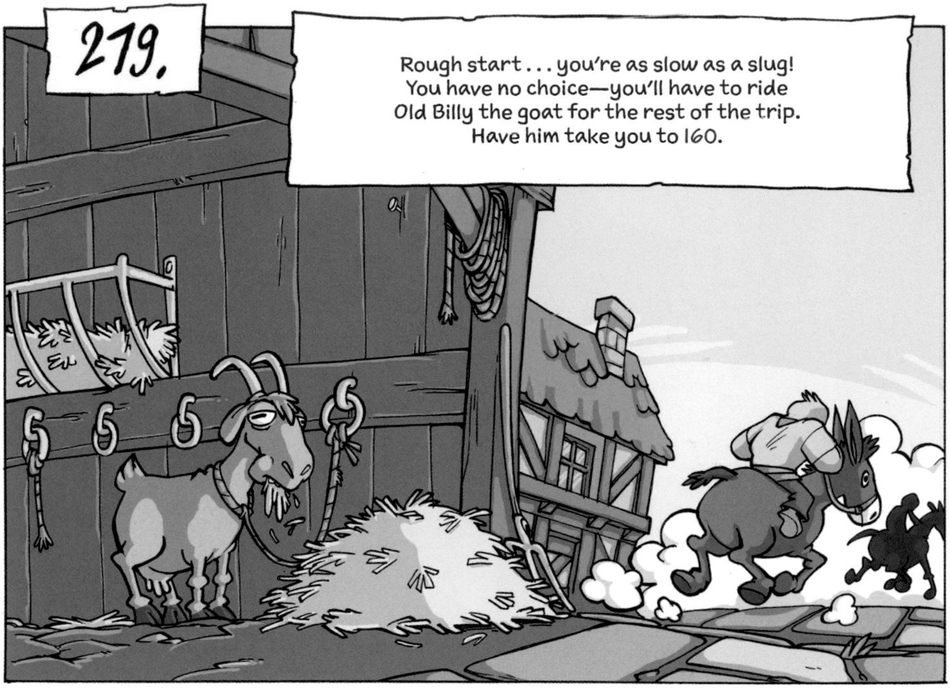
279.
Rough start . . . you're as slow as a slug! You have no choice—you'll have to ride Old Billy the goat for the rest of the trip. Have him take you to 160.

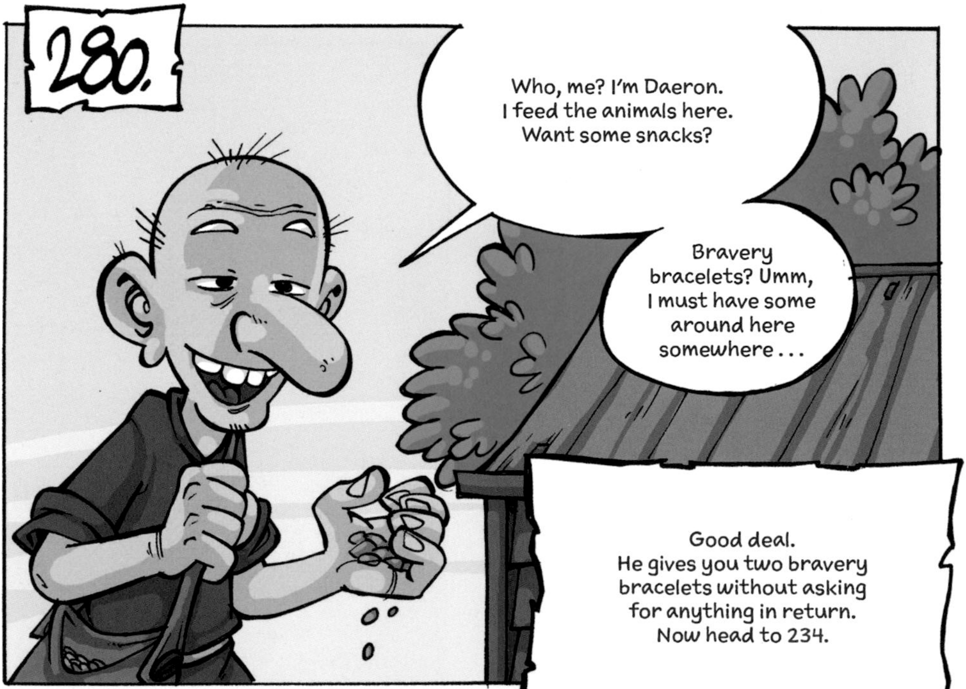
280.
Who, me? I'm Daeron. I feed the animals here. Want some snacks?
Bravery bracelets? Umm, I must have some around here somewhere . . .
Good deal. He gives you two bravery bracelets without asking for anything in return. Now head to 234.

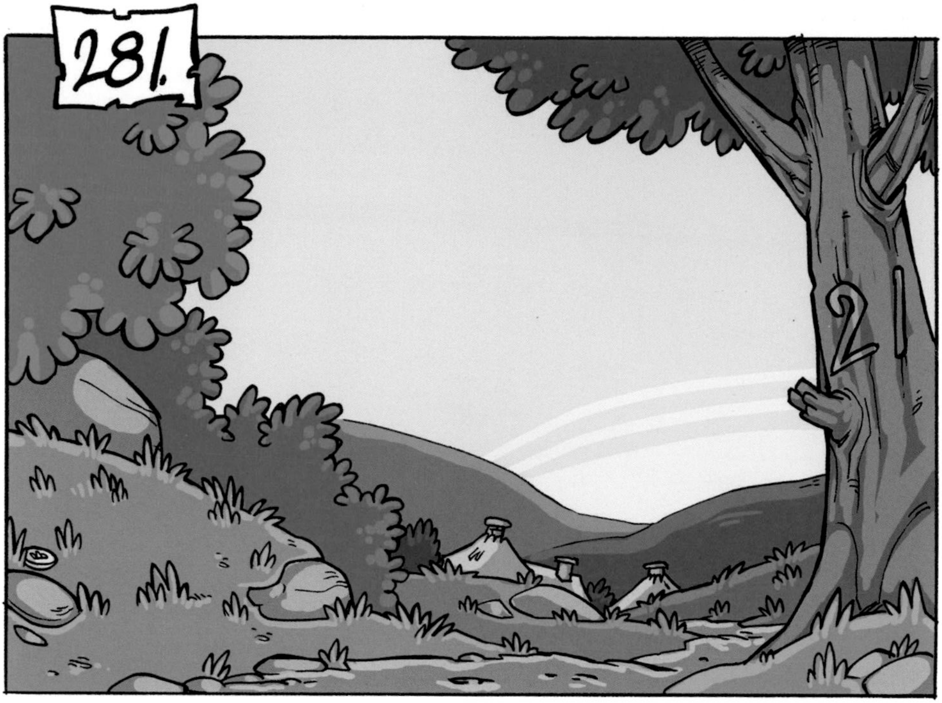
281.

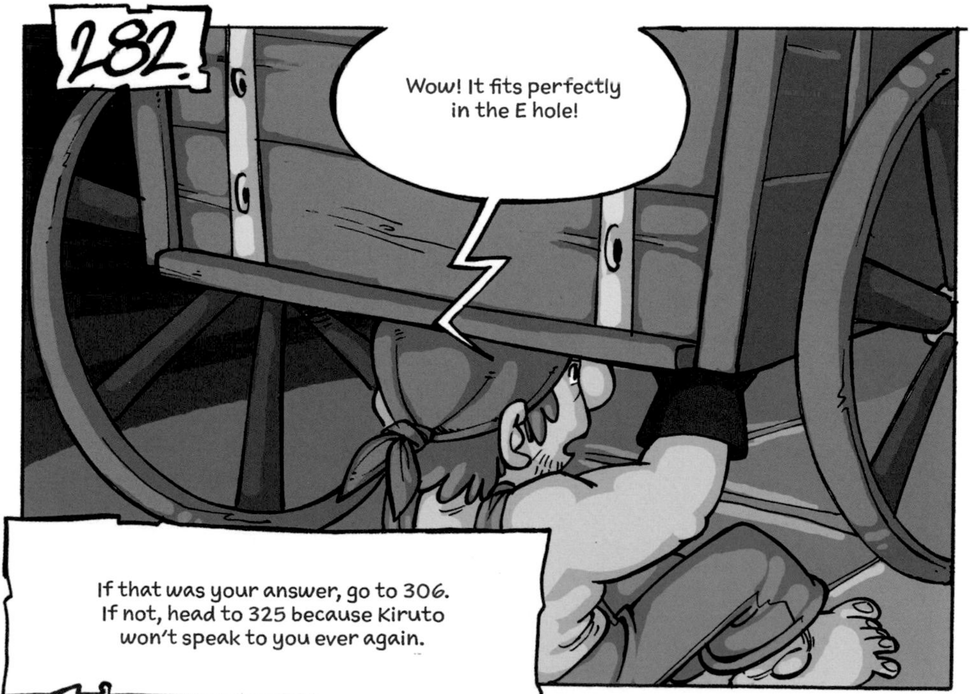
282.
Wow! It fits perfectly in the E hole!
If that was your answer, go to 306. If not, head to 325 because Kiruto won't speak to you ever again.

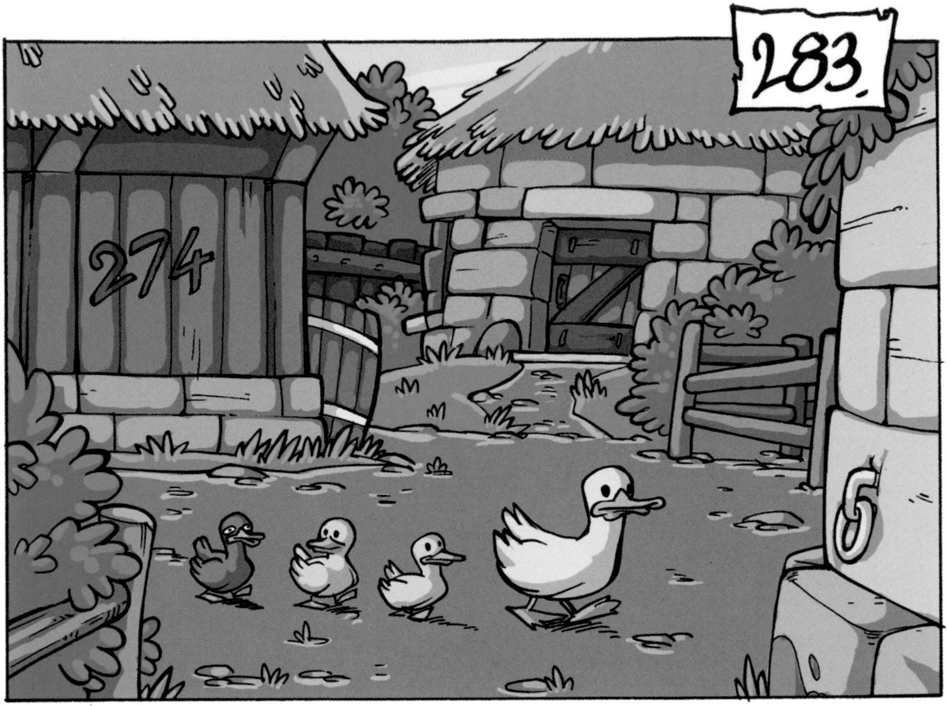
283.
274
6

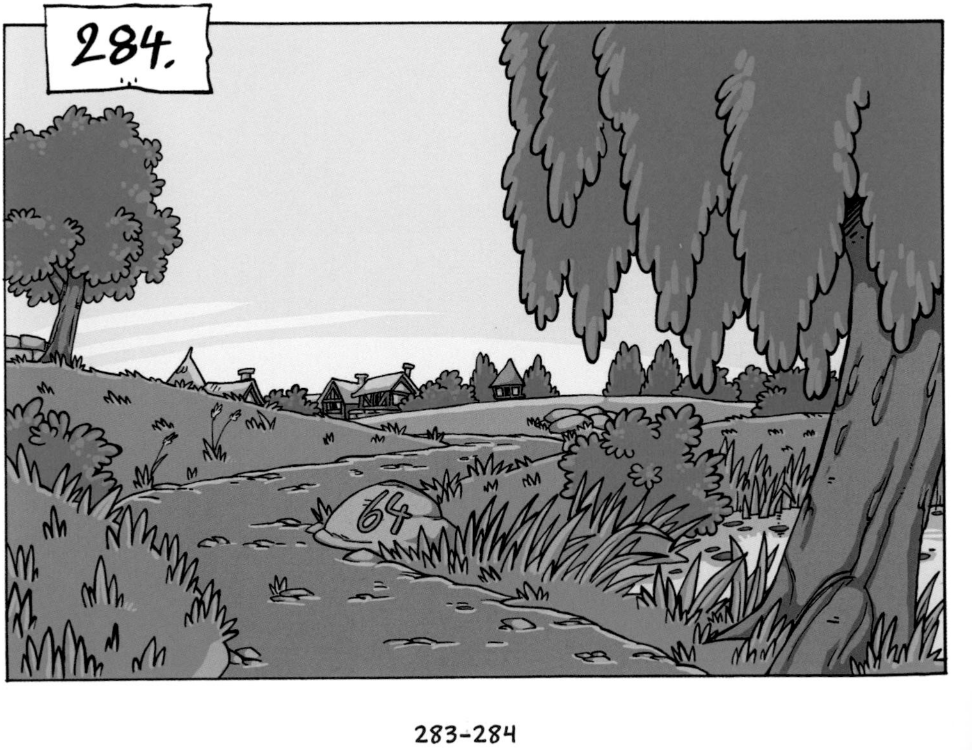
284.
64

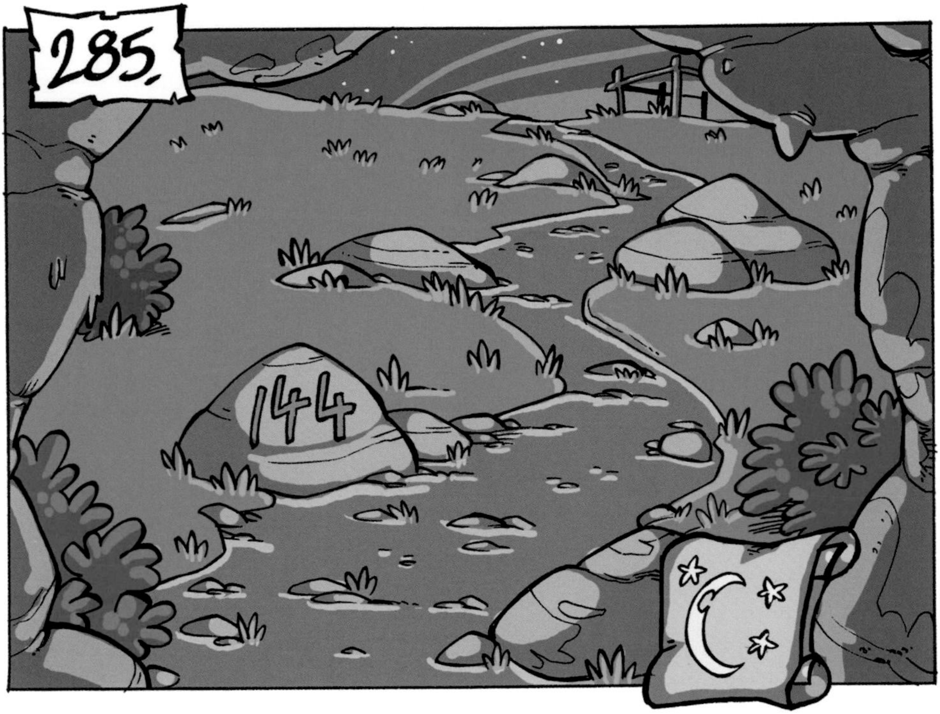
285.
144

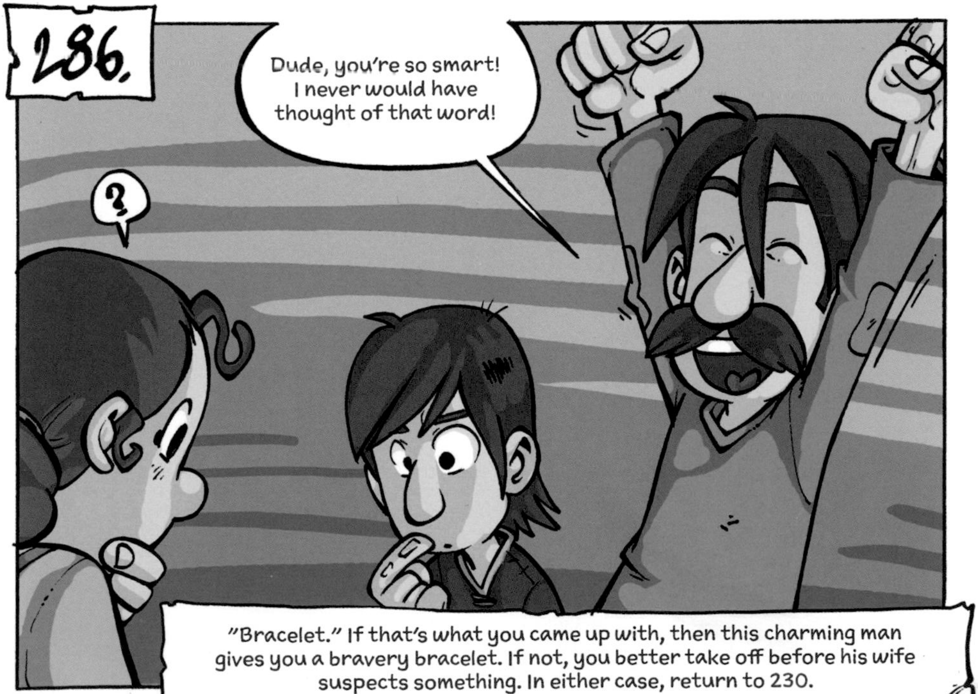
286.
Dude, you're so smart! I never would have thought of that word!
?
"Bracelet." If that's what you came up with, then this charming man gives you a bravery bracelet. If not, you better take off before his wife suspects something. In either case, return to 230.

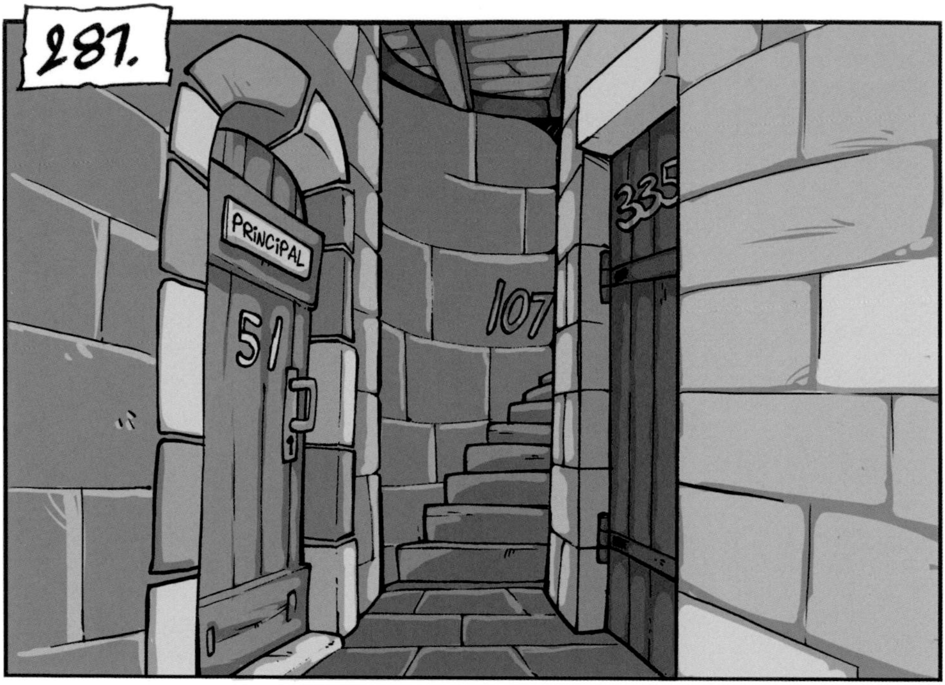
287.
PRINCIPAL
51
107
335

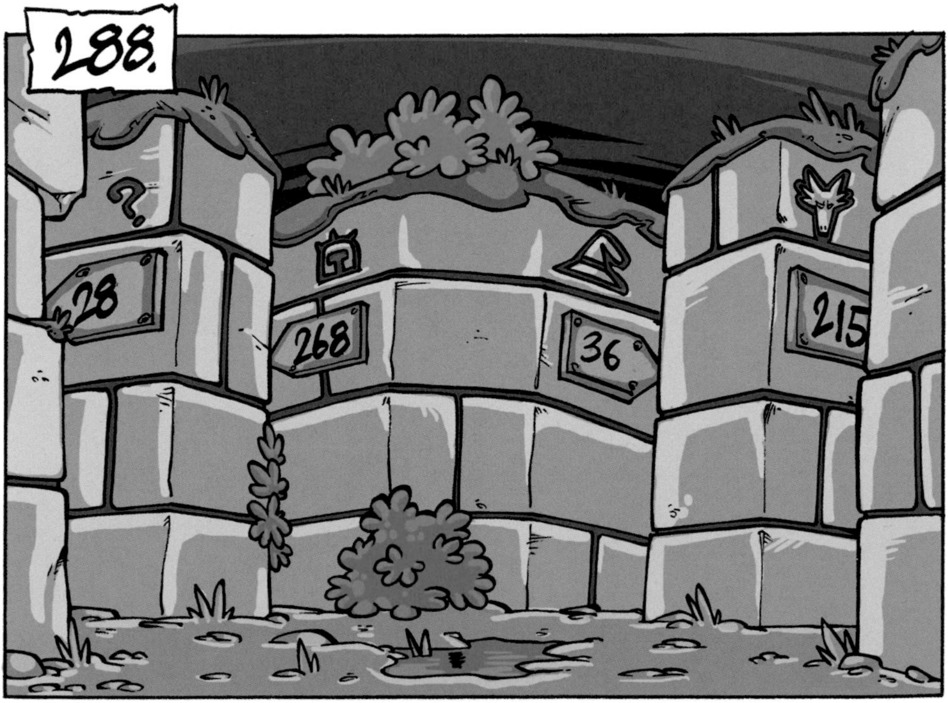
288.
28
268
36
215

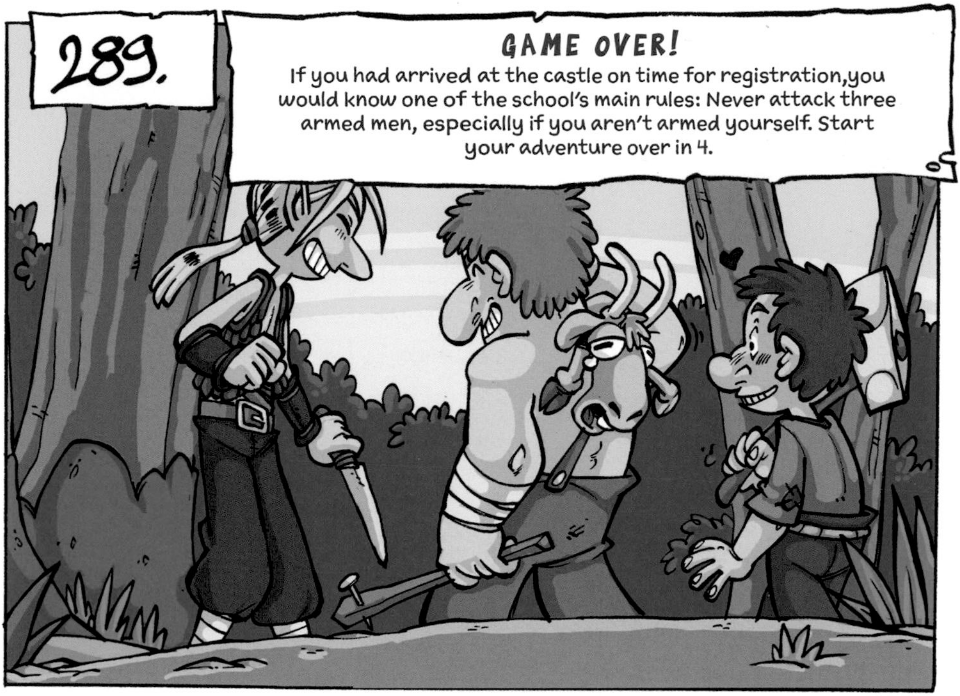
289.
GAME OVER!
If you had arrived at the castle on time for registration,you would know one of the school's main rules: Never attack three armed men, especially if you aren't armed yourself. Start your adventure over in 4.

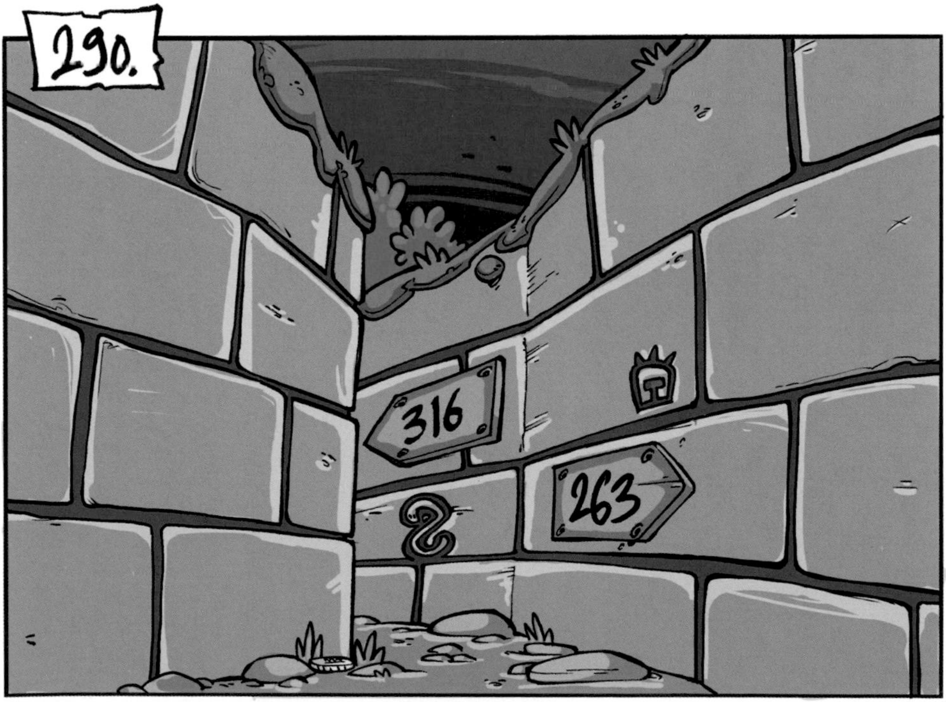
290.
316
263

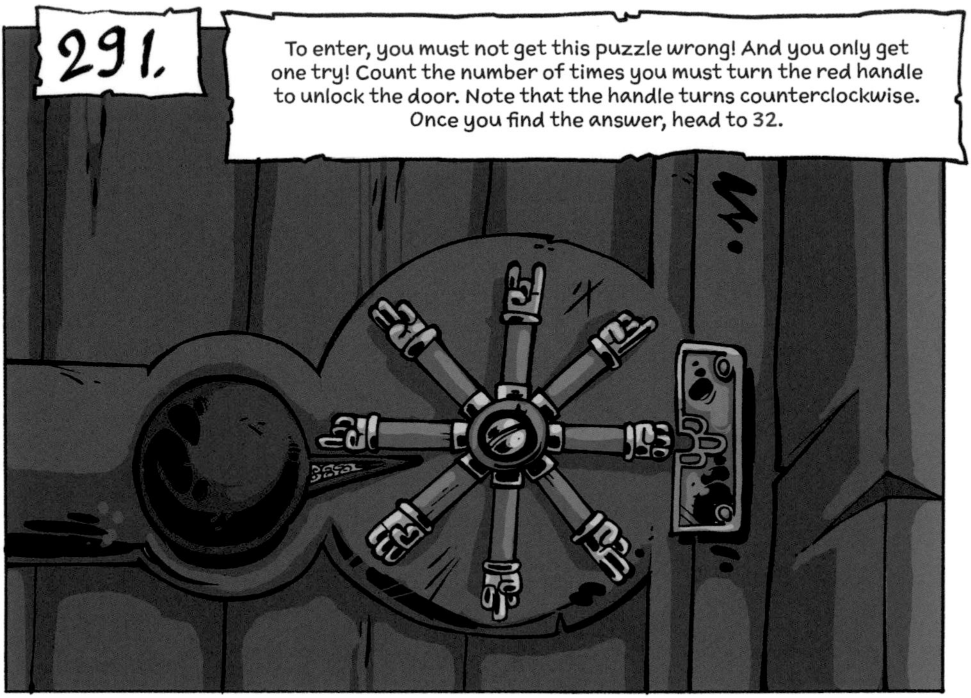
291.
To enter, you must not get this puzzle wrong! And you only get one try! Count the number of times you must turn the red handle to unlock the door. Note that the handle turns counterclockwise. Once you find the answer, head to 32.

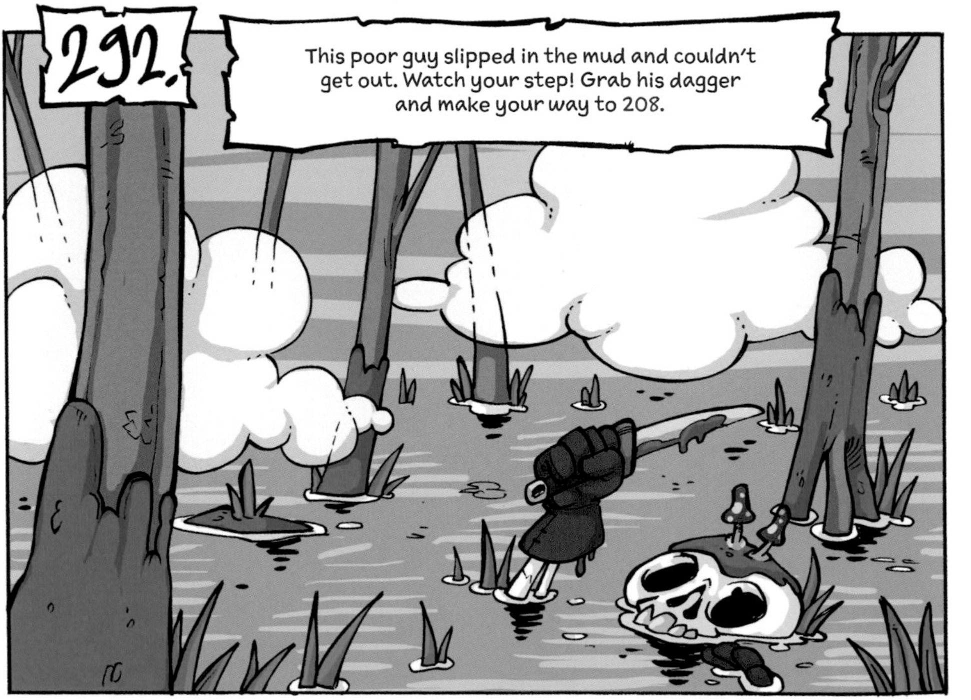
292.
This poor guy slipped in the mud and couldn't get out. Watch your step! Grab his dagger and make your way to 208.

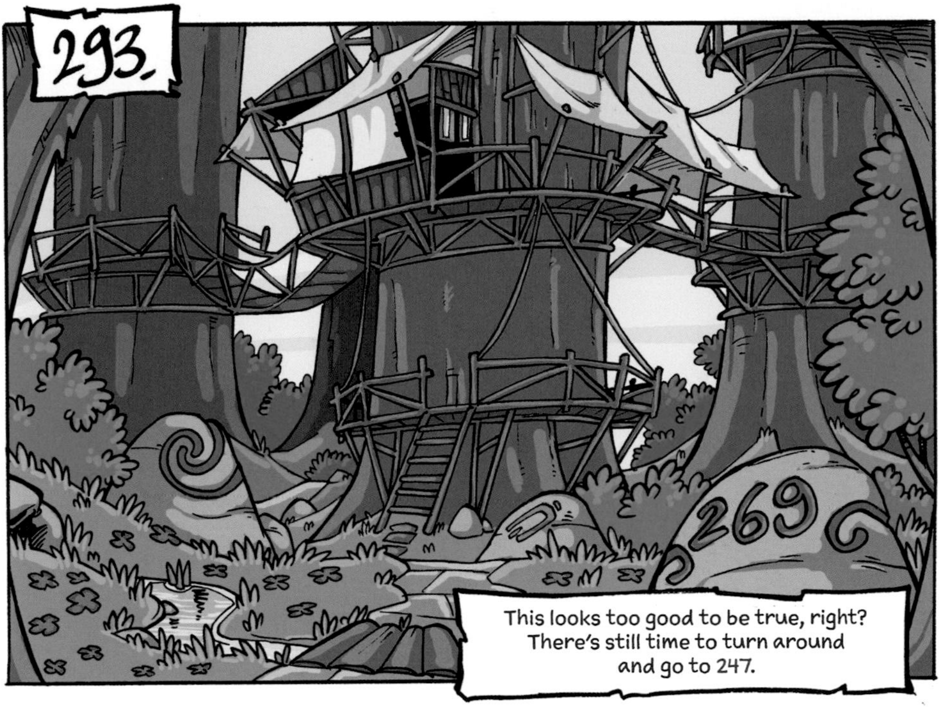
293.
269
This looks too good to be true, right? There's still time to turn around and go to 247.

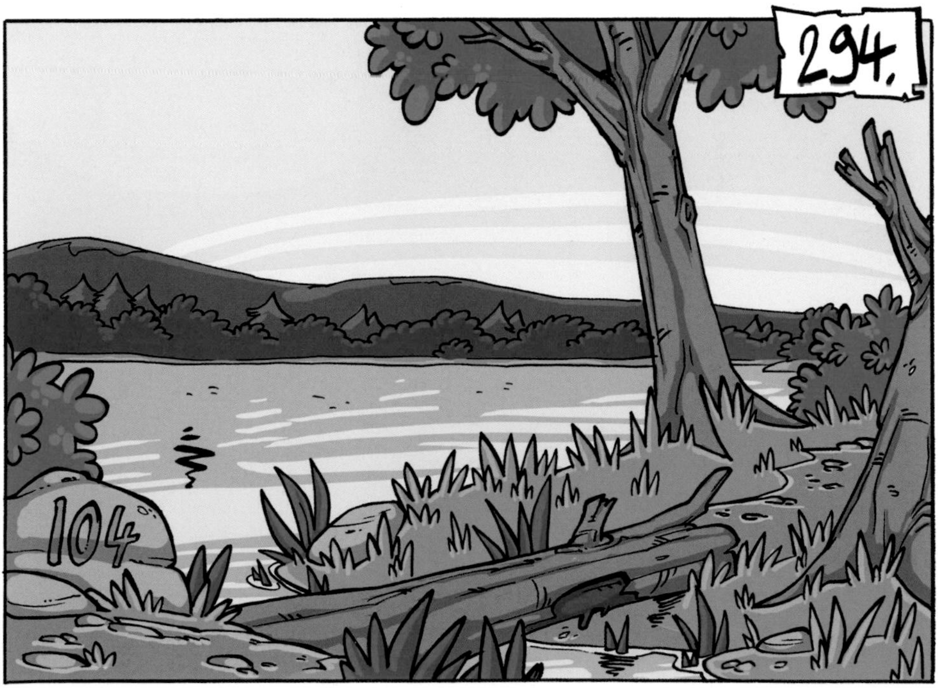
294.
104

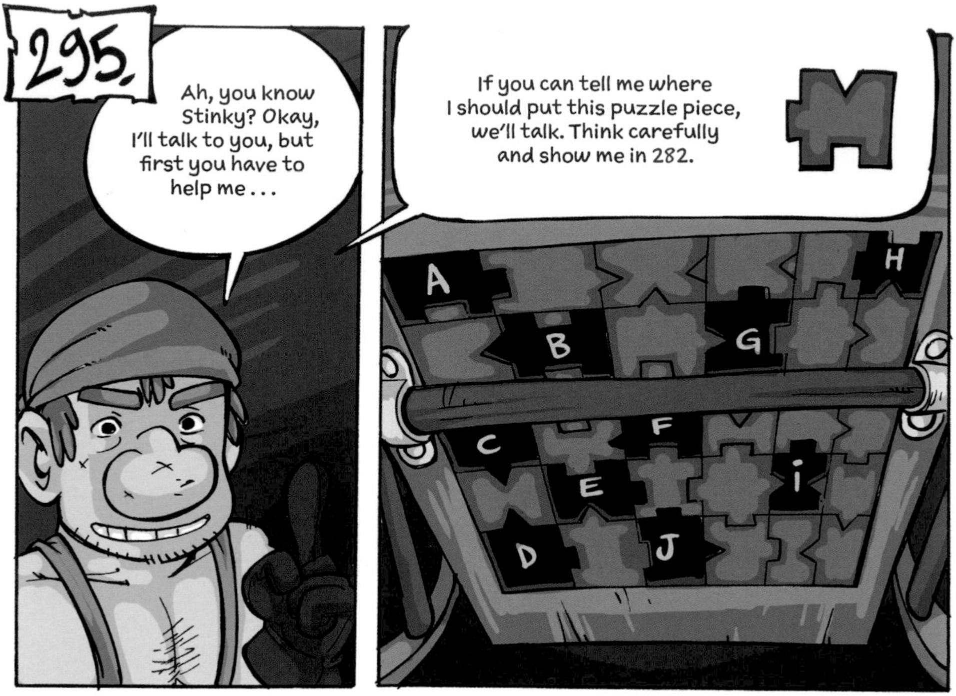
295.
Ah, you know Stinky? Okay, I'll talk to you, but first you have to help me . . .
If you can tell me where I should put this puzzle piece, we'll talk. Think carefully and show me in 282.
A
B
C
D
E
F
G
H
i
J

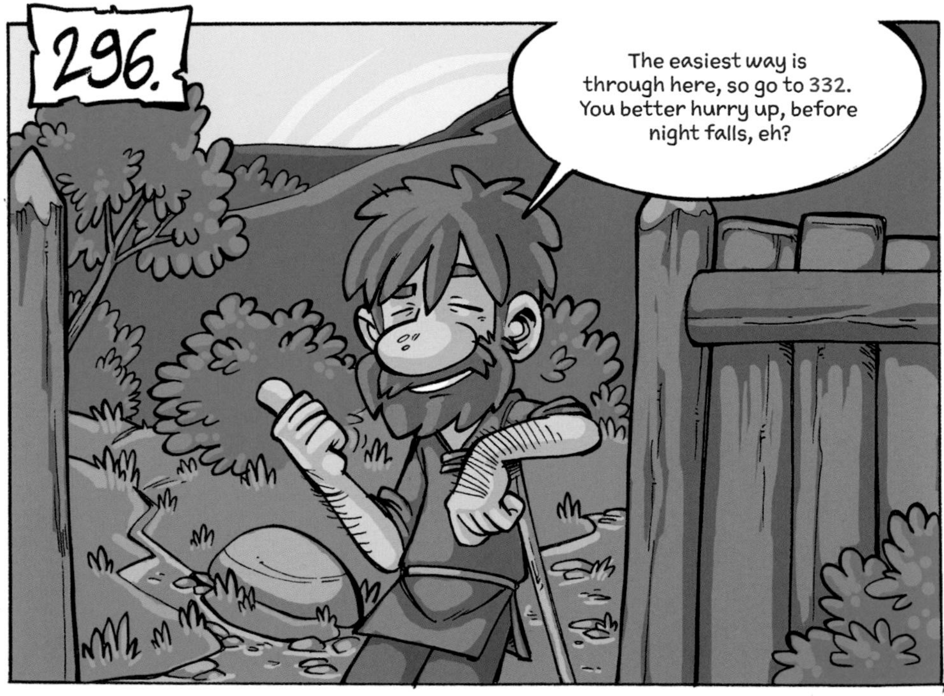
296.
The easiest way is through here, so go to 332. You better hurry up, before night falls, eh?

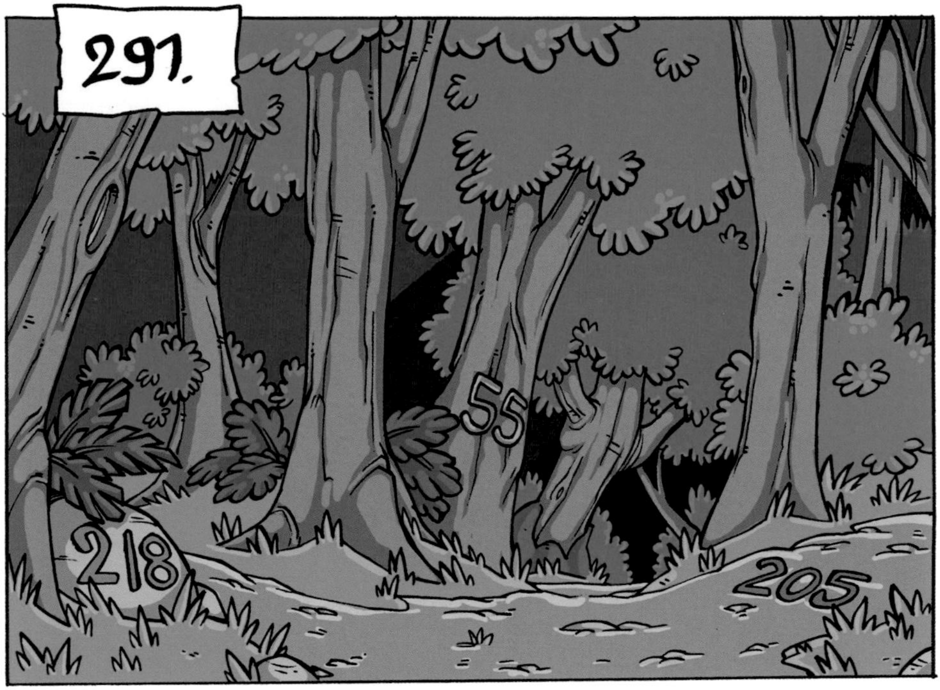
297.
55
218
205

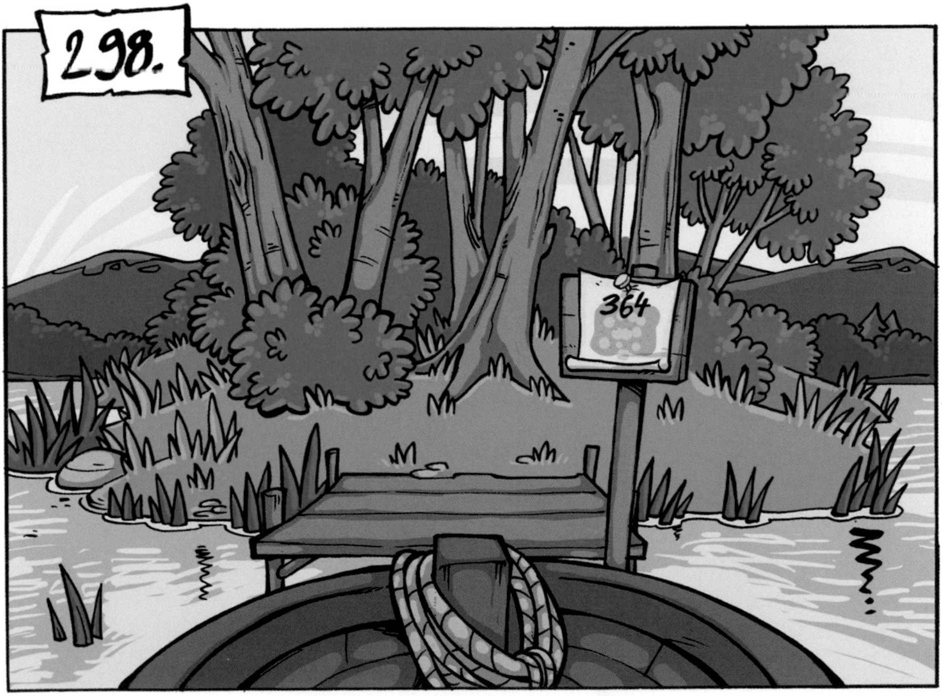
298.
364

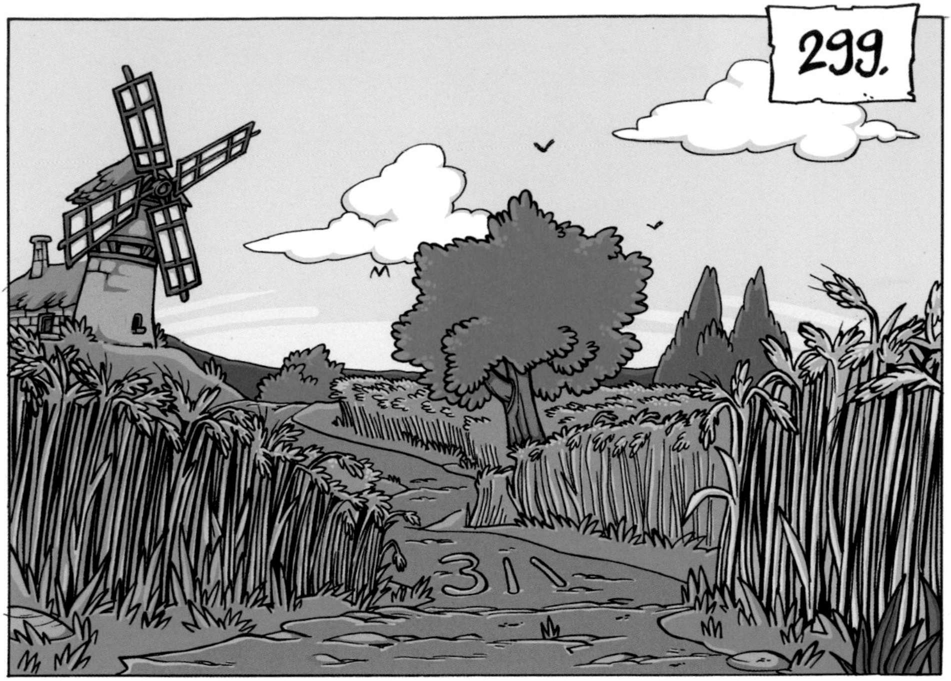
299.
311

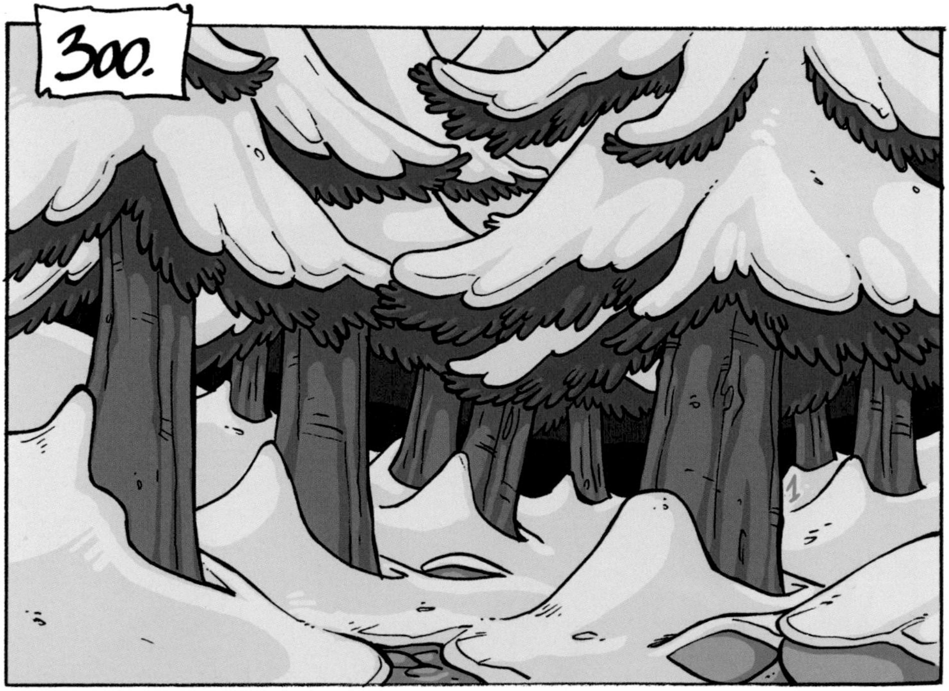
300.
1

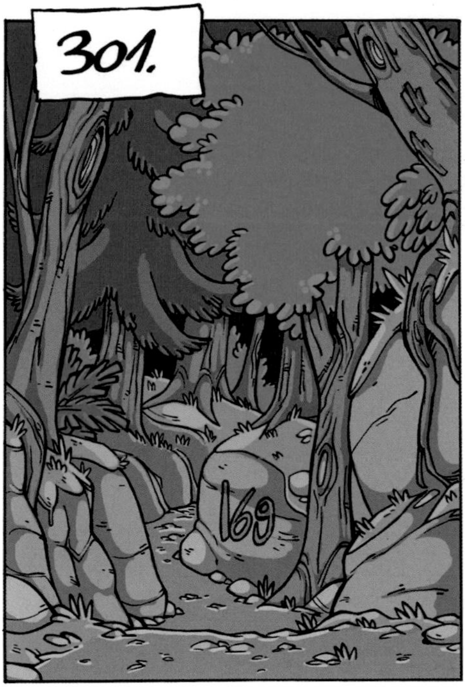
301.
169

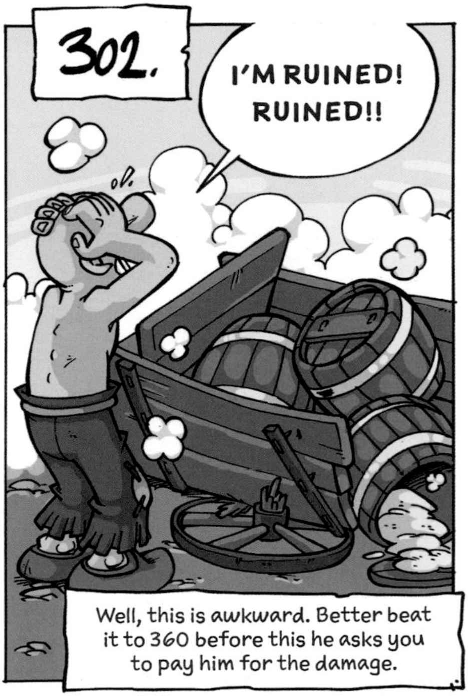
302.
I'M RUINED! RUINED!!
Well, this is awkward. Better beat it to 360 before this he asks you to pay him for the damage.

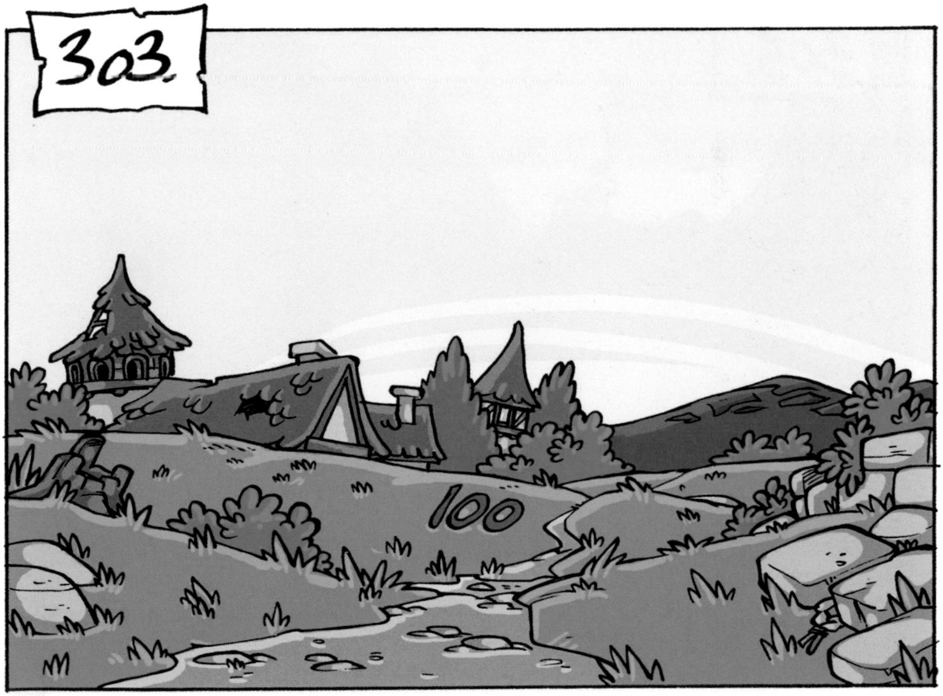
303.
100

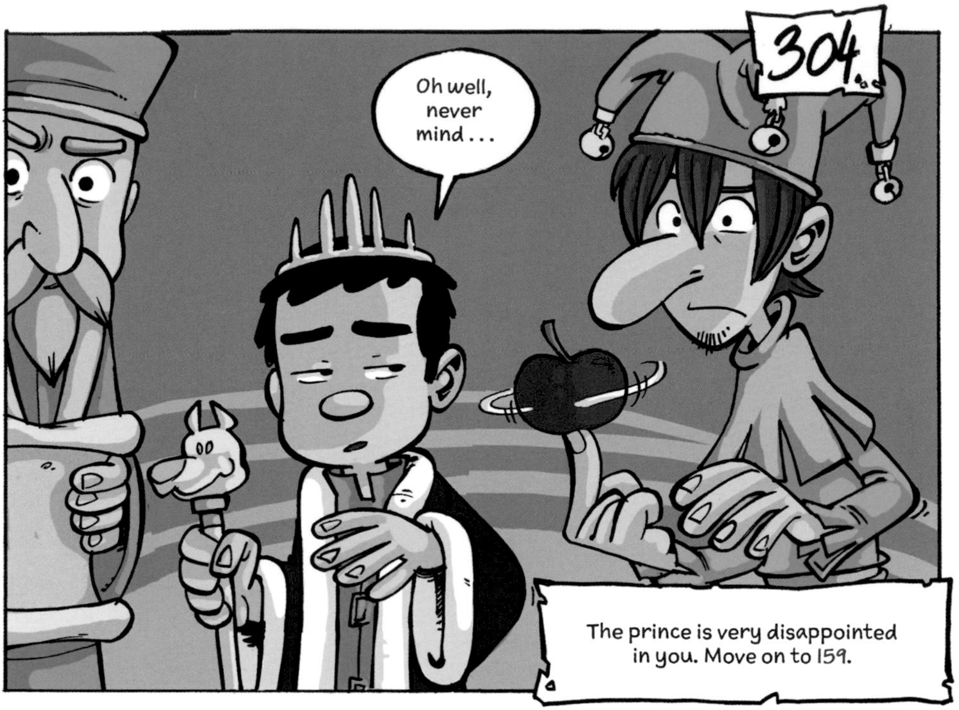
304.
Oh well, never mind . . .
The prince is very disappointed in you. Move on to 159.

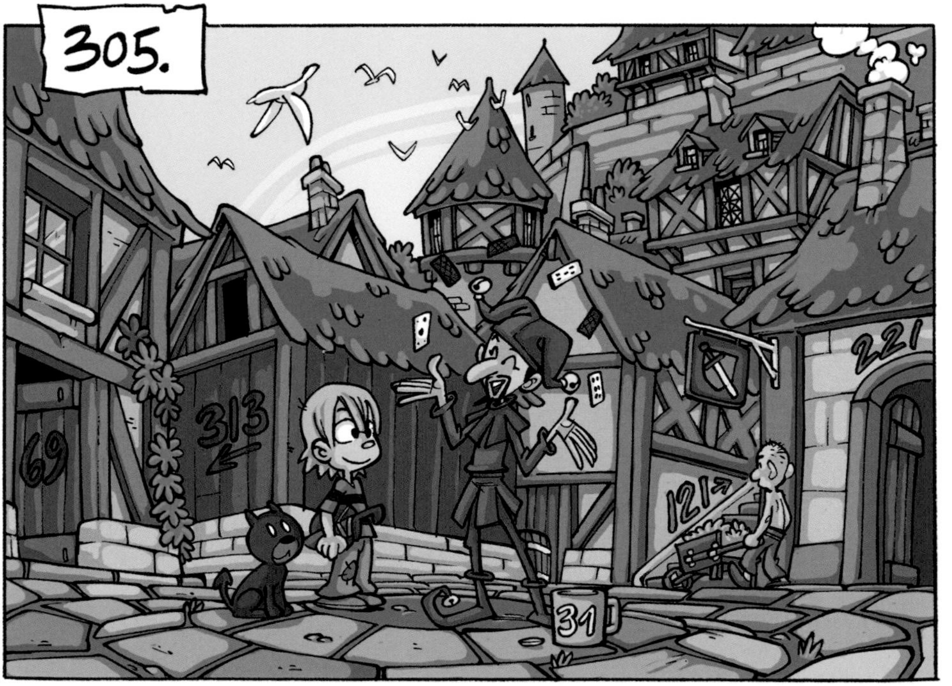
305.
69
313
221
121
31

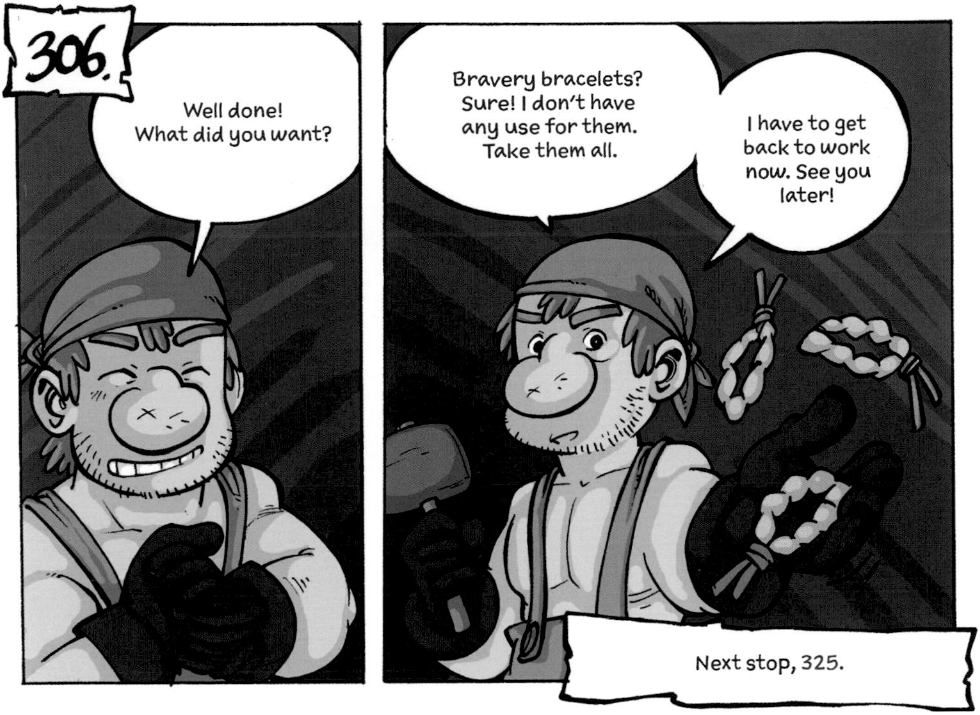
306.
Well done!
What did you want?
Bravery bracelets? Sure! I don't have any use for them. Take them all.
I have to get back to work now. See you later!
Next stop, 325.

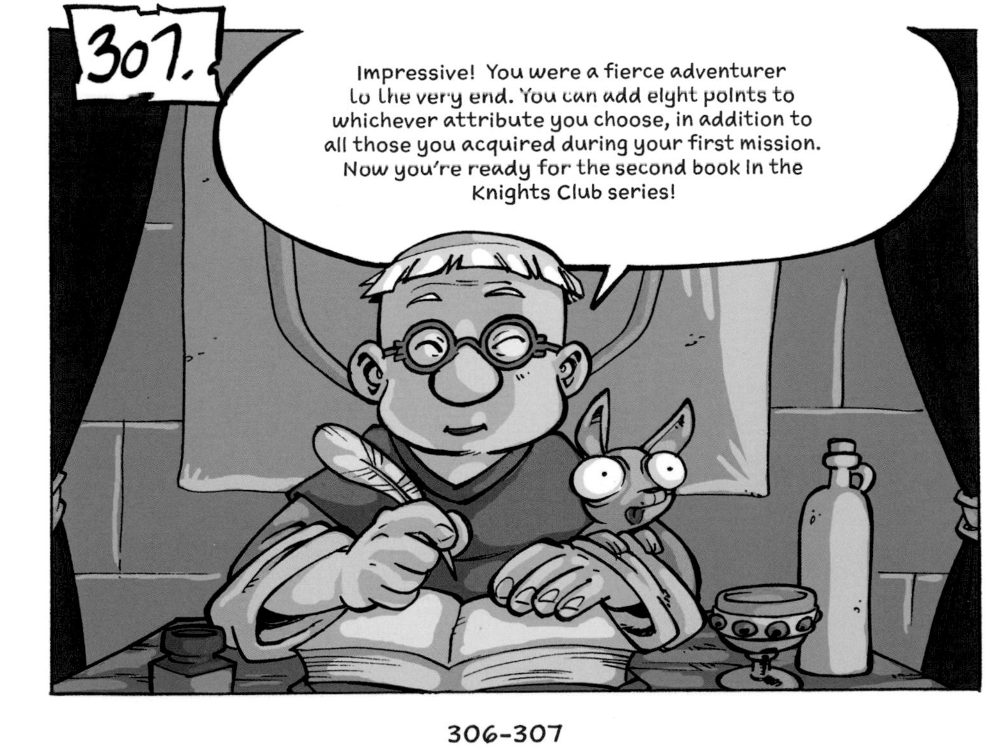
307.
Impressive! You were a fierce adventurer to the very end. You can add eight points to whichever attribute you choose, in addition to all those you acquired during your first mission. Now you're ready for the second book in the Knights Club series!

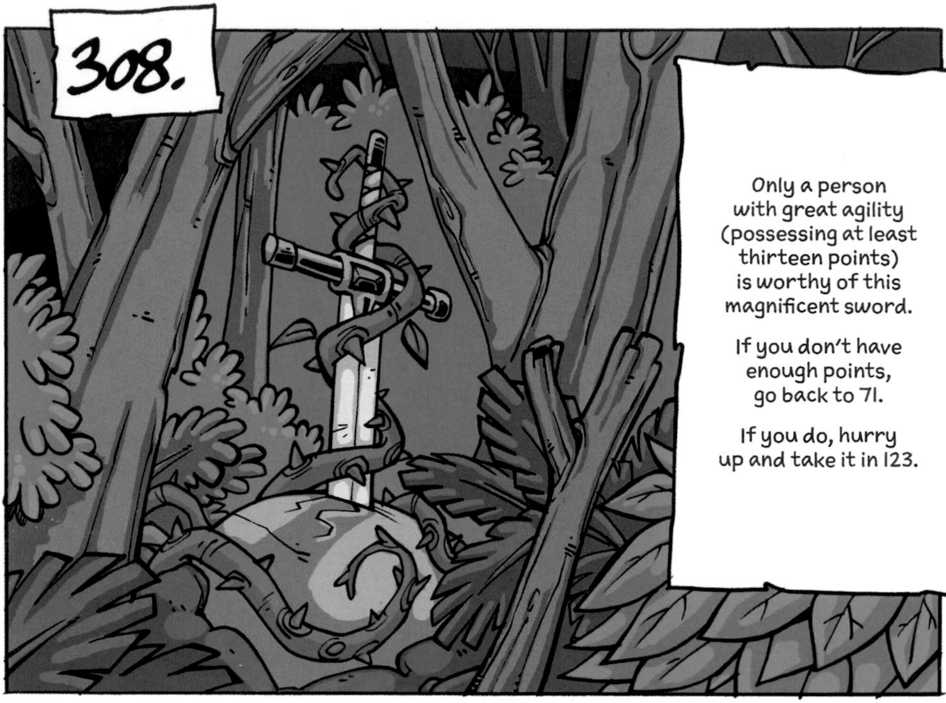
308.
Only a person with great agility (possessing at least thirteen points) is worthy of this magnificent sword.
If you don't have enough points, go back to 71.
If you do, hurry up and take it in 123.

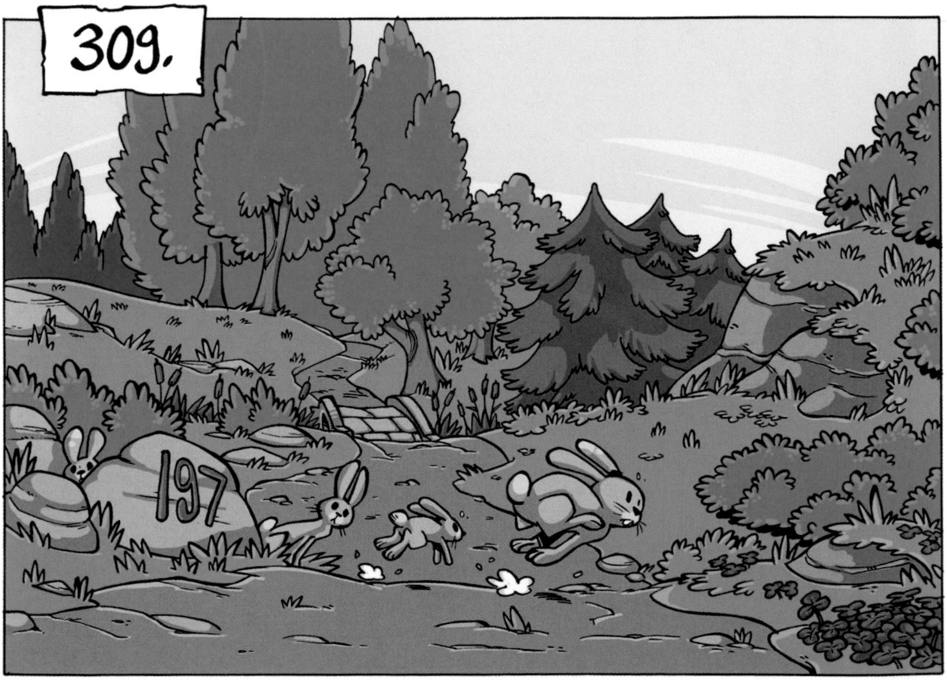
309.
197

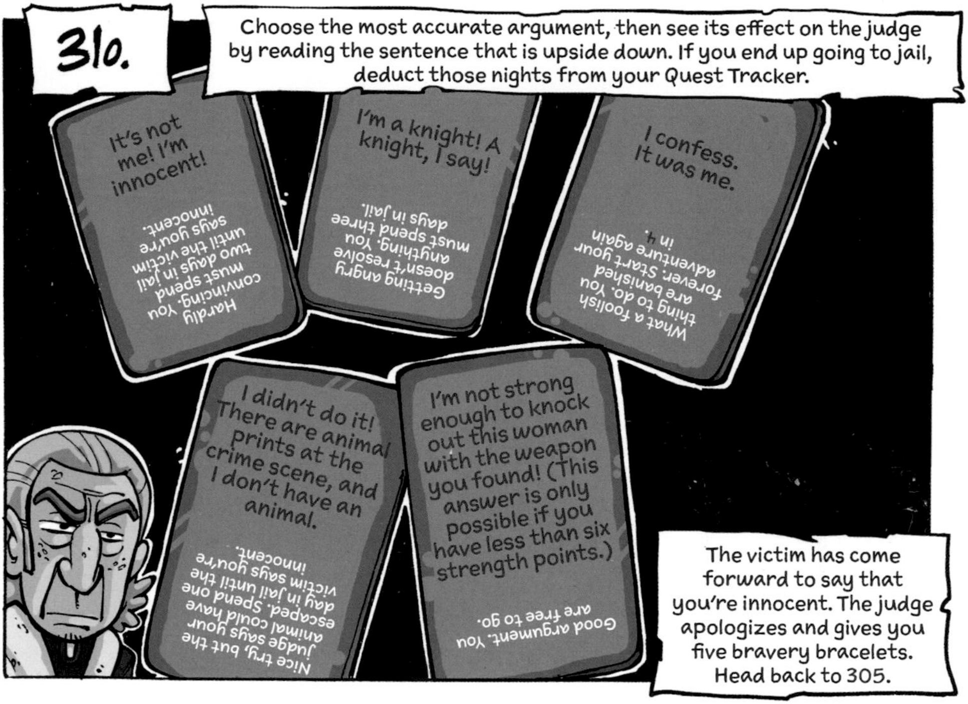
310.
Choose the most accurate argument, then see its effect on the judge by reading the sentence that is upside down. If you end up going to jail, deduct those nights from your Quest Tracker.
It's not me! I'm innocent!
Hardly convincing. You must spend two days in jail until the victim says you're innocent.
I'm a knight! A knight, I say!
Getting angry doesn't resolve anything. You must spend three days in jail.
I confess. It was me.
What a foolish thing to do. You are banished forever. Start your adventure again in 4.
I didn't do it! There are animal prints at the crime scene, and I don't have an animal.
Nice try, but the judge says your animal could have escaped. Spend one day in jail until the victim says you're innocent.
I'm not strong enough to knock out this woman with the weapon you found! (This answer is only possible if you have less than six strength points.)
Good argument. You are free to go.
The victim has come forward to say that you're innocent. The judge apologizes and gives you five bravery bracelets. Head back to 305.

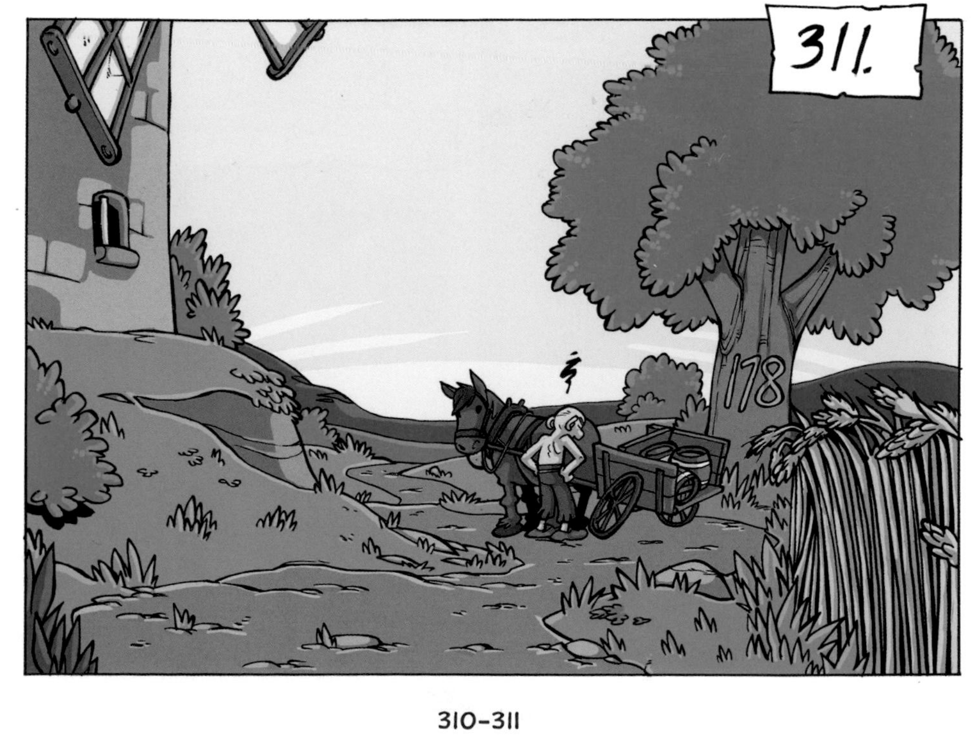
311.
178

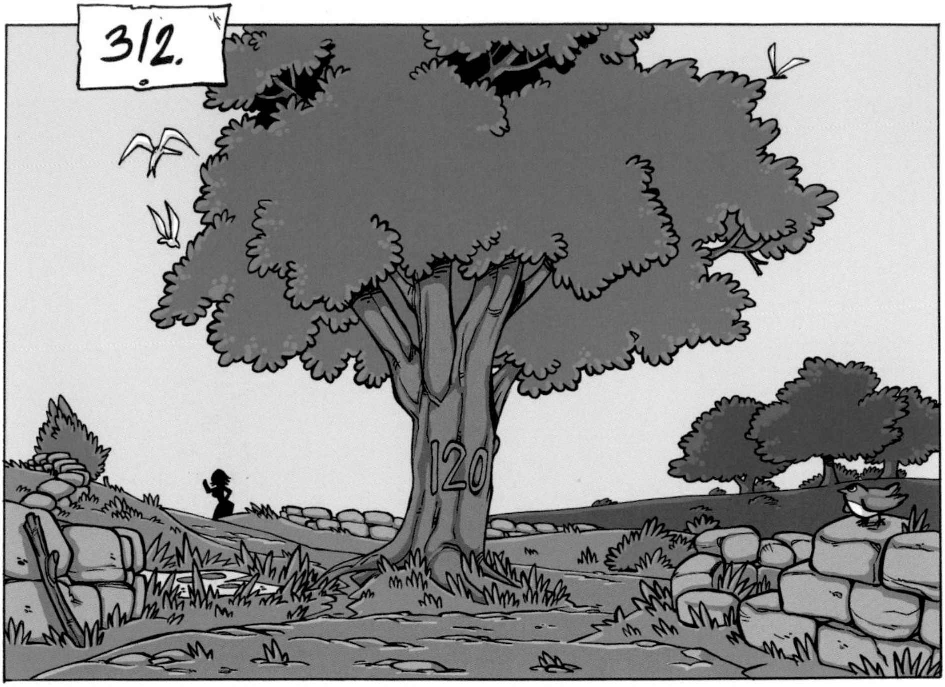
312.
120

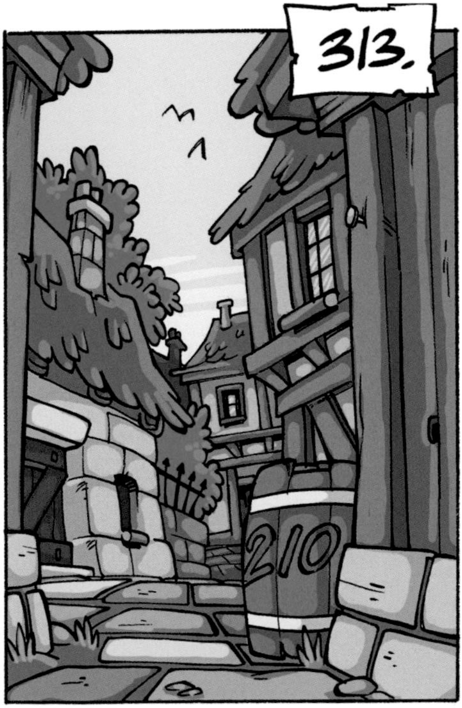
313.
210

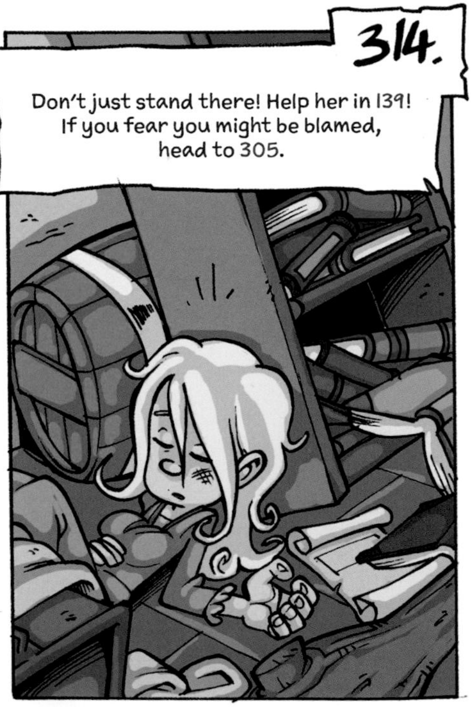
314.
Don't just stand there! Help her in 139!
If you fear you might be blamed,
head to 305.

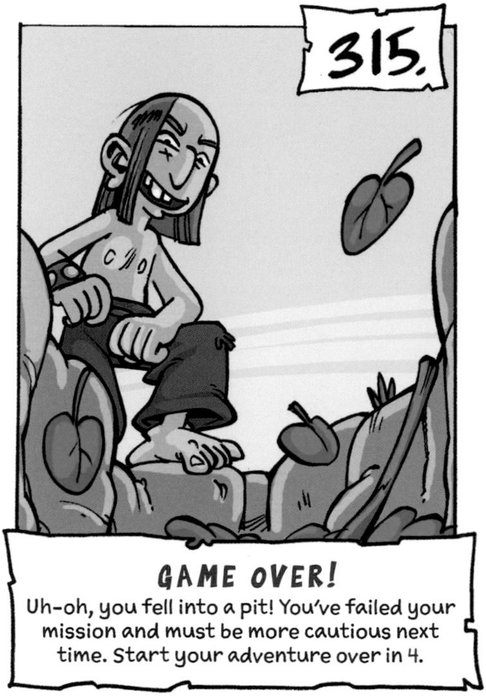
315.
GAME OVER!
Uh-oh, you fell into a pit! You've failed your mission and must be more cautious next time. Start your adventure over in 4.

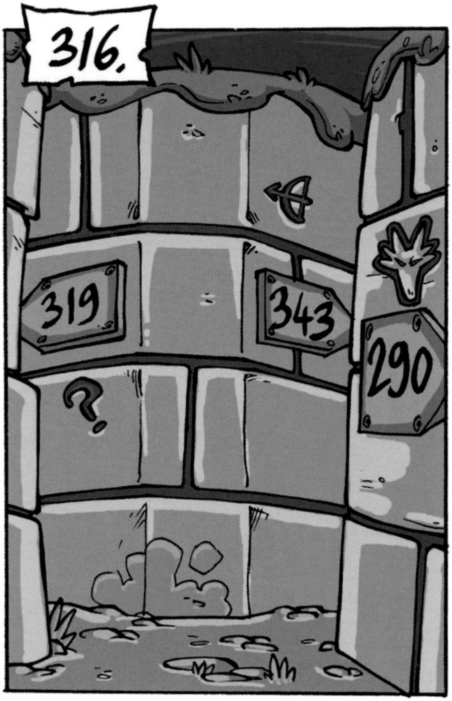
316.
319
343
290
?

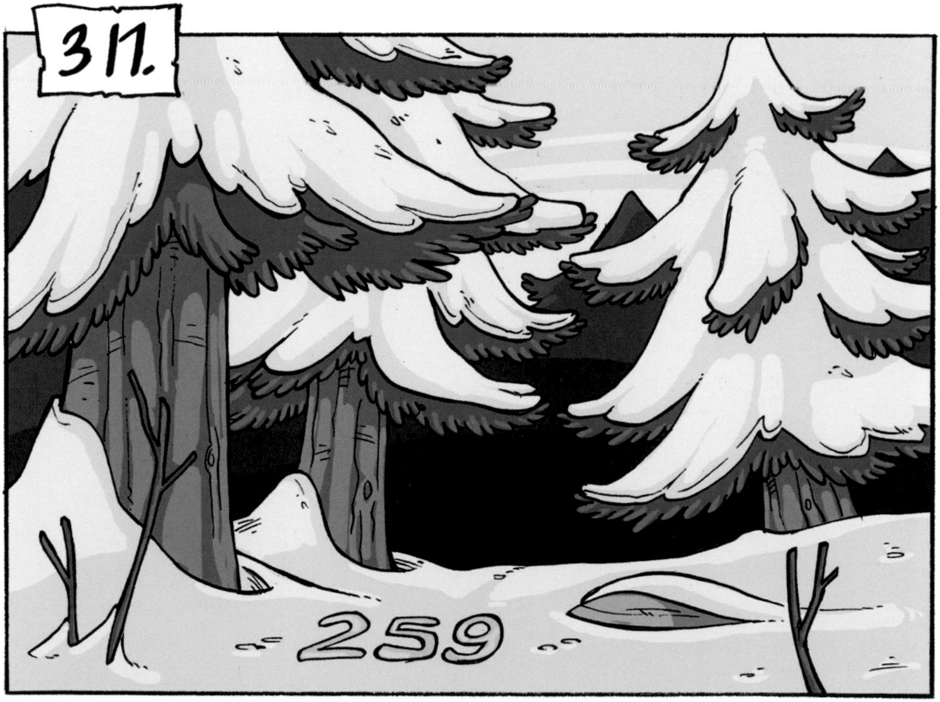
317.
259

318.

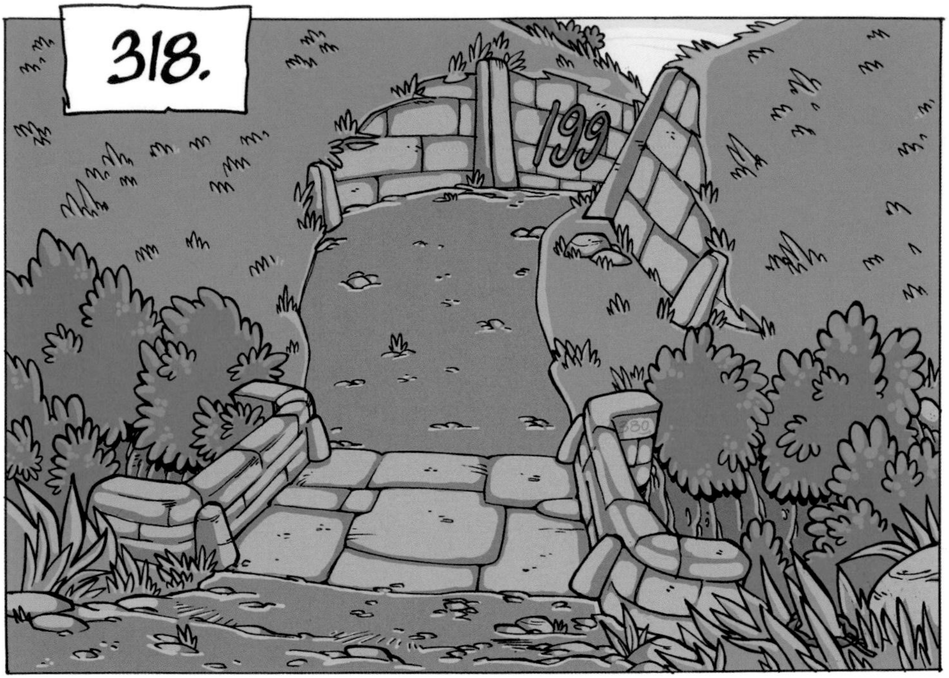
199
380

319.

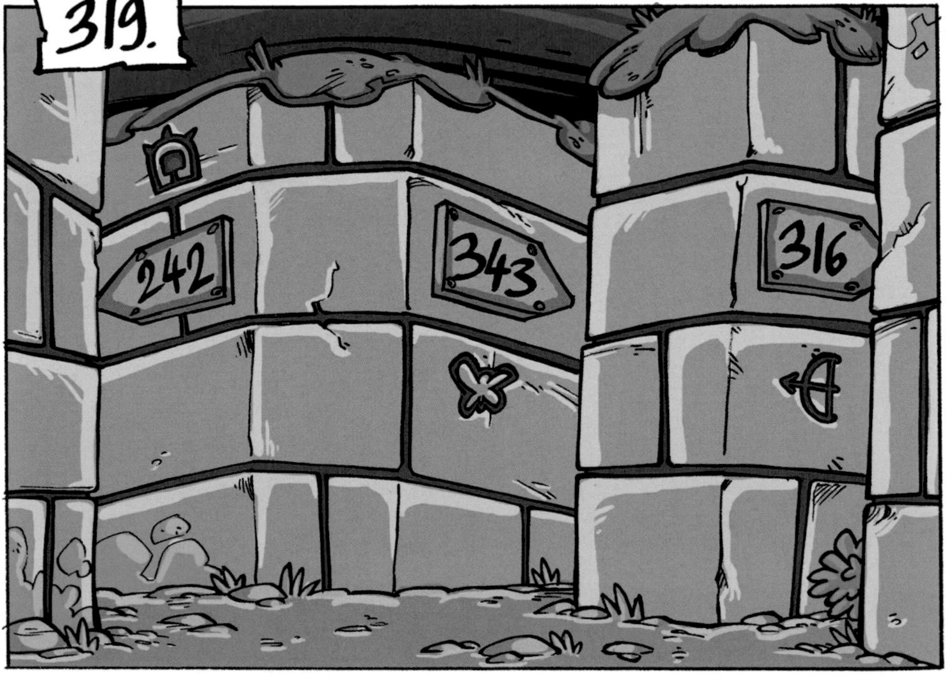
242
343
316

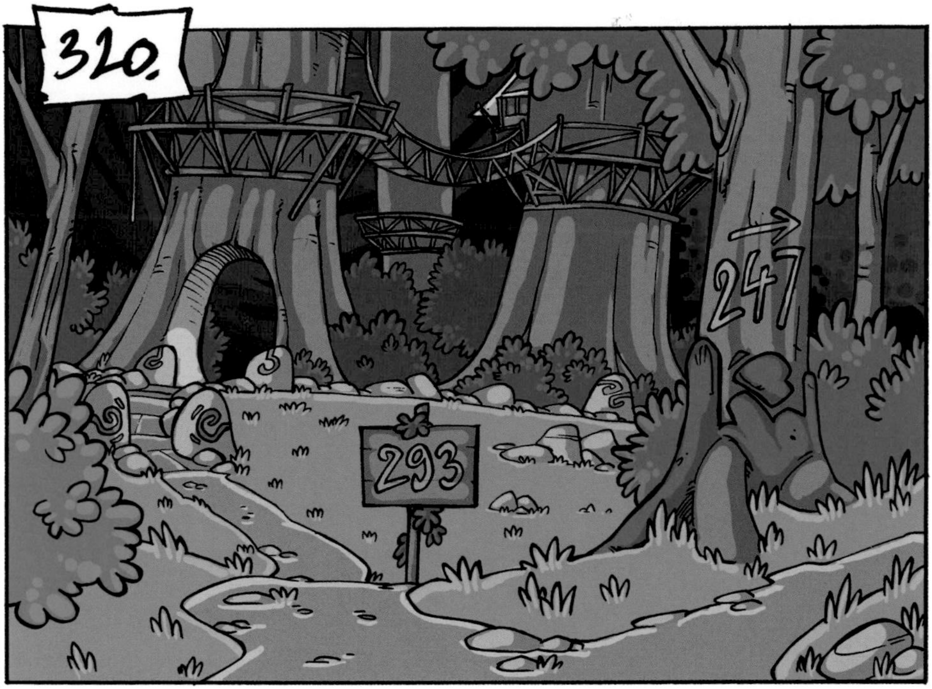
320.
247
293

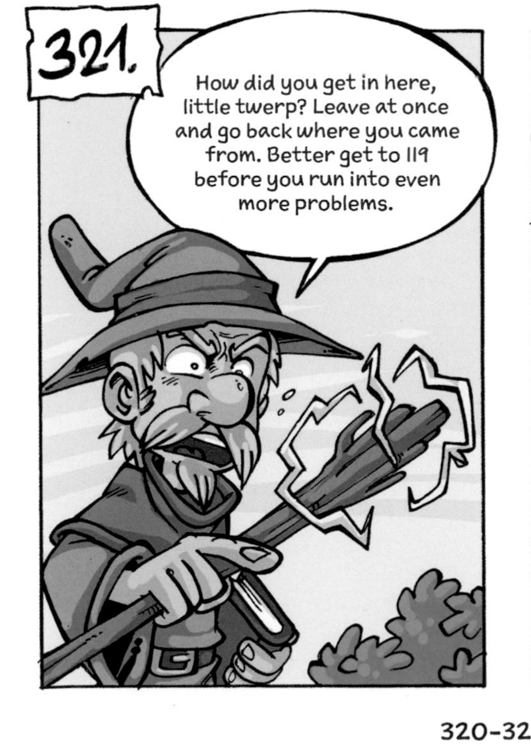
321.
How did you get in here, little twerp? Leave at once and go back where you came from. Better get to 119 before you run into even more problems.

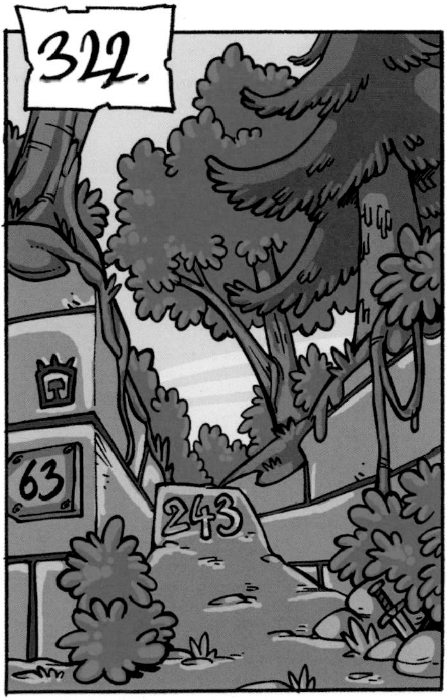
322.
63
243

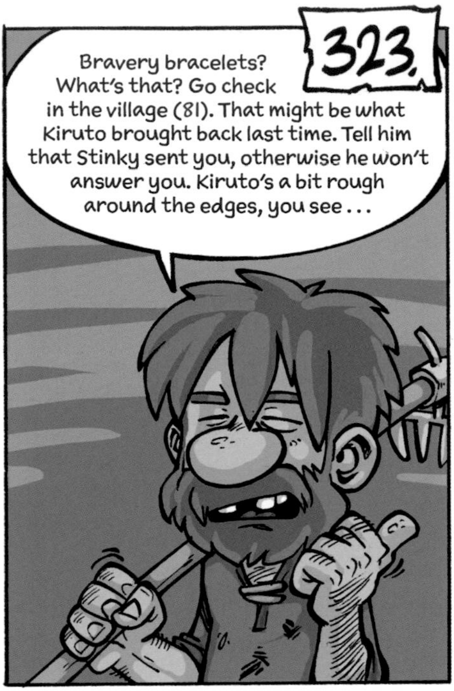
323.
Bravery bracelets? What's that? Go check in the village (81). That might be what Kiruto brought back last time. Tell him that Stinky sent you, otherwise he won't answer you. Kiruto's a bit rough around the edges, you see . . .

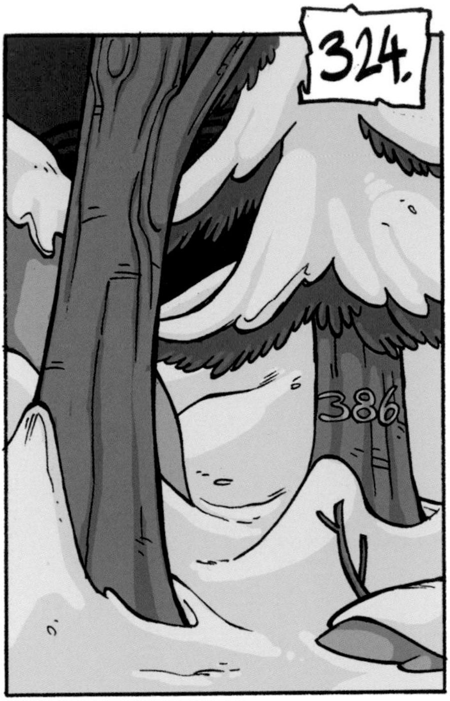
324.
386

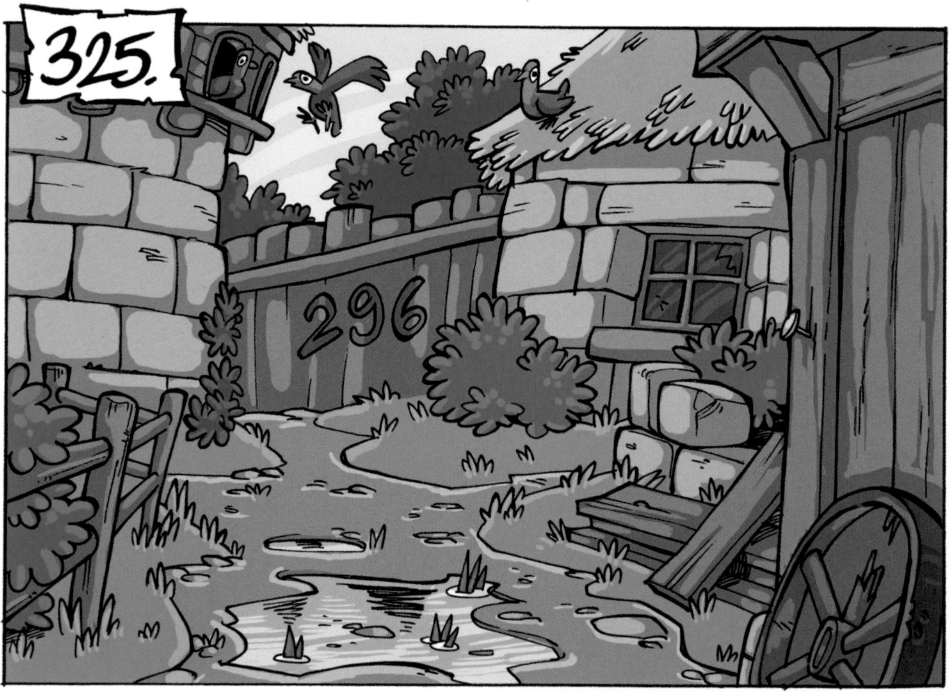
325.
296

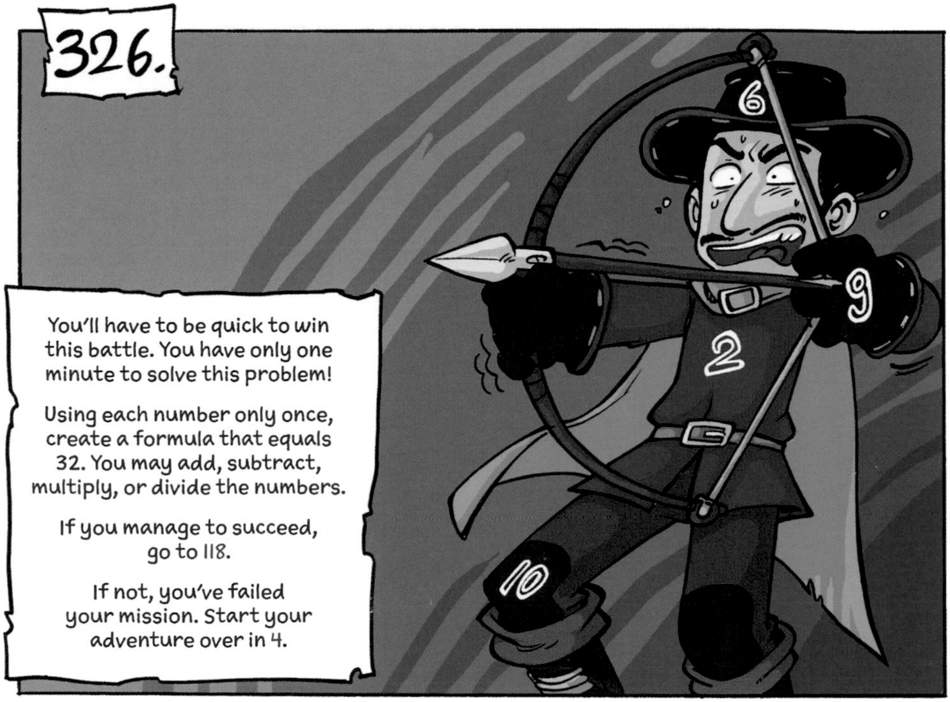
326.
6
9
2
10
You'll have to be quick to win this battle. You have only one minute to solve this problem!
Using each number only once, create a formula that equals 32. You may add, subtract, multiply, or divide the numbers.
If you manage to succeed, go to 118.
If not, you've failed your mission. Start your adventure over in 4.

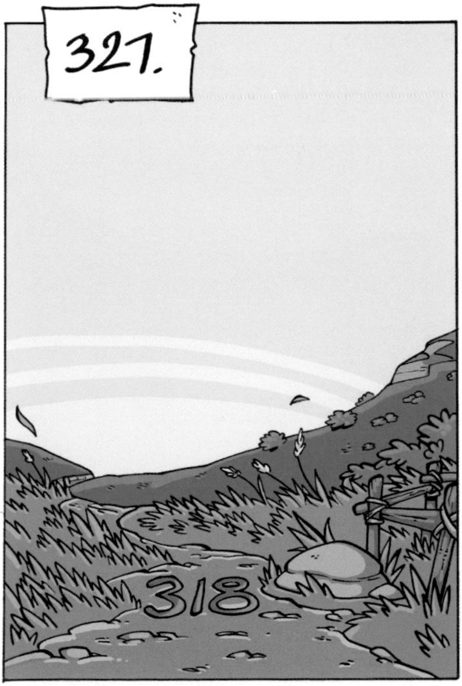
327.
318

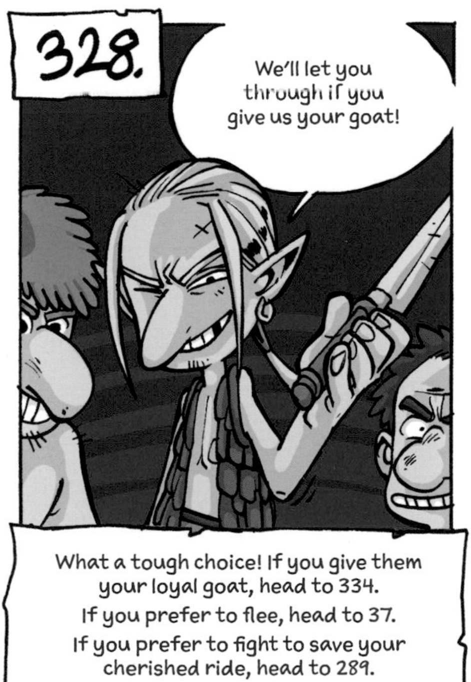
328.
We'll let you through if you give us your goat!
What a tough choice! If you give them your loyal goat, head to 334.
If you prefer to flee, head to 37.
If you prefer to fight to save your cherished ride, head to 289.

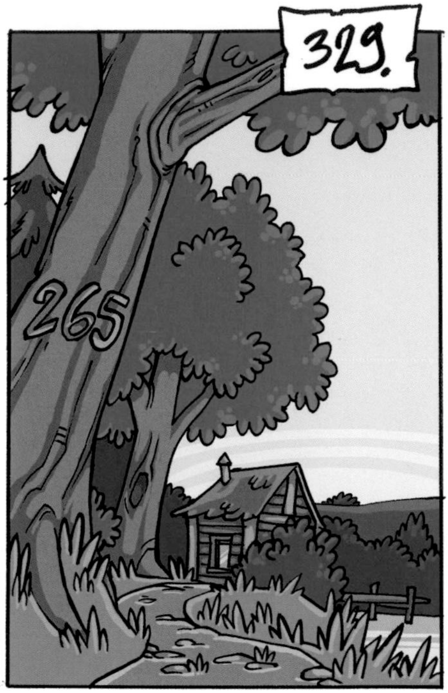
329.
265

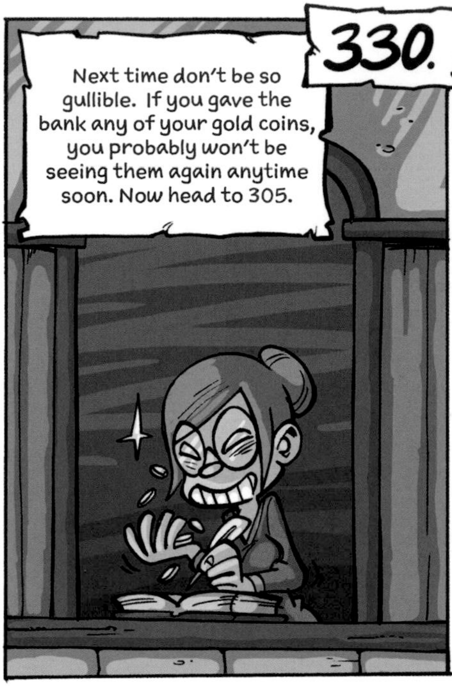
330.
Next time don't be so gullible. If you gave the bank any of your gold coins, you probably won't be seeing them again anytime soon. Now head to 305.

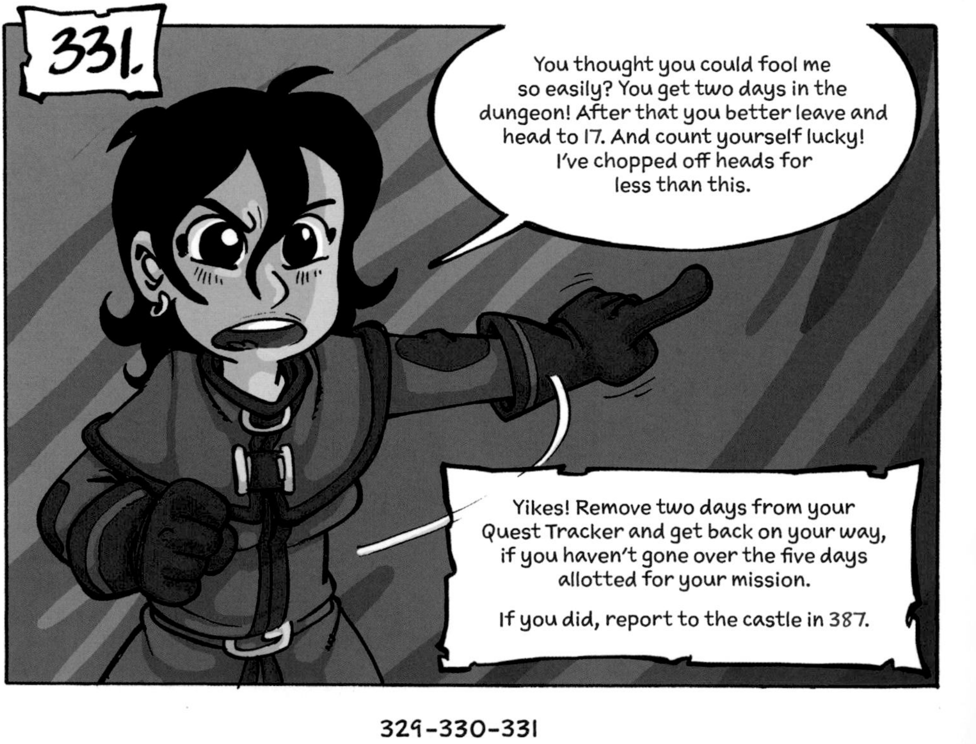
331.
You thought you could fool me so easily? You get two days in the dungeon! After that you better leave and head to 17. And count yourself lucky! I've chopped off heads for less than this.
Yikes! Remove two days from your Quest Tracker and get back on your way, if you haven't gone over the five days allotted for your mission.
If you did, report to the castle in 387.

332.

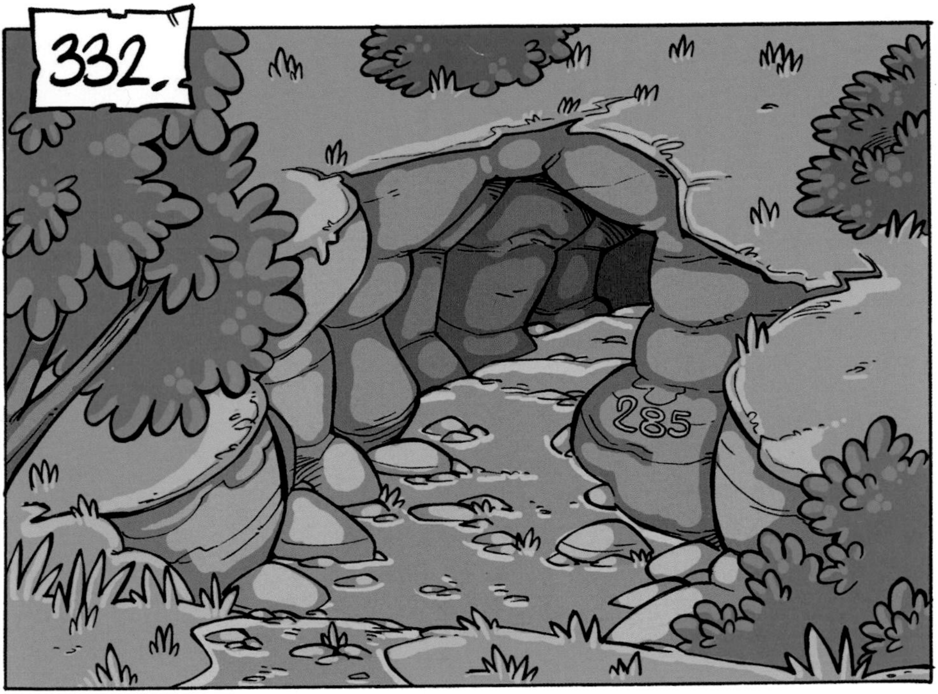
285

333.

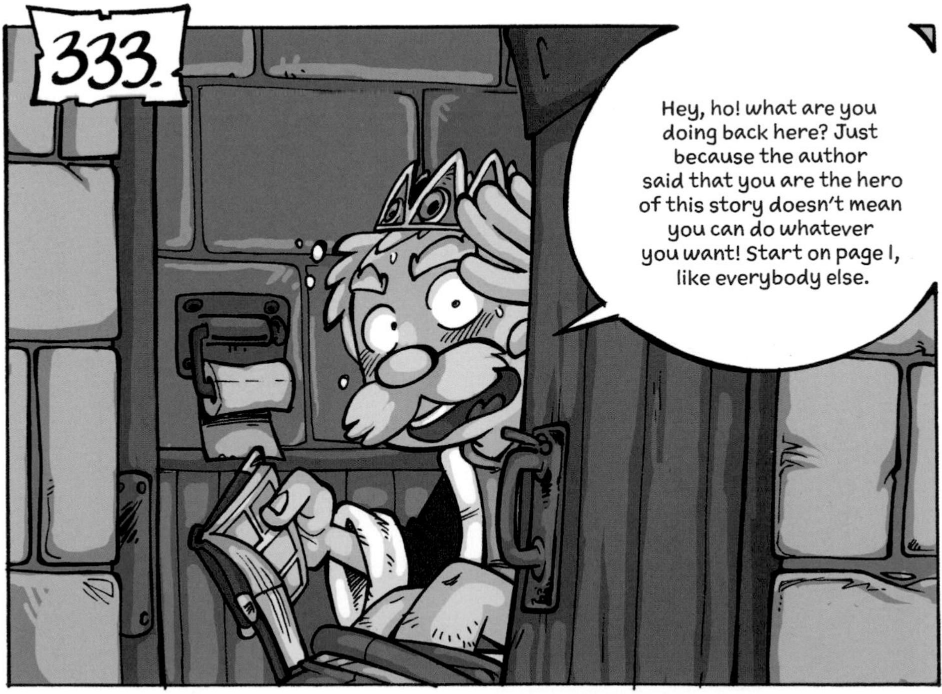
Hey, ho! what are you doing back here? Just because the author said that you are the hero of this story doesn't mean you can do whatever you want! Start on page 1, like everybody else.

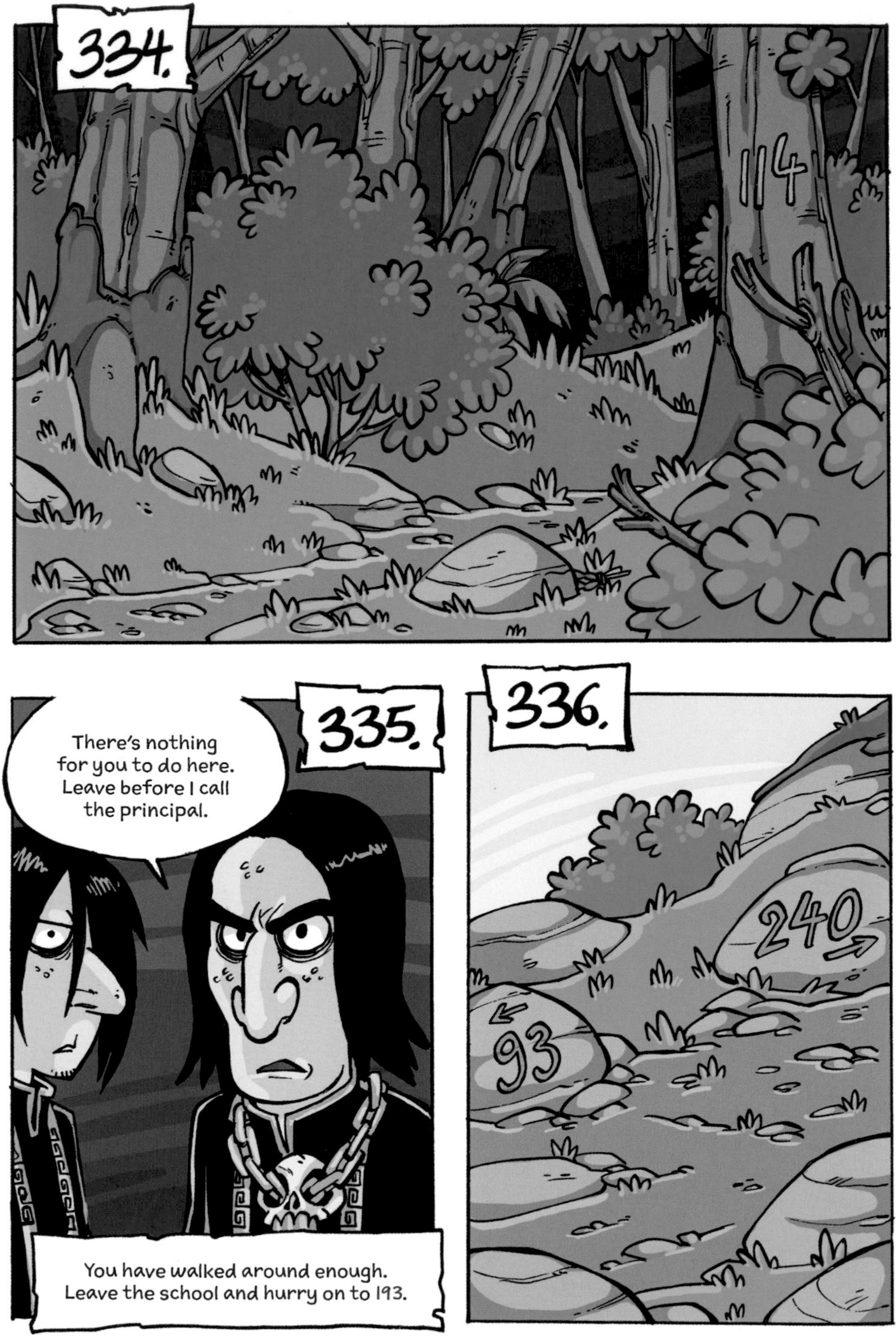
334.
114
335.
There's nothing for you to do here. Leave before I call the principal.
You have walked around enough. Leave the school and hurry on to 193.
336.
240
93

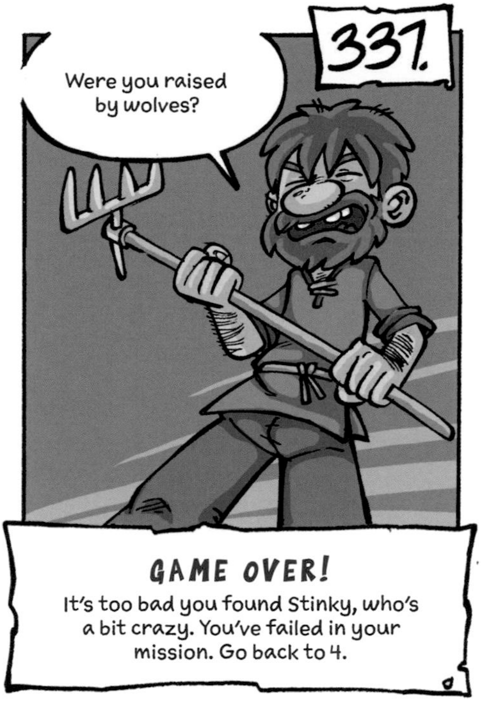
337.
Were you raised by wolves?
GAME OVER!
It's too bad you found Stinky, who's a bit crazy. You've failed in your mission. Go back to 4.

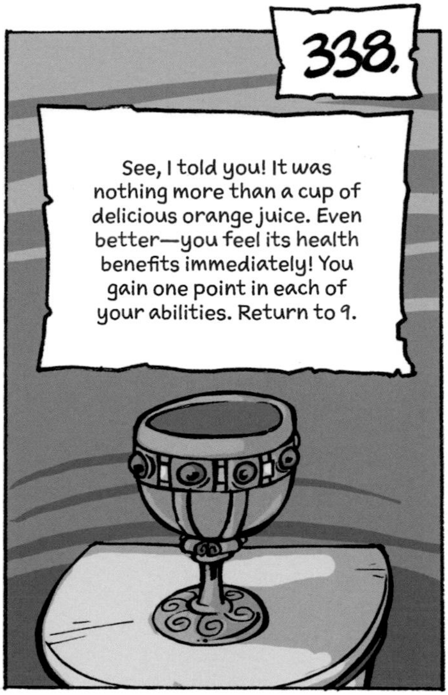
338.
See, I told you! It was nothing more than a cup of delicious orange juice. Even better—you feel its health benefits immediately! You gain one point in each of your abilities. Return to 9.

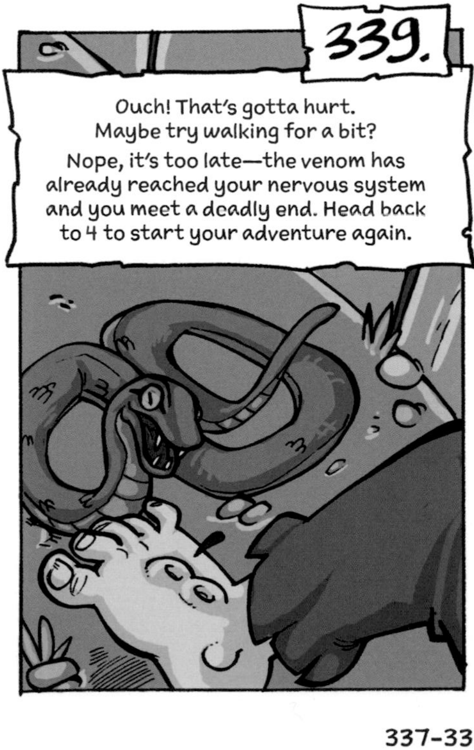
339.
Ouch! That's gotta hurt. Maybe try walking for a bit?
Nope, it's too late—the venom has already reached your nervous system and you meet a deadly end. Head back to 4 to start your adventure again.

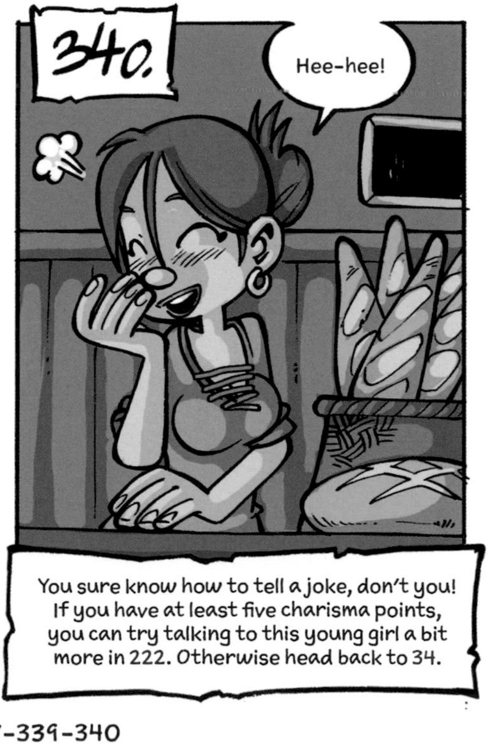
340.
Hee-hee!
You sure know how to tell a joke, don't you! If you have at least five charisma points, you can try talking to this young girl a bit more in 222. Otherwise head back to 34.

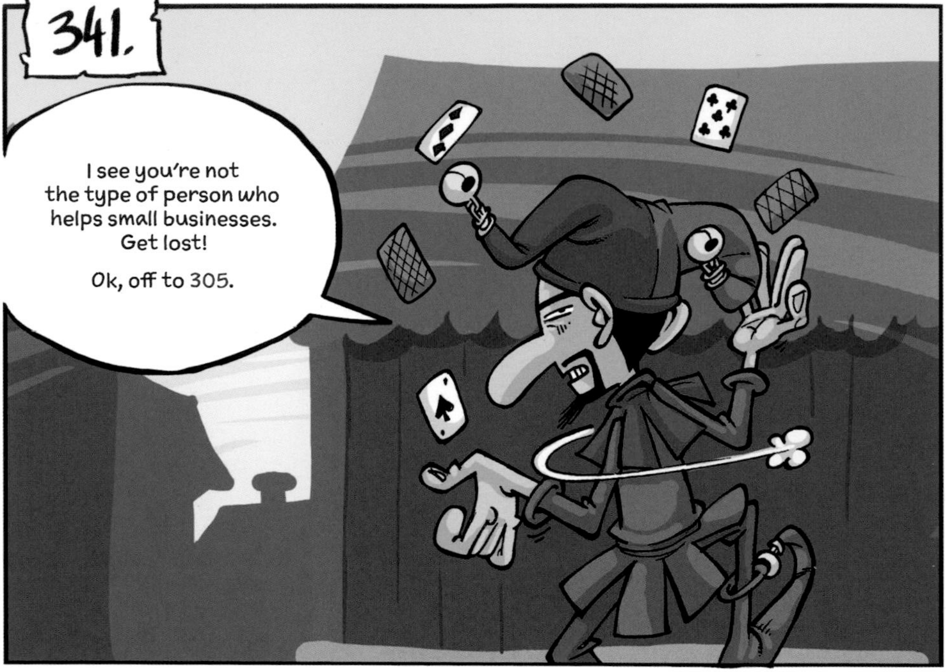
341.
I see you're not the type of person who helps small businesses. Get lost!
Ok, off to 305.

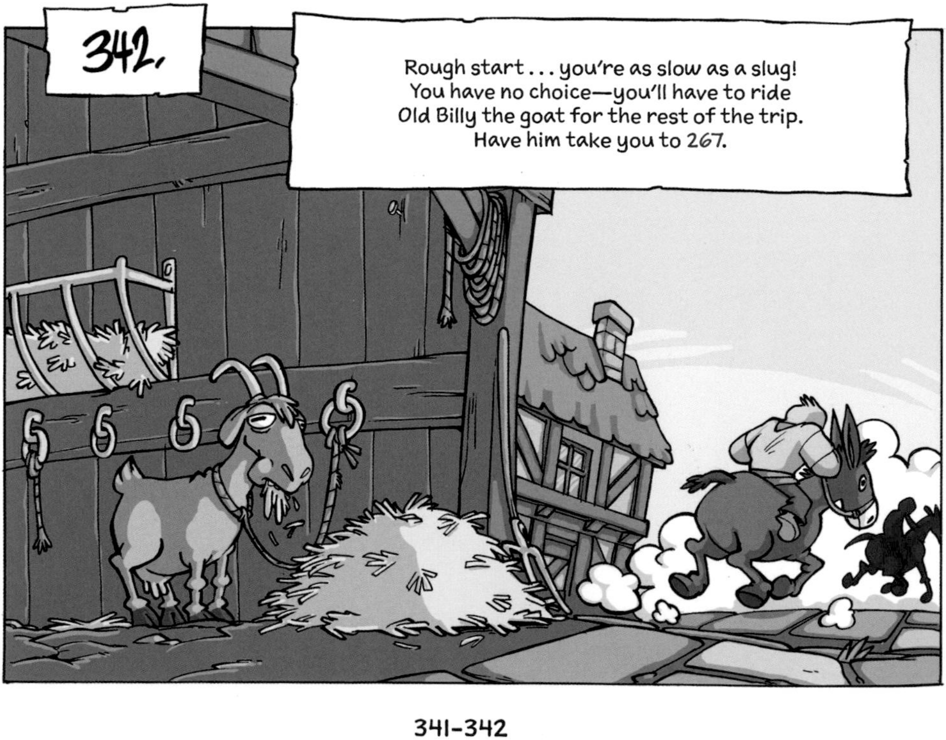
342.
Rough start . . . you're as slow as a slug! You have no choice—you'll have to ride Old Billy the goat for the rest of the trip. Have him take you to 267.

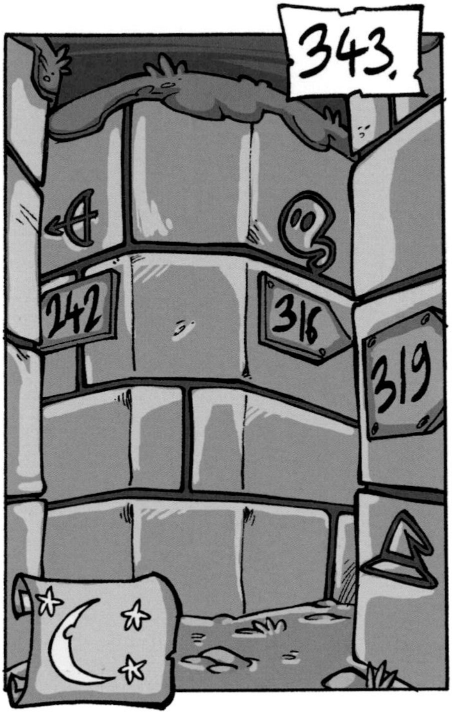
343.
242
316
319

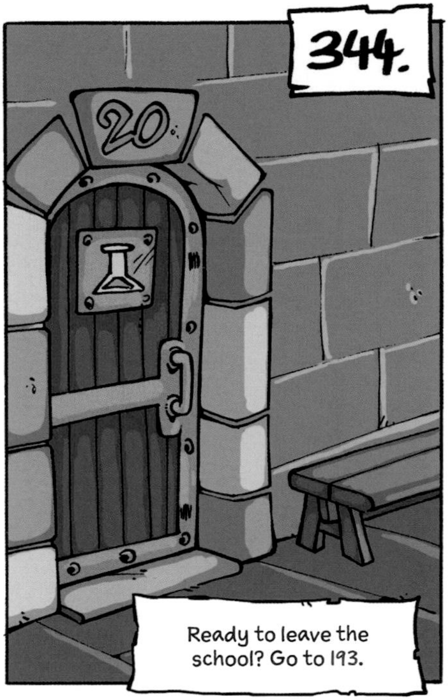
344.
20
Ready to leave the school? Go to 193.

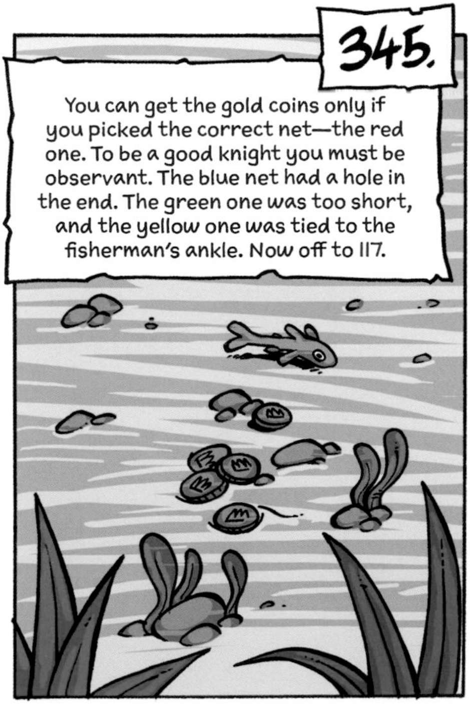
345.
You can get the gold coins only if you picked the correct net—the red one. To be a good knight you must be observant. The blue net had a hole in the end. The green one was too short, and the yellow one was tied to the fisherman's ankle. Now off to 117.

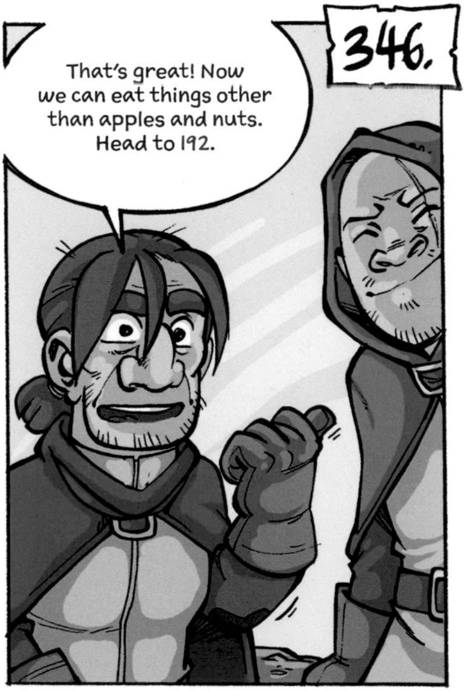
346.
That's great! Now we can eat things other than apples and nuts. Head to 192.

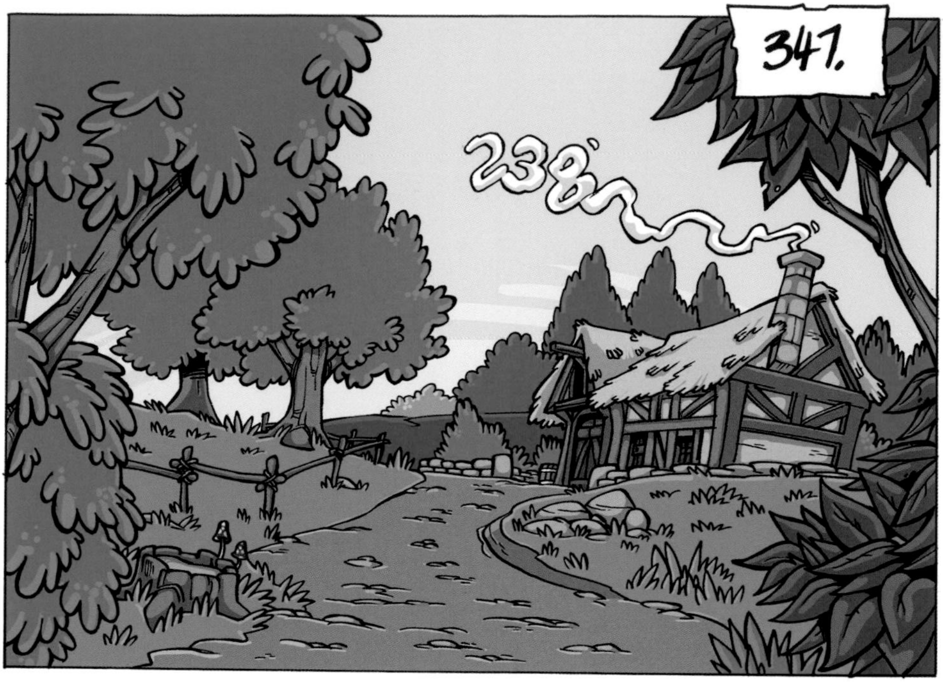
347.
238

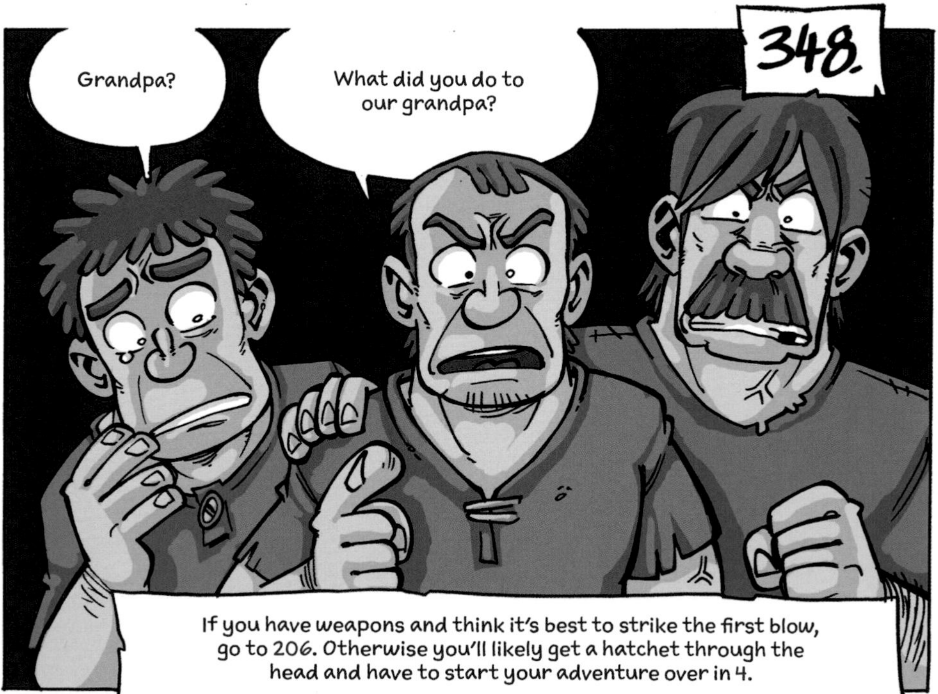
348.
Grandpa?
What did you do to our grandpa?
If you have weapons and think it's best to strike the first blow, go to 206. Otherwise you'll likely get a hatchet through the head and have to start your adventure over in 4.

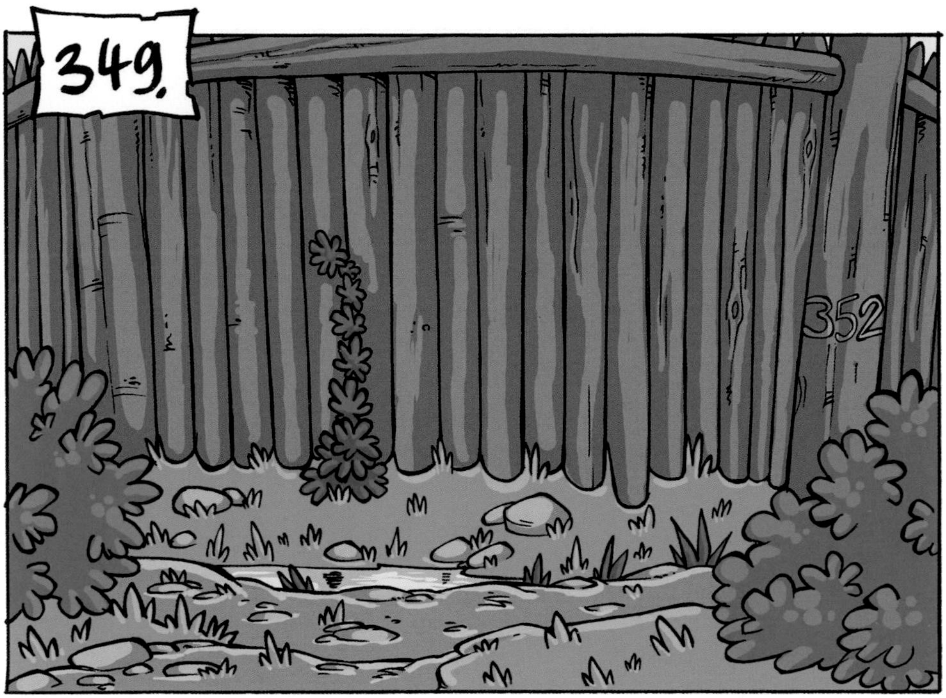
349.
352

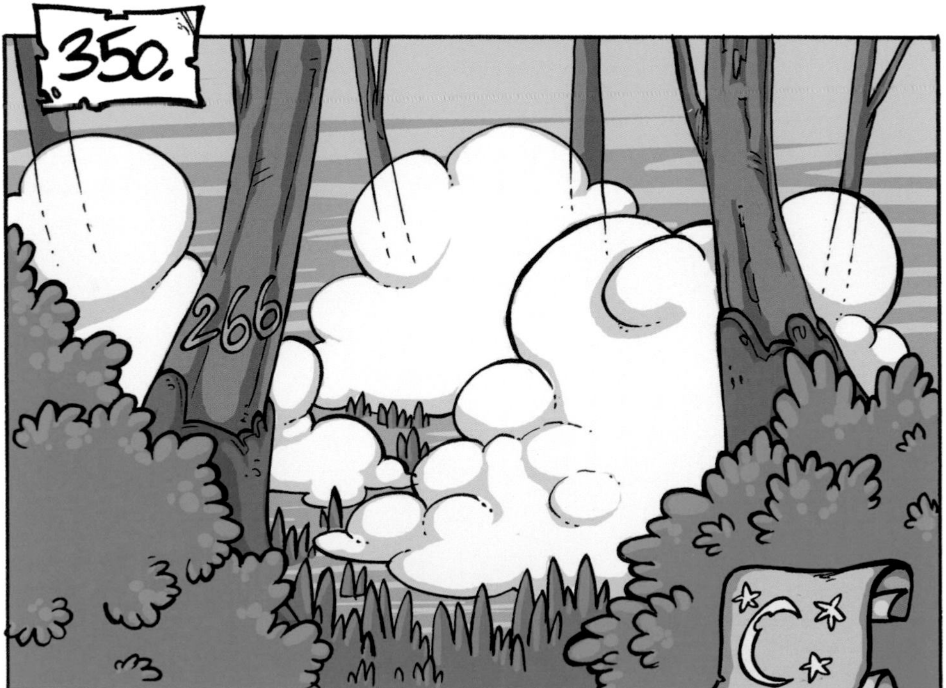
350.
266

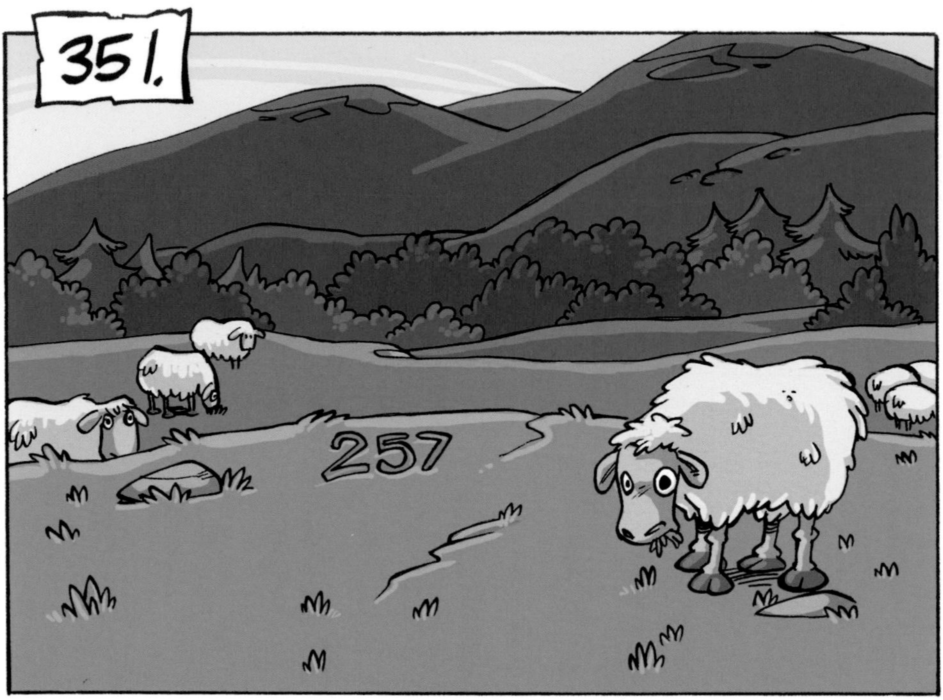
351.
257

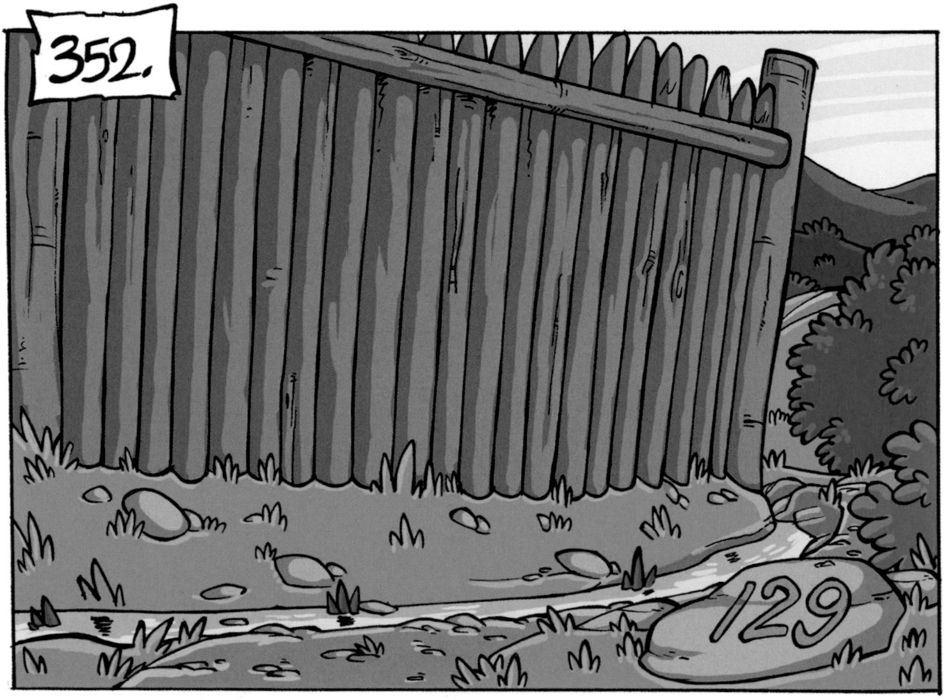
352.
129

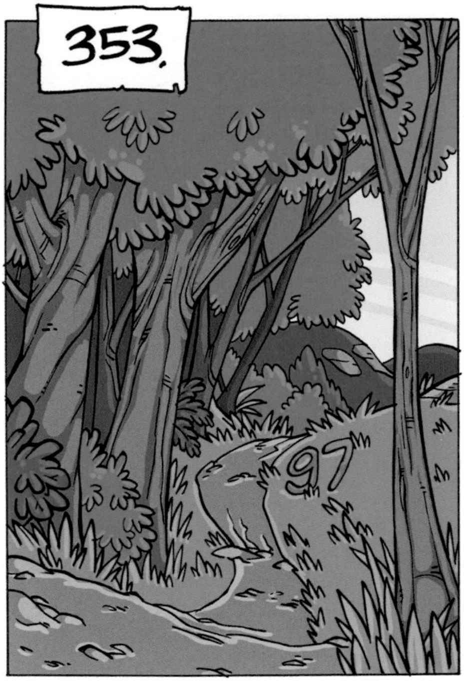
353.
97

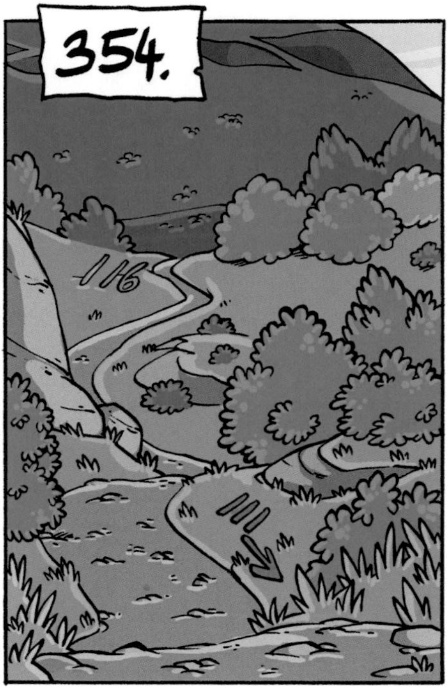
354.
116
111

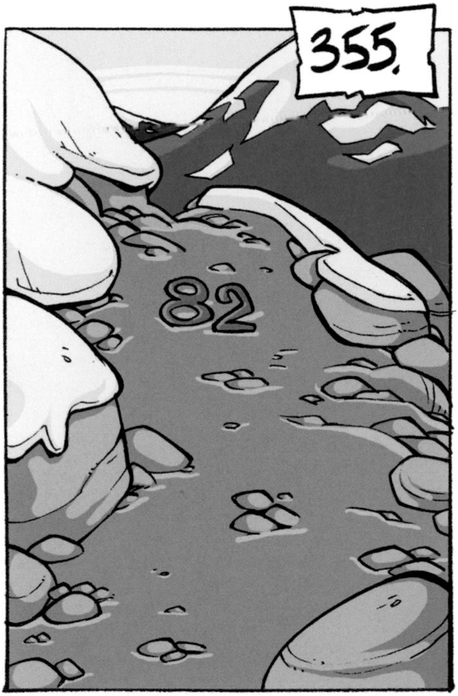
355.
82

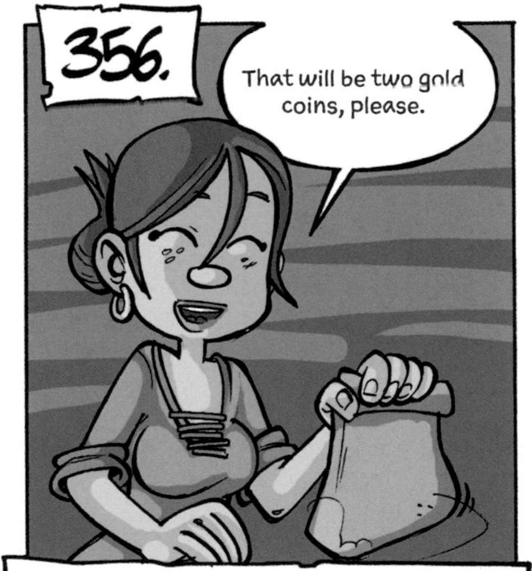
356.
That will be two gold coins, please.
Two gold coins?! Talk about inflation! Do you want to buy the croissants? Note that they will give you one extra permanent strength point. Decide what you want to do and then head to 121.

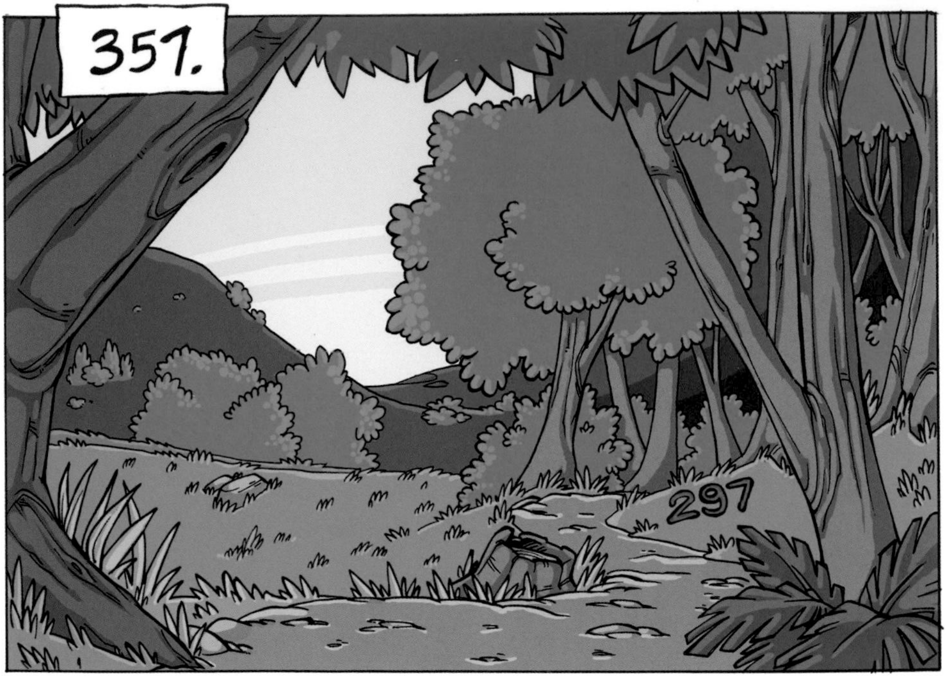
357.
297

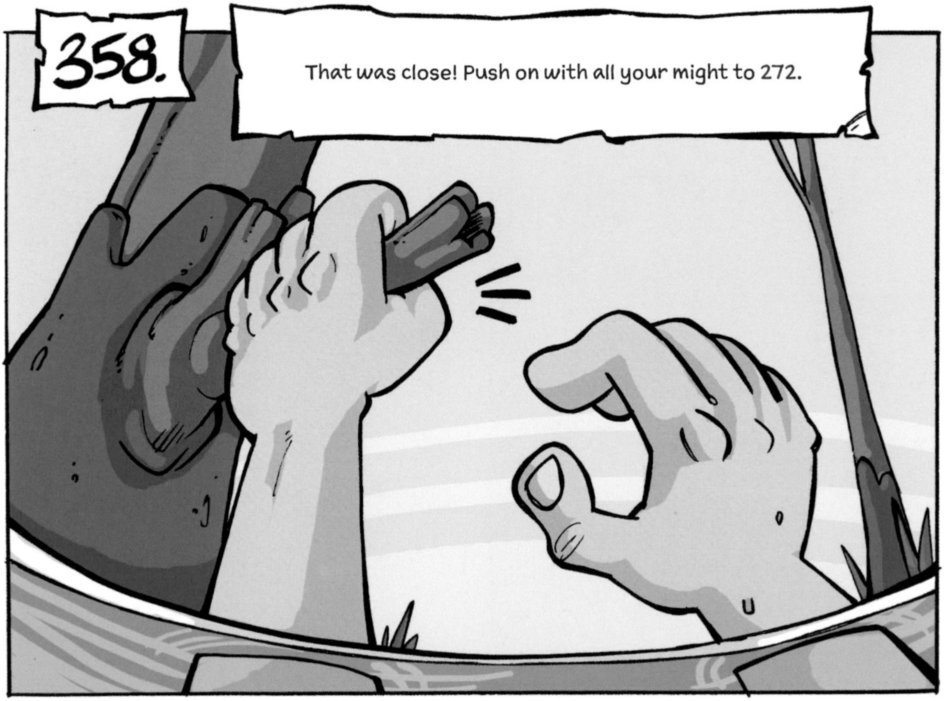
358.
That was close! Push on with all your might to 272.

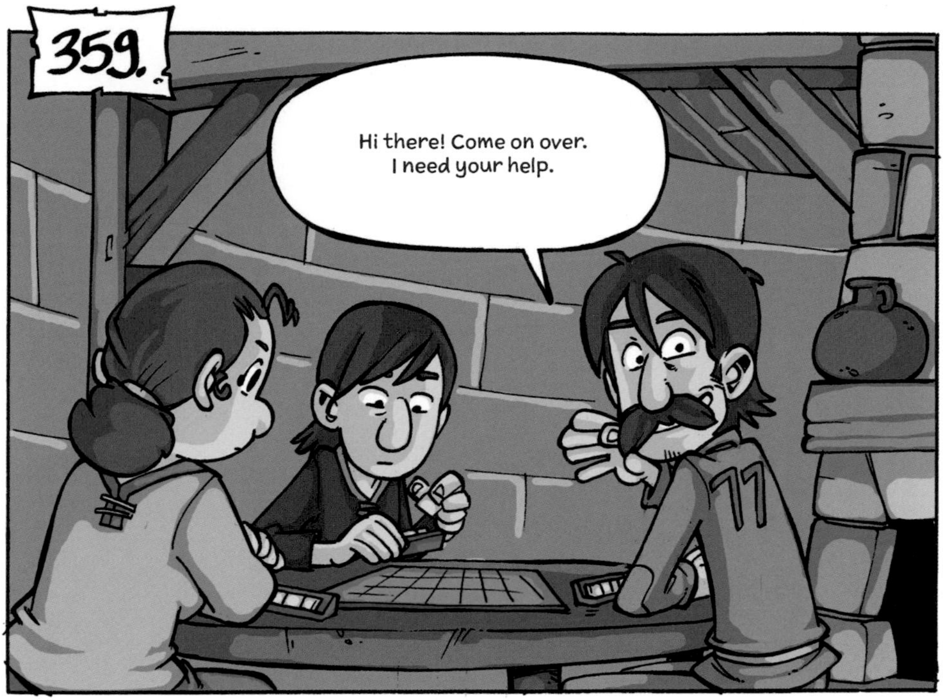
359.
Hi there! Come on over. I need your help.

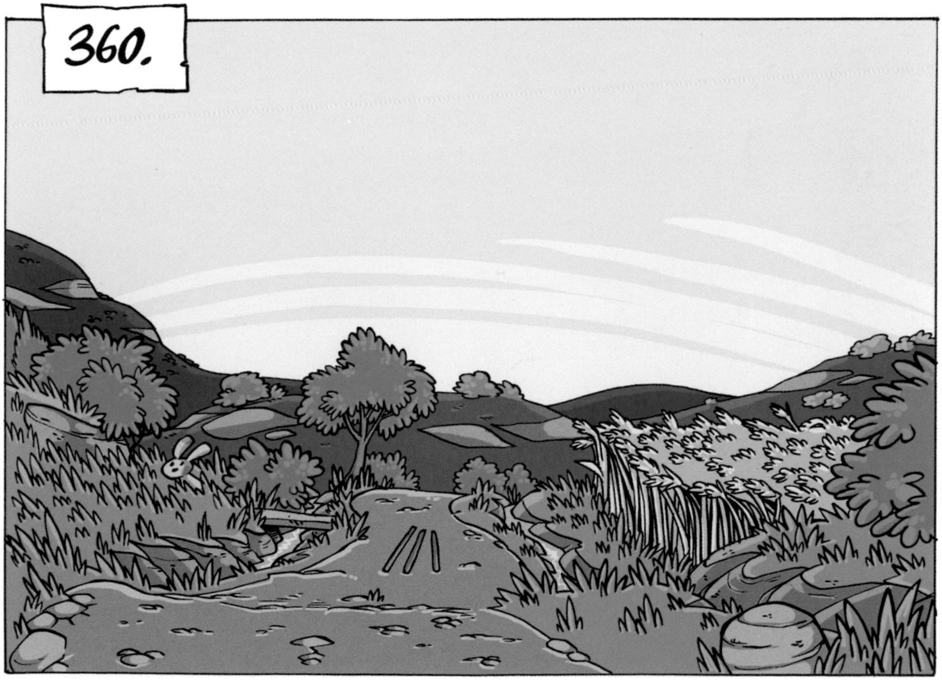
360.

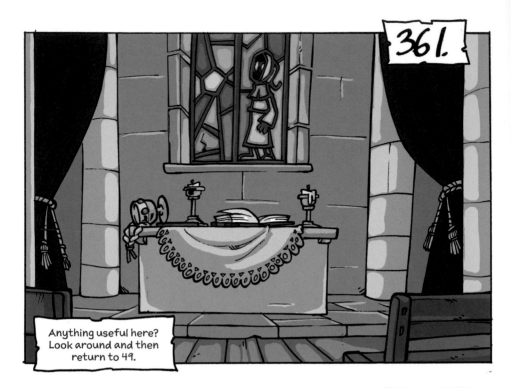

Anything useful here? Look around and then return to 49.

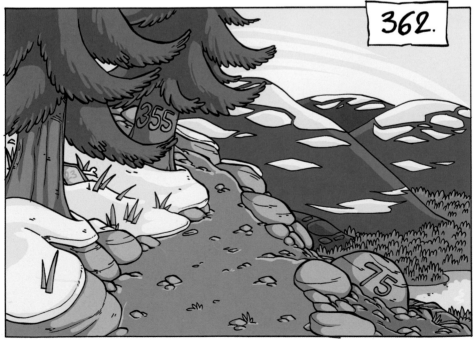

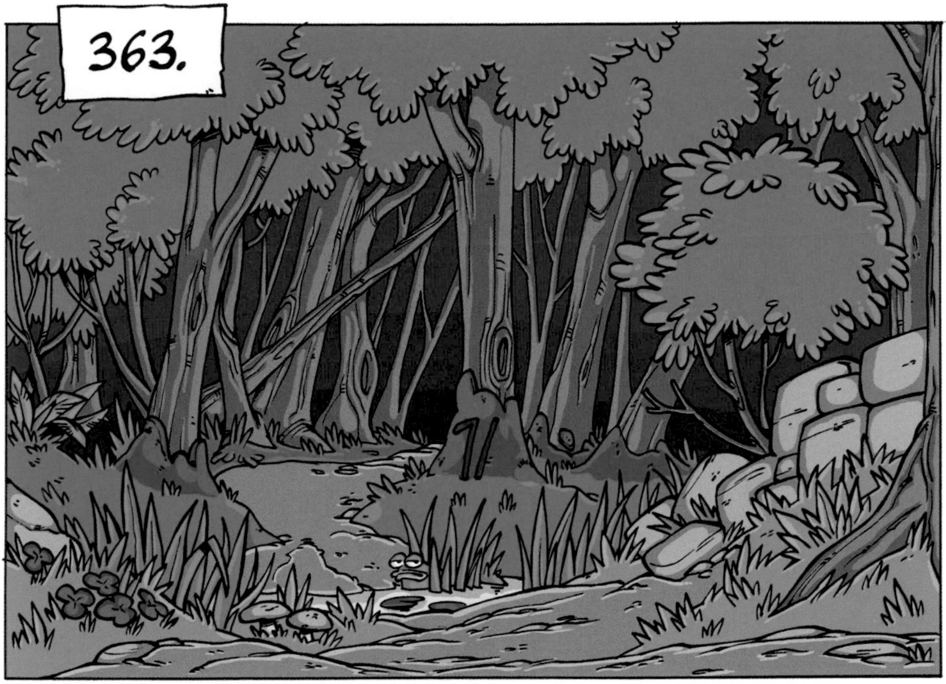
363.

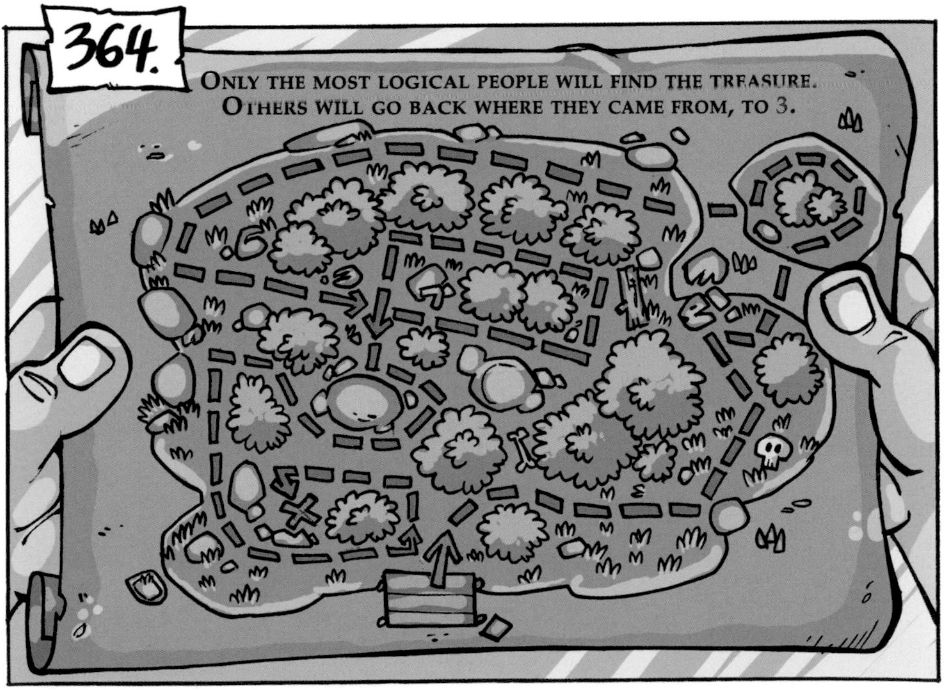
364.
ONLY THE MOST LOGICAL PEOPLE WILL FIND THE TREASURE.
OTHERS WILL GO BACK WHERE THEY CAME FROM, TO 3.

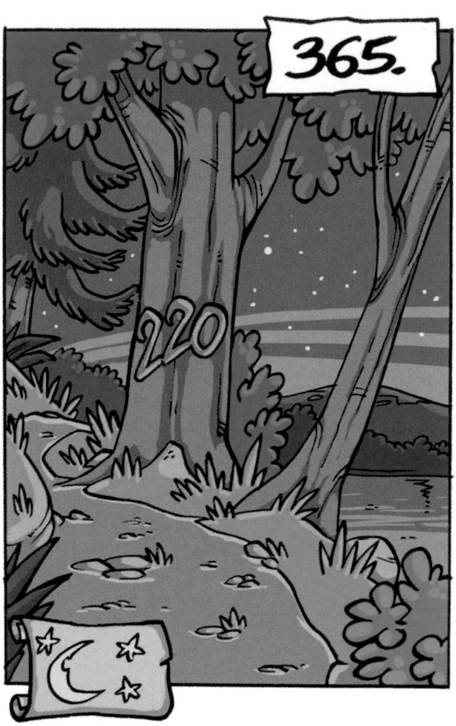
365.
220

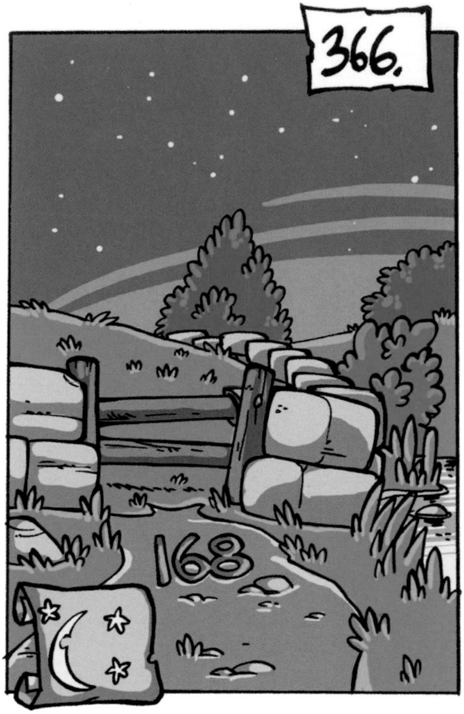
366.
168

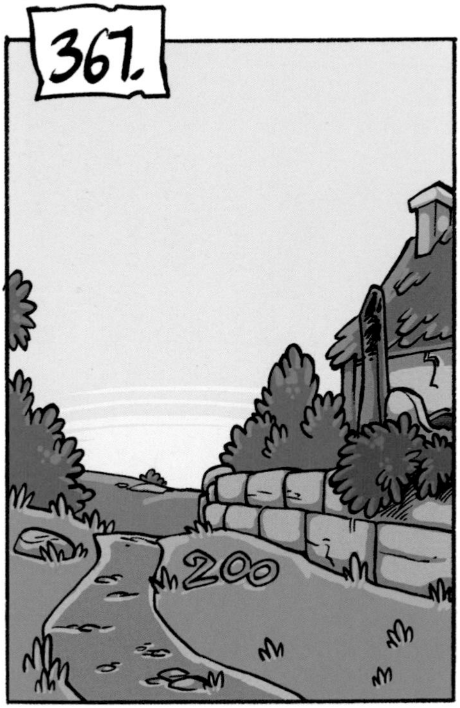
367.
200

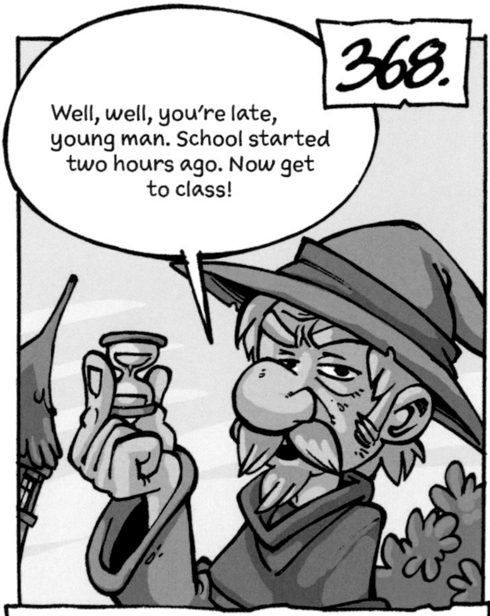
368.
Well, well, you're late, young man. School started two hours ago. Now get to class!
If you want to explain that you are not a magic school student, head to 321.
If you want to go to magic class for a while, head to 101.

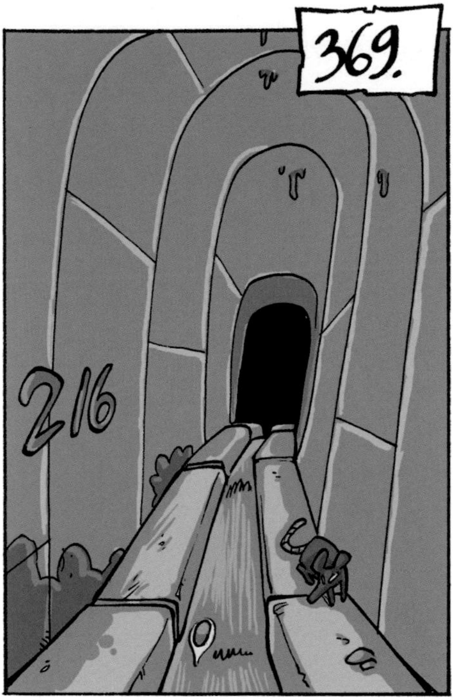
369.
216

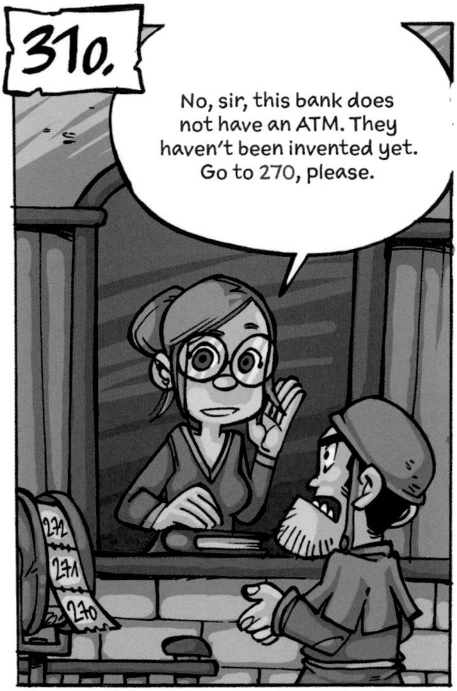
370.
No, sir, this bank does not have an ATM. They haven't been invented yet. Go to 270, please.

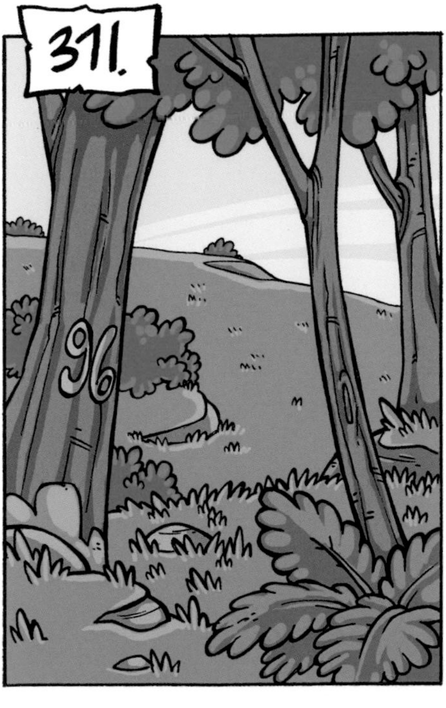
371.
96

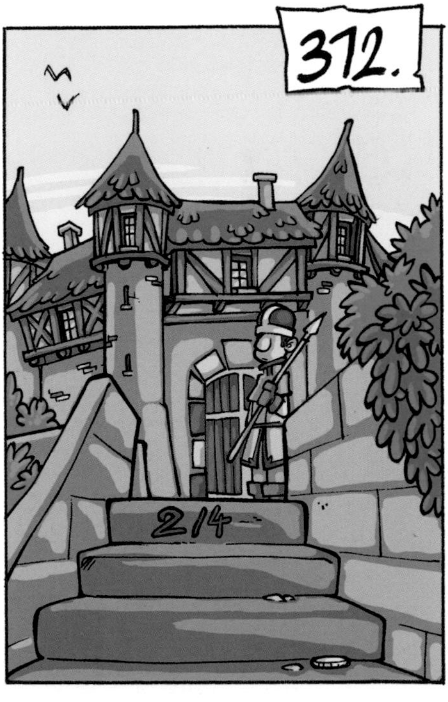
372.
214

373.

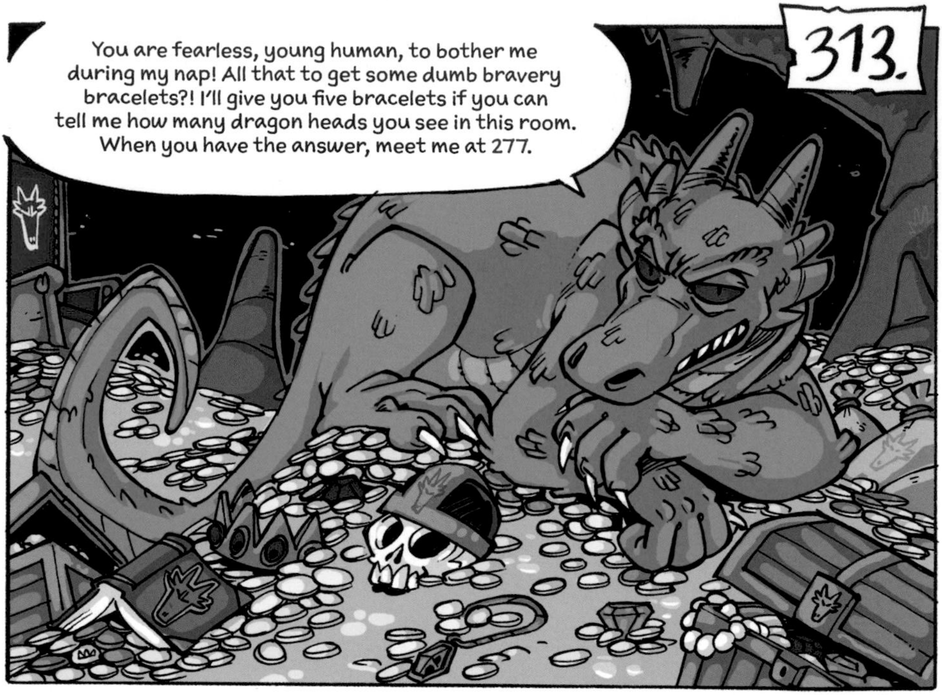
You are fearless, young human, to bother me during my nap! All that to get some dumb bravery bracelets?! I'll give you five bracelets if you can tell me how many dragon heads you see in this room. When you have the answer, meet me at 277.

374.

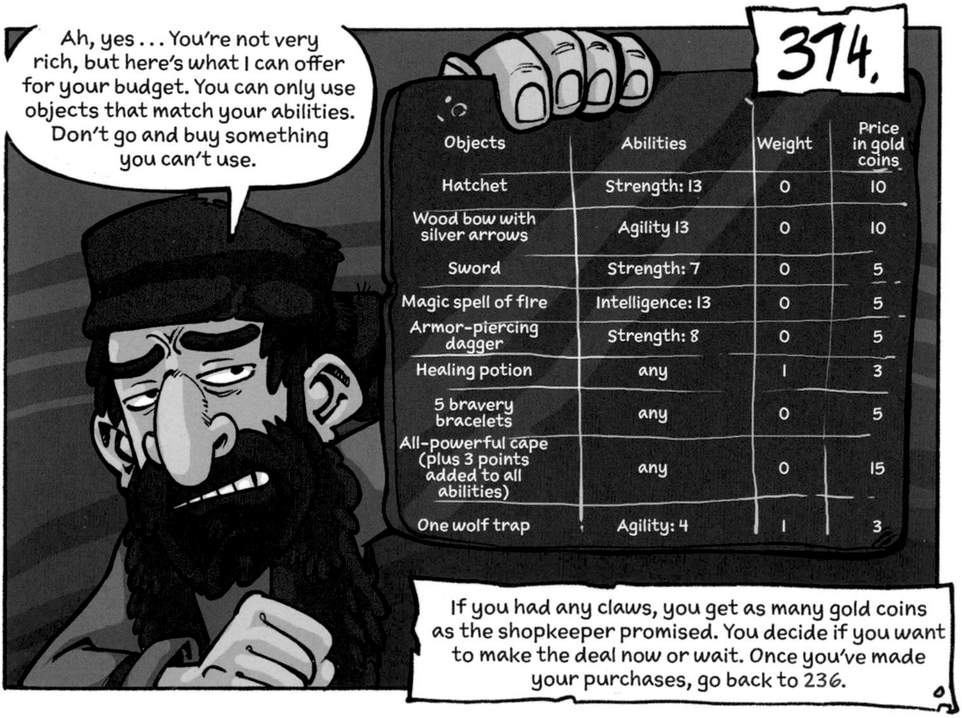
Ah, yes . . . You're not very rich, but here's what I can offer for your budget. You can only use objects that match your abilities. Don't go and buy something you can't use.

Objects	Abilities	Weight	Price in gold coins
Hatchet	Strength: 13	0	10
Wood bow with silver arrows	Agility 13	0	10
Sword	Strength: 7	0	5
Magic spell of fire	Intelligence: 13	0	5
Armor-piercing dagger	Strength: 8	0	5
Healing potion	any	1	3
5 bravery bracelets	any	0	5
All-powerful cape (plus 3 points added to all abilities)	any	0	15
One wolf trap	Agility: 4	1	3

If you had any claws, you get as many gold coins as the shopkeeper promised. You decide if you want to make the deal now or wait. Once you've made your purchases, go back to 236.

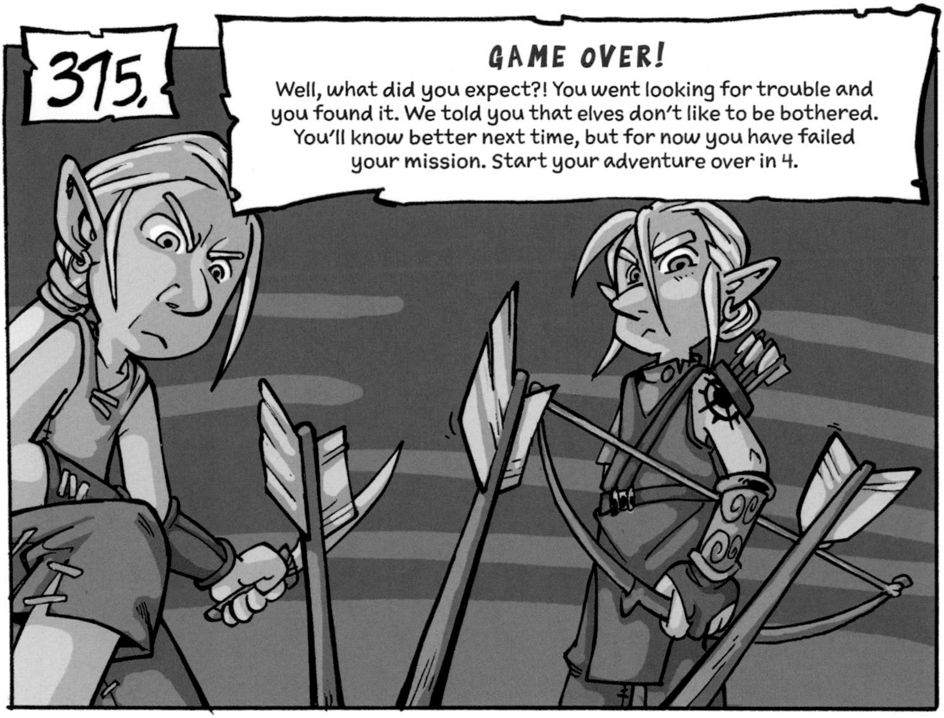
375.
GAME OVER!
Well, what did you expect?! You went looking for trouble and you found it. We told you that elves don't like to be bothered. You'll know better next time, but for now you have failed your mission. Start your adventure over in 4.

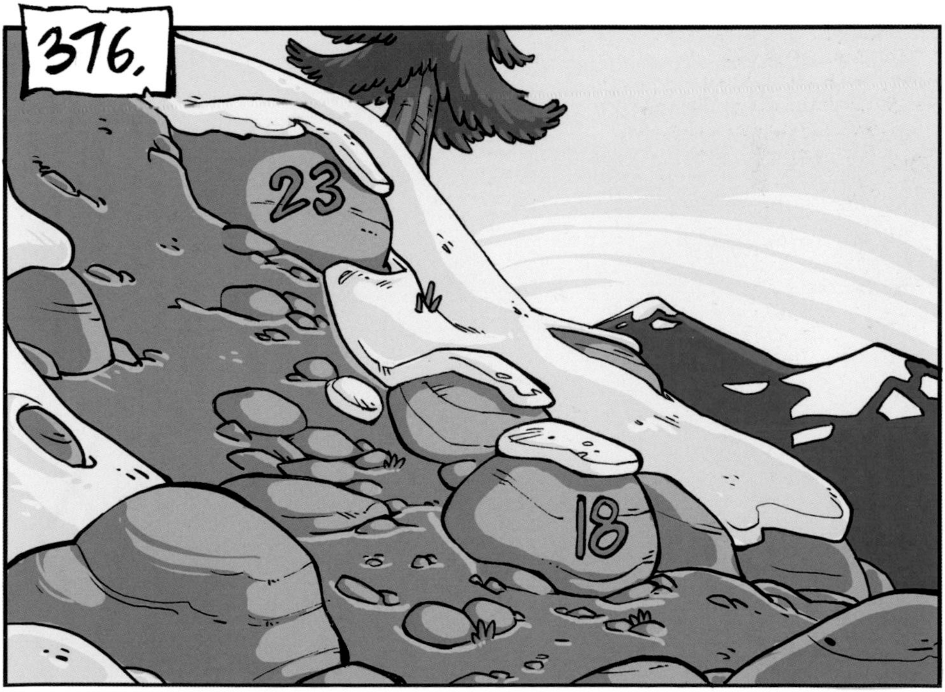
376.
23
18

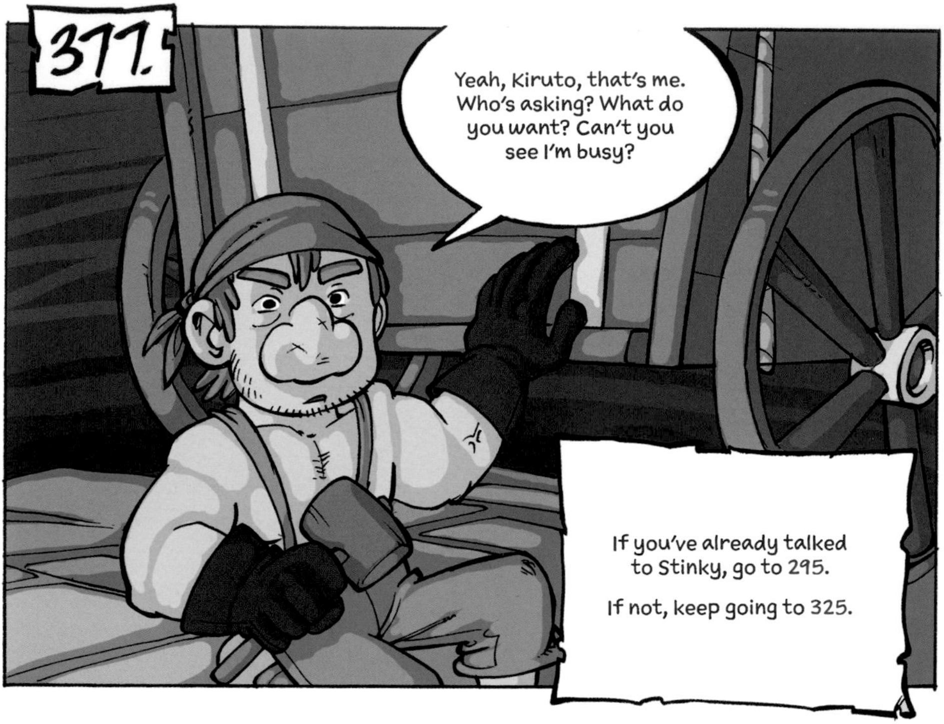
377.
Yeah, Kiruto, that's me. Who's asking? What do you want? Can't you see I'm busy?
If you've already talked to Stinky, go to 295.
If not, keep going to 325.

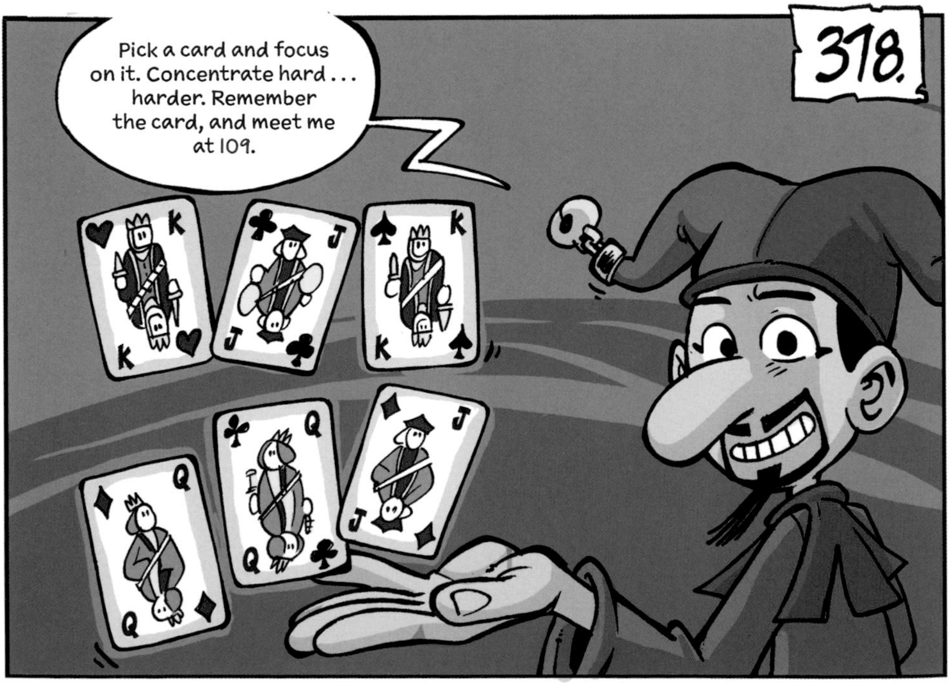
378.
Pick a card and focus on it. Concentrate hard . . . harder. Remember the card, and meet me at 109.

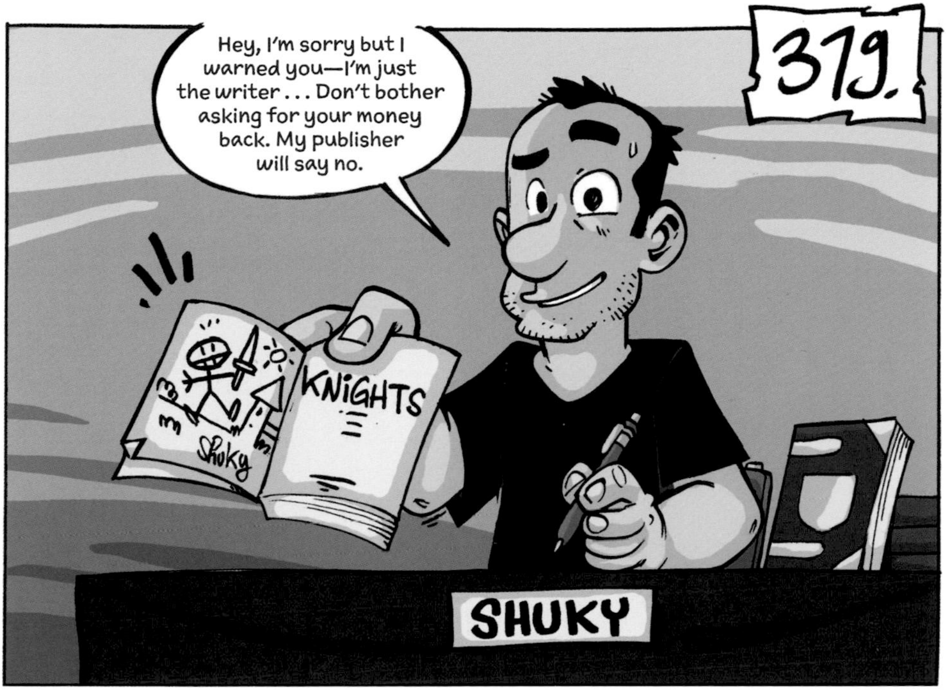
379.
Hey, I'm sorry but I warned you—I'm just the writer . . . Don't bother asking for your money back. My publisher will say no.
KNIGHTS
Shuky
SHUKY

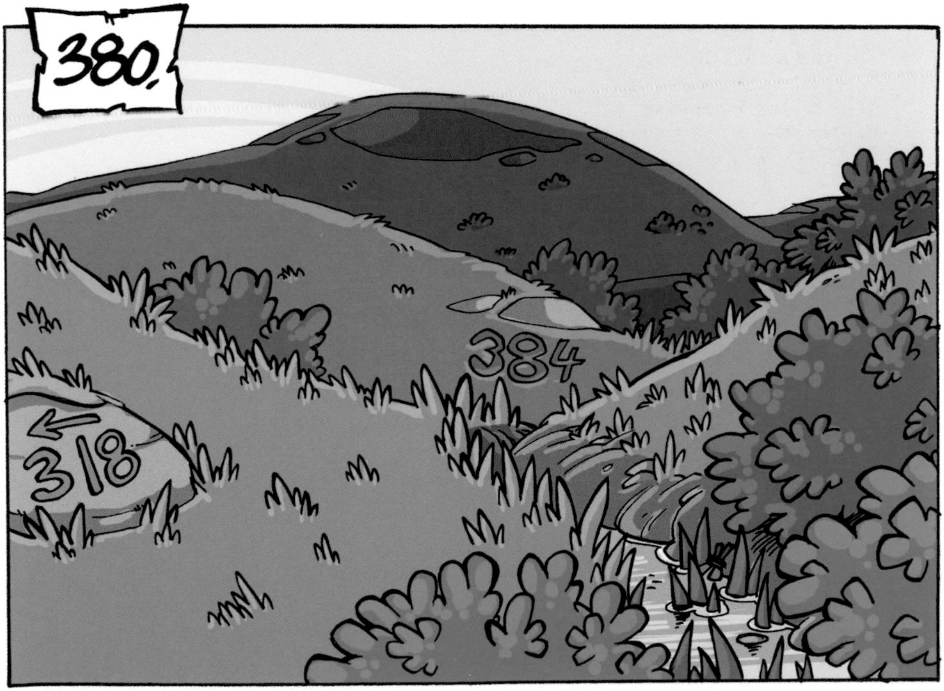
380.
384
318

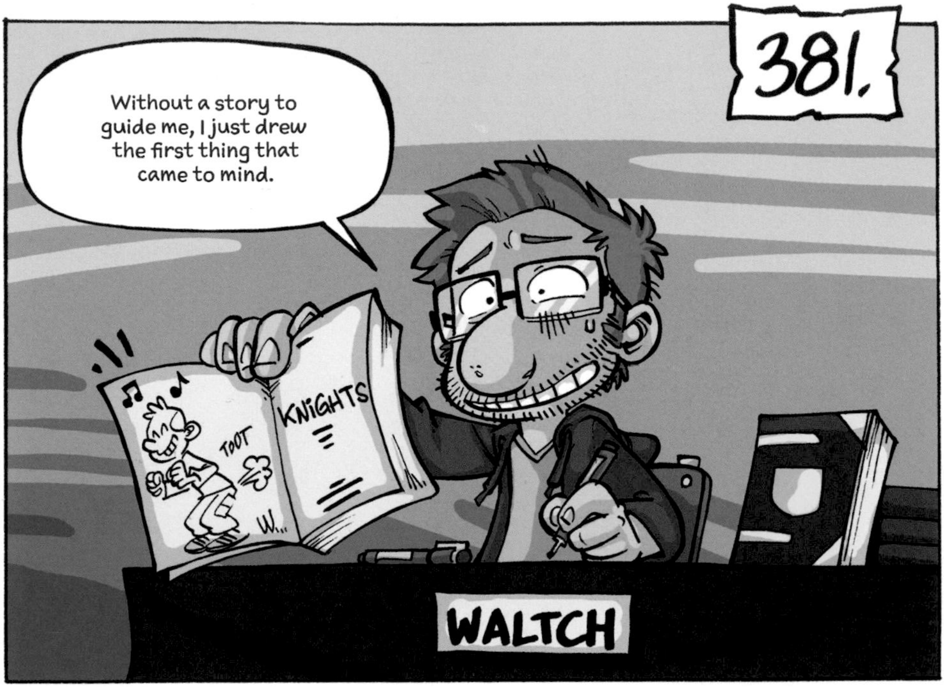
381.
Without a story to guide me, I just drew the first thing that came to mind.
KNIGHTS
TOOT
WALTCH

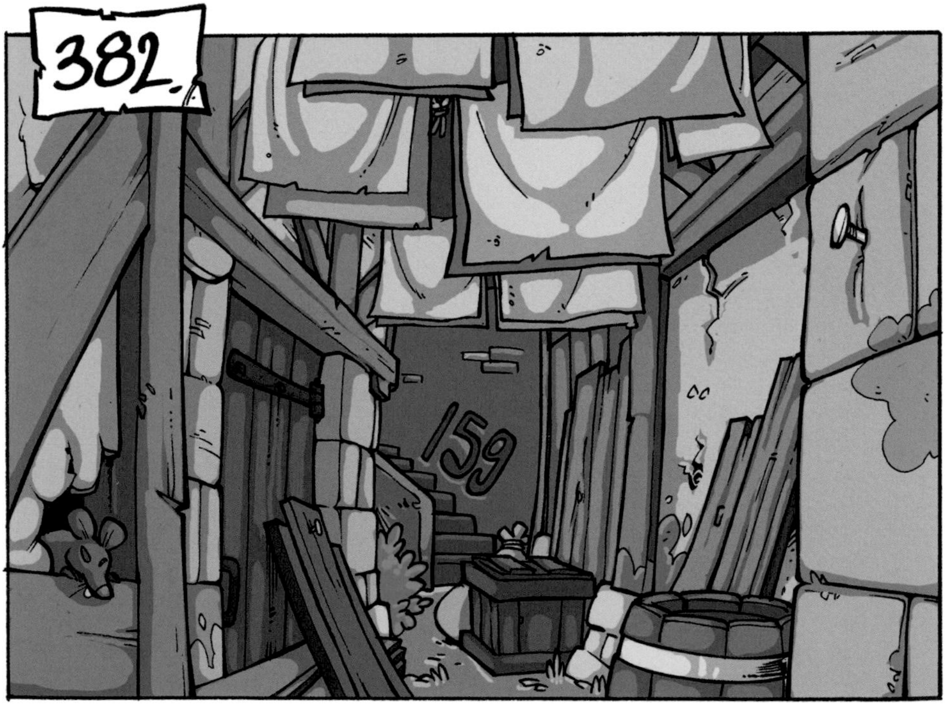
382.
159

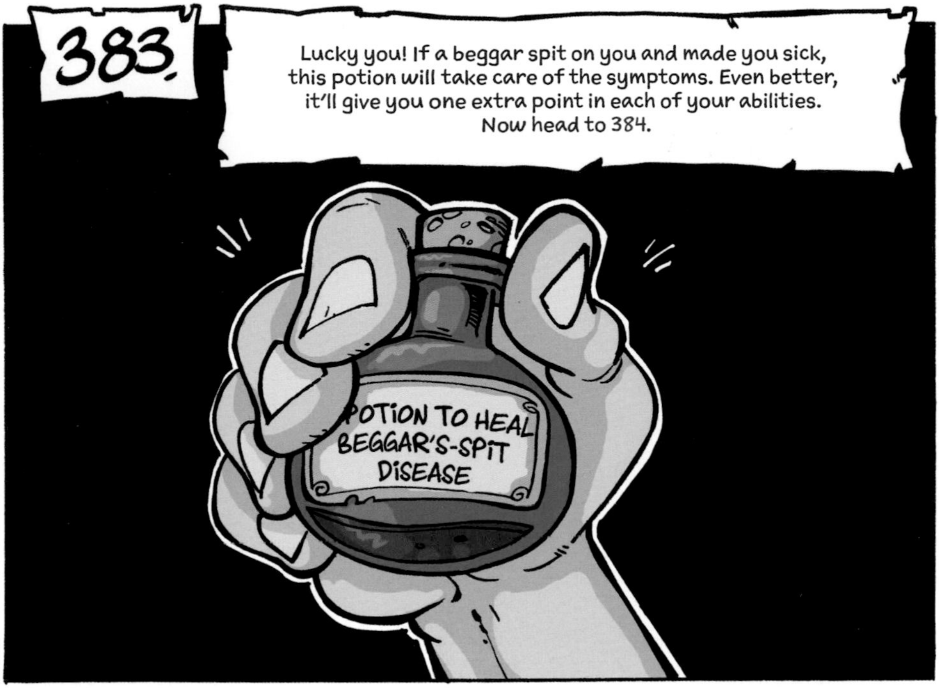
383.
Lucky you! If a beggar spit on you and made you sick, this potion will take care of the symptoms. Even better, it'll give you one extra point in each of your abilities. Now head to 384.
POTION TO HEAL BEGGAR'S-SPIT DISEASE

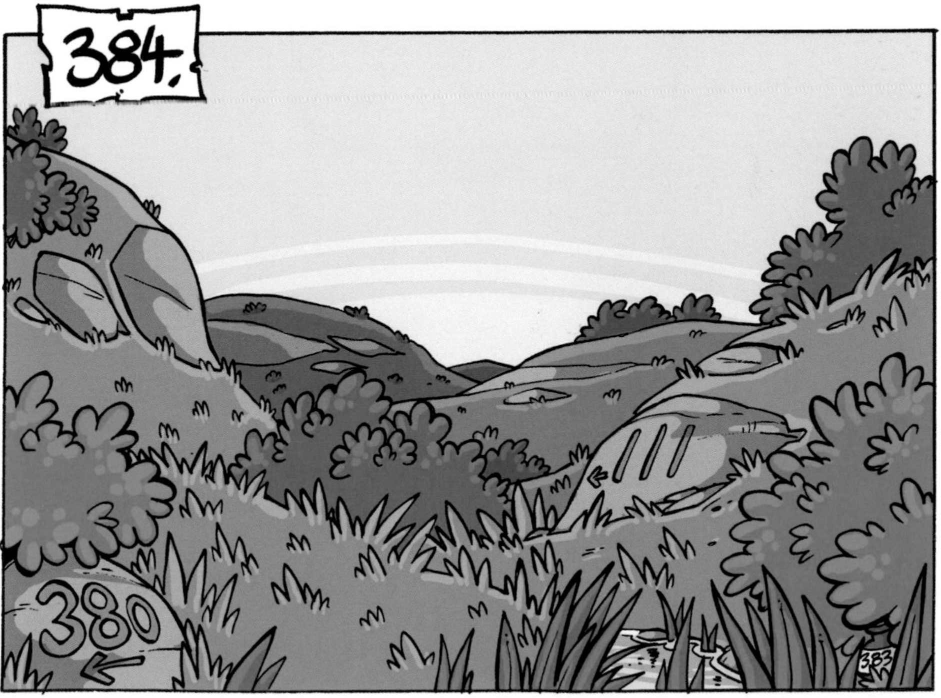
384.
380
383

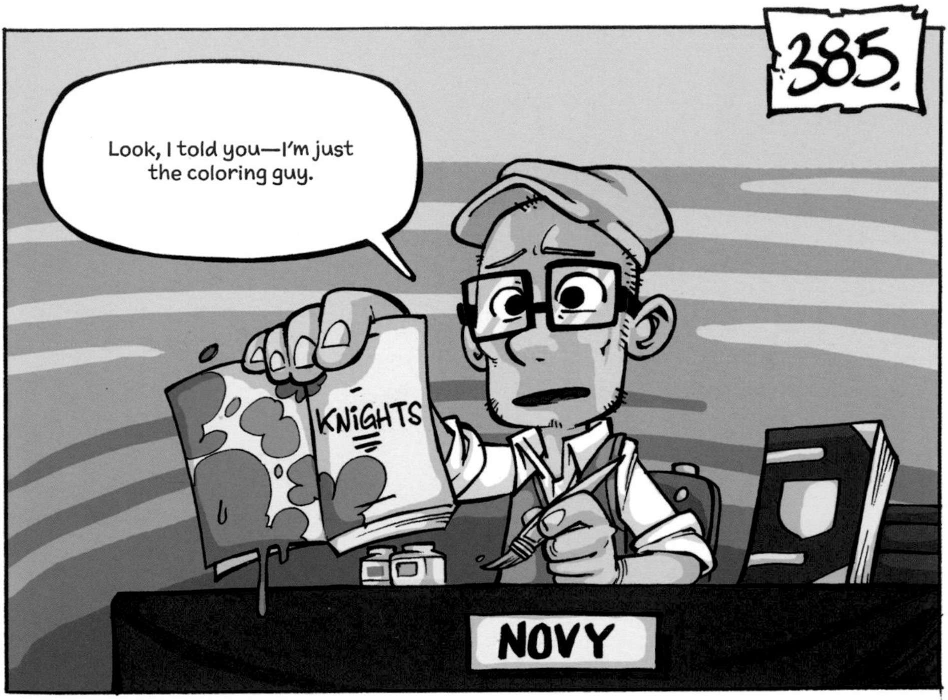
385.
Look, I told you—I'm just the coloring guy.
KNIGHTS
NOVY

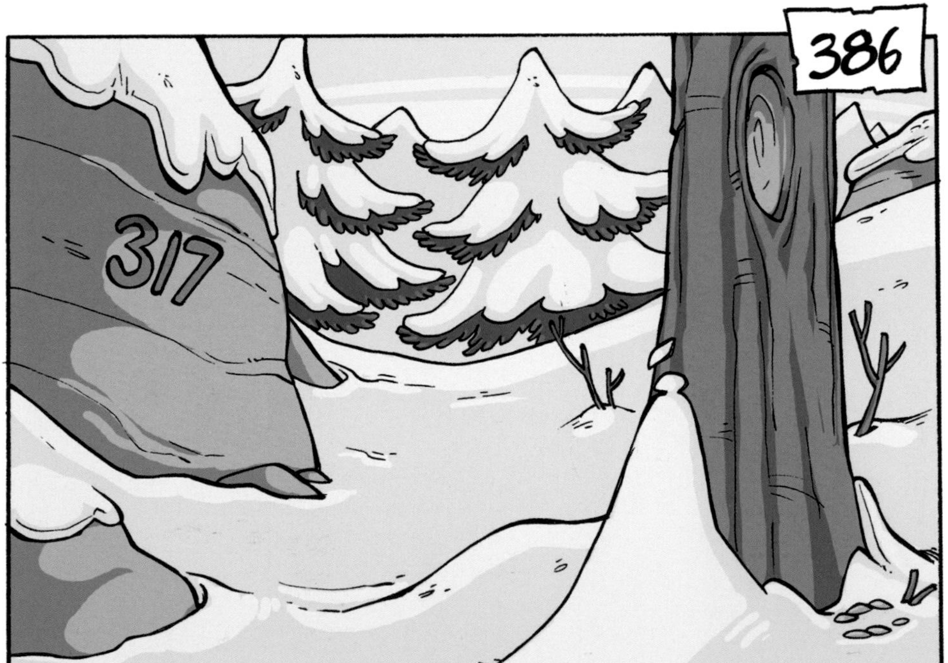
386
317

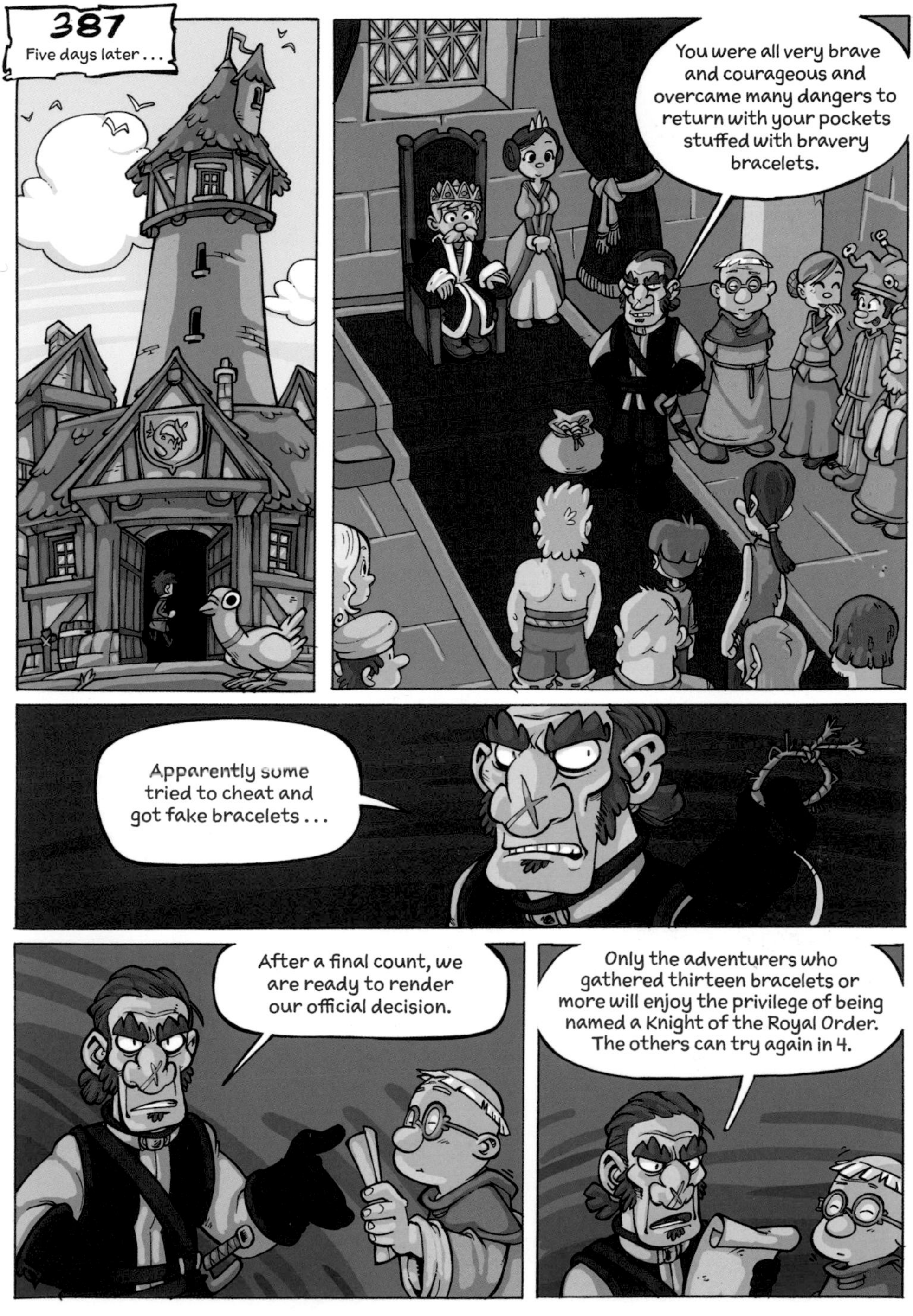
387
Five days later . . .
You were all very brave and courageous and overcame many dangers to return with your pockets stuffed with bravery bracelets.
Apparently some tried to cheat and got fake bracelets . . .
After a final count, we are ready to render our official decision.
Only the adventurers who gathered thirteen bracelets or more will enjoy the privilege of being named a Knight of the Royal Order. The others can try again in 4.

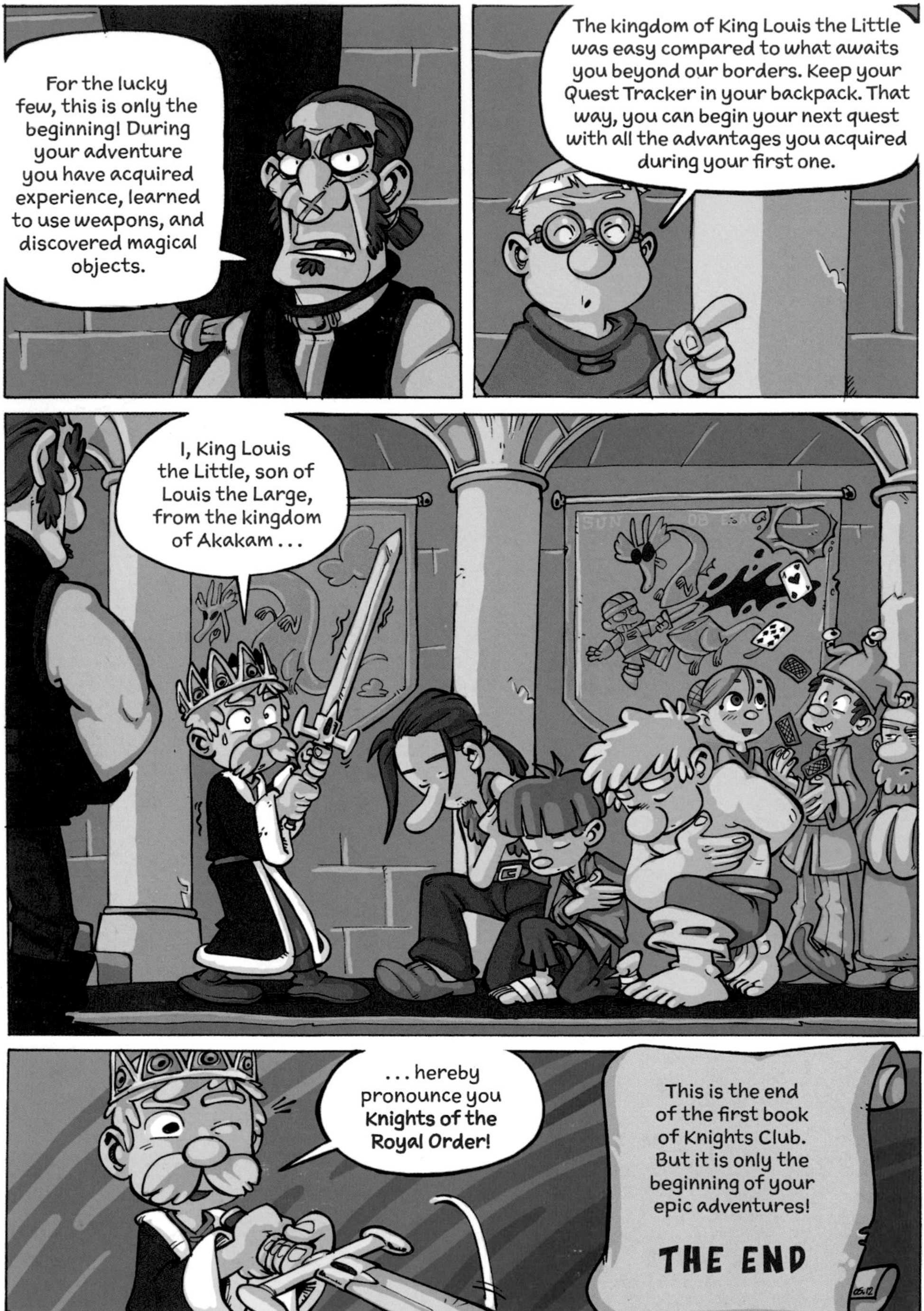
For the lucky few, this is only the beginning! During your adventure you have acquired experience, learned to use weapons, and discovered magical objects.
The kingdom of King Louis the Little was easy compared to what awaits you beyond our borders. Keep your Quest Tracker in your backpack. That way, you can begin your next quest with all the advantages you acquired during your first one.
I, King Louis the Little, son of Louis the Large, from the kingdom of Akakam . . .
. . . hereby pronounce you Knights of the Royal Order!
This is the end of the first book of Knights Club. But it is only the beginning of your epic adventures!
THE END